Riddle of Alexandria

Peter Bowman

LUNA CITY FREE PRESS—Womelsdorf, PA
ISBN: 979-8-218-23600-7
Library of Congress Control Number: 2023912636
Title: *Riddle of Alexandria*
Author: Peter Bowman
Digital distribution | 2023
Paperback | 2023

This is a work of fiction. The characters, names, incidents, places, and dialogue are products of the author's imagination, and are not to be construed as real.

Dedication

To my family who continually supported and encouraged me throughout my life. My deepest respect and appreciation to Robert Heinlein whose stories and imagination created a desire in me to write my own stories.

Prologue

Levi Thurman finished his scan of the papyrus scroll in his hand. Lovingly he replaced it in its rack. He turned off his recorder with relief. Levi stared bleary-eyed at the many racks of scrolls before him. Just one more small section left to record and catalog, thought Levi with relief and sadness. A white robed scholar drifted over to a rack of scrolls in from of the Temporal Historian. Levi stepped aside before the man bumped into him. The scholar found the scroll he sought. He grabbed it and walked away muttering to himself.

Levi smiled. He recorded the writings of so many ancient libraries like an invisible spirit, it no longer seemed strange. No one had thought to recover the lost records of the Great Library of Alexandria until he pointed out the omission to the Time Council. One week later, it approved the mission to the first library that the Romans had torched. To Levi's surprise and delight, he received the assignment for the Alexandria mission and as Team Leader.

The Alexandria I mission was nearly finished. Even with modern technology, it had taken over three months to finish the job. Levi worked unseen by the ancients thanks to his invisibility cloak. He sat down wearily and eased himself against the cool stone chair.

Maybe the Romans torched the library because it offended them that the library hadn't been made by them. Wanton destruction of books and historical records left so many gaps in Terran history. Book burnings by barbarians appalled Levi, but he understood their rationale. Calculated obliteration of the past by civilized men disturbed him much more. Often the final injury of a conqueror was the destruction of its defeated foe' past, as Rome had done with Carthage.

Levi glanced at the flickering flames of the torches stirring in the cool night breeze. Shadows of patrons danced on the walls. Levi rubbed his overworked eyes. How did anyone ever find anything in the Alexandria library with such a primitive classification system?

I have the best job in the Alliance, thought Levi with deep satisfaction. He brought history to life for mankind, improving life as well as increasing knowledge. Alliance scientists eagerly awaited the fruit of Levi's labors. Half of genius was seeing the obvious. Some lost technology of the ancients hadn't been recreated in the twenty-third century. Modern scientists would soon learn to appreciate the knowledge of their ancient colleagues.

Levi experienced a rush of euphoric triumph. A deep sadness quickly replaced it. Did Sir Galahad feel that way after he found the Holy Grail? Levi took comfort from the knowledge that he still had other Holy Grails to find. Levi enjoyed traveling through time. Nevertheless, every trip through the Time Door made him a little uneasy. Although the time continuum wasn't as frail as a spider's gossamer web, the temporal tapestry might unravel if someone pulled the right threads.

Levi suddenly felt a sensation like insects crawling all over him. He felt a few seconds of dizziness followed by a manic rush. Levi recognized the familiar symptoms of desynchronization psychosis. Most Temporal Historians experienced it after ninety days of a mission. Then they needed a week break to fully recover from it. Levi would be back at Time Control before it set in.

Levi sighed. "We're stuck with the fruits and dangers of your genius, Dr. Warner. Heaven help the galaxy if the guardians of time ever fail."

"Bowen to Team Leader. Do you copy?"

"I guess the medical scanner roused you from your nap, Bobby," surmised Levi.

"You're close to your desynchronization limit, Boss," acknowledged Bowen. "You are officially notified according to regulations. Have you found anything interesting since your last check in?"

"Most of the scrolls I've recorded since then are dull clerical tomes and local history.. The remaining scrolls are probably more of the same. I'll return in a couple of hours after I finish the last five racks."

"Your humble subordinate looks forward to your return with joy, Team Leader. Bowen out."

It annoyed Thurman and his fellow Temporal Historians that occasional desynchronization psychosis was an occupational hazard for them. Time Control had learned from unpleasant experience that being in another time for more than ninety days caused historians to experience paranoia and delusions. Soon Time Control doctors would be able to treat the historians' brains so they would not suffer from it again. Thurman looked forward to the end of desynchronization psychosis.

Levi returned to work. He read the translation off his recorder, looking for technological references. Halfway through the first scroll of the next rack, something very unexpected grabbed his complete attention. His blood raced as he read some ancient blueprints: blueprints of a fusion reactor! Levi grabbed the next scroll. It contained the list of all the weapons used by Atlantis including submarines.

Levi quickly grabbed the next scroll. He read the opening words with trembling hands. An account of the survivors of Atlantis.

The mighty Mistress of the Atlantic has fallen! Her power and glory once the envy of the world, are now just a memory. In the end, her wisdom and wizards failed her. In just three terrifying days, the gods sundered the Golden Isle and buried her in the depths of the sea. Remnants of her people traveled to the shores of our country. They came in their marvelous flying machines. They left behind most of their treasures bringing provisions and some changes of clothes.

No longer will mankind behold the glorious beauty and wonders of Atlantis. Never again will mankind sail beneath the seas or fly through the heavens. For their wise and unknown reasons, the gods judged Atlantis. They swiftly executed their terrible judgment.

The discovery made Levi's head spin. Neither the Greeks nor the Egyptians could fathom the deep science of Atlantis. It had lain in dusty obscurity until it finally vanished into deep memory. A disturbing question dampened Levi's delight: how did Atlantis acquire such technology?

Sentinel Point
Salkun Province
Kem.
Plain of Numar
Varlock
Holy City of Algona
Verant River
Fr.
...t of Arvira
Mount Darkfire Volcano
Army Base
Project Skybridge
Rutania Province
Kimmaren Province
Naval Base
Sylvon Forest
Dirl
Valoth
Mou
Calima River
Shrine
Stiel River
Irramar
Mount Starock Volcano
Ermak Province
Gal-Rian
of
Sadona Province
Skymount
Alaya
Base
Caldor
Temple of the Moon
High View
Ekal Hills
Caldor Forest
Kiral Pass
Atlantis
Plain of Zor
Teyron
Stiel
Shanya River
Erkun
Army Base
Castle Rock
Falls
Naval Base
Noda Province
Plain of Teanor
Fr

Chapter One

Gideon and Amara Warner lingered in the Time Council meeting room after the other members left at the conclusion of their daily meeting. Warner removed his Council robe and draped it over his chair. The only time he wore it was during the Council meetings as protocol dictated. When the Warners organized Time Control, they decided that the members should wear black robes like judicial robes. It served to remind all the members of the seriousness of their responsibilities.

Regularly they had to sit in judgment of Time Control personnel. Sometimes the Time Council members had to make decisions that might affect the time continuum. Gideon Warner served as President of the Time Council; Amara Warner served as Vice President. They assumed their responsibilities because they couldn't risk allowing the Time Door to be in the hands of people who might be more interested in power rather than protecting the time continuum. It was a continual battle Time Control dare not lose.

For half a century, the Warners had guided the Time Council and protected the time continuum. Once a less wise Solar President tried to seize control of the Time Door. Time Control security managed to foil the effort. Gideon Warner threatened to destroy the Time Door rather than let it fall into government or military hands. The government knew Warner well enough to know he meant what he said. Since that time, the government and Earthfleet left Project Timestream alone.

Most Council business concerned more mundane matters. Today's agenda had one very important item of business: whether to make Atlantis I an interaction mission. Normally the Council members discussed things in a calm, scholarly fashion. This time the discussion had been very heated. Important Council decisions had to be unanimous. After six hours of discussion, the Council approved the interaction mission.

Gideon sighed. "It seems like just yesterday that I made the first journey through the Time Door. So many journeys have been made since then. I insisted on making the first journey. I knew it would not be permitted once the Time Council was organized."

Amara smiled. "I have no regrets about passing on that opportunity. Neither do I regret our many years together in Time Control. The fifty years of our marriage have also flown by. I think we have aged like fine wine. Gideon, our days are not endless. We are drawing near the wood, as the Chinese would say. We need to choose and prepare our successors as soon as possible. A succession fight is unacceptable."

"This has weighed heavily on my mind the past year," confessed Gideon. "What do you think about Levi Thurman as my possible successor? He's the best Temporal Historian the Time Control Academy ever turned out. Levi has made some excellent suggestions to improve mission protocols. Making the Atlantis I mission an interaction mission was his idea. He's the kind of son I wish we had had."

Amara smiled slyly. "This doesn't surprise me. You tipped your hand when you started to invite Levi regularly to Time Council meetings. The Council discussed some very serious issues during some of those meetings. Levi has contributed a new and refreshing perspective. Why else would you involve him with Time Control administration?"

Gideon chuckled. "Nothing escapes you, dear. I've followed Levi's career closely. He has the wisdom and integrity the President of the Time Council needs. The fact that he finds the idea of being the Time Council President horrifying shows the right attitude and good judgment. Hopefully, we can get the rest of the Council members to approve Levi's nomination when the time comes. I think they are sufficiently impressed with him too."

"They are," agreed Amara. "I've often wondered how the time continuum might be affected if someone died in the past. The possibility exists on every mission."

"Would that cause some kind of temporal paradox?" wondered Gideon. "The team's experiences in Atlantis should reveal whether time is mutable. If it is, teams on interaction missions must be even more careful not to change history. Even a small change might have a huge impact. We just don't know."

Amara frowned. "The Atlantis I team should have personal shields. I don't understand why President Harrison and the Commanding Admiral have so far refused to give them to us. Hopefully, we can soon persuade them to give us those shields."

"We'll keep twisting their arms until they do, Amara," decided Gideon. He glanced at his watch. "It's time to give Levi his mission briefing."

"Don't forget to act surprised when the Temporal Historians shout surprise at our surprise Golden Anniversary party, Gideon," Amara reminded him.

Gideon chuckled. "Have I ever failed to be surprised at any of our surprise parties? I hope Levi and his future wife also have a Golden Anniversary."

Jerrel Dark checked his hair and suit in the bathroom mirror. Perfect. The Telmierian Special Observer needed to look his best when he met the galactically famous Gideon Warner. He sat down on the luxurious couch and waited for his ride to arrive. The room wasn't exactly the Imperial Hotel of the Telmierian capital, but still most worthy.

Dark eagerly awaited his journey through the Time Door. No one outside of the Solar Alliance had ever been permitted to travel through time. Finally, the Time Council changed its fifty-year-old policy. Previously, Telmierian VIPs had only been granted tours of Project Timestream. Only Jerrel Dark would travel the time stream!

The Telmierians understood the reluctance of the Terrans to allow outsiders to step through the Time Door. They knew that the Empire would have done the same in the Terrans' place. Imperial scientists had debated for centuries whether the past was mutable or not. After half a century of time travel, the jury was still out. Dark resolved to be as agreeable and cooperative as possible to ease the way for the next Telmierian time traveler.

Dark checked the time. The government shuttle should soon arrive to take him to Project Timestream. A minute later, someone knocked loudly on the door. Dark opened the door and blinked at the sight of a double of himself flanked by two thuggish looking Rigellians. He reached for his stunner. Before he could pull it out, the Rigellians jumped him. The double injected Dark with a hypo. In seconds, all of Dark's voluntary muscles were paralyzed.

One of the Rigellians pulled out a dagger. The pseudo-Dark knocked him down with a back hand slap. "Dog! The Confederacy needs him for a prisoner exchange. Besides, Mr. Dark is a diplomat, even if between assignments."

The second Rigellian scowled. "Why can't we carve him up a little?"

Aran Var contemplated his uncouth fellow Rigellians. An involuntary expression of distaste momentarily appeared on his face. Purposeless violence and cruelty no longer amused him. Civilization has advantages that we Rigellians have overlooked, decided Var.

Levi Thurman hurried to Gideon Warner's office. Being late for a mission briefing was a cardinal sin for Team Leaders. Normally, Levi would stroll leisurely along the winding paths of the Time Control Garden. He had been so lost in thought he had forgotten about the time. Being late would be rude as well as impolitic. By practically running, he managed to arrive at Dr. Warner's office with a minute to spare. Levi hoped that he didn't look sweaty.

He had not even been born when President Alexander Harrison unveiled the Time Door to the galaxy back in 2266. The news caused a tsunami of panic on many worlds. Only the Telmierians remained calm although apprehensive. President Harrison and Gideon Warner held a series of town meetings to calm and reassure the citizens of the Solar Alliance. Only a man of Harrison's stature could have pulled it off.

In time, many people became history buffs. The recovered artifacts of many centuries fascinated the people of the Telmierian Empire as well as the Alliance. People wanted to visit and vacation in the past. Many of them became very angry when Gideon Warner informed them that only Temporal Historians would pass through the Time Door. He bluntly refused the entreaties of the rich and powerful. In time, the Time Council permitted civilian observers to go on historical missions.

Levi knocked on the door of Gideon Warner's office. Warner buzzed him in and directed him to sit down. Although eighty-five and physically wearied by time, Warner's spirit and enthusiasm seemed as young as when he created the Time Door. His eyes shone with merriment and intelligence. At a distance, he seemed like the leader of an arcane brotherhood. Up close, he seemed like an ordinary man.

"Levi, all my life I've been fascinated by the legend of Atlantis," began Warner. "Until your discovery of the Atlantean records in the library of Alexandria, no serious scientist would dare express belief in it. Documented history has always been our priority. It will be a long time before we devote resources to chasing down doubtful myths and legends. Alexandria has presented us with a very intriguing riddle."

"I never expected Atlantis to have technology like ours," confessed Levi. "How could those people develop it thousands of years before us?"

Warner sighed. "That's one of the big questions you and your team must find the answer to. We must face the possibility that someone else has developed their own Time Door and seeks to use it against us. We have determined when Atlantis was destroyed. Your team will arrive there ninety days before the end. Our first timeship will be ready to pick you up by the end of your mission. I'm afraid that you will have a bit of a walk to the Atlantean capital."

Levi smiled. "The exercise will do us good, Dr. Warner."

"Waiving the Non-Interaction Directive will make it easier to learn what you need. You may not kill or seriously injure anyone, not even in self-defense. Your stunners and tranquilizer darts are more than adequate protection. I'm doing my best to acquire personal shields from Earthfleet. Hopefully, you will have them for Atlantis II. First, let's go over the special protocols for the Atlantis mission."

After the mission briefing, Levi returned to his quarters to get ready for the Warners surprise Golden Anniversary party. Everyone knew the Warners wouldn't be at all surprised. It was understood that they desired no gifts. The Temporal Historians wore their Time Control uniforms with the all-seeing eye over infinity on the blouse. Other Time Control personnel wore their best clothes.

Levi had read the dossiers of Jerrel Dark and the three soldiers who would participate in the Atlantis I mission. Dark was a respected former soldier, explorer, and diplomat. He had a very distinguished career for a man of thirty-five. Reading between the lines, Levi got the impression that Dark was a bit of a maverick. He reminded Levi of the famous British explorer and former soldier Sir Richard Burton.

As soon as Levi arrived at the party, he spotted Lisa Stern, the Temporal Historian assigned to him by Gideon Warner. She finished filling her plate with food and sat down at an empty table to eat it. Lisa was the first Telmierian to enter the Time Control Academy. Her family had a close relationship with the Imperial family. Lisa stood out with her loveliness and blue skin. Levi figured she was about 28 and 175 millimeters tall. He was only a few years older. Lisa had a distinguished Time Control career. Bad timing kept him from meeting her earlier.

Levi heard that Lisa was unmarried. She had turned down many well connected Telmierian and Alliance suitors. Apparently, Lisa planned to marry for love rather than advantage. Levi felt a bit intimidated by Lisa's history and her family's importance. The choice of Lisa for the Atlantis I mission surprised Levi. She was a part Karani dual citizen of the Alliance and the Empire. Alliance law treated her as a Telmierian citizen.

Lisa's grandfather, William Stern, received the Solar Council Medal of Honor for his service during the Marauder War. Her grandmother, Dawn Mellicos, played a key role in rescuing President Harrison from the Rigellians. Hopefully, Lisa believed in noblesse oblige like most Telmierian aristocrats.

Levi walked over to the table where Lisa sat and introduced himself. "Levi Thurman, Temporal Historian and Team Leader for the Atlantis I mission, I presume," responded Lisa. "I'm glad to finally meet you." Lisa smiled slyly. "I've heard a lot about you, Levi. I look forward to working with you."

"I've looked forward to having a Karani historian on a mission. I never imagined it would be you. Now that I think about it, you are the logical choice."

"I'm a dual citizen of the Alliance and the Empire so I served practically and politically to go on this mission," noted Lisa with amusement. "Emperor Marcellus wants Professor Mirak to be a member of the next Atlantis mission."

"It would be a privilege and a pleasure to work with such an eminent Telmierian historian," said Levi. All Temporal Historians knew of Professor Mirak. Levi hadn't had the pleasure of meeting him.

Levi noticed his good friend Bobby Bowen observing him and Lisa from across the room. He looked very annoyed. Bowen drifted over to Levi and Lisa. He looked over Lisa approvingly. "I haven't had the pleasure of meeting you, Miss Stern. My name is Bobby Bowen, Temporal Historian extraordinaire." He shook Lisa's hand. "You, unlike your fellow Telmierian, Jerrel Dark, will be of great use on the Atlantis mission."

Bobby's undiplomatic dig at Dark surprised Levi. He understood how his friend felt being left off the Atlantis I team because it included four Special Observers. Bobby brightened. "It's not a total loss. I've been named Team Leader for the Alexandria II mission." Levi had quietly recommended his friend for the job to compensate for losing his place on the Atlantis mission.

"Congratulations! It's Bobby's first time as Team Leader," Levi informed Lisa. "When is your team leaving?"

"Alexandria II will run concurrently with Atlantis I," said Bowen. "My mission will probably finish about the same time. I'd like to see you guys off tomorrow. Unfortunately, I'm having my mission briefing when you step through the Time Door."

"Why don't you ask President Warner to reschedule your briefing so you can see Lisa and I off?" suggested Levi waggishly.

"Are you crazy?" Bobby practically shouted. "He would probably reassign me to the janitorial staff. If you guys will excuse me, I have some important brown nosing to do."

"Bobby is quite a character," observed Lisa after Bobby was out of earshot. "I wish he was going with us."

"Bobby aspires to become a member of the Time Council," said Levi. "Not me. I guess it's time to pay our respects to the Warners."

Levi suddenly remembered that Lisa was a full telepath. He hoped she would never read his thoughts without permission, but his thoughts were mostly pure. Levi read an article about telepaths in a Telmierian scientific journal. All of them were female. They could only read the thoughts of their fellow Karani if the subjects willed it. The psychic gifts came from unique physical and biochemical conditions that couldn't be duplicated.

Before Levi and Lisa reached the Warners, Jerrel Dark intercepted them. "It's a great pleasure to meet you, Miss Stern, Mr. Thurman. I am pleased and grateful to be included on your mission to Atlantis. Telmieria has no similar legend or myth. Why doesn't the Alliance share the Time Door with its greatest ally and galactic friend, Mr. Thurman?"

Levi blinked at the blunt question. Usually, diplomats phrase such questions more delicately. "Frankly, Mr. Dark. We barely trust ourselves with the Time Door."

Annoyance appeared briefly on Dark's face, then he chuckled. "Such refreshing candor. I think I'm going to like you. Your Temporal Historian oath states, 'I swear to gather historical records and artifacts without revealing my identity or purpose to anyone in the past. To protect the time continuum, I will sacrifice my life if necessary.' How many Temporal Historians have been required to make the ultimate sacrifice?"

This guy is a character, thought Levi appreciatively. "None so far, I'm happy to report. I'll do my best to see that neither I nor Lisa will need to. That oath is not required of you or the soldiers."

Dark smiled. "I am glad to hear it. It has been a long day. I think I will retire. I'll see you and Lisa at the Time Door tomorrow. Good night." Dark bowed and left the room.

After briefly speaking with Gideon and Amara Warner, Levi spoke with the Earthfleet soldiers who would accompany him and Lisa on the mission. Levi read the names off their uniforms: Major Trent Kinsey, Sergeants Colin McNeil, and Galan Kelly. He couldn't believe it. A Scotsman, an Irishman, and a Sassenach. Someone in Earthfleet had a perverse sense of humor.

Kinsey, tall and pale, exuded an aristocratic hauteur. Clearly he was no peasant. McNeil and Kelly were friendly and apparently enthusiastic about being a part of the mission. Kelly had the delicate features of an Irish poet, but he was all soldier. Kinsey succinctly expressed his opinion about the mission. "We are here to observe and serve, sir."

And serve the soldiers would, thought Levi with amusement. Neither he nor Gideon Warner believed in wasting manpower. He hoped that Kinsey's attitude would improve over time. It irritated him that anyone, even a non-historian, failed to appreciate the great privilege of being part of a mission every Temporal Historian would kill to be on.

Chapter Two

Levi and his team gathered in front of the Time Door. Everyone made a final check of their weapons and equipment. All team members carried an invisibility cloak, dragon medallion com-link and tranquilizer dart guns strapped to their arms. Their long sleeves covered the dart guns. The tranquilizer could stop an elephant. Everything was fully functional. Levi brought a holo-thought imagizer disguised as a bracelet to entertain himself and the team.

The team waited patiently as the generators powered up the Time Door. Levi had gone through the Time Door many times. Each time he experienced the same anxiety, anticipation, and exhilaration of his first trip. Levi suspected it was the same for Lisa. The soldiers acted like it was no big deal for them, but their eyes revealed fear and uncertainty.

They would soon learn that nothing they experienced before could prepare them for the experience of the Time Door. The probe that Time Control sent back to Atlantis revealed architecture reminiscent of New Washington. As it passed over the harbor of the capital, it recorded wooden and metal ships. Some of the wooden ships appeared to be yachts of the wealthy. Unfortunately, the color circuits of the probe failed. Levi couldn't determine the race of the darker skinned people. They looked like aristocrats and businessmen. Many of them wore loose-fitting robes.

The probe revealed that Atlantean men wore pants and shirts. Women wore dresses yet curiously they didn't seem to wear skirts. Younger women and girls revealed more of their bodies than they covered. Levi figured it was the warm season because the majority of the Atlanteans wore sandals and open shoes.

Both Levi and Lisa had misgivings about having Dark and the soldiers on such an important mission. No doubt Gideon Warner gave them a lecture about doing anything that might negatively impact the time continuum. Lisa figured that the risk of damage was minimal on the Atlantis mission. Dark and the Sergeants appreciated the adventure they were about to begin. Kinsey saw the mission as something he did because he had been ordered to do. Hopefully, the sergeants' enthusiasm would rub off on Kinsey.

"Everyone ready?" asked Levi. They assured him that they were. "We have a general idea of how to behave in public. Gentlemen, to be safe, do not speak to respectable women unless they first speak to you. Feel free to speak to the less respectable women as you choose. Lisa, Atlantean society is most likely conservative and patriarchal. It is best that you don't initiate conversations with male strangers."

The opening of the Time Door startled the soldiers and Dark. Swirling waves of temporal energy appeared over the platform before them. The regular blue and red patterns seemed to mesmerize Dark and the soldiers. The psychedelic effects and sensory illusions never failed to delight Levi. He and Lisa walked up the steps to the temporal doorway. "Follow us, boys!" called out Levi. He and Lisa stepped through the door together and vanished. After a moment of hesitation, Dark and the soldiers followed them.

After what seemed like minutes, Levi and Lisa abruptly slipped into synchronization. Happily, it proved less jarring than usual. Dark and the soldiers appeared beside him a moment later. "This is better than all the wildest roller coaster rides combined," whispered Kelly.

A pleasantly cool breeze balanced out the warmth of the sun. The team stood on a hill overlooking a two-lane road that snaked its way to the Atlantean capital. Levi led the team down the hill to the road. He touched the smooth surface of the road while Lisa scanned it. It felt smooth and cool.

"The road is composed of similar materials we use on Telmieria," announced Lisa. "Terra didn't have anything like this before the Empire shared them with the Alliance."

"I suspect that this will be one of many mysteries we will encounter in Atlantis," commented Dark.

Levi checked his temporal scanner. "It looks like unusually strong temporal currents stopped us five days past our target. We'll just have to make sure we get the job done in eighty-five days."

Lisa studied Atlantis' tectonic plates and fault lines. "Hm. Higher than normal stress levels, but nothing to be presently concerned about."

Major Kinsey scanned the distance to the city. "We have a five mile walk as the crow flies. We'll cover the distance quickly enough if we maintain a good pace."

The complete absence of traffic on a main road puzzled Levi. By 1700, he expected heavy traffic heading to and from the city. Could the city be sealed off due to plague? A slow-moving vehicle approached the team from behind. To everyone's surprise, it was a floater hovering four feet above the road. A sullen white robed priest sat behind his equally disagreeable looking driver. The team moved quickly off the road. Both occupants of the floater ignored them as if they were invisible. Gradually, it disappeared in the distance.

"Hopefully there will be a few friendly and cheerful clerics," commented an amused Dark.

The team walked toward the city at a quick pace. Occasionally, they looked over their shoulders. The floaters were so quiet they could run one over before he knew it. Two miles down the road, the team heard a shuttle rapidly approaching. They hurried off to the side of the road. The family size shuttle had two occupants: a male driver and a female passenger who was probably his wife. They looked like well-off commoners.

The shuttle came to a stop beside the team. The Atlanteans warily scrutinized the team. They smiled after they decided that the strangers posed no threat.

"Good journey!" greeted the man. "People do not usually travel to Aurelin on foot."

Levi was shocked to hear the man speaking Telmierian. He hoped that he managed to contain his surprise. "Thieves," he explained. "We rented a shuttle in Aurelin to visit the local sights. Unfortunately, thieves surprised us, took our shuttle, and stranded us."

"Normally this road is perfectly safe," said the woman uneasily. "Please allow us to give you a ride. My husband and I do not want you to be victimized twice."

Levi thought it was curious that the couple wore matching gold rising sun pendants. He figured that it was some kind of fashion. The driver and Levi took care of the introductions as he and his team boarded the shuttle. Once everyone had secured themselves, the driver resumed the journey. The driver and his wife maintained a steady and informative stream of chatter. Levi recorded everything. The Atlanteans asked the team questions and answered the team's questions. Levi did most of the talking. He warmed the hearts of the Atlanteans with his sincere praise of their country and civilization.

The team anxiously awaited its first look at Aurelin, even Kinsey. Levi hoped it would be as glorious as he had imagined. Some ancient cities had been a great disappointment to him. Some had been more magnificent than he expected. Rome, mistress of the Mediterranean world for many centuries, dazzled Levi with its magnificent marble buildings and statues and engineering wonders. Levi could hardly recall an ancient city without waste and offal in the streets. Modern sanitation facilities wouldn't exist for many centuries.

The view of Aurelin had been blocked by the hills surrounding it for most of the drive. It came into full view after the shuttle passed the final hill. The city with its large harbor spread out as far as the eye could see. Rows of multi-story buildings lined the straight streets and broad boulevards. Aurelin looked much like New Washington. Levi figured that the city had electricity, but he saw no electrical lines.

Lisa discreetly scanned the buildings. She contacted Levi's mind. "Levi, the buildings are constructed of the same materials used in the Alliance and the Empire. The serenium is as pure as anything found in our time."

Levi stared at the ships docked at the piers and anchored in the harbor. Side by side, sail and engine driven ships loaded and unloaded their wares. Different races worked together in apparent harmony and cooperation. None of the men seemed to be slaves. Fair skinned Atlanteans swiftly and efficiently loaded supplies into military shuttles. Merchants and ships captains haggled and argued to the amusement of the team. Customs officials painstakingly inspected goods being imported and exported.

Most of the people Levi and his team had seen wore the same gold pendant as the couple who gave them a ride. Neither he nor Lisa thought it was coincidental. It was very unlikely that it was a popular fashion. Hopefully, someone would explain it to them without being asked.

It suddenly hit Levi how quiet the city and harbor were. He never expected Atlantis to have noise suppression technology. The Alliance only got theirs from the Telmierian Empire less than a century ago.

Scans revealed little air or water pollution. The levels were the same found in the Alliance and Empire.

The road passed near the harbor and led into the business district. After passing the commercial center, the shuttle came to several inns. Some looked very elegant. Others looked like they catered to the poorer classes. At regular intervals trees, bushes and small gardens broke up the concrete monotony. The streets teemed with humbly but neatly dressed people.

Levi noticed a sign on a rundown inn to the right: Inn of The Seventh Ecstasy. "Please stop here," requested Levi. The driver stopped and allowed the team to disembark. Both the driver and his wife gazed disapprovingly at the team.

"May the blessings of Father Sun be with you," said the driver. He quickly drove off.

Dark looked at Levi with a puzzled expression. "I wasn't expecting the Grand Hotel of New Washington, but I expected a bit better than this."

Levi glanced at Lisa. She seemed as unimpressed as Dark.

"How did the people of Atlantis come to speak Telmierian?" asked Dark in consternation. "We have no Time Door!"

"That you know of," countered Kinsey. "Something very strange and disturbing is going on in Atlantis. The sooner we find out what it is the better."

Dark regarded the facade of the inn before them with distaste.

"We want to keep a low profile," Lisa reminded him. "What better place to do it than a place like this?"

The door of the inn opened to a bar and dining room. A host of customers at the bar and tables clamored for service. Barmaids rushed around trying to take care of customers as quickly as possible. Levi led the team to the only unoccupied table in the dining room where the team sat down. Seedy looking men with pleasure ladies at the bar took occasional gulps of their drinks.

A slutty looking barmaid wearing a dress that covered little of her body noticed the team. She looked over the men and smiled. Immediately she turned her attention to them.

She leered at Levi. "What will you and your party have, sir? Coffee, wine, tea, ecstasy?"

Cute in a degenerate sort of way, thought Levi. "A round of your best wine for me and my friends. We will have supper later."

After the barmaid left to get the wine, the team listened to the conversations of customers at nearby tables.

"Who is worse: the army or the priests? The army is always looking to find newer and better ways to kill and destroy. At least the priests are more concerned with their pleasures and privileges than bothering us peasants."

"Children of the Sun. Hah! No doubt solar energy flows through their veins."

"Quiet you fool! Too many priests have large ears and small hearts."

"Damn High Command! Our trade houses control or influence most of the western world, but Garai the Great wants a military conquest of everything. That power-hungry bastard will not be fighting and dying. He will not be paying the increased taxes to finance military operations either."

"Atlantis is a land of contradictions," reflected Lisa. "The Atlanteans are apparently sun worshipers, yet they have an advanced civilization and a modern technological state."

A grumbling, sixty-something man burst out of the kitchen unexpectedly. He wore an apron and appeared to be a cook. Unlike the barmaids, he looked like a man of quality. He smiled when he noticed the team. The man hurried over to them.

"Have you and your party been served?" he asked Levi.

"Our order of wine has been taken. Hopefully, it will soon arrive."

"My name is Gallo," revealed the man. "I own the Inn of The Seventh Ecstasy."

"I thought you were the cook," admitted Levi with embarrassment.

Gallo laughed. "Sometimes necessity forces me to fill in for one of my cooks. Will you and your friends need rooms? The entire second floor is vacant. I have two sets of adjoining rooms, if you like. How long will you be staying?"

"Indefinitely," replied Levi. "How much are the adjoining rooms?"

Gallo studied the team for a moment. Levi suspected that Gallo figured that the team was a bunch of country bumpkins or tourists he could take advantage of. "Four rooms are twenty golden sovereigns a week. Meals are not included. There is a fifteen percent discount for long term guests." Gallo's eyes widened when Levi paid him with gold coins without inscription.

The barmaid finally arrived with the team's wine. She placed all the glasses on the table. "Jinny, show our guests to their rooms after they finish their wine," ordered Gallo. "They will be occupying the adjoining rooms on the second floor. See to all their needs."

Jinny's lustful eyes suggested that she served pleasure as well as food and drink. After the team finished their wine, she took them to their rooms. She winked at Levi. "If you require anything when I am off duty, do not hesitate to call on me." She handed him the room keys and returned to her usual duties. Everyone gathered in the room Levi had chosen for himself.

"Lisa, job number one is identifying all sources of historical records and prioritizing them," decided Levi. "Job number two is giving our observers a crash in history recording. Its technology is simple enough for anyone to learn, although like good photography it is art as well as science. After I get a city map of Aurelin, we will divide it into sectors that each of us will have responsibility for. Gentlemen, please remain here until Lisa and I return. Occupy yourselves as you choose."

Dark chuckled. "Our Earthfleet friends and I will do our best to entertain ourselves while staying out of trouble. Major Kinsey, I noticed some soldiers at the bar. Perhaps you and your men might learn something useful from them."

Kinsey smiled. "An excellent idea, Mr. Dark. With your permission, Mr. Thurman."

"By all means, Major," replied Levi.

"Do you think that Dark and the soldiers will stay out of trouble?" asked Lisa doubtfully after they left.

"I think so," figured Levi. "President Warner gave them the same reminders to be careful about everything they do that he gives to all Special Observers."

"Levi, would you mind sharing a room with me?" asked Lisa unexpectedly and unabashedly. "I've had private quarters since I've been in Time Control. It would be nice to share my quarters with someone for a change."

Levi had enough experience with Karani women to know Lisa was perfectly serious. He also understood that her need was emotional, not physical. Neither of them would break the fraternization rule and jeopardize their careers for momentary pleasure. Levi found living alone as tiresome as Lisa did.

"All right," agreed Levi. "Let's make a deal. You won't attack me, and I won't attack you. Deal?"

Lisa laughed. "Deal, boss. Before we leave, let's check out the room."

The room was decent overall. A maid clearly serviced the room on a regular basis. It had a nice shower and a hot tub that could accommodate three adults. Levi suspected that it had and more than once.

Lisa sniffed the soap and shampoo. "Very nice. I look forward to using them. Boss, may I make a suggestion?"

"By all means."

"We need to get some clothes," Lisa reminded him. "All we have are the clothes on our backs. I think I can tell what will fit you guys."

Levi chuckled. "Thank you for reminding me of this important detail. You are a lady of excellent taste; I leave it to you to pick out the clothes for the men."

"That's very good thinking for a bachelor," approved Lisa.

Levi and Lisa bought everyone six days of clothes. They needed a taxi to transport everything back to the inn. When they returned to the inn, Jinny saw them. Immediately she rushed over to help them. She informed them that the inn provided a reasonably priced laundry service. Levi decided that he had made a good choice with the Inn of The Seventh Ecstasy. He and Lisa placed the observers' clothes on their beds.

The historians then went into the city to find the main sources of historical records: libraries, religious meeting places and government offices. Although most of the records seemed to be computerized, the libraries still contained many printed books. Levi scanned the books to determine their age. To his amazement, most of them were centuries old. Somehow the Atlanteans managed to preserve them very well.

Levi and Lisa were very tired when they returned to their room. They had walked around a great deal of Aurelin. Levi felt they could get a better feel for the place and the people that way. Most of the residents were friendly, even the higher-class ones. It struck Levi that they hadn't seen any stray dogs or cats. He suspected that the city government took great pains to keep it that way.

Levi and Lisa showered separately, then slipped into the hot tub. They sighed with contentment. "Now this is civilized living!" commented Lisa.

Levi smiled. Lisa had been raised Telmierian. Telmierians had no hangups about shared nudity with the opposite sex. They managed to separate nudity from sex. When the Karani were cast out of their Eden, they wisely dumped all the shame on the serpent. Levi heard that Telmierian houses had communal baths shared by family members and guests.

After soaking in the hot tub, Levi decided to go to bed. The king-size bed gave him and Lisa enough space to stretch out without invading the other's space. They quickly fell asleep. The alarm jolted Levi into wakefulness at 0800 after what seemed like only a couple of hours. Nevertheless, he felt sufficiently refreshed. Levi and Lisa showered and dressed quickly. They discovered that the observers had already gone to the dining room for breakfast. The food was already prepared and waiting for the team.

"Good morning," greeted Dark. "My fellow observers and I thought you might have overslept. Now that you are here, let's eat so we can get to work."

After the team finished eating and the barmaid had cleared the table, they got down to business. "Right now, it's more important to learn how the Atlanteans came to speak Telmierian than how the island was destroyed. Major Kinsey, I want you and your men to give me a rundown on all the army and navy facilities of the greater Aurelin area. Study all the commercial ships docked and anchored in the harbor. Report to me when you are finished. Check in with me every four hours."

Kinsey acknowledged the orders with a salute and departed with the sergeants. The major seemed to be pleased with his assignment. Levi figured that the major would eventually get into the proper historical spirit.

"With your permission, I'd like to spend a day or two schmoozing the locals, Mr. Thurman," said Dark. "That's something I'm good at. Over the years, I learned a lot of useful information that way."

"Sounds good," decided Levi. "A Telmierian diplomat should be able to stay out trouble. Check in with me every four hours. Have some fun while you can. Soon I will be putting you to work."

Lisa watched Dark as he left the room. "I don't think you need to worry about him, Levi. He impresses me as a man who knows how to avoid trouble and deal with it when he can't."

"Let's visit the marketplace," suggested Levi. "Perhaps we will have some interesting opportunities for discussion with some of the natives. Socrates showed us how useful that can be."

Levi chose to take an indirect route to the main marketplace. Not far from the business district, he and Lisa passed through the old quarter. The narrow winding streets looked like they hadn't changed in centuries. Surprisingly, even the poorer section of town had little trash messing up the streets and sidewalks. Regularly the historians passed street vendors peddling a variety of food and wares, haggling with customers.

The stone and wooden buildings of the old quarter appeared to be holdovers from a much less technologically advanced time. The newer, wider streets ran north to south, east to west. They were composed of the same material as the road the team had taken into Aurelin. Occasionally, the historians encountered pairs of policemen walking beats. Soldiers manning checkpoints closely observed people as they passed through. They only stopped people who looked suspicious or behaved suspiciously.

"Is the city under martial law?" wondered Levi.

"Maybe it's the military that helps to keep things so peaceful," speculated Lisa. "The vast majority of visitors are barbarians. If I was the mayor of Aurelin, I'd want a military presence too."

"Curious," commented Levi as he scanned the highest buildings. "No habitable structure in city we passed is higher than fifteen stories. The limits don't seem to be because of earthquakes. It would take a hell of an earthquake to bring those buildings down."

"All buildings on Telmieria in high-risk earthquake zones have the same height restrictions," said Lisa. "Sometimes we have very severe earthquakes."

Not far from the poor quarter, the historians encountered commercial buildings. They gazed in admiration at the polished white marble. Statues of civilian and military leaders stood at the entrances of the buildings like sentinels. Just like on Telmieria, noted Levi.

"Lisa, what was it like growing up Telmierian?" asked Levi as curiosity overcame him.

The question surprised her. "I never really thought about it, Levi. Growing up on two different worlds has been a unique mind-expanding experience. Family and duty to the Empire are paramount. Family duties, education and public service occupied most of my time when I was growing up." Lisa smiled in wistful remembrance. "I still had time for fun and mischief. There are no closed doors in imperial schools. We were taught how to think, not what to think. Virtues are cultivated, not imposed. Parents use positive reinforcement, not shame, to teach their children. That's what it's like growing up Telmierian."

Finally, Levi and Lisa arrived at a bustling square filled with many stands. Prosperous looking commoners tried to sell their wares to the rapidly growing crowds. The historians stopped at a stand filled with all kinds of fruits including tropical fruits. The vendor had no shortage of customers.

The short, crewcut vendor eyed Lisa appreciatively. "You are obviously a lady of taste and discernment. My fruit is the best in Aurelin." He pointed to a fruit stand a few stands away. "Not like the wormy trash of my competitors."

"How much are the mangoes?" asked Levi.

"For people of quality like you and your lady, one silver sovereign apiece."

Levi was about to pay the vendor, but Lisa stopped him. "You're supposed to haggle," whispered Lisa into his ear. "He'll be offended if you don't."

Levi and the vendor haggled until they reached agreement on the price of the mangoes. The vendor sighed and told Levi that he was taking advantage of a poor man. After the sale, he asked the historians to come back soon.

"Levi, look over there," said Lisa when she spotted something interesting on the other side of the marketplace. A crowd of people sat down around a silver haired man. When the historians got closer, they found that the man was telling stories to the people.

"An old-fashioned oral storyteller!" exclaimed Levi with great delight. The oral storytelling tradition had nearly died out in the Alliance. Telmierian storytellers triggered a Renaissance of the tradition on Terra. Both adults and children listened to the elderly man in rapt attention. An idea popped into Levi's mind. At the conclusion of the performance, Levi and Lisa approached the storyteller. Levi bowed respectfully.

"My sister and I love your wonderful stories, grandfather. May I tell you and your people a story about the mysterious empire of Chin?"

Interest shone in the old man's eyes. "Where is this empire of Chin?"

"The glorious land of Chin lies on the far side of the world. During my travels abroad, I encountered a storyteller from Chin. He taught me stories from his country.

"I have never heard of the land of Chin," confessed the old man. "Please share your story with us."

Levi had studied with one of the best Telmierian storytellers. He researched all the extant books of Chinese Fairy Tales. Occasionally, he told stories to appreciative audiences at Time Control parties. Levi used his holo-thought imagizer to bring the stories vividly to life. Within a minute, he had the crowd hooked. At the end of the story, people applauded and tossed coins to him. They implored him to tell another story. Levi obliged them with the tale of the Divided Daughter.

Halfway through the story, a royal floater approached Levi. The commoners quickly moved out of the way. Lisa gasped when she saw the attractive blue skinned couple in the open floater. Both wore the same gold pendant as the other people. The woman listened intently to Levi's story. She played unconsciously with her long raven hair. Her handsome escort, an athletic looking aristocrat, silently fumed. He glared at Levi. Lisa glanced at one of the coins that had been given to Levi. The woman's image was on the silver coin. Levi suspected that she was a princess.

The woman called Levi over to the floater. Levi bowed to her. He completely ignored her escort. "Your obedient servant, Lady."

"I am Princess Nura, descendant of the Sun Lords," announced the princess imperiously. The twinkle in her eye belied her haughty tone of voice. "By happy chance, I heard your wonderful story. I wish to hear more of them."

Princess Nura removed her signet ring and pressed it and her hand against Levi's palm.

"Come to the palace at the fifteenth hour tomorrow. Present my ring to the guard at the main gate of the palace. Inform him that I summoned you."

Levi bowed. "You greatly honor me, princess."

Princess Nura favored Levi with a smile. She ordered her driver to resume the journey to the palace. Levi watched the floater disappear in the distance. He wondered if he was awake or dreaming.

Lisa took Levi aside. "While you spoke with Princess Nura I scanned her DNA. She is part human and part Karani, mostly Karani."

"Karani?" echoed Levi in consternation. "Has the Empire found its own door to the past or has there been a splintering of the timeline?"

Lisa sighed. "I have no idea. There is an answer. We must find it before we return home."

Chapter Three

Levi and Lisa's sleep was restless and fitful. They woke early the next morning, having gotten little refreshment from their rest. He had discussed the Telmierian connection to Atlantis with Lisa late into the night. The Empire's insistence of having Dark on the mission now seemed very sinister to both historians. Levi recalled his joke to Dark at the party. We hardly trust ourselves with the Time Door. Levi put that issue on the back burner. The team had historical work to do.

Levi and Lisa studied the soldiers' reports. The army had a base near Aurelin. It contained soldiers and tanks that could occupy the city quickly should the need arise. Soldiers had apparently been deployed in the city to assist local law enforcement, not supplant it. Atlantis had a naval base nineteen miles up the coast from Aurelin. Twenty cruisers and destroyers were currently anchored there. Each ship was armed with cannons and solarite tipped missiles.

Kinsey reported that twenty foreign merchant ships, all sail propelled, were currently loading or unloading cargo. Half the number of Atlantean freighters were docked or anchored in the harbor. Kinsey had engaged people working on the dock in conversation. He learned that ships loaded and unloaded around 24/7 except on the Day of Rest at the end of the week and important holidays. Kinsey also learned that many yachts occupied a privileged place in the harbor. Levi was surprised that they were powered by engines and sail.

Levi summoned Dark and the soldiers to give them their assignments. "Major Kinsey, I want you and the sergeants to study local law enforcement and security forces. I would also like you to begin collecting as many different weapons as you can for the Time Control Museum."

"Yes, sir!" replied Kinsey enthusiastically. The soldiers saluted and left. "Mr. Dark, I want you to continue indefinitely to hobnob with the blue bloods. You might learn some valuable information about the Atlantean government and diplomatic affairs. I'm confident that you can pass yourself off as a man of importance."

Dark smiled. "I won't disappoint you. It's strange and disquieting to deal with Karani in Atlantis." He laughed as Levi's joke finally sank in. "Ah, blue bloods. Very good. I will check in with you every four hours." Dark left without further comment.

"Let's get moving, Lisa. I want to get as much work done before my date with Princess Nura."

"I have a bad feeling about this, boss," said Lisa uneasily.

"It's risky," agreed Levi. "I don't have much choice. Royal requests are little different from royal commands."

At the end of the day's work, Lisa returned to the inn. Levi went alone to the palace. Four guards dressed in scarlet and white uniforms observed him very carefully as he approached the main gate. Diffidently, he presented Princess Nura's ring to the guard who seemed to be in charge.

"Princess Nura has summoned me," Levi informed the guards.

The guard placed the ring in a pouch hanging from his belt. "We have been expecting you, foreigner," said the guard with an evil grin. "You are very punctual."

Uh-oh. There is nothing in the Historians Manual to cover this, thought Levi uneasily. The guards seized and bound Levi. They dragged him to a cell deep within the palace. Stone faced stationary guards and roving patrols gave the prisoner disdainful or indifferent glances as he passed them. When Levi's escort reached his assigned cell, they removed his binders, opened the door, and unceremoniously tossed him inside.

No wall shackles, relatively clean and dry, noted Levi in his historical log. The sound of squeaking, scurrying rats alarmed Levi. He scanned the cell and was relieved to find nothing else living in the cell. Very subtle, these Atlanteans, thought Levi appreciatively. Hopefully, Atlantis hadn't discovered the rack or thumbscrews. He made a note to find out if Atlantis had shock rods and other delightful high-tech toys.

Levi contacted Lisa. "How is your visit with the princess going, boss?" asked Lisa.

"Not very well," confessed Levi. "Instead of regaling Princess Nura with my stories, I was dumped in the dungeon to warm a cold cell. The cell isn't too bad as cells go, but I wouldn't give it four stars."

"Remember that sourpuss guy with the princess?" asked Lisa. "His name is Maric. His father is the Supreme Commander of the Atlantean army. Maric was very angry that Princess Nura invited you to the palace. He would have you killed without reluctance or hesitation."

"A real charmer," commented Levi. "Right now, I wish we had personal shields. For the moment, I will sit tight and wait to see what happens. I think Princess Nura will eventually figure out what happened and spring me."

"I wish I was that confident," said Lisa. "If you want to talk, you know my number."

The silence of the cell was a little unnerving. Sounds of tortured prisoners screaming and begging for mercy or the relief of death would have been more unnerving. Levi scanned the rest of the dungeon. To his surprise, he discovered that he was the only prisoner. Solitude and silence often drove prisoners mad. They often served as a crucible for the strong minded. Levi hoped that he wouldn't be around long enough for that to happen to him.

As the minutes passed, memories of his early life welled up unbidden to his consciousness. For some reason, he thought of childhood memories and his mistakes, bumbles, and other things he preferred not to think about. Levi was becoming less thrilled by the interaction part of his mission. A Fairy Tale princess and a land of legend come to life in its magnificence and splendor, was not what he or the Time Council expected.

Levi wondered if Atlantis had been destroyed by some preventable event. He knew he would be tempted to keep it from happening despite the possibility that his life and reality might change drastically. In the end, he knew that he wouldn't save Atlantis even if he could. Levi didn't doubt that he would do a poor job playing God. He hadn't thought much about it before, but why wasn't the Time Door a portal to the future as well as the past? Did the future even exist? For the half century of its existence, the Time Door had been closed to the future. As Gideon Warner regularly reminded Temporal Historians, the temporal sword cuts both ways.

The opening of the cell door interrupted Levi's musing. A tall, athletic looking man about thirty entered the cell. His plumed helmet and insignia of office revealed him to be the Captain of the Palace Guard. He carried a short sword and a sidearm. At least it wasn't the headsman with his ax.

"Have I received a royal pardon, sir?" joked Levi nervously.

The captain acted as if he had heard nothing, but Levi thought he detected amusement in his eyes. "Come with me, sir," he requested respectfully.

Levi struggled to keep up with the captain's long swift strides. He never looked back to see if his charge was still with him. The captain led Levi on a direct path to the southern side of the palace. The servants stared at them and whispered to each other. They seemed very curious, but chose not to question the captain. Apparently, guests like Levi were not common. The unpretentious elegance of the palace greatly impressed Levi. Its statues, paintings and vases would grace any emperor's palace. The murals of gardens and mountains showed an almost oriental respect for nature.

The captain took a short cut through the Hall of Audiences. The panorama of the solar system moved Levi to stare in open mouthed wonder. It contained not just all the planets, but their moons and the asteroid belt. Had Atlantis traveled beyond Terra? As far as Levi could tell, Atlantis had the necessary technology for space flight. So far, the team hadn't discovered any spaceships or heard news about spaceships under construction.

The captain led Levi to Princess Nura's apartments. He knocked on the door. A cute female servant opened the door and allowed them to enter. She eyed Levi with suspicion. The captain presented Levi to Nura in her Receiving Room. He saluted her and left. Nura's servant remained. She eyed Levi like he posed an immediate threat to the virtue and safety of the princess.

Princess Nura's apartments were as magnificent as Levi had expected. The spacious rooms had been decorated with expensive furniture, paintings, vases, and statuettes. Nura had a Receiving Room that could comfortably accommodate ten people. Levi doubted that she had ever had more than a few friends or cousins during any visit. Beautiful animal sculptures adorned the Receiving Room. Blue carpets covered all the rooms Levi had passed through.

Princess Nura smiled and rose from her chair. "Welcome to the palace, storyteller. I am glad that Captain Etor found you alive and well. The officer who arrested you will be punished. He acted on orders of Lord Maric, the man who was with me yesterday. Regrettably, he is too important to be punished as he deserves." Nura turned to her servant. "You may leave us now, Seren." For a moment, Seren looked into Levi's eyes like she was trying to determine his character and intentions. Reluctantly, she left the room.

"You may call me Nura when we are alone," announced the princess. "What is your name?"

"I am Levi, son of Jacob," replied Levi. "I come from a small country on the far side of the Inner Sea. The Atlantean name for the Mediterranean Sea was very appropriate, thought Levi.

Nura indicated with a nod that she understood the reference. "How long do you plan to stay in Atlantis, Levi?"

"My sister, my friends and I will be here at least a few months," responded Levi truthfully. "We heard of the beauties and wonders of Atlantis and had to experience them for ourselves. I want to learn Atlantean stories and tell my own as well."

"Excellent!" exclaimed Nura in delight. "Hopefully, you will stay longer. Maybe you can make Atlantis your home."

Nura was so unlike what Levi expected from Atlantean royalty, warm and open, happily devoid of royal airs and arrogance. Levi felt that she was starving for simple human contact that was a rare pleasure for a princess. He could imagine how tiresome it must be for her to have people constantly sucking up and seeking advantage and favors.

"Please tell me more of your stories of Chin," asked Nura. "Your performance in the marketplace was too brief."

Levi performed five of his favorite Chinese stories. Nura listened in wide eyed wonder, hanging on every word. Before each story, he explained the Chinese customs and references. He drank some wine when his throat became dry. To make the stories more real, he created images using the holo-thought imagizer.

"I wish there were magical foxes, dragons and fairies," said Nura after Levi finished his performance. "How did you create those amazing images?"

"Magic," replied Levi with a wink.

Nura laughed. "Of course. A magician never reveals his secrets." Nura gazed thoughtfully at Levi for a long moment. "Levi, commoners enjoy simple pleasures denied to princesses. You can go to the marketplace, shop, hear stories and even tell stories. A princess can only dream of these things. I only heard your stories because the main marketplace was along the way to the palace. I want you to take me there now disguised as a commoner."

"I do not think the king or the captain would like that," said Levi uncertainly.

Nura's gazed sternly at Levi. "It is my will!" she stated with finality.

"Your will, princess," murmured Levi.

Nura ordered Seren to get her a white pigment to cover up her blue skin. While Seren applied the pigment to Nura's exposed skin, another trusted servant brought one of her own dresses with a hood to cover her face. The disguise couldn't hide Nura's beauty.

"What do you think, Levi?" asked Nura hopefully.

Levi studied Nura for a long moment. "Most likely, the guards will not even give you a second look. People outside the palace will probably not look closely at you either."

Nura reflected for a moment. "I will risk it," she decided.

Nura and Levi walked past many guards and servants on the way out. As Levi figured, no one paid much attention to them. They both breathed a sigh of relief when they passed by the guards at the main gate. They said nothing until the guards were out of earshot.

Nura sighed. "Free at last, even if only for a short time! Levi, thank you for the chance to forget about Princess Nura and royal duties. Sometimes, I get so tired of my golden cage I could scream." Nura slipped her hand into Levi's. "I have often wondered what it would be like to walk hand in hand with a man. It is even nicer than I imagined. Aurelin looks so different from a sidewalk's point of view. How pleasant to be a part of the city rather than an observer."

"Most people do not have a floater's view of Atlantis, Nura," noted Levi. "It is good to be able to look life in the eye."

Nura gazed up at the clear cloudless sky. "Perhaps blue is the favorite color of Father Sun. Why else would he crown his creations with it?"

"Perfect combustion is a blue flame," noted Levi.

Nura smiled. "Our color may be perfect, but we Children of The Sun are not. My father often reminds me that even a king and princess are imperfect people."

"A wise king and father," approved Levi. "Heaven pulls down the proud. It is best that we humble ourselves rather than move heaven to humble us."

"You speak like a follower of the Sun Path," noted Nura with surprise. "Have you read our Book of Commandments?"

"I have not," admitted Levi. "Nura, not all foreigners worship idols and spirits."

When they arrived at the main marketplace, Levi and Nura found the old storyteller that Levi had encountered the day before. Forty people, mostly women and children, had gathered around him, enjoying his performance. The storyteller noticed Levi and smiled. Other people who recognized Levi joined the audience. Levi and Nura approached the storyteller at the end of the performance.

The storyteller bowed to Nura and shook Levi's hand. "My name is Mikel. I am happy that you returned to the marketplace today, my son." He gazed curiously at Nura. "You seem very familiar to me, daughter. Have we met?"

"No, grandfather," replied Nura demurely.

"My name is Levi, son of Jacob. I come from a land on the far side of the Inner Sea. This is my friend, Manara," explained Levi. "I got acquainted with her on an earlier visit to Atlantis." Levi noticed that the audience was gazing expectantly at him.

Mikel smiled. "They remember you from yesterday, Levi. They will not leave unless you perform some of your stories."

Levi told five new stories. The audience, especially the children, listened quietly to the performance. Levi entranced everyone with the holo-thought projector's vivid images. He greatly enjoyed performing his stories. It gave him as much enjoyment as his historical work.

At the end of his performance, Levi felt mentally tired from using the imagizer.

Levi thanked the people for the coins they gave him. A short, sour looking man walked up to Levi and glowered at him. "I am Rinan, Membership Officer of the Storytellers Guild," he announced with practiced arrogance. "No one may perform in public as a storyteller without being a member of the guild."

"I was not aware of this, sir," apologized Levi. "I would be delighted and honored to join the guild."

"Foreigners have never been allowed to join the guild," declared Rinan pompously. "You will cease and desist immediately, or the guild will take legal action against you!"

Rinan stopped his tirade when he noticed that the sullen looking audience had surrounded him. He gazed nervously at the people. A rough looking man in his twenties shoved Rinan, almost knocking him down. "Who do you think you are, you ridiculous runt? Let the storyteller perform in peace!"

"The guild has its rules and regulations!" persisted Rinan.

A young mother with three small children kicked Rinan in the shin. "The only time I get any peace and rest is when my children listen to the storytellers. You want to take this away from me because you won't allow this man to join the guild!"

The woman's words seemed to set off the crowd. One person, then another began to pommel Rinan. Mikel silently watched. Levi thought Mikel seemed unable to believe what he was seeing. The people ignored Levi's entreaties to desist. The crowd chased the unexpectedly fast Rinan out of the marketplace with jeers and volleys of stones. Nura watched it stunned to speechlessness.

"I hope my new fans' love never turns to hate," murmured Levi. "Rinan was lucky there was no tar and feathers handy."

Mikel chuckled. "Rinan is a self-important, second-rate guild bureaucrat. When he reports to the Guild Master what happened, I do not think the guild will bother you again. Most likely, you will be granted a Professional Courtesy Dispensation as a member of a foreign guild. That will permit you to perform as you chose for the remainder of your stay in Atlantis. You will have to pay prorated dues while you are here."

"That is fair and reasonable," figured Levi.

Mikel watched the slowly dispersing crowd and shook his head "I have never seen an audience ever get so angry at a guild official. I hope that I never see anything like this again."

A security shuttle from the palace rushed into the square. It forced the people to get out of the way. The shuttle stopped short of Nura. Captain Etor with six palace guards jumped out with weapons drawn. They ordered Levi and the people to back away from her. The captain glowered at her. "Did you enjoy your unauthorized, unprotected visit to the marketplace?" he demanded angrily. "You might have been injured in that riot!"

"I was very careless about my safety, captain," realized Nura. "I just had to be free, even if just for a moment."

The captain's anger subsided a bit. "Please do not travel without an escort again, princess." The guards hustled her into the shuttle, then got in. The captain turned his ire to Levi. "You will not be punished for this incident, storyteller. You had no choice but to obey the princess. Do not come to my unwelcome attention again!" With that pronouncement, the captain got into the shuttle. It took off and soon disappeared from Levi's sight.

Levi sighed. "Princess Nura is as surely a palace prisoner as anyone occupying a cell in the dungeon. She just has some freedom of movement, better quarters, better clothes, and better food. It was nice to meet her and spend some time with her. I doubt that I will see her outside of the palace again."

"Truly royalty lives in a golden cage," agreed Mikel. "We need not envy anything of her life. Please perform regularly, Levi. You can perform every day except Seventh Day. It is our Day of Rest."

Levi didn't have the time to perform every day, but he decided that he could perform three or four times a week. He either earned good money by storytelling, or the team had to finance itself through robbery or burglary. His choice was clear.

"Let us discuss that over dinner." Levi sniffed. "Is that ribs I smell?"

Mikel smiled. "It is. I think you will enjoy Zelek's Ribs. They are the best in Aurelin. It will be my treat."

Chapter Four

Levi quickly established the team's work routine and schedule. After a few days, the Special Observers became more interested in their recording. As Levi expected, they learned quickly. He felt that they had real potential as historical workers. For the historians, the mission was almost as much fun as it was work. Interaction was proving to be as helpful to the history gathering as Levi had hoped and expected. No perusing of historical records and tomes could have revealed the heart and spirit of the Atlanteans.

It had been two weeks since Levi had his visit with Princess Nura. The rest of the team regularly kidded him about it. Everyone had quickly become comfortable with each other. They were all on a first name basis. By necessity, Levi had to press the observers into service to get the recording job done. The observers did not complain. They understood and appreciated that no other Earthfleet personnel would step through the Time Door after them.

The team discovered that Atlantis had technologies spanning centuries. It appeared that everything had developed mostly in the past six centuries. The video and communication networks of Aurelin were as good as those of New Washington. No one had found a spaceport. The Atlanteans used anti-gravity transports, both civilian and military, instead of helicopters. Atlanteans were very safety conscious. Floaters seemed to be limited to royalty, aristocrats and the very rich.

The soldiers spent much time studying and researching the Atlantean military. They didn't need to travel around the island to learn what they desired. Dark showed an unexpected talent for hacking into computer and communications networks. His schmoozing helped him to learn a lot about the lives and activities of the higher classes of Atlantis. Overall, they seemed little different from modern Karani and Telmierians.

Levi decided that he wanted to have Dark with him on the Atlantis II mission. He was an excellent scrounger. Levi thought Dark would have made an excellent intelligence agent. The man had boundless energy and enthusiasm. Levi decided that Bobby was very wrong about Dark. His presence on the team was not a gift but a reward. Dark never spoke much about his life or past. He skillfully deflected most personal questions with witty responses. Levi and Lisa were aware of Dark's nocturnal adventures. It didn't bother them because he always did his job well.

Dark began to lead a double life within a week of the team's arrival in Atlantis. By day, he schmoozed and recorded. By night, he roamed the streets of Aurelin looking for pleasure and entertainment. Dark soon found all the pleasure and entertainment he could handle. He resorted to burglary to pay for it. The historians would not have approved of his misuse of the invisibility cloak.

Dark had no interest in using the services of the inn's pleasure ladies. On all his assignments, he only enjoyed high class pleasure ladies. On his third day in Aurelin, he discovered the Palace of Celestial Delights. He was shocked to find two beautiful Karani women working there. Pleasure service and giving birth to an illegitimate child were the most disgraceful things a Karani woman could do.

Dark had never had the chance to bed a Karani woman. He wasn't about to waste the opportunity. Dark observed and studied the Karani women. Not surprisingly, they wore masks to help shield their identities. Unlike the other pleasure women, they had the right to choose the men they gave themselves to. Dark casually moved within range of their conversations with customers. Rigellians had unusually good hearing. It didn't take him long to size up the blue skins.

The younger one appeared to be not much over twenty. Her expression often seemed bored and disinterested. The woman's voice had an irritating whiny quality. Without her blue skin, she probably wouldn't have as many customers. Dark turned his attention to the other Karani woman. Her beauty had fully blossomed. He guessed that she was twenty-five or twenty-six, an old maid by Atlantean standards. She spoke pleasantly and intelligently. Her voice sounded like music to Dark's ear. She bore herself with an unpretentious dignity.

When Dark spoke to the women, he bowed and called them lady. He noticed that none of the other men did. Dark's respectfulness to the women didn't go unnoticed. The madam, a very attractive woman named Muna, chose him for herself on his first visit to the Palace of Celestial Delights. She didn't disappoint Dark. This time he wanted to enjoy the Karani woman of his choice.

When Dark entered the common area, the older Karani woman walked over to him. She ignored three other men who attempted to engage her in conversation. Her smile and body language indicated interest in Dark.

"You are a true gentleman, sir. Your courtesy to the palace ladies is sadly lacking in most of our clients. My name is Dawn. I am certain that we have never met."

Dark bowed. "My name is Jerrel, lady. You are correct. We have never met."

Dawn gave Dark a long appraising look. "You are neither Atlantean nor Lemurian, yet you are no stranger to civilized manners. What barbarian country could have produced a quality gentleman like you?"

Dark smiled. "Pockets of civilization exist throughout the world. The gods kindly placed me in one of them."

"Have you come to Aurelin for business or pleasure?"

"In Aurelin it is possible to do both," parried Dark.

"You would have made a good diplomat, Jerrel."

"I came to the golden isle seeking business opportunities that cannot be found anywhere else in the world," began Dark. "I also wanted to see the beauties and wonders of Atlantis, not the least of all its beautiful ladies."

Dawn nodded. "There is no flattery. You only state a fact. If you are not in a hurry, I would like to talk for a while." She smiled mischievously. "No extra charge. You are a man of intelligence and wit."

Dawn took him by the hand and led him to a couple of empty chairs away from the rest. Her movements were smooth and purposeful. Dark admired her independence. A man would only have Dawn on her terms. He wanted to know her much better. Dark ordered wine for himself and Dawn.

Dawn sipped her wine. "Like your conversation, subtle and delicate. Opportunities can be made as well as sought."

"As my people say, 'the roast duck does not fly into your mouth.'"

Dawn laughed. "A delightful saying. I will remember it. Jerrel, you impress me as a man who would succeed and prosper even without connections. Still, I think a partnership with an Atlantean businessman is best for you. What do you bring to a partnership?"

"A fair question," acknowledged Dark. "Some money, some talent and great determination."

Dawn leaned closer to Dark. "Talent and determination are great assets. They make up for deficiencies in other areas. The ability to create wealth is more important have having wealth one has not created or worked for. Many aristocrat families lost or squandered their inherited money. The Palace of Celestial Delights began with Muna's dream. Hard work and determination made it come true. How do you rate Muna as a lover? She rated you very highly."

The question totally took Dark by surprise. He gazed at Dawn with admiration. She knew how to throw a man off stride and gain advantage. It was a shrewd test. If he answered the question directly, it would make him look boorish. If he refused to answer, she might dismiss him.

"No words can do justice to her," replied Dark carefully. "It is difficult to imagine greater mutual pleasure with a woman."

Dawn unexpectedly kissed Dark. "Well spoken, Jerrel. Muna taught me bedroom arts. Let us see if the student can equal or surpass the teacher."

Dark had made love with women of many races on more worlds than he cared to remember. Some had pleased him more, others less. He had touched their passion but never their thoughts. Dawn's passion was refined, unlike the passion of women like Jinny. Dawn gave all of herself in pleasuring him, holding back nothing. He experienced a tide of pleasure that seemed to flow from the depths of his being. In inundated him like a tsunami. For a moment, Dark felt fear. It quickly vanished.

Dark felt emotionally naked when he and Dawn looked deep into each other's eyes. It seemed like their spirits and emotions were joined. Dark let the experience fully embrace him.

It felt like he had been spiritually joined with Dawn. A feeling of wholeness flowed through him. The deep joy and delight seemed to last for hours. Eventually, the pleasure ebbed away leaving a pleasant afterglow.

They silently savored the memory of their joining. Dark knew that something strange and wonderful had happened to him. The hate, anger and pain that had driven him throughout this adult life had been purged. Dawn seemed to have had a similar experience. For the first time in his life, logic and reason utterly failed him. His joining with Dawn had a spiritual quality that evoked a feeling of reverence in him.

Suddenly Dark understood. The intense passion and pleasure were Dawn's as well as his. Empathic Karani women had the ability to create a psychic link with their lovers. It more than doubled their shared pleasure. Telmierians rarely spoke about to outsiders. Dark and Dawn lay together in no hurry to dress. Dawn didn't have to ask who pleased him more, herself or Muna. She knew fully without words.

"Never before have I been at such a loss for words, Dawn," confessed Dark. "After tonight, I can never enjoy another woman as I have enjoyed you. No one else could compare."

Dawn kissed Dark. "That sounds very eloquent to me, Jerrel. There is no charge for tonight. For what you have given me, taking payment would be wrong and insulting. You and I are now joined together, heart, mind, and spirit. I am yours and you are mine, in life and in death. I never suspected that I had the gift. This Joining only happens between people who are meant to be joined. Tonight, my time in the palace ends. I am yours alone. Next Sixth Day, meet me at the Grand Hotel at the nineteenth hour."

"I look forward to it, Dawn."

Dark sighed. Whether Time Control liked it or not, the ride home would include Dawn.

He smiled with wry amusement. Dark went on the mission to work mischief on it. The mission unexpectedly worked mischief on him. The Divine surely had a sense of humor. Dark appreciated the joke even if it was on him. Although the joining with Dawn had greatly changed him, Dark had to continue with his mission. He was honor bound to perform his duty. Now it was extremely unpleasant and distasteful to him.

After seeing the security around the Time Door during his tour of Project Timestream, Dark realized that he had no chance to destroy the Time Door. An attempt to do so would only result in his useless death. Dark had no fear or reluctance to sacrifice his life to accomplish something very important or necessary. He refused to throw away his life for nothing. It suddenly occurred to him that there was one blow he could strike against Time Control. He could arrange for a bomb to wipe out the Time Council. Of course, it would also cause his death. Dark knew he could no longer do it. King Eikel had to be content with the death of two Temporal Historians.

Chapter Five

Levi decided to visit the harbor and talk to some of the barbarian sailors. Lisa insisted on accompanying him. After Dark and the soldiers left to complete their assignments, Levi and Lisa walked leisurely, having no need to hurry. Levi wanted to see international commerce from a foreigner's point of view. The historians regularly talked to foreigners who ate and drank at the inn as well as people on the street. Foreigners had mixed feelings about Atlantis.

The historians followed a serpentine ancient street that led to the harbor. Warehouses and import shops catered to both locals and foreigners. Small groups of foreign sailors drifted past Levi and Lisa, seeking cheap wine and cheap women. They laughed and told dirty jokes. Pairs of policemen patrolled the harbor keeping close eye on the sailors. They dealt harshly with men who bothered respectable women.

"Hearing barbarians speak Telmierian sounds so strange to my ear," said Levi.

"Mine too," said Lisa. "I don't know if I'll ever get used to it."

As on the day of the team's arrival in the city, foreign ships filled the harbor and lined the docks. Every berth appeared to be occupied. Visitors and Atlantean dock workers labored together to load and unload goods with astonishing efficiency. When one ship left, another soon replaced it. Levi and Lisa walked over to a foreign ship that had just finished unloading its cargo.

The burly captain finished negotiations with an Atlantcan businessman. They sealed the deal with a handshake. In Atlantis, a handshake was as legally binding as a written contract. Six sailors including the First Mate turned their attention to the historians while the captain dealt with a Customs officer. The officer took care of business with cheerful efficiency. The sailors left the ship and gathered around the historians.

"We rarely see nice, pretty ladies around the docks," commented the First Mate. He elbowed one of his men who moved too close to Lisa. "They do not care for our rough company."

"Or our smell," cackled a grizzled, bandy-legged sailor. The others laughed raucously.

The First Mate chuckled. "The commoner women like us well enough when they see our gold and silver. They do insist that we shave and take baths. I do not like shaving, but the baths are all right, especially when you have good female company."

"Do the Atlanteans harass or mistreat you?" asked Levi.

"Most of the time they are all right," admitted the First Mate. "Many blue skin men are arrogant and treat us like dirt."

"The voyage to Atlantis from the Inner Sea was long and tiresome," complained Lisa. "It took more than two moons. We had no sight of land after passing through the Pillars of Atlan. Sometimes I feared we would never see land again."

"A journey to Atlantis by sail is long and tiresome," agreed the First Mate. "Were it not for the magic engines the captain bought in Aurelin, our journeys would be longer and less profitable."

"Until Atlantis came into view, I often feared that we would reach the edge of the world and fall off," said Levi.

The sailors laughed uproariously. "We sailed across the Murian Ocean to Lemuria," said one of the sailors. "We bear witness that the world is not flat."

"Thank the gods for that," said Levi with relief. "My sister and I will take an Atlantean ship on the voyage home if we can. I did not expect the Atlanteans to share their magic with foreigners."

The First Mate scowled. "We must take an Atlantean with us on every voyage to operate and service the engines. He costs plenty of money. In all fairness, he tried to teach many crewmen how to do it. None of them were able to master the machines. The engines have increased the ship's profits fivefold."

The captain finished with the Customs man and joined his men. He bowed to the historians. "I am Badrik, captain of the Sea Dragon." He turned to Lisa. "You honor us with your presence, lady."

"My sister Lisa and I live far from the sea, Captain Badrik," said Levi. "We have been fascinated with ships since we were children. Your ship is much larger and nicer than the one that brought us to Atlantis."

"And better smelling," sniffed Lisa.

"You will have to go very far to find a better ship than the Sea Dragon," Badrik proudly informed the historians. "We also carry passengers. Maybe you can return home with us if the timing is good."

"I was surprised to find that most Atlanteans are nice and friendly," said Lisa. "So far, no one has made my brother and I feel unwelcome."

"The common people are agreeable," allowed Badrik. In a lower voice he said, "A lot of the blue skin men I deal with are arrogant bastards. Often I wanted to take a couple of them and knock their heads together." Badrik sighed. "I would love to bed one of the blue skin beauties. They are pleasant if we remember our place."

"The biggest surprise of my visit so far has been the absence of slaves," mentioned Levi casually.

"That's more than I can say for my country," said Badrik. "Atlantis condemns criminals and prisoners of war to their mines. Those men are little better than slaves."

The First Mate's face darkened. "I do not care much for the Atlanteans magic weapons. One of them is a machine that creates and throws fire the length of my ship."

"It's true," confirmed Badrik. "About a week's journey from Aurelin, a marauder ship overhauled us. Out of nowhere, a metal navy ship appeared and intercepted the marauders." He shivered at the memory. "The Atlantean warship shot liquid fire at the marauder ship. The entire ship was engulfed in flames in seconds. All the marauders were burned alive. If the Atlantean captain had been in a benevolent mood, he would have just rammed the ship and let the crew drown."

"I did not feel sorry for those scurvy dogs," admitted the First Mate. "They kill good men who work hard for their living. They deserved what they got."

"Let me buy you and your men some wine," offered Levi. "In exchange, you can tell me and my sister some of your sailor stories."

"It is early in the day for wine," noted Badrik.

"Only for getting drunk," disagreed Levi.

Badrik laughed and slapped Levi roughly on the back. "You are a wise man, Levi. I accept the gift of your wine and your lovely sister's company."

At Badrik's suggestion, they went to the Blue Whale saloon, a favorite of foreign sailors. It served a noisy but mostly well-behaved clientele. The First Mate said the saloon watered down their wine much less than its competitors. The barmaids were all friendly and open to offers. Levi couldn't believe how full the saloon was before noon. Six barmaids rushed around constantly trying to keep up with all the orders. The historians and the sailors sat down at the last unoccupied table.

An intricately carved wood blue whale hung on the wall behind the bar. Four bouncers with shock rods watched over the customers to prevent trouble and deal with it when it occurred. After the crewman drank their wine, they left to take baths before seeking female companionship.

Badrik pointed to nets hanging from the ceiling. "Those nets are not for decoration Levi. When fights break out, the bartender drops a net on the men who are fighting. Then the saloon's guards use their shock rods on the offenders. No one is foolish enough to risk a second experience."

"Do the Customs men take a big bite out of your profits, captain?" asked Lisa.

"The Atlanteans are not greedy," admitted Badrik. "In truth, the duties are bearable. The benefits of paying them do much to ease the pain. They buy us the protection of the army and navy in the Sea of Atlan and all the places where Atlantean merchant ships sail. Trade would be much more dangerous without the Atlanteans."

Atlantis strongly reminded Levi of the British Empire of the nineteenth and twentieth centuries. It had a similar form of imperialism. People under Atlantean dominion appreciated the benefits. They deeply resented the control. Their position would always be inferior. Except for some machines like the merchant ships engines, Atlantis fiercely guarded its technology. Other countries resented that Atlanteans placed themselves above local laws. They also showed little respect to local customs and sensitivities.

Levi found it curious that Atlantis had made no attempt to convert people in other countries to their religion, although they felt strongly that their god was the only true one. They allowed people to join the Brotherhood of Father Sun, but never proselyted. Atlantis had zero tolerance for human sacrifice or abuse of women and children. They left idol worshipers alone if they didn't bother anyone. Badrik didn't believe in his own gods, but he made sacrifices to them occasionally just to be safe. He warned Levi and Lisa never to speak disrespectfully of Father Sun.

"I am very worried about the future, Levi," whispered Badrik. "General Garai, the Supreme Commander of the Atlantean army, has been trying for years to convince King Adeil to conquer the western world. He has been pressuring the king to marry Princess Nura to his jackal son, Maric. I heard rumors that the king will eventually agree to the marriage. An Atlantis ruled by those two men would be a great sorrow to the world. Lord Kal is the man I prefer for to succeed King Adeil. He has long been a voice of reason and peace. Heaven help Atlantis and the world if Maric ever becomes king."

"Lord Kal must be a great man if he impresses a foreigner so much," said Lisa. "Captain Badrik, you call your ship the Sea Dragon. Are there sea dragons?"

"I cannot say that I ever saw one," confessed Badrik. "I have met some men who swear by all the gods that they did." Badrik told the historians of the sea creatures that he saw on his sea voyages like whales and Great White Sharks. Badrik checked the time. "My First Mate and I must go now. I need to get enough gold to pay my men before they get mad and cause trouble. It has been a great pleasure to visit with you and Lisa. Maybe our paths will cross again."

"I think it's time to get back to work, Lisa," decided Levi. "We are having far more fun than Temporal Historians should have. Hopefully, we won't run into Princess Nura or Lord Maric."

"Amen to that," agreed Lisa.

At 1400, the historians returned to the inn. They saw two palace guards were waiting by the door. Levi suspected that they were looking for him. There was just one way to find out. The historians walked up to the guards who blocked the entrance.

"We seek the storyteller Levi," said one of the guards.

Levi suspected the guards knew perfectly well that he was the man they sought. Security cameras had probably recorded him when he visited Princess Nura. "I am Levi. Can I help you with something, sir?"

The guard with an officer insignia came to attention. "We have been ordered to escort you to the palace. Princess Nura commands your presence."

"I do not think you should wait for me, Lisa," said Levi. "Let us go, gentlemen. We do not want to keep the princess waiting."

The officer summoned a floater that arrived a few minutes later. It had the royal crest painted on the sides. The floater flew at an alarming speed, but managed to avoid hitting other vehicles and pedestrians. Levi got the impression that the guards were annoyed by having to wait so long for him to return to the inn. When the floater reached the main gate of the palace, it stopped. Levi and his escort disembarked. The guards at the gate checked him for weapons. Fortunately, Levi forgot to take his stunner and dart gun.

Levi's escort took him to the palace library. One of the guards opened the door and directed Levi to enter. They then returned to their duties. Levi found Nura sitting at a table reading a book. She noticed his presence and told him to sit down beside her.

"Welcome again to the palace, Levi. I want to enjoy another one of your performances, but my father ordered me to be confined indefinitely to the palace. The only way I could enjoy another performance was to have you brought to the palace. Thank you for accepting my invitation."

"Invitation?" echoed Levi in surprise. "The guards said, come with us, so I came."

"The guards were to convey my invitation, not treat you like you were under arrest," said Nura irritably. "I must have a long talk with them. Some of the palace guards lack good diplomatic sense. Being with you two weeks ago was one of the most enjoyable times of my life. I like that you treated me just like an ordinary person. When I am with you, I feel that I am free to be just Nura rather than Princess Nura. Almost everyone I see wants something from me or my father. It is so rare to meet a man like you who is content with what he has. Being with you makes me feel free although I am not."

Levi wasn't sure what to say. Nura seemed sincere. "You honor me, Nura. Your company and conversation are very pleasing to me as well. It feels strange and a little uncomfortable to enjoy you like you were a commoner like me."

Nura smiled and placed her right hand on his. "Relax, Levi. You will not be punished for your familiarity with me. It is my wish. You are here with my father's permission and approval." Nura checked the time. "Our dinner should be waiting for us in my apartments. I am sure that you will enjoy it."

Levi followed Nura down the corridors until they arrived at her apartments. The guard at the door saluted her and opened the door for her and Levi. As Nura predicted, dinner was ready. They sat down at the table and began to eat. Levi savored the steak and the vegetables. The cook who prepared the food was an artist. Levi had never enjoyed a better meal or a finer wine. He and Nura talked about their families and countries.

When they finished their meal, servants removed all the dishes and leftovers. Nura took Levi by the hand and led him to her bathing pool. To Levi's astonishment Nura took off all her clothes. Levi hesitated a moment before he disrobed. Nura slipped into the pool and beckoned him to join her. She pressed her body against his.

"Nudity is another kind of freedom," murmured Nura. "The unclothed state is the most natural. It is difficult to be proud or pretentious without clothes. Few people have ever been invited into my apartments. You are the first man outside of my family to enter here. This has not happened by chance. Father Sun has brought us together. For a season, we will be friends and maybe more than friends. You will be my special guest at the palace for a few days. My servants and I will do all that we can to make your stay in the palace one you will happily remember."

Part of Levi felt delighted to spend time with a beautiful and charming princess. The Temporal Historian in him felt very annoyed that Nura would be keeping him from doing his historical work for days. All he could do was gracefully accept it. When he retired to his guest room, he informed Lisa that she and the observers had to temporarily pick up the slack. On the bright side, he could freely study and record the books and royal records as a guest instead of an intruder. Why fight it?

Chapter Six

Levi used his provident sojourn in the palace to look through the books and records in the palace library. To his surprise and delight, Nura was willing to let him read books and records at length. His interest in the library greatly pleased her. Viewing the video records proved entertaining as well as informative. Nura happily answered all of Levi's endless questions. She seemed to have become a bluestocking for lack of more useful things to occupy herself with.

The dehumidifiers in the library helped to preserve the hardbound books and records. It helped to prevent the mustiness of libraries that Levi disliked. Levi checked the titles as he browsed. The library's classification system eluded him. It was the Library of Alexandria all over again. Even the ancient Dewey Decimal System would be a big improvement.

Levi missed exploring Aurelin. It had much less stress and social friction than one would expect in a city of its size. Aurelin spread out with enough space between buildings that people didn't feel squeezed. Never had Levi experienced a modern city so quiet in the Alliance. New Washington didn't come close to Aurelin's cleanliness. In all fairness, Aurelin punished littering severely. One didn't have to go far to find a garden. The clean air and water made the city very livable.

The government of Atlantis had a surprisingly small bureaucracy for a modern state. Government employees seemed to perform their duties cheerfully and efficiently. The people Levi and Lisa dealt with were as pleasant and helpful as if it was an election year. As in all ages, the rich and the aristocrats had the playing field tilted heavily in their favor in business and the courts. To a large degree, laws and regulations applied equally to all citizens of Atlantis.

Atlantis was a Constitutional monarchy with a Senate that had much power and influence in the country. The king's rule was not absolute. The Code of The Kings guided government and the judiciary. It preceded and greatly exceeded the Code of Hammurabi. Yet tradition, often stronger than law, strongly encouraged noblesse oblige in the king and aristocracy. Atlantis had capital punishment. It was applied only for treason and heinous crimes. A convicted person had just one court of appeal before the king. His judgment was final.

Nura had achieved good conditioning through careful diet and daily workouts in the palace gym. She insisted that Levi join her in the gym. For three days, he experienced a lot of soreness. He didn't visit the Time Control gyms regularly. Nura eagerly accepted Levi's suggestion that they do some jogging. Apparently the thought hadn't occurred to her. They ran four miles on a track in Aurelin Stadium. Levi decided that physical conditioning before going on an interaction mission was a good idea.

Levi and Nura bathed daily in her pool at the end of the day. He wondered if she was testing her own self-control, his or both. The thought of making love to a woman of the past intrigued him. Levi decided that if Nura eventually chose to attack him, he would gracefully surrender. Time Control regulations only forbade sexual relations between team members during a mission. Regulations permitted Temporal Historians to take some souvenir artifacts home with him. Princesses of the past didn't qualify as souvenirs.

When Levi commented that he missed telling stories in the marketplace, Nura decided to permit him to resume his schedule of performances with one proviso. She would accompany him. After Nura twisted Etor's arm very hard, he permitted her to accompany Levi in disguise. Plainclothes palace guards would watch over her very carefully.

Etor's attitude toward Levi began to change as he watched his performances. Gradually he grew less suspicious of Levi. He occasionally engaged Levi in conversation. Etor was intrigued that a barbarian as well-mannered and educated as an Atlantean gentleman. It both pleased and puzzled him. Etor began to understand why Nura enjoyed Levi's company and conversation so much. He enjoyed the anger and frustration of Lord Maric who greatly resented Nura's relationship with the storyteller.

It had been many years since Etor had seen Nura as happy as she was since getting acquainted with Levi. Her golden cage was a lonely place for her. Etor understood it very well. He hardly had a life outside of his job. Etor couldn't begrudge Nura her brief happiness with the storyteller. Before the end of the year, Nura would be betrothed to Lord Maric. Nura's happiness was the least of his concerns. Etor couldn't help but respect and appreciate someone who gave Nura much yet asked nothing in return.

Levi awoke early on the fourteenth day of his stay in the palace. He felt surprisingly refreshed both mentally and physically. As usual, he found his clothes laid out and his bath prepared. Everything was done while he was still sleeping yet the servants always managed to avoid waking him up. After bathing and dressing, Levi waited for a palace guard to escort him to Nura. When he heard a knock at the door, he hurried to respond. When Levi opened the door, he found Nura rather than the guard.

"May I come in, Levi?"

Levi's brain froze for a moment. "Uh, certainly, Nura."

Levi watched in curiosity and confusion as Nura walked through his apartment carefully examining it. "I am glad that your servants have taken good care of you. Levi, I know that you have felt more like a prisoner than a guest. It is not much different for me. From this day forward, you may come to my apartments without an escort as a true guest should be free to do."

Levi bowed. "You are very thoughtful and considerate, especially to a commoner like me."

Nura shook her head. "I have been very selfish keeping you here away from your sister and friends for two weeks. Today I release you from your prison. Please visit me for an evening every three days."

"Your will, Nura," agreed Levi with alacrity.

Nura looked earnestly at him. "Levi, ask any favor of me that you like, and it will be granted immediately. Take a moment to decide."

Levi wondered if Nura was testing him or simply trying to do something nice for him out of appreciation for their friendship. "I appreciate the thought, but I lack for nothing. A man with simple desires and tastes enjoys more peace and contentment. My only indulgence is visiting other countries."

Nura looked pleasantly surprised. "Someday you must bring your sister with you to the palace. If she is anything like you, I know that I will like and enjoy her."

"Soon," promised Levi. "Nura, may I ask you a personal question?"

"Go ahead, Levi."

"Why does almost everyone wear a gold rising sun pendant?"

Nura smiled. "Everyone who belongs to the Brotherhood of Father Sun is required to wear it. It reminds them of their spiritual covenants and duty to him. Hopefully, someday you will wear the pendant too. I will escort you to the main gate."

They said nothing as Nura led him down corridors until they reached the main gate. She hugged Levi before he exited the palace. "I look forward to your return."

Levi decided to walk back to the inn rather than taking a taxi. It would save money and he could use the exercise. Levi decided to surprise the team. When he entered the inn, he saw Lisa and the observers eating breakfast. Levi checked the time. It was 0900. Everyone should have left already. None of the team noticed his approach until was a few steps away from their table.

"When the Team Leader is away, the team members will play," said Levi in feigned annoyance. "You guys better get moving or I'll have your pay docked!"

Lisa, Dark and the soldiers enthusiastically welcomed Levi back. "It's about time you got back to work and start pulling your own weight, Boss," chided Lisa.

"What were you doing all that time, Levi?" asked Dark.

They all sat down. "I wasn't just having a good time with a beautiful Karani princess. I was also working," insisted Levi.

"Working?" asked Lisa skeptically.

"You wouldn't believe what the palace library has!" began Levi enthusiastically. "It has video records, computer records, digital books, hardbound copy books and palace records that go back over a thousand years. The library has a large Atlas as accurate as any of our time. Beneath the palace, they keep the original papyrus scroll records from before Atlantis achieved modern technology. Lucky for me, Nura is an avid reader and history buff. Eventually, we'll all have to do a few overnighters to record it all. What I didn't find is as intriguing as what I did find. The religious history practically stops six hundred years ago."

"It's like someone brought down the stage curtain on King Lear, then revealed the set for Romeo and Juliet when the curtain rose again," observed Kinsey.

"An appropriate comparison," agreed Dark.

"It looks like in the short run that we will find as many questions as answers," figured Kelly.

"That's why we will have other Atlantis missions to find the answers," said Levi. "Gentlemen, perform the tasks Lisa assigned you for today. After I have some breakfast, she and I will get to work on the task she assigned to herself. Check in with me every four hours and stay out of trouble."

Dark decided to rest in Aurelin Park after stopping for lunch. He didn't mind helping Levi and Lisa with their historical work. Before his current mission, Dark hadn't been very interested in any world's history including his own. Working as a history recorder during the mission made him desire to learn about his own world's past. Few Rigellian men cared about history. Their minds were focused on the schemes, dreams and work of the present.

Unknown to the rest of the team, Dark usually took a break at the park after lunch. He especially enjoyed the beautiful and fragrant flowers that had been carefully and lovingly cared for. The Rigel Home World had much beauty of its own. Dark hadn't paid any attention to it. An intelligence agent had many more important things to focus his attention on.

Dark moved to a bench near the fountain at the center of the park in a shady spot. Occasionally he spoke with commoners as he wandered on the winding paths. He especially enjoyed talking to young mothers as they relaxed with their small children. Their laughter as they played was far different from his own childhood. He never knew his mother. Often Dark wondered what she was like.

Atlantis is so different from the Home World, thought Dark enviously. The Rigel System seemed very colorless and drab by comparison. Utility and efficiency determined everything, never beauty. No wonder the Telmierians called the Home World the prison planet. Here on Terra, people knew and cared about their neighbors and often trusted them. On the Home World, a man necessarily viewed his neighbors with suspicion and distrust.

The Home World had no place like Atlantis in its past or present. Being schooled in Telmierian culture and customs, Dark realized the sterility of his own. The Home World had made real improvement during his lifetime. It happened from one single, but ultimately fatal mistake made by his grandfather, King Zukar. He abducted the Solar

President to persuade him to agree to an alliance with the Confederacy.

The effort failed in the end when a joint Terran-Telmierian team rescued him. While on the Home World, the President carefully and quietly sowed the seeds of a cultural revolution among the women. Its effects had been great and continued to increase with each passing year. Dark had come to believe that Rigellian men might someday achieve a degree of civilized thought and behavior.

Dark's mind kept returning to the Telmierian influence in Atlantis. Only the Empire could have recreated itself in Atlantis. Did they have their own Time Door? Were they using it against Terra while pretending to be the Alliance's friend? For almost half a century, the Alliance had made no effort to attack the past of any worlds of the Empire, Sirian Alliance or the Rigellian Confederacy. That could change when Gideon and Amara Warner were gathered to their fathers. Neither the Empire nor the Confederacy had any idea who would succeed them. This uncertainty weighed heavily on King Eikel's mind.

Despite centuries of bad blood and brief wars between the Confederacy and the Empire, the Telmierians had never tried to destroy it. The Empire only resisted efforts by the Confederacy to bring unwilling worlds under their control. Thanks to its efforts, the galaxy had maintained a balance of power that all the powers could live with. As Kelly observed, the team seemed to be finding as many questions as answers.

Dark became instantly alert when he noticed a casually dressed man sit down on a bench a couple of hundred feet away from the fountain. The man tried to act naturally, but Dark recognized him immediately as some kind of security or intelligence man. Dark wondered what could have aroused interest in him. He reflected on what he had done since arriving in Atlantis. Nothing should have aroused any interest or suspicion. Possibly law enforcement or army security checked out all foreign visitors to some degree. Dark looked directly at the stranger and smiled.

The man realized that he had been made. He got up and slowly walked over to Dark. "Good afternoon, friend. It is a perfect day to spend outdoors."

Dark regarded the stranger with amusement. He could easily rid himself of the man. The man would never know what hit him. It would be entertaining but counterproductive to his mission. "Have I unwittingly broken some law or committed an offense, sir?" asked Dark innocently.

"Not at all, sir," responded the man. "Let us say that you are associated with a man who has come to Lord Maric's unwelcome attention. We just want to ask you a few questions. Please come quietly."

Dark smiled unpleasantly. "Fortunately for you, I will."

The army security man sensed that Dark was not an ordinary man. He respectfully searched Dark for weapons but found none. Dark needed no weapons to defend himself. The security agent walked Dark over the parking lot where an unmarked security shuttle was waiting. The agent loaded Dark into the shuttle. It drove to the army base outside of Aurelin. The agent took Dark to an unmarked building. He left Dark alone in an interrogation room. Dark sat down and waited for the interrogator.

Just fifteen minutes later, a Lieutenant came in and sat down across from Dark. For a moment he studied Dark. He smiled pleasantly. "Your name is Jerrel Dark. You are staying at the Inn of The Seventh Ecstasy with your friend Levi the storyteller, his sister and three other friends. Have you come to Atlantis for business or pleasure?"

"Pleasure of course," replied Dark smoothly. "We heard of the beauty and wonders of Atlantis and wished to experience them for ourselves. We will be staying a while unless the government decides otherwise."

The interrogator eyed Dark with curiosity and suspicion. "Your friend Levi seems to have very good luck. By chance, if chance it was, he was performing in market square when Princess Nura's floater passed by. The performance intrigued her, and she invited him to the palace for a private performance. For two weeks she entertained him. This may be completely innocent, but we cannot make any assumptions. We take no chances with the safety of the royal family."

Dark didn't believe the army or civilian security truly believed Levi to be a threat to anyone. Levi would have been arrested if security truly feared that he might be a threat to Nura or the king. Disappearing peasants, especially foreign peasants, was easy enough. Dark figured that he had been picked up to serve two purposes. The first was to warn Levi to stay away from Princess Nura. The second purpose was to remind all the team members to continue to behave themselves if they knew what was good for them.

"You may go now," decided the interrogator. "Please forgive the inconvenience." The interrogator summoned a soldier. "Drop off Mr. Dark wherever he desires with the exception of the palace or military installations."

The soldier took Dark to the exclusive club frequented by the most important businessmen in Aurelin. A week ago, Dark bluffed his way inside. A group of men got together to play a high stakes game like Terran poker. Dark obtained a sufficient stake through nighttime robberies to be permitted to join the game. Wisely, he made certain that he won, but not too much to avoid wearing out his welcome. Today's game was in the afternoon. The next day was Seventh Day, the Day of Rest. All the members visited the Palace of Celestial Delights earlier in the evening on Sixth Days to spend some time with their wives and children.

When Dark entered the game room, his new friend Janno got up from the table and greeted him warmly. "You're late," noted Janno reproachfully. "Will you be joining us at the Palace of Celestial Delights this evening?"

Dark smiled. "No, I have a lady who is more pleasing than any of the women there. I feel very lucky today, so bet wisely."

Maric hurried to his father's home office after receiving the summons from General Garai's aide De camp. When the general said immediately, he meant immediately. Maric knocked on the office door. He didn't enter until the General Garai said, "Come." Maric walked over to his father who sat at his desk pretending to read some paperwork. Maric came to attention and saluted the general like any other man in his command.

Garai ignored his son for a moment, then finally looked up at him. Maric noted with concern that his father didn't give him leave to sit down. Garai gazed impassively at Maric.

"You seem to presume much lately, Force Commander," began Garai with deceptive calmness. "First, you presume to give orders to King Adeil's guards to throw Princess Nura's storyteller friend into the palace dungeon. Now you presume to take one of his friends into custody and interrogate him without justification or my authorization. What were you thinking, Force Commander?"

Maric heard the menace in the easy tone. The general expected no less of his son than he expected of every other soldier. "I did not think, General."

"I had to humble myself before the king to save you from punishment," growled Garai. "He was about to announce your betrothal to Princess Nura. Now he will leave me twisting in the wind indefinitely. I schemed and maneuvered for many years to put you on the throne. Your foolish jealousy may have ruined everything. If I did not have a majority of the Army and Navy in my pocket, the king would marry Princess Nura to Lord Kal. Now there is a chance that he may do so."

"Has the king pardoned my presumption, general?" asked Maric uncertainly.

Garai forcefully slapped Maric's head. "The king has pardoned your offense to him, thanks to my intercession. I have not yet pardoned your offense to me. Never forget that an offense to a Friend of the Crown is an offense to the king. You will only concern yourself with the storyteller and his companions if I decide that it is necessary. Concern yourself with your assigned duties lest I increase them so much you will not have time or energy for pleasure. Go! General Urian awaits you."

Maric saluted and left for his meeting with General Urian, his father's crony, and head of Army Intelligence. When Maric arrived at Urian's office, Urian made him wait for thirty minutes before seeing him. Maric felt intimidated by Urian who treated him like an importunate child. When the general called him lord, it sounded like sonny. Maric looked forward to making him pay heavily for the offense. Nevertheless, Maric felt a grudging respect for the craggy faced battle-scarred combat veteran.

Finally, the secretary ushered Maric into Urian's office. He walked over to the general and saluted. "Give me your report, Force Commander," ordered Urian.

"Lord Kemen has sent agents to find Project Sky bridge," began Maric. "We have not learned who informed him about it. Providently, the High Priest's source did not learn the project's location. So far, we have discovered and disappeared all of his agents. The Chief

High Priest continues to tempt fate. General Garai thinks that we may soon need to consider a replacement for him."

Urian smiled. The office of High Priest was a lifetime appointment. Only death or incapacity ended his service. "I agree with General Garai, but I do not think that is presently necessary. When it becomes necessary, Gotzon will have the pleasure of expediting Kemen's retirement."

Maric smiled. "I look forward to that day, general."

Chapter Seven

King Adeil waited patiently for Captain Etor in his office. For weeks, Etor had shadowed Nura and Levi while they were together outside of her apartments. Now Adeil wanted to know what Etor had learned about the storyteller and his intentions. At fifty-seven, he looked more like Nura's brother than her father. It would be many years before he started to show his age.

In thirty minutes, Adeil had to endure the wearisome parade of courtiers, sycophants, and toadies again. Every day they annoyed him with their endless complaints and requests for favors, most of which they didn't deserve. Only his incapacity or death would bring it to an end. Adeil sighed. He and his daughter had spent all their lives in their golden cage.

A knock on the door interrupted Adeil's train of thought. A guard ushered in Etor and closed the door behind him. Etor saluted Adeil who ordered him to make his report on Levi.

"I had an agent discreetly investigate the storyteller during his stay in the palace," began Etor. "He casually approached the storyteller's sister and their friends. Smoothly he engaged them in conversation to learn what he could. My agent also spoke with barmaids to get a complete picture of the foreigners. They are the innocent tourists they appear to be."

"Is anyone ever as innocent as they appear?" reflected Adeil.

Etor smiled. "Occasionally, sire. Levi is no killer. I can see that in his eyes. He is more likely to be a diplomat than a warrior. Princess Nura and Levi spent all their waking hours together during his two-week visit to the palace. He performed his stories for the princess and her maid servants. Levi tells strange and wonderful stories never heard before in Atlantis. He somehow conjures up marvelous images while telling his stories. He has spoken much about his travels throughout the world. Levi speaks our language very fluently and can also read it."

"Much to my surprise, Levi has spent many hours in the palace library. Curiously, he seems familiar and comfortable with our technology. When he looked through the Atlas, nothing seemed to surprise him. Levi and Nura have discussed the Sun Path at length. He seems very interested in our religion. I do not believe Levi is Atlantean or Lemurian. I know it sounds foolish, but it is like he came from another world."

"Very curious and fascinating," murmured Adeil. "Perhaps time will give us greater understanding of this unusual man. If Levi poses no danger to Nura, I will permit her to continue to enjoy his company as she pleases. Our true concerns are Garai and Maric. The general is very unhappy with me because I do not share his desire to create a world empire. He seems to have forgotten that Lemuria would oppose us. I want no conflict with Lemuria. To the contrary, it is time for us to finally make peace with Lemuria."

"That would be best for both countries and the world," agreed Etor. "That is not likely to happen if you give Maric Nura's hand in marriage. Lord Kal is the man Atlantis needs on the throne. He is everything Garai and Maric are not."

Anger and frustration welled up in Adeil. "Then a peace treaty needs to be negotiated and signed before he inherits the throne. Once the Senate ratifies the treaty, he cannot change it unilaterally. Two thirds of the Senate is completely loyal to me. Garai and Maric could do nothing. I am confident that you will see to it that I am not a victim of an unfortunate accident like my son. Is Levi currently visiting Nura?"

"Yes, sire."

"Bring him to me immediately, captain," decided Adeil. "I want to make my own judgment on him."

"Sire, I– Etor hesitated to broach a delicate subject. "Princess Nura seems very attracted to Levi. I fear that eventually that they, uh, will eventually become intimate."

At first, the idea greatly displeased Adeil. Then a pleasant thought came to him. "Maric would be very angry and offended if he found that his bride was no longer a virgin. His displeasure is my delight. Do nothing to discourage intimacy between Nura and Levi. If it occurs, please avert your eyes."

Etor blushed. "I would never, sire!"

Adeil shook his head. "I am the most powerful man in the world, yet I am powerless to do what I most desire. I cannot allow my only daughter to marry a man she loves, one who will love her and try to make her happy." Adeil took two scrolls out of his desk. "After you bring Levi to me, take these scrolls to Kemen. Tell him to give these to the Lemurian negotiator when he arrives."

Etor saluted. "I will not fail you, sire."

Just as Levi and Nura arrived at her apartments, they saw Etor appear around the next intersecting corridor. Etor called out to them to wait. He hurried over to them. "The king desires to speak with Levi immediately in his Private Audience Chamber!" he announced gravely. "He is very angry." Nura became very alarmed. "But with Garai and Maric, not Levi," added Etor.

Nura glowered at Etor. "I will accompany Levi and wait for him. I want to be ready to intercede if it becomes necessary."

When they reached the Private Audience Chamber, Etor ushered Levi inside. Nura waited anxiously to learn how the audience went.

Levi bowed to Adeil. The king didn't seem angry or annoyed. Adeil seemed more curious than displeased.

Adeil studied Levi. "You interest me, storyteller. Few men do. You are not Atlantean or Lemurian, yet with your bearing, speech, and behavior you could pass for either one. Certainly, you are no barbarian. You tell stories unlike any found in Atlantis or Lemuria."

Levi took a moment before replying. "For the most part, I am just an ordinary man, Your Majesty. Through the grace of Father Sun, my father had an Atlantean business partner. Through his teaching machine, my sister and I learned to read and write your language. My father is wealthy enough to send me on journeys throughout the western world. This is my first visit to Atlantis."

"Our science and technology intimidate and frighten most foreigners," observed Adeil. "Even visitors who have sojourned in Atlantis for many years still feel very uneasy about them. According to Nura and Captain Etor, you seem very comfortable with our technology."

Levi suppressed a smile. "Ignorant, superstitious people fear what they do not understand. Science and technology are not magic or evil."

"Is your country ruled by a king?" asked Adeil, unexpectedly changing the subject.

"Every four years all adult males choose a thirteen-member Council of Elders. The Chief Elder is chosen by the council members."

"Rulers chosen by the people," marveled Adeil. "This has never happened in all recorded history in Atlantis. What do you think of our form of government?"

"If the king is a good and able man as you are, Your Majesty, having a king is the best form of government," replied Levi judiciously.

Adeil chuckled. "Diplomatically put. You have brightened the life of Princess Nura. I thank you for that. Understand that in the coming months, I will announce her betrothal to Lord Maric. Until her wedding, she may enjoy your company as she pleases."

For a long moment Adeil said nothing. Levi saw a strange light in the king's eyes.

"Lord Maric is very displeased about your relationship with Princess Nura. Your life is in great danger. I am surprised that he has not yet tried to kill you. Outside of the palace, his agents could strike you down at any time in any place. Nura's friends have always been under my protection for she has unavoidably had few. Until now, none of her friends needed my protection. Only one thing can protect you."

Adeil took his scepter and commanded Levi to kneel before him. He placed the scepter on Levi's head. "Levi, son of Jacob, I, Adeil, king of Atlantis, declare you Friend of the Crown with all attendant rights and privileges. An insult to you is an insult to me. An injury to you, is an injury to me. For the remainder of your life, you are under the protection of the crown. Now not even a general or lord dares to harm you. You will receive a medallion attesting to your new status. When someone is made Friend of The Crown, they are granted one favor from the king. What do you desire?"

"I would like to have a floater of my own, Your Majesty," replied Levi boldly.

The request surprised Adeil. "So be it. Your floater will be ready for you tomorrow. It is not hard to drive. One of my guards will teach you how. I have heard that you conjure up amazing images as you perform your stories. Soon you will perform some of your stories for me. You may return to the princess."

Levi bowed and left the king. "What did my father want with you, Levi?" asked Nura anxiously as soon as he rejoined her.

"The king expressed concern that Lord Maric might try to have me killed," said Levi. "Understandably, Maric is very angry that you are spending so much time with me. The king informed me that the only way he could prevent my assassination was to make me Friend of The Crown. He bestowed that honor on me."

Nura sighed with relief. "Thank Father Sun!"

Levi smiled. "I think he put me under his official protection more to annoy Lord Maric than to benefit me."

Nura laughed gaily. "You can be certain of that, Levi. It seems that you have made a good impression on my father. I have only known you a short time, but something tells me that you are a good friend, one I can trust completely."

Levi suddenly realized that Nura had a rudimentary telepathic ability. It hadn't been developed but it was there, nevertheless. She could read his emotions and probably got impressions of some of his thoughts. Levi knew that he and Nura were beginning to feel more than friendly toward each other. It had begun innocently and unintentionally. Levi wished he could go back in time. He would just have listened to Mikel's stories. Nura would have passed by without even noticing him.

When it was time for Levi to return to the inn, Nura asked him to stay for the night. Mysteriously, she told Levi that she wanted him to experience the fullness of palace hospitality. Levi sensed that it was a request rather than a command. He couldn't imagine what he had missed. When Levi returned to the room, he found Navad, supervisor of the palace guest suites, waiting for him.

Navad appraised Levi. He seemed to like what he saw. Navad bowed. "It is customary to provide bedroom companions to all gentleman guests of the royal family. Princess Nura asked me to convey her apology for this oversight." Navad handed Levi seven photos of some of the loveliest women he had ever seen. "Please choose one of these ladies to serve as your bedroom companion when you stay overnight at the palace."

Atlantis was proving to be a source of endless surprises to Levi, most of them pleasant. He hadn't planned to know any ladies in the

Biblical sense during the mission. Nura decided that he would. Levi looked over the ladies very carefully before making his choice. He handed a photo to Navad. "She is not only fair but agreeable looking as well."

"An excellent choice, sir!" agreed Navad enthusiastically. "I will send her to you without delay. My daughter will not disappoint you."

For a moment, Levi couldn't process what Navad had told him. He seemed happy and proud that his daughter served the palace in that fashion. Levi decided to investigate the matter.

Navad bowed and departed. Twenty minutes later Levi heard a soft knock on the door.

When he opened the door, he found the lady from the photo. She looked even better in person. The woman smiled and bowed. "I am Zira, handmaid to Princess Nura. She asked me to convey her thanks for honoring her humble servant."

"Please come in, Zira," invited Levi. "I was going to relax in my bathing pool before retiring for the night."

"I will prepare everything for you."

Zira quickly laid out two towels and Levi's night clothes. She led him to the bathing pool, where they both undressed. Levi sighed with contentment as they slipped into the pleasant warmth of the water. Zira expertly massaged his neck and shoulders.

"How long have you served in the palace, Zira?" asked Levi.

"Next month it will be four years," replied Zira. "Our basic training lasts one year. I began mine on my nineteenth birthday. Those of us fortunate enough to serve the royal family get another year of training. Only a small number of ladies earn the privilege of serving as bedroom companions. After three years of service, I earned this privilege. It has its rewards."

Levi had heard of the bedroom companion service from other servants. It never occurred to Levi that it applied to him. Many second and third sons of highborn families chose bedroom companion servants for wives. The highly prized women were not only beautiful but intelligent and educated. Levi didn't doubt that a lady as nice and pleasant as Zira would fail to find a rich or aristocrat husband through her bedroom service.

"Princess Nura told me that you share many beliefs of the Sun Path," mentioned Zira casually. "That is very unusual for non-Lemurian foreigners."

Levi chuckled. "Thank you for not saying barbarian."

Zira laughed. "You are as civilized a gentleman as any born and raised in Atlantis. You have been greatly blessed by Father Sun. Most Atlanteans take for granted the blessings we received from the Sun Lords."

Levi almost jumped at the mention of the Sun Lords. So far neither he nor the team had learned much about them. People became quiet and clammed up whenever Levi or Lisa asked about the Sun Lords.

"You are the only person except for Princess Nura who would even speak of them," said Levi. "Are they the gods of Atlantis?"

Zira stared at Levi in amazement, then she laughed. "Many centuries ago, the Sun Lords came to Atlantis from heaven. They all had wondrous blue skin. The Sun Lords took Atlantean women for wives. The firstborn daughter of our last native king married the most powerful Sun Lord. King Adeil is his direct descendant. We do not speak of these things to foreigners, Levi. I share this with you because you are not an idol or spirit worshiping heathen. Do you think that you will join the Brotherhood of Father Sun someday?"

"It is possible," allowed Levi. "I think I am ready to go to bed, Zira."

They got out of the bathing pool and dried off. Zira led him to the bed. Levi smiled. He decided that this incident would be left out of his historical reports although not his personal log. Most likely, the Warners and the rest of the members of the Time Council would be happier not knowing.

Chapter Eight

General Garai slipped unobtrusively into the Half Moon saloon, favored by sailors and assassins. He wore a gray hooded robe like those worn by commoners. It cloaked him in anonymity. He frowned as the odor of a long unwashed body that assaulted his nose. Garai disdainfully brushed off low class pleasure ladies who offered him their services. The men in the saloon ignored him.

Garai's eyes scanned the saloon until they locked onto the subject of his visit; Gotzon, the master of the Assassins Guild. The man sat by himself at a table facing the door. Garai thought he looked more like a bureaucrat than the most skilled hired killer in Atlantis. Only his fellow assassins and customers knew who he was.

The man became alert when he noticed the stranger's scrutiny. He eyed Garai warily as he approached him. His eyes widened in recognition. "I am honored by your visit, general. Please sit down and have some wine."

Garai sat down and studied the wine bottle. "I think I will pass on the wine. I have a job that requires exceptional skill, a challenge worthy of Gotzon, Master of the Assassins Guild."

Gotzon grinned. "Who will it be this time. The princess? The king himself?"

"That kind of talk can get you disappeared and buried in an unmarked grave," warned Garai.

Gotzon was not troubled or offended by the threat. He leaned back on his chair and balanced it on the back legs. "It is true that you can kill me with impunity, Lord Child of The Sun, but you will not. There is no one else you dare trust."

Garai relaxed. Carelessly he tossed a bag of coins in front of Gotzon. "Ten thousand gold sovereigns. Consider it a down payment."

Gotzon quickly and efficiently counted the money. He confirmed Garai's count. Garai smiled. "They are all good. Passing counterfeit currency is a serious offense." The same could be said for regicide, reflected Garai with amusement. "No king since the coming of the Sun Lords has ever been assassinated."

"Then history will be made," declared Gotzon solemnly. "When and where do you want the job done?"

"I will let you know."

After some perfunctory traditional haggling, Garai and Gotzon agreed on a price of one hundred thousand gold sovereigns half to be paid one week before the job and the rest on completion. They sealed the deal with a handshake. The Assassins Guild assigned numbers for all the guild's customers. Gotzon personally kept the records. Only he knew who had assassinated the heir to the throne and who paid for it. Most people still thought the prince's death was an accident.

So far, Gotzon hadn't tried to blackmail Garai. With very few exceptions, the general reserved his complete trust for the dead. Once the job was done, Garai planned to eliminate the entire Assassins Guild to ensure that his secrets remained safe permanently. He would then confiscate all the guild's money for himself. King Maric wouldn't have any objections.

The day had finally come for Dark to see Dawn again. He struggled to keep his mind on his mission and his historical chores. Dark had chosen to rob thieves during the night to get money for his entertainment. It drove the Thieves Guild crazy that someone was effortlessly robbing guild members. It incensed and frustrated the Guild master that the criminal disappeared like a ghost after committing his crimes. Dark was enjoying himself so much that he felt almost guilty. The Alliance and the Empire would have been happier if he had just been a thief.

Levi permitted Dark to use his floater so he could travel to his dates with Dawn in style. It impressed and pleased her. As he drove to the Grand Hotel, he noticed that other drivers gave him plenty of space. Everyone could see that the floater belonged to someone of consequence. Along the way to the hotel, Dark passed the Palace of Celestial Delights, he recalled the intense pleasure of his Joining with Dawn. Just contemplating the memory felt like he was experiencing it all over again.

Six blocks later, Dark pulled up in front of the Grand Hotel. He noticed both aristocrats and rich commoners leaving and entering it. As soon as Dark got out, Dawn exited the hotel. Seeing her without the mask was strange. During the time they spent together at the Palace of Celestial Delights, she never removed it. The Joining unmasked her heart and spirit. All the men around her stopped to take a long admiring look. Dawn's elegantly simple white dress with blue star flowers revealed much skin, but no more than usual for a respectable Atlantean woman.

Dawn greeted Dark with a hug and a kiss. Her star flower perfume enticed him. She checked her watch. "You are very punctual, Jerrel."

"Only a fool takes a woman like you for granted," said Dark. "You look as lovely without your mask as I imagined."

Dawn smiled. "I only used my mask to conduct business with my former clients. It is no longer necessary. I have a special surprise for you. Tonight, we will sail on my family's yacht. The weather is perfect for a night sail."

After they got into the floater, Dawn inputted the location of the yacht into the navigation system. Traffic was light so the floater made good time. Streetlamps and outdoor building lights brightly lit up the night and streets. They conversed about many things on the way to the harbor. Dawn had much business knowledge. Her family had rich lands throughout Atlantis. Dark suspected that Dawn's mention of these things had a purpose. Her family was very important. Dark figured that Maric might have sought to marry her had he had not sought the throne.

The floater approached the docks used exclusively by the aristocrats. Most of the docks were empty. Dawn's father's yacht was the one of the few remaining. The captain waited for them by the gangplank. A crewman parked the floater.

The captain bowed to Dawn and Dark. "It is a pleasure to serve you and your guest. Lady Kanya. Too long you have been away from the Stream of Gold. Dinner will be ready within the hour."

So, Kanya is the name of my lovely Karani star flower, thought Dark. For reasons he couldn't even imagine, she had lived a dual life as Dawn the courtesan and Kanya the scion of wealth and privilege. Letting him know her real name told Dark two things. Her Dawn life was truly over. It also told him that Kanya was including him in her real life.

The running lights had already been turned on. As soon as everyone had boarded the yacht, the crew cast off. The Stream of Gold moved slowly out of the harbor. It turned to port to avoid a Coast Guard ship. Dark and Kanya leaned on the guard rail and inhaled the sea air.

"Kanya is a much lovelier name than Dawn," commented Dark. "It suits you."

"We are going to Sentinel Point on the windward coast," announced Kanya. "Then we will return to Aurelin. Even at night, the coastline is beautiful, especially with a full moon."

"I wonder if anyone lives on the moon," mused Dark. "Will anyone ever travel there and find out?"

"I have often wondered that myself," said Kanya. "We have the technology to travel to the moon, but Father Sun has forbidden space travel. He promised that someday the ban would end. Hopefully, we will live to see it."

"You seem much more relaxed here than you did in Aurelin, Kanya," observed Dark.

Kanya sighed. "Only when I am away from the city can my spirit fully breathe. Even a noblewoman has some tiresome social expectations and customs to endure. At least I am not expected to save myself for marriage. It is comforting to know that in a barbarian society, I would be little more than a servant of my father or a husband. In Atlantis, any woman can own property and control her own money independently after she comes of age. No woman can be compelled to marry against her will."

Dark frowned. "That is not the case in my country. I suppose that love is not a consideration for marriage with most people of your class."

Kanya looked into Dark's eyes. "It is for me."

Dark smiled. "I know. Until our Joining, I had no interest in marriage. All week I have wondered what we will do when your parents find out about us. Your father will have me thrown out of the country at the very least. Perhaps I should buy a grave."

Kanya pinched Dark's cheek. "I am confident that you will win over my parents. Our family only considers the quality of people, not their class."

Dark decided to see how Kanya would react to the truth about himself with some embellishment. "Kanya, I am the illegitimate son of my king. My mother was a peasant woman he took to his bed for a season. He dumped her when she became pregnant with me. The king did provide her with enough money to live on and take care of me. My mother only told me this when I came of age. One day the king summoned me to the palace."

"He gave me a large sum of money and ordered me to leave the country and never return during his lifetime. If I refused, he would lock me in the dungeon and throw away the key. His legitimate children knew nothing about me. If I ever told them that I was their half-brother, my father would kill me. I took him at his word. Since that time, I have wandered throughout the world. Before I left for Atlantis, I learned that my mother had died."

"Yet despite having been cast off and exiled by your father, you became a successful, civilized man," marveled Kanya. "Illegitimate or not, royal blood is royal blood. Too many highborn men behave as badly as your father."

Dark gazed up at the moon. "I believe that the gods expect men to live higher than the beasts. I want to believe they care about justice and hold men accountable for the injuries and wrongs they commit against others."

"Father Sun will balance all accounts whether here or after this life," Kanya assured him. "Often I wish He would prevent wrongs rather than right them."

"As do I."

"Like you, your friend Levi is also a remarkable man," noted Kanya. "He seems to be a favorite of Father Sun. I would like to hear his stories in a private rather than public performance. Can you arrange it, Jerrel?"

"I can. I will check with him to see when he can accommodate you."

Kanya sighed. "Levi's priority is Princess Nura. I recently visited her at the palace. I have never seen her so happy and content. She deserves more than a loveless state marriage. If only she was as blessed as me to choose the man she will marry."

Levi and Lisa gazed in wonder and delight at the Temple of The Sun. They had visited the temple on their second day in Aurelin, but they hadn't gone inside. They planned to visit and explore it earlier. Levi's unanticipated stay at the palace forced him to postpone the visit. Other things crowded it out for weeks. Finally, nothing stood in the way. They chose to visit late in the evening when there would be little or no activity there. Having the invisibility cloaks allowed them to easily and safely gain access to explore.

The Temple of The Sun rose in white marble splendor in the heart of Aurelin. A rising sun flag atop the five-level pyramid flapped in a stiff breeze. As the twilight deepened, circles of lights on each level lit up. The temple stood alone and aloof from the rest of the neighborhood. Pedestrians passing by stopped to admire the temple before moving on.

"I think the temple looks more beautiful lit up in the night," commented Levi.

Lisa scanned the temple. "Curious. The structure is about one thousand years old, but the heating and electrical systems are less than fifty years old."

"The temple must have been built before the Atlanteans acquired or developed their technology," figured Levi.

"Something tells me that the advanced technology was a sudden development rather than a gradual one," said Lisa.

"You could be right."

Levi tried the door. To his surprise, it was open. Inside the door, they found a hallway lined with torches on both sides. A smell of incense increased as Levi and Lisa moved deeper into the temple. Levi scanned the walls and ceiling. "The temple has no cameras, snoop devices or alarms, not even motion detectors. Either the clerics are extremely traditional, or they felt that no one would dare trespass for fear of the consequences."

The historians stopped when they entered a large chamber. Friezes of kings, ancient knights and filled the supporting columns. Their weapons and attire predated the present civilization. The paintings on the walls took Levi's breath away. One painting depicted blue skinned people descending from the skies on anti-gravity platforms. A man on the closest platform held up a staff with a glowing blue orb on the top. Other paintings depicted blue skinned people teaching farming and construction to the white skinned Atlanteans.

Lisa sighed. "The Children of the Sun are part Karani. These paintings as well as the DNA scans of Nura and Maric bear witness. How did they get here? The Empire has no Time Door that we know of. Having a Time Door and acting upset about ours makes no sense. Terra has the only known temporal rift in our section of the galaxy."

"Is there some long-lost group of Karani who could have reached Terra?" asked Levi.

"According to the ancient histories, all the surviving Karani scattered throughout the old Alliance gathered on Telmieria. Almost all present-day Karani live in the Empire or in the Alliance. The answer is somewhere here in Atlantis. I hope we can find it before the end."

Levi and Lisa took the lift to the highest level of the temple. They checked out the Holy of Holies. At the center of the room, the historians heard voices coming from the next room. They found the door open, so they walked inside. Braziers with cold fire brightly illuminated the room. The middle-aged High Priest knelt before a rectangular altar. An acolyte holding a golden chalice stood to his right. A group of ten priests wearing scarlet robes stood behind them. The acolyte handed the chalice to the High Priest who held it up chest high.

"This is the symbol of the covenant between Father Son and His people," intoned the High Priest. "It purifies and sustains us." The High Priest took a sip of sacramental wine from the chalice. He handed the chalice to the acolyte who did the same. One by one the other priests partook of the wine.

"Be merciful and forgiving, Father Sun!" chanted the priests in unison. "Blot out our sins and remember them no more. Let thy favor rest always on thy obedient servants."

"For your service and devotion, your sins are forgiven," pronounced the High Priest. "Be faithful unto death and be received into eternal bliss with Father Sun. Let thy Emissary return and open the stars to us."

Who was this Emissary? Where did he come from? Why had he forbidden Atlantis to travel to the stars? Atlantis had no space capability, so another Emissary never came to remove the ban. It seemed that some alien civilization wanted humanity earthbound. That would make it harder for Terra to protect itself from a space attack, yet no attack had ever come. A couple of generations ago, wreckage of a spaceship had been found on Terra. The Telmierians couldn't determine what world the ship came from. Could it have been the ship of the promised Emissary?

The historians quietly left the room. They took the lift down to the ground floor and hurried out of the temple. When they found a private spot, they deactivated their invisibility cloaks. They caught a taxi that took them back to the inn. As Levi and Lisa got out, a ground shuttle suddenly flew around the corner and stopped beside them. Two gray suited men jumped out with blasters drawn. One of the men held his gun against Lisa's head. "Get in the shuttle," he ordered. "Resist, and she dies."

The gray suited man hustled the prisoners into the shuttle. It sped off toward the center of Aurelin. The driver drove quickly but carefully through traffic. Levi noticed that the rear doors had no inside controls. He scanned the windows. They were all made of unbreakable glass. None of the pedestrians the shuttle passed showed any interest in it.

Lisa established a mind link with Levi so they could communicate telepathically. "These men are not cops, Levi. They would have frisked and bound us if they were."

"I don't think they are security or intelligence men either, Lisa. Could they be the private security of some powerful businessman?"

Lisa shrugged. "At first, I thought that they were Maric's men. They would be dressed like soldiers if they were."

The historians couldn't believe it when they saw that their destination was the Temple of The Sun. Their captors looked puzzled when their prisoners started to laugh. The shuttle pulled up in front of the temple and stopped. Two of the historians' captors marched through them to the door to the lift. Everyone got out on the fourth level. One of the men took them to a room at the end of the hall. They ushered them inside. The robe and medallion the man wore indicated that he was the Chief High Priest of Atlantis.

"Leave us," the High Priest ordered the historians' escort. He studied Levi and Lisa for a moment. "Please have a seat. So, you are the foreign storyteller Levi I have heard so much about. This lovely lady must be your sister. I am Kemen, the Chief High Priest of Atlantis. I have been looking forward to your arrival. The long trip from Suminar must have been very exhausting. It was very shrewd of you to use Princess Nura to learn more about King Adeil. That is when I realized who you were. I waited for the right moment to make contact. Now it is time to get down to business."

Levi checked and found the mind link with Lisa had not been severed. "Kemen obviously thinks I am someone from Lemuria he has business with. This could get awkward. I'll play along and see what happens."

Kemen smiled. "I regret the need for strict secrecy, but General Garai and Lord Maric must not learn of the treaty before it is signed, sealed, and delivered to the Senate for consideration and ratification. Regrettably, the forty-five-year armistice never led to a peace treaty. Once the treaty is signed, it will not be long before full diplomatic relations are restored between Atlantis and Lemuria."

"I look forward to that day, Kemen."

Kemen gazed at Levi with admiration. "Using storytelling as a cover was brilliant. No one would imagine that you are a Lemurian diplomat. Please forgive me for having you and your sister brought here at gunpoint. That was to throw off any intelligence or security men who may have been watching you. Staying at a peasant inn was also brilliant."

Levi smiled. "You are also very shrewd, Kemen. I need to see your authorization from King Adeil to conduct negotiations in his name."

Kemen handed Levi two scrolls. Levi read them carefully. The first named Kemen as the king's authorized negotiator. The second was the agenda the king had decided on. "Everything seems to be in order. When would you like to begin the negotiations?"

"How about after dinner tomorrow here in my apartments?" suggested Kemen.

"That will be fine," agreed Levi. "My sister serves as my secretary. She has the highest security clearance. I want her to attend our sessions."

Kemen looked over Lisa approvingly. "Your lovely sister is very welcome to attend. My secretary will not attend. Only King Adeil and I know about these negotiations. I want to keep it that way. This treaty must be win-win if it is going to work. I will be tough but just, Levi."

"As will I, Kemen."

Seren watched Levi and Princess Nura talking and joking as they ate dinner. It greatly annoyed her to have been supplanted by the foreign storyteller. Seren had been very close to the princess for many years. Suddenly, this foreigner appeared out of nowhere. Smoothly and easily, he ingratiated himself with the princess. Zira had also been relegated to second place in Princess Nura's affections although she gracefully endured it. Day by day, Seren became more displeased about the situation. Princess Nura was falling in love with the storyteller. Only she seemed to be unaware of it.

An idea came to Seren. She knew Maric was very angry about Nura's relationship with Levi. Why not get back at Levi and profit from it as well? At the end of the day, Seren disguised herself and went to General Garai's estate. She boldly told the guards that she needed to see Lord Maric immediately. At first, they denied her request. Seren told the guards that her business concerned the storyteller Levi. Immediately the guards became very cooperative.

One of the guards escorted her to Maric's apartments. The guard knocked on his door. He opened and door and gazed at the guard and Seren with annoyance. Maric dismissed the guard. He immediately recognized Seren. His annoyance changed to curiosity. "What do you want of me, Seren?"

"I have bad tidings for you, Lord Maric," began Seren haltingly. "As you know, Princess Nura has become very close to the foreign storyteller. The princess spends much of her free time with him. She has even taken him into her bedroom!"

"Her bedroom?" repeated Maric angrily.

"Princess Nura also shares her bathing pool with him!"

Maric struggled to rein in his anger. He didn't want to lose control in front of a servant. Although reason told him that he and Nura were not yet betrothed, she should not insult him by such familiarity with a foreign peasant.

"Please let me be your eyes and ears in the palace," entreated Seren. "I can learn things of much use to you."

Maric gazed warily at her. "Your first loyalty is to the king and the princess."

"My first loyalty is to the future king of Atlantis!" disagreed Seren. "My lady has allowed her loneliness and romantic nature to overcome her better judgment. In this instance, both your best interests and hers coincide."

Maric couldn't suppress a smile. Seren was a lot smarter and sneakier than he imagined. "And what reward do you desire for your service to me?"

"Do you think I desire pay for doing my duty?" asked Seren with feigned indignation. She smiled slyly. "Three hundred gold sovereigns a week."

"Done," decided Maric. For years, he had tried to plant spies in the palace. Etor always sniffed them out and quietly discharged them. None of the other servants of the royal family could ever be persuaded to serve him. Today one of them came to him unbidden. "Give me weekly reports about the activities of the princess and the storyteller and anything else that might be of interest to me. One of my soldiers will be your contact. He will identify himself with the code words night wings. Find out if Princess Nura is still a virgin. If she becomes pregnant, there will be no uncertainty."

Seren blushed. "That will not be easy, Lord."

Maric smiled unpleasantly. "I trust that your ability is equal to your nerve. Do not disappoint me."

Chapter Nine

The team relaxed for a while after finishing their dinner. Gallo's food was good, but Lisa thought it could be even better. One evening, she went to the kitchen and shared some Alliance and Telmierian recipes with the cook. At first, the presumption annoyed and offended her. When Lisa showed her how certain spices and ingredients could greatly enhance the flavor of the food, the cook became very interested. After the cook sampled the General Tso's chicken Lisa had prepared, she became very open to culinary suggestions. They also proved popular with the customers.

"Tonight, Lisa and I will attend a performance of the Aurelin opera," announced Levi to Dark and the soldiers. "All of you are welcome to join us. I guarantee that it will be a cultural experience you will never forget."

The soldiers and Dark looked at each other uncertainly. Levi detected no interest or enthusiasm in them. "I appreciate the offer, Levi," said Dark, "but I have a date with a special lady. In any case, I am not an opera kind of guy. My taste is more plebeian."

Dark excused himself and left the table. The soldiers claimed to have other plans and quickly left the historians behind. "It looks like it's just you and me for a night at the opera," noted Lisa. "This the perfect combination of historical work and play. The recording of this opera will be a Time Control first."

As a rule, Levi didn't have much interest in Terran opera. It seemed artificial and stilted to him. Lisa, on the other hand, loved both Terran and Telmierian opera. Levi enjoyed some opera music. He especially liked the music and vocals of The Merry Widow. The people of the art history division focused solely on art. Levi chose to take a taxi to the opera house rather than use his floater. He didn't want to call attention to himself and Lisa. Hopefully, none of his fans would be there.

Levi had the taxi driver drop off him and Lisa one block from the opera house. They arrived there without anyone recognizing Levi.

Curiously, the opera house had been built in the ancient style rather than the modern. It balanced beauty and practicality. The historians presented their tickets at the door, then went to their seats in the balcony. They were close enough to the stage to get an excellent view. Most of the people in the audience quietly conversed with other people. Everyone ceased talking when the performance began.

Unlike modern Terran opera houses, the Atlantean ones had no orchestra. Levi's scanned the area and discovered that an incredible synthesizer, rather than an orchestra, produced the music. He figured that the Atlanteans didn't want an orchestra to distract the audience from the performance. The opera was based on an ancient love story. It balanced comedy and drama well. Levi suspected that a story like Hamlet would have been incomprehensible to Atlanteans. They despised weakness, vacillation, and indecision.

Levi was grateful that he knew Telmierian as well as his native English. He needed no universal translator. Like most Telmierians, Lisa spoke Telmierian and English well. They only used the translator to adjust for the Atlantean variant of Telmierian. Levi marveled that the Telmierian language had not changed all that much in thousands of years. His missions showed him that art revealed much about a people and their culture.

Like the Telmierians, Atlanteans were upbeat and optimistic. They had the old American can-do mindset. In the historians' brief time in Aurelin, they learned that most of the people, high, low, and middle, strove to balance work and pleasure. Duty always came first. The story of Romeo and Juliet would fall flat in Atlantis. Suicide and defiance of parents seemed to be rare from what Levi had read and seen. Atlantean lovers would have found an imaginative way to accomplish the fulfillment of their love.

Levi and Lisa thoroughly enjoyed the opera. So did the Atlanteans as their thunderous applause attested. Levi and Lisa waited until most of the audience left before they got up to leave. Levi inhaled deeply of the pleasantly cool air after they left the opera house. He was impressed by the efficiency of the people in getting their rides. Many people had chosen to walk home. Opera goers in New Washington would not have.

"That performance was incredible, Lisa," said Levi. "I think Dark and the soldiers would have enjoyed it."

"I agree, boss. Maybe you can get them to watch part of the recording you made. If they like it, they can attend a live performance."

"You know, I think Emperor Marcellus would appreciate a copy of the opera," decided Levi. "When we get home, I'll send him one. I think Empress Zaya would like it too. She's Rigellian by birth, but Karani in spirit. It's my way of thanking the Empire for everything it has done for the Alliance."

"That's very thoughtful and appropriate. That will make you very welcome on Telmieria the next time you visit."

The historians took a taxi back to the inn. When they arrived, they found that Dark and the soldiers hadn't returned. They went to the bar and bought some wine. Levi had suggested to Gallo that serving better quality wines would bring in more business. The innkeeper did as Levi suggested and enjoyed the increased business and profits predicted by Levi. From that time on, Gallo gave the historians free wine. They didn't abuse the privilege.

"Lisa, we have visited every section of Aurelin except one," noted Levi. "The Night Kingdom."

"Because it's the section where the criminals and poorer classes live," noted Lisa. "I don't mind the poor people. I don't care much for the criminals."

"The common people also have their story," said Levi. "It's our historical duty to record it."

"I suppose a little slumming won't kill us," decided Lisa.

"Don't worry, Lisa. I have two aces up my sleeve."

The historians took their stunners and dart guns with them. This time, Levi took his floater. He used it sparingly because it brought him too much attention. Levi drove to the Night Kingdom and parked one block away from it. He didn't lock the floater. The dullest and most ignorant resident of Aurelin knew that it belonged to someone they would better leave in peace if they knew what was good for them. The historians stopped at the border of the Night Kingdom for a moment. In earlier drives around the city, they noticed that it was like there was an actual border separating the Night Kingdom from the rest of Aurelin. The transition to the Night Kingdom was very abrupt.

"Where do we begin," mused Levi. "Jinny told me that she sometimes works at the Last Chance Saloon. As a pleasure lady, no doubt. Let's start there." Levi checked his map of Aurelin. "The saloon is just four blocks ahead. Time to thrill, delight and charm the locals."

The historians passed a few people as they walked to the saloon. Younger women smiled inviting at Levi. The men regarded him sourly. People kept their distance as if the visitors were something outside of their experience and understanding. A man stood at the door of the Last Chance saloon screening prospective patrons. People whose looks he did not like he ordered to move along. One man tried to barge his way past. He got dumped in a puddle of dirty water for his trouble.

The screener looked over Levi and Lisa as they approached him. He immediately discerned their quality. His surprise indicated that he rarely encountered higher class visitors in the Night Kingdom. The man bowed and allowed them to pass. Every table was occupied. Slutty looking barmaids served drinks. Pleasure ladies plied their trade. Poor men socialized with friends as they enjoyed some drinks.

Levi gazed at a short, wiry man dressed in flowing gypsy like clothes chatting with a woman who sat on his lap. They noticed Levi and Lisa observing them. Levi thought they weren't certain what to make of the well-dressed strangers. Lisa followed Levi's lead. Everyone in the saloon stopped talking as Levi approached the flamboyantly dressed man.

Levi bowed. "May we join you, friend?"

The man seemed suspicious, but after some reflection he said, "Please sit. We do not have many quality visitors like you. What brings you to the Night Kingdom?"

"We were once poor too," explained Levi. "Only through the grace and mercy of Father Sun did we improve our lives. I have not forgotten where I came from."

The man smiled. "My name is Zaki, Master of the Thieves Guild. This my friend, Sira."

"Friend!" snorted Sira. "My friends do not share my bed as you do, Guild Master."

Levi couldn't suppress a smile. "My name is Levi. This is my sister Lisa. We came to Atlantis to see its beauties and wonders."

"Are you the storyteller Levi all of Aurelin has been talking about?" asked Zaki excitedly.

"I am," replied Levi modestly.

Zaki called out to everyone in the saloon. "My friends, tonight the storyteller Levi honors us with a visit!" Everyone else in the saloon ran over to Zaki's table and surrounded it. "We never imagined that you would deign to grace us with your presence. Father Sun be praised! Please perform a few stories for us. We will never have the chance again."

Levi rose from his chair. "It is my pleasure, Zaki."

After getting the crowd back off to a comfortable distance, Levi began a story. The enthralled audience listened in silence as he performed. They watched in delight as he conjured up images with the holo-thought imagizer. He concluded his performance after four stories. When the people took coins from their purses to pay him, Levi held up his hand and said, "Keep your money. This is my gift to you."

The people cheered and called on Father Sun to bless him. Zaki sighed. "Master Levi, we will always remember this night and your gift to us. I would like to give you and your sister a gift in return. I will personally show you places in the Night Kingdom that outsiders rarely or never see." Zaki looked over the clothes of the historians and shook his head. "You must change into more appropriate clothes."

Zaki sent Sira to fetch suitable attire for the Night Kingdom. Ten minutes later, she returned with it. The historians went to the room Zaki shared with Sira to change their clothes. Lisa wore a skintight, low-cut blue dress while Levi wore an outfit like Zaki's. He and Sira nodded approval.

"Our first stop is the Thieves Court, Levi," announced Zaki. "You and Lisa are the first outsiders to be granted this privilege. I am sorry that I must blindfold you. Outsiders are not permitted to know the court's location. I promise that you will not stumble or slip along the way."

The historians allowed Zaki and one of his friends to cover their eyes. The thieves took Zaki's guests by the hand. Levi and Lisa found themselves led along with the utmost care. They could estimate the distance, but not the direction they walked. Occasionally they were spun around to keep them from knowing what direction they were moving in. The smells told the historians what kind of places they were passing.

Levi and Lisa listened with great interest as Zaki explained the guild system. The guilds jealously guarded their territory and prerogatives. One joined a guild and if accepted, he paid his dues and learned his trade. If he tried to work independently, he would get hurt or worse. Some offenses were punishable by death. Zaki didn't elaborate. The guilds and the authorities reached an unofficial agreement centuries ago.

Children Of the Sun were sacrosanct. Even the Assassins Guild left them alone. The Guilds permitted no overlapping. The Thieves Guild forbade pleasure ladies to steal from their customers. Thieves could prey upon all Atlantean and foreign commoners. Guild masters received a degree of sufferance from the police and security forces. Regular payments maintained their privilege. Zaki complained that too few policemen were on the take.

"How many guilds are there?" asked Lisa.

"Twenty-two," replied Zaki. "The largest ones are the Thieves Guild and the Pleasure Ladies Guild. We also have a Storytellers Guild. My guild oversees them all. I heard that the Guild Master initially denied your request for a Professional Courtesy Dispensation so you could perform legally in Atlantis. After his lackey Rinan was rudely driven out of market square by your angry fans, he changed his mind. The Assassins Guild is the smallest guild."

"Assassins Guild," echoed Levi. "Why does the government tolerate an organization of hired killers?"

"What an innocent!" laughed Zaki. "Corrupt government officials, Army leaders and businessmen are the guild's best customers."

"I am surprised that Atlantis has a system as old fashioned as the guilds," commented Levi.

"They are a holdover from the days before the arrival of the Sun Lords," explained Zaki. "We Atlanteans hold tightly to tradition. The Sun Lords also decided that the guilds served a useful purpose. Guilds have not changed much since then. Originally guild membership and leadership were hereditary. Three centuries ago, it was abolished."

"What caused the change, Zaki?" asked Lisa.

Zaki hesitated before replying. He looked very embarrassed. "The old arrangement brought in so many deadbeats, the rank and file revolted. They forced the Guild masters to abolish hereditary privilege. Merit became, as it should be, the main consideration for guild membership, especially leadership. Under great pressure, the guild reduced initiation fees and dues. Most of the Guild masters grumbled about it. Personally, I think the members pay more than enough for the privileges of guild membership."

"Do you have loan sharks or protection rackets?" asked Levi.

Levi had to explain the terms to Zaki. "What an imaginative concept: forcing people to pay for protection from you! Atlantis has nothing like that. The Ministry of Public Safety would take a very dim view of such enterprises. We are practical people, Levi. The government knows it cannot eliminate the guilds and certain illegal activities, so it regulates and taxes them, endlessly."

Levi nodded. Government regulation, taxation and extortion were the downside of civilization. Humanity hadn't grown past them until after the Outer World Rebellion two generations ago.

"We have arrived at the Thieves Court," announced Zaki. He removed the historians' blindfolds. He laughed at the confused looks on their faces. "The outside of the building is not impressive. That is by design. It discourages the government and police from snooping around. Building inspectors rarely come to the Night Kingdom. They do not look very closely at things after we slip them a few gold sovereigns."

"More than a few," grumbled the bartender. "

As soon as they entered the building, the historians marveled at the elegance of the design and décor. It hardly looked like a court. A man dressed in a green robe sat on a bench outside of the first of four courtrooms. He was so absorbed with his paperwork that he didn't notice the approach of Zaki and the historians until they were almost on top of him.

Zaki glanced at the red triangular badge with a black cross on the man's robe. "I see that you have prosecutor duty this month, Damon. It is probably the first real work you have done this year."

Damon jumped up and gave Zaki a bear hug. "Where have you been the past two months, you second rate pickpocket? I thought you might have turned respectable."

Zaki looked aghast. "Do not even say that in jest! These are my new friends, Levi, and his sister Lisa. I thought that they would be entertained and enlightened by viewing a trial."

"Levi the storyteller!" exclaimed Damon. "I saw one of your performances. You put all our storytellers to shame. It seems that you are also a magician. If we had a Magicians Guild, you would be invited to join. You are just in time for a robbery-murder trial. Never reveal to anyone what you see and hear."

Zaki looked deeply troubled by the unusual crime. "Three robbery-murders this quarter," he murmured.

Damon sighed. "All senseless murders too."

A bailiff opened the courtroom door. "The judge is ready," he announced solemnly.

Damon took his place while a guard led the defendant, a pallid young man with crazy eyes, to the judgment bar. The blue robed judge sat on the bench. He wore a ceremonial eagle mask that covered most of his head and face. Zaki and the historians sat down in the gallery.

"Only the Guild masters know the identities of the judges," Zaki whispered to Levi and Lisa. "They serve a five-year term."

Flickering torches lined the gray walls of the courtroom. It reminded Levi of the cell he briefly occupied in the palace dungeon. He suspected that the court's justice was swift, without any appeal. People had clear and protected rights in official Atlantean courts. Judges protected them zealously. The Night Kingdom operated autonomously for the most part. Lines had been clearly drawn. Smart people didn't cross them.

The judge banged his gavel. "The Thieves Court is now in session. Beld the thief, you are accused of murdering a respectable citizen while plying your trade. How do you plead?"

"Uh, not guilty, Your Honor."

Damon and the people in the gallery chuckled like the thief had just told a good joke. Damon succinctly presented his case against the defendant. He read the police report and entered it into evidence. Afterward, he called his only witness to the stand, the pleasure lady whose customer he had killed. She stated clearly and simply what she had seen.

"You were not close enough to identify me!" insisted Beld.

"My morals are bad, not my eyesight!" retorted the woman. "He was a good customer of mine, always paying more than I asked for. He never resisted or insulted you, Beld. The guild and I lost a lot of money because of you!"

Beld continued to strongly deny his guilt. He had no one who would support his claim. Levi suspected that the man's word wouldn't carry much weight. Beld didn't even have a character witness.

"How can the judge be sure she is telling the truth?" whispered Lisa.

"False swearing in the Thieves Court is a very serious offense, Lisa," said Zaki gravely. "The punishment is death."

"Then he is guilty," said Lisa with relief.

Zaki seemed miffed that she would think otherwise. "Do you think we prosecute innocent men? No one faces the judge until the court detectives have a solid, convincing case against him."

"Does the defendant have an advocate?" asked Levi.

"Who would defend a person he thinks or knows is guilty?" asked Zaki incredulously. "The accused can speak for himself, offer evidence in support of himself and call witnesses on his behalf. We have no sufferance for guild members who murder respectable citizens. Their actions might provoke the government to retaliate against innocent guild members. To forestall that, we deliver the offenders body to the police along with a blood tribute for the victim's family. They are almost always content with it."

Beld continued to insist that he was innocent. He claimed the woman lied about him because she had a grudge against him. No one spoke in his defense. He only defense was his word.

Everyone became quiet when the judge announced his verdict. "Beld, the court finds you guilty of murdering a respectable citizen and good guild customer, offending every guild member, and placing their lives in danger. You have dishonored the Thieves Guild. Since you are unmarried and without issue, all your monies and property will be given to the family of the man you murdered in compensation."

"The court sentences you to death." A murmur of approval rippled through the gallery. The bailiff placed a black hood over Beld's head. "Deliver the condemned to the Assassins Guild with the usual fee for carrying out the execution. Bailiff, tell Gotzon to make his death slow and painful."

"You can count on that!" cackled Zaki. "The fee is one hundred silver sovereigns, courtesy of the Assassins Guild. Our next stop will be much more pleasant. The last stop will be the most pleasant of all. First, we will visit the Temple of Fortune."

Lisa regarded Zaki skeptically. "You do not impress me as a religious man."

"I devoutly worship the Goddess of Fortune," swore Zaki solemnly. "Regularly I lay sacrifices on her altar."

Zaki guided the historians through the maze of winding streets. Thieves regularly appeared out of nowhere several times. Each of them backed off when they recognized Zaki. The Master of the Thieves Guild served better than a safe conduct pass. They entered the heart of the Night Kingdom. Zaki stopped at a three-story circular building. It had a modern design. The Temple of Fortune was the most impressive building in the Night Kingdom the historians had seen so far.

As soon as the historians entered the building, they knew that it was not a religious structure. "This is a gambling house!" realized Levi.

"We do not have a Goddess of Fortune," Zaki confessed merrily. "If there was one, I would be her most faithful devotee. I pray to her daily as well as all the other gods, just to be safe."

"We have a goddess of fortune in our country," Lisa informed him. "We call her Lady Luck."

The so-called Temple of Fortune was a surprisingly nice casino. Zaki and his guests went to the desk where a guard sat screening visitors. They arrived in time to see a man rejected by the guard. The guards standing by the desk seized the man and escorted him out of the casino. Levi noticed that all the guards carried dart guns rather than deadly weapons.

"Welcome to the Temple of Fortune, Master Zaki!" greeted the guard behind the desk. "Are these people friends of yours?"

"New friends but friends," explained Zaki. "I guarantee their behavior."

After Zaki signed the guest register and stamped it with his Guild Master chop, he and his guests were permitted to pass. They stopped by a statue of a beautiful woman with long wavy hair. She was clad in a robe more appropriate for the goddess of love than the goddess of fortune. Gamblers bowed to her when they passed. Panoramas of Aurelin and mountains covered the walls. Bright ceiling lights illuminated the tables for the players.

The manager came to Zaki. He greeted him and his guests. As a courtesy, he ordered three hundred silver sovereigns each in chips to be given to Levi and Lisa. Zaki took them on a quick tour of the casino before they played. Levi noticed the casino had no Roulette wheel. The casino had a horizontal version of the wheel of fortune. There were no craps tables. Atlanteans played Blackjack with different face cards. A standard deck had kings, queens, wizards, and knights. Priest cards served as aces. People even played a game like Poker.

"The only women in the casino are barmaids and pleasure ladies," observed Lisa with annoyance.

"Gambling is not an appropriate activity for ladies," declared Zaki as if it were a commandment from God not to be questioned by anyone.

"Many of the players look so serious, Zaki," observed Levi. "They do not seem to be enjoying themselves."

"The happy players are the ones who are just here for the pleasure of playing," explained Zaki. "The serious ones are here to make their living. For them, the games are serious business. None of them drink alcohol while playing. Their glasses contain fruit juice, not wine or hard liquor."

Levi smiled. In every age, one thing remained the same: the house always won. "There are Pyramid tables!" exclaimed Lisa. Zaki seemed surprised and displeased that she knew about the game. All the seats at the Pyramid tables were taken. A man at the nearest table got up and gave his seat to Lisa. Levi thought the players were intrigued and pleased rather than offended to have a woman at the table. Levi gave Lisa his complimentary chips to work with.

The game of Pyramid was found in Alliance and Telmierian casinos. Levi had seen enough games to know it was the most challenging game humans ever played. Players drew gold and silver pieces to build their pyramids. The more gold pieces a player had the more valuable the pyramid. Ten pieces completed the pyramid. Each player kept two pieces turned over until the end. They could draw two new pieces and discard two during each hand. The players never knew completely what the other players had until the final play when the remaining pieces were revealed. Luck was just as important as skill.

Levi and Zaki watched in fascination as Lisa worked on her pyramid. Unbeknownst to the other players, she had drawn a blue orb, the most valuable piece of all. There were two blue orbs. If two players drew one in the same round, the game would be decided by one draw. Every two pieces the players made bets. Larger bets sometimes turned out to be bluffs. A couple of players lost their nerve and folded. The dealer and players gasped when Lisa uncovered the blue orb.

Lisa raked in her winnings. "Seventy-five gold sovereigns!" she announced triumphantly. "I am quitting while I am ahead."

"What game do you want to play, Levi?" asked Zaki.

"I will pass," decided Levi. "I only gamble in love."

Zaki smiled slyly. "Then we will go to our final destination."

Instead of walking, Zaki summoned his shuttle and driver. They took the historians on a ten-minute trip to an elegant stone building that stood out from the rest of the buildings like a cactus in a rain forest. The driver stopped at the front door. Zaki and the historians approached the doorman. Zaki tossed the man a five-gold sovereign coin. The doorman thanked Zaki profusely.

"This hotel is as nice as any we have seen in the rest of Aurelin," declared Lisa.

The doorman looked at Zaki in puzzlement. "It is her first time," explained Zaki.

"It is not Ladies Night tonight," he muttered, but allowed Lisa to pass.

Perfect crystal chandeliers lit up every corner of the spacious common area. The Ming like vases, nude statues of beautiful women and rainbow crystals would have graced an aristocrat's home. Women dressed like higher class pleasure ladies sought the company of well-dressed men. Levi realized that it was an economy version of the Palace of Celestial Delights. Levi thought that Lisa's expression was like that of a customer who just found rat droppings in his soup. "This is a pleasure house!" spluttered Lisa.

Zaki's eyes sparkled wickedly. "Second only to The Palace of Celestial Delights." He called out to a woman standing at the top of a winding staircase. She smiled and waved back. Quickly she descended the stairs. Levi guessed that she was about forty. Her yellow gown contrasted sharply with the dresses of the other women. She threw herself into Zaki's arms and hugged him. The woman then turned her attention to Lisa. She looked over Lisa approvingly. "If you want a job, you can start your training tomorrow night. Zaki, you have a lot of nerve staying away from here so long!"

"Guild business," apologized Zaki. "A Guild Master's work and headaches never end. Alita, this my new friend, Levi, the storyteller. This is his sister Lisa. They paid me an unexpected visit at the Last Chance Saloon."

Alita looked embarrassed about the misunderstanding but was too proud to apologize or even acknowledge her mistake. "All friends of Zaki are welcome here." She moved closer to Levi. "It is my honor and pleasure to give you a night of delight you will always remember."

"It would not be fair for me to enjoy a night of pleasure while my sister has nothing," demurred Levi.

Alita sighed. "You are a rare gentleman, Master Levi. We have Ladies' Nights twice a week. It will be four days until the next one. Please return as soon as you can. You are always welcome at the Golden Palace."

After conversing a while with Alita, Zaki and the historians left the Golden Palace. Zaki's shuttle and driver waited for them in front of the door. Zaki drove the historians to Levi's floater. He looked at the floater, then at Levi. "The marketplace gossips spoke truly. You really are a friend of Princess Nura, Levi." Zaki hugged Levi. "Thank you for showing friendship to the low as well as the high. If I can ever do anything for you, just come to the Last Chance Saloon. Someone can contact me if I am not there."

When the historians arrived at the inn, Levi parked the floater a few spaces away. He could have parked it by the front door but chose not to abuse his privilege. That further endeared Levi to Gallo and his people. When the historians entered the dining room, they found Dark and the soldiers waiting. Levi wondered why they, the barmaids and the other customers stared at them with curious and puzzled expressions.

Lisa laughed. "It's just like my parents waiting up for me the night of my first date."

Levi chuckled. "It wasn't that way with me. I didn't have my first date until I was nineteen. I was a bit of a late bloomer."

The historians joined Dark and the soldiers at their table. A barmaid brought them wine without being asked.

"Have you found a sideline too, Lisa?" asked Dark innocently.

"Sideline?" repeated Lisa. "Why do you ask—" She looked at her dress and understood why people had stared at her. Lisa laughed.

"We visited the Night Kingdom after we left the opera house," explained Levi. "We met the Master of the Thieves Guild. His name is Zaki. I performed a few stories for him and his friends. In gratitude, he took us to see the main attractions of the Night Kingdom. Zaki had Lisa and I change into more suitable clothes for the tour. Zaki's woman looked like a pleasure lady. I guess that's why she chose that kind of dress for Lisa."

Everyone laughed heartily. "How much of what we have experienced her will go into your final report, Levi?" asked Dark.

"Technically, just about everything," admitted Levi. "If I report everything that I have done and experienced, would the Time Council even believe it?"

Chapter Ten

Seren watched at a distance as Princess Nura and Levi ate dinner. She smiled as she anticipated Maric's reaction to her next report. Except for bathing with Levi, Princess Nura's relationship with him seemed to be innocent. Seren knew Nura was still a virgin. She would tell her handmaids if she had shared her bed with the storyteller. Seren felt it was just a matter of time before they became intimate. She admitted to herself that she also found Levi attractive.

Maric was so easy to manipulate, His ego wouldn't let him seriously question why Seren betrayed her mistress. The fact that she didn't drive a hard bargain should have made him suspicious. Once a woman found a man's weakness, he could be easily turned to her purpose. Seren greatly enjoyed stringing Maric along.

Seren felt very annoyed with herself. Her petulance at being supplanted by Levi as Nura's chief companion and confidant strained her relationship with Nura. Seren also squandered an opportunity to learn something useful about Levi. She needed to learn more about this mysterious stranger who suddenly appeared out of nowhere. Effortlessly, like a well-trained, experienced agent, Levi had placed himself at the center of Nura's life.

The storyteller fascinated Seren. He didn't look Atlantean or Lemurian. Levi's manners and speech were too sophisticated for any barbarian to have accomplished. Could there be some other presently unknown civilization in the world that had managed to remain hidden from both Atlantis and Lemuria? Seren had missed a golden opportunity because of jealousy. Perhaps something could still be salvaged.

Levi and Nura talked for hours. She enjoyed listening to Levi's experiences from his travels throughout the world. Seren pretended indifference, but listened very carefully to everything he said. She felt envious of him. He had visited far more places than she had or likely would. Finally, Levi decided to retire for the night. Nura escorted him to the door and kissed him good-bye.

"Will that be all for the night, Nura?" asked Seren.

"I think I will retire for the night," decided Nura.

"Nura," began Seren diffidently, "may I ask a favor of you?"

"Of course, Seren. What is your desire?"

"May I serve as Levi's bedroom companion for one night?"

The request took Nura aback. "Are you serious, Seren?"

"Very serious, Nura."

Nura frowned. "You had a chance to be chosen as his bedroom companion. Your former unfriendliness toward him cost you your chance. He has chosen Zira. That is the end of the matter."

Seren knelt at Nura's feet. "I was jealous and resentful because you spent so much time with him," she sniffled. "I feared that our former closeness would never return."

Nura sighed and raised Seren. "Seren, we have been close friends for many years. Nothing will change that. I wish you had spoken with me before Levi chose his bedroom companion. Now it is too late."

Seren burst into tears. "Please make an exception for me, Nura for the sake of our friendship! All I ask is one night. It will allow me to make amends for my failure to show Levi proper palace hospitality."

Nura gazed searchingly into Seren's eyes. "That decision is Zira's. Let us see how she feels about it."

Zira came out of the next room. "If that is all for the night, I will join Levi now."

"Zira, Seren desires to be Levi's bedroom companion for one night," announced Nura. "If you agree, I will permit it."

The request surprised Zira. She frowned at Seren. "You did not find Levi so desirable earlier," noted Zira pointedly.

Seren sniffled. "I felt hurt and angry that Nura spent much time with him and much less time with me. I felt that our former closeness might not return."

Zira was unimpressed and unmoved.

Seren played her trump card. "I pretended to be sick when Lord Kal asked for me to be his bedroom companion so you might have your chance with him. And he chose you."

Zira sighed. "I owe you much for that favor," she acknowledged. "The least I can do is let you have the night with Levi you desire."

"Can it be tonight?" begged Seren.

Nura looked at Zira who nodded. "If Levi permits it," added Nura.

Seren hugged Nura and Zira. "Father Sun bless you!" She ran to the door then stopped and turned around. "With your permission, Nura."

Nura laughed. "Go!"

She hugged Zira. "I would not have blamed you if you had denied Seren's request."

Zira smiled slyly. "I think Lord Kal wants to marry me. When he asks for my hand, Levi will need to choose another bedroom companion anyway."

"Will Levi permit the substitution?" wondered Nura.

Zira smiled. "I would not bet against Seren. She can be very charming when she wants to be."

Levi hopped off his bed when he heard a soft knock on his door. Zira usually arrived sooner. Levi found Zira pleasing in every way. No doubt some man of consequence would choose her to be his wife. When Levi opened the door, he found Seren rather than Zira. Her warm smile disarmed him. She had slipped into something much more revealing and comfortable than her work dress. Seren's star flower perfume drove out all memory of her earlier sour attitude toward him.

"May I come in, Levi?"

"Uh, certainly," replied Levi after a moment of hesitation. They sat down on the couch in the receiving room. "Is Zira sick?" asked Levi with concern.

Seren shook her head. She placed her hand on his. "Please forgive me for not making you feel welcome earlier as duty required. I would like to make up for it. I want to serve as your bedroom companion tonight to make amends."

Levi suppressed a smile. Wrath is cruel, and anger outrageous; but who can stand before envy? Without an unfriendly attitude, Levi found Seren very pleasing. "As the princess and Zira desire," decided Levi.

Seren took Levi to his bed and undressed. She laid her clothes neatly on a chair. After helping Levi to undress, she laid his clothes on top of hers. Levi felt like a driver that had just been eased out of the driver's seat by his passenger.

Seren, like Zira, had been trained in the bedroom arts in Aurelin's best school: the Palace of Celestial Delights. Meeting the high expectations of gentlemen palace guests frequently led to marriage. Seren had learned well how to please a man in bed. Levi forgot about Nura and Zira. Seren acted like she was trying to outperform all the other women Levi had ever shared his bed with. If so, it was a competition she was determined to win. When they finished their lovemaking, Levi acknowledged that she had.

They lay together in silence for a few minutes. Seren sighed. "It is like being allowed to eat a delicious food just one time, then not be allowed to enjoy it again."

"An appropriate analogy," agreed Levi. "Do you have any regrets?"

Seren smiled and shook he head. "It saddens me that Princess Nura will never be pleasured by a man as I have been pleasured by you, Levi. Her cruel fate is marriage to Lord Maric. Nura's pleasure will be of no concern to him. You said that your country is on the far side of the Inner Sea. What is it like?"

"It is most flat with hills," said Levi. "We live away from the desert so we can grow various grains. Our country's value lies more in its location than the things it produces. It is a starting and transfer point for caravans to the eastern world. Many people in my country have large herds of sheep."

"How did you come to speak our language and know our culture so well?"

Levi smiled. Unlike Seren, Nura just happily accepted it without question. "I had an excellent teacher, an Atlantean trader who lived and conducted business near us. My parents did many favors for him. He decided that my sister Lisa and I had higher than normal intelligence. He taught us your language and customs. Our brothers and sister were not interested in learning them."

"Do your people have a written language?" asked Seren.

"No, but we adapted Atlantean writing to our language. Our family is wealthy enough to pay for my travels throughout the western world."

"I love to travel, but I have had few opportunities since I entered palace service," said Seren wistfully. "Only when Princess Nura travels can I travel. She does not travel often or for very long."

"I rejoice daily that I am just a commoner," said Levi. "Our king has two empty-headed daughters whose faces would turn a man to stone if he gazed upon them too long. I am spared the unhappy fate of the men who will be condemned to marry them."

Seren laughed gaily. "There should be laws requiring all princes to be handsome and all princesses to be beautiful. Levi, what kind of ship brought you to Atlantis?"

Nura had not been interested in that detail. Seren on the other hand was interested in many details. "Lisa and I wanted to sail on an Atlantean ship. Unfortunately, none would be available for weeks. Our ship made many stops along the way to Atlantis. Some of the people we met were, well, an unforgettable experience."

Seren smiled. "I can imagine the culture shock. Even more civilized visitors to Atlantis find the experience quite a jolt."

"Civilized baths and palace hospitality would shock most of my people," admitted Levi. "Our women rarely share their beds with men without marriage. But I, as an unmarried man—"

"Can sleep with unmarried women as you please without condemnation." finished Seren. "Commoner Atlantean women save themselves for marriage as the Sun Path requires. Father Sun distinguishes between being a pleasure lady and a palace bedroom companion in service to the king."

"Surely," agreed Levi. Seren was very serious.

Seren inquired at length about women's clothes and hairstyles in his country. Levi told her about the twenty-fourth century hairstyles and clothes of the Alliance and the Empire. They fascinated Seren. She found the idea of women wearing pants scandalous.

Seren kissed Levi. "It is late, and my day begins very early in the morning." Levi and Seren showered quickly then went to bed. Seren hugged him. "Thank you for a night I will happily remember always. Levi, if you decide to make Atlantis your home, my family would not object to having a foreign storyteller in it."

Levi suspected that she was just being polite although she sounded sincere. "My family would not object to having an Atlantean palace handmaid in it either."

Ximin, President of the Science Council, impatiently awaited the arrival of Lord Maric. Maric's upbringing and training lacked many things including punctuality. Ximin checked his watch. The careless lordling was already thirty minutes late. Shiftless aristocrat scions continually wasted his precious time. Maric's attitude toward scientists irritated him most of all.

In the minds of children like Maric, the men who designed weapons rated more respect than those built them and made them work. The Marics fawned on the theoreticians who never worked up an honest sweat. Like their masters, they looked upon all physical work with distaste. On the other hand, General Garai appreciated and rewarded Ximin. This time Maric's tardiness irritated him more as a matter of principle. Presently, the solar gun was not working.

Techs worked feverishly to get the solar gun working. They wanted to avoid Maric's temper tantrums. They already had enough headaches. The glow of computer and radar screens lit up the faces of the techs. Ximin's greatest problem and concern was the solar gun's cooling system. It had been problematic from day one. Some of the weapon's delicate circuits got cranky when they reached the limit of their heat tolerance.

Presently the temperature was just six degrees above normal. Ximin knew that meant nothing. The gun usually overheated just before they were about to fire it. A day ago, they almost got a shot off. The techs kept Ximin continually running to deal with problems that sprang up like heads of the Hydra. He wished that he was thirty years younger.

Maric walked leisurely into the control room flanked by two guards. He gestured carelessly to Ximin to join him. Ximin had made the controls simple enough so even a drone like Maric could use them. Maric checked the status of all the systems. He cursed when the red light of the cooling system came on.

"Ximin, you have been working on this accursed gun for four years," complained Maric. "Will I need to tell General Garai that it will be another four years before the solar gun becomes fully functional?"

Ximin bristled at the casual contempt in Maric's voice. He was as much a descendant of the Sun Lords as Garai. "The solar gun is the most complicated weapon ever devised. We had to develop new alloys to cope with the great heat it generates. General Garai doubted that it would get even this far."

Maric raised an eyebrow at the implied criticism of his father. "This is a work of genius," he conceded in an oblique apology. "The

Lemurians have nothing like it. Once the solar gun works, we can force Lemuria to bow to our will. Then Atlantis will rule the world!"

Much of the Sun Lords scientific knowledge had been placed in the custody of the Chief High Priests. Over the centuries they doled it out in small increments. Kemen bluntly informed the general that the Chief High Priests would continue to decide what scientific knowledge would be released and when. Ximin strongly suspected that some militarily useful knowledge might never be released. Most of the clerics opposed the creation of an Atlantean Empire.

Maric slammed his fist against the control panel in frustration. Ximin and the techs gasped in shock and horror. To everyone's astonishment, the red warning light winked out. All the function indicators down the line turned green. "Let us test it now before something else goes wrong!" ordered Maric.

"We should test the gun on a stationary target," suggested Ximin. "General Garai has given us a list of targets to choose from."

"We will test the gun on a moving target," decided Maric. "We can kill two birds with one stone using the Lemurian flagship Pendaran. A spy ship has been tracking it in the South Murian Ocean."

The communications officer got the coordinates of the Lemurian warship. They were inputted into the targeting computer. The computer automatically aligned the space mirrors. Maric powered up the solar gun. He targeted the first mirror. Maric savored the moment. One sipped a fine wine like an aristocratic gentleman, not gulp it down like an ill-bred peasant. Ximin and the techs tensed in anticipation. Maric fired.

The flash of light passed across the viewscreen. A concentrated blast of energy bounced off four mirrors.

"Missed," reported the communications officer with disappointment after receiving the report from the spy ship.

The gun fired a second shot. Maric cursed when the spy ship reported another miss. The tension level in the control room soared as everyone waited for the result of the third shot.

"Pendaran is huge for a ship but it's like trying to shoot a squirrel at one thousand yards," pointed out Ximin. To his surprise, Maric didn't argue the point.

Pendaran's captain uneasily watched the Atlantean spy ship that had shadowed his ship for the past week. It remained just barely visible on the horizon near the setting sun. The Atlanteans and Lemurians regularly followed each other's warships to remind each other that few ship movements escaped their notice.

At present, no state of war existed between the world's superpowers. King Bakri wanted to keep it that way. The captain's orders were clear. Do not fire on Atlantean ships except in self-defense. Atlantis had an unprecedented number of spy ships operating in both the North and South Murian Oceans. The Atlanteans were up to something but what? Could Atlantis be planning to end the armistice and return to an active state of war? If so, the Atlanteans must have some new capability that emboldened them.

A flash of light and a blast four thousand yards off the starboard bow startled the captain. He searched the ocean for the source of the blast. He saw nothing. Less than a minute after the first blast, a second blast struck the ocean two thousand yards off the port bow. The captain ordered the helmsman to take evasive action. He feared that it might already be too late.

A third blast struck Pendaran dead center. The very air seemed to catch fire. All the fuel and magazines of the ship simultaneously ignited. The cruiser turned into a fireball as explosions ripped it apart. Flaming pieces of the ship scattered across the water. When the smoke cleared, Pendaran was gone.

The techs in the control room whooped in delight when the spy ship reported that the target had been obliterated. Maric heartily congratulated Ximin. "If King Adeil does not know about the solar gun, the Lemurians do not know about it either. It makes a clean surgical strike unlike atomic weapons. When I become king, my first act will be to demonstrate the power of the solar gun on a Lemurian military installation. Then I will demand Lemuria's surrender."

Fire and coolant suddenly erupted from the gun. Techs immediately killed the power and put out the fires. Ximin and the techs braced themselves for a tirade from Maric. Maric was too excited and happy about the successful test of the solar gun to be angry about some short-term problems. In time, they would work out of the bugs. Maric hurried off to personally deliver the good news to his father.

Chapter Eleven

The first month and a half of the Atlantis mission had passed by like the scenery outside of the windows of a bullet train for the team. They had learned very much about Atlantis and its people, but the biggest questions remained unanswered. The biggest was how the Karani got to Terra. Could a Karani Colony Ship have accidentally broken the time barrier in some unknown, unexpected way? Gideon Warner believed that there might be other pathways to the past. None had yet been discovered.

Normally, Time Control went back to the beginning of a country or civilization, then worked forward to its end. Gideon Warner decided to start with the end of Atlantis rather than the beginning. The Time Council desired to learn the level of Atlantean technology at its zenith. Levi appreciated the useful, willing hands of the Special Observers. Nevertheless, he decided to urge the Time Council to limit the number of observers on future interaction missions to three. He didn't want another Temporal Historian to lose his or her place on a mission as Bowen had.

Before Levi left on the mission, he suspected that the Warners had given in to government and Earthfleet pressure to include the soldiers. Understanding slowly dawned on him. The government and Earthfleet needed to learn why the Time Door had to be independent of them.

Kinsey, Kelly, and McNeil had become enthusiastic participants in the mission. Kinsey privately told Levi that he agreed that the status of Project Timestream should permanently remain as it was.

The Time Council hadn't included a Telmierian just as an expression of gratitude for all the Empire had done for the Alliance. Although the Telmierians didn't publicly complain or press the Alliance for access to the Time Door, the Time Council understood that it deeply concerned them. Dark would help to allay those fears.

For weeks, Mikel had pressed Levi to visit him. Nura and exploration of Aurelin took up almost all his waking hours since he met Mikel. Levi decided that it was time to accept the hospitality of his fellow storyteller. Mikel had been the most popular storyteller in Aurelin. Levi immediately overshadowed him. Mikel sincerely didn't mind Levi's success. He became Levi's biggest fan.

The historians went to see Mikel after dinner. The navigation led Levi and Levi efficiently to Mikel's apartment. He lived in an apartment complex reserved exclusively for veterans. The Atlantean military was the best paid and cared for in history. Government took care of the men and women who had faithfully and honorably served their country. Atlantis had no homeless veterans on the streets.

Levi knocked on the door of Mikel's first floor apartment. Seconds later, Mikel opened the door. He hugged Levi and Lisa. "Thank you for accepting the hospitality of my humble home, Levi, Lisa. Come in and make yourselves comfortable."

A lovely young woman left the kitchen and joined Mikel and the historians. "This is Adira. She is my only unmarried daughter."

Adira bowed. "Father has told me much about you, Levi. You are a magician as well as a marvelous storyteller."

Levi looked closely at Adira. "I swear that I have never seen you in my audiences. My eye for beauty misses little."

Adira smiled at the indirect compliment. "Let me get you and your sister some wine."

After Mikel and the historians sat down, Adira returned with their wine. She sat down next to her father. "Levi, I, and most of Aurelin would like you to make your home in Atlantis. We feel that Father Sun has brought you to us. Is there a wife waiting for you in your country?"

"I am not married or betrothed," admitted Levi. "The idea of staying in Atlantis the rest of my days is very tempting. I am in no hurry to return home."

"A man your age should have a wife," observed Mikel in a fatherly tone. "You will not find a more desirable wife than a fine lady of Atlantis. Adira possesses the most important attributes of a good wife, chief of which are virtue, a good disposition, and a good sense of humor."

"Good attributes for a husband as well," commented Lisa. "As Solomon the wise said, 'it is better to dwell alone in the wilderness than with an angry and contentious woman.'"

"A wise man indeed," murmured Adira demurely.

"Adira is also an excellent cook," added Mikel.

Levi never expected an Atlantean man to offer his daughter in marriage to a foreign man. For a moment, he wasn't sure how to respond. "I am afraid to get married," parried Levi. "Father Sun might curse me with a son like Maric. Better to be childless than to have offspring like him."

"Truly, my son," agreed Mikel. "Adira would give you sons you could be proud of."

"And daughters," added Lisa.

Levi glanced at Adira. Her radiant smile and the light in her eyes told him that marriage to him was agreeable to her. It might have been her own idea. How could he say no or even delay giving an answer to Mikel and Adira? An idea came to him.

"I am in Atlantis to conduct important negotiations with Aurelin companies for my city," began Levi. "That, my time with Princess Nura and my storytelling take up most of my time. In a month and a half, the negotiations will be completed. Then Adira and I can get better acquainted."

"I look forward to that, Levi," said Adira. "I respect and appreciate a man who places his duty to his family and country above everything else. At least we can spend some time together in between your performances. Do not fear, Levi. I am not jealous of your friendship with Princess Nura. I am glad that you are giving her some happy memories to comfort her after she marries Maric. A woman is greatly blessed who can marry as she desires. How sad it is to be someone for whom a simple visit to the marketplace is a rare privilege."

After the historians left Mikel's apartment, they went straight to the Temple of The Sun for another round of negotiations with Kemen. The negotiations proved both enlightening and entertaining. The historians hoped that the real Lemurian negotiator didn't show up unexpectedly and at the worst possible time. Levi figured that any time before the last day of Atlantis was the worst possible time.

Levi found it strangely satisfying to do a good job negotiating with Kemen. He never suspected that he had it in him. The fact that it meant nothing, practically speaking, was irrelevant. Dealing with Kemen gave the historians much insight into the thinking of the priests and aristocrats. The Karani influence was unmistakable.

Atlantean aristocrats and clerics seemed more worldly and self-interested than present day Karani.

When the historians arrived at the temple, they received a much warmer welcome than the first time. Levi suspected that his floater had something to do with it. Levi enjoyed horse trading with Kemen. His pragmatism made the process much smoother. Even if it was just a game, Levi always played to win. Surprisingly, Kemen was not angry or offended that Levi had been named Friend of The Crown. "Father Sun has a strange sense of humor sometimes," commented Kemen.

Levi presented his counter proposals to the trading concessions they discussed during their last session. Kemen read the proposals then placed the papers on his desk. He smiled. "You represent King Bakri well. Let us split the difference between the two proposals?"

Levi pretended to consider the offer. "That is more than we wanted to pay, but it is acceptable. They shook hands on it. Lisa prepared the documents in the office of Kemen's secretary. Levi and Kemen signed the papers when they were ready. They moved on to the next item of business."

"Your mooring and offloading fees are much too high," declared Levi bluntly. "Our Shipmasters Guild suggests these figures." He handed the paper to Kemen. The High Priest's face grew dark as he read it. Levi's low figures were insultingly low.

Levi and Kemen argued for ten minutes like a customer haggling with a market vendor. Neither wanted to budge from their position. Lisa's father was a very successful negotiator. She shared some of his strategies with Levi. Kemen felt that he had bested Levi when he agreed to his terms. Kemen didn't know Levi would have agreed to a higher figure if it had been necessary.

Levi sighed. "You are a fearsome negotiator, Lord. We want your uranium, but at a fair price. Your latest offer is a big step in the right direction."

For an hour and a half, they wrestled until they reached agreement. Levi and Lisa had to do a great deal of research to know what the current prices of fees, commodities and minerals were. Manufactured goods were next.

Levi expected the military issues to be the most contentious of all. Atlantis didn't want to concede any real or imagined advantage to its pacific rival. Levi sought the fairest agreement for both parties like it was real. The final negotiations would be for a peace treaty between Atlantis and Lemuria. Those could easily be dragged out until the end of the mission. Levi wondered what Lemuria was like. He and Lisa had to visit at least once to find out.

Atlantis wanted badly to have an oceanographic research station in the South Pacific Ocean. Before the last conflict with Lemuria, the two countries were close to an agreement. The brief war prevented that. Kemen refused to offer anything of equal value in return. Levi suggested an even up trade: an Atlantic research station for Lemuria in return for the station Atlantis wanted.

"Let Lemuria establish a research station in OUR ocean?" asked Kemen incredulously.

"Why not?" asked Levi. "To sweeten the deal, we will give you access to all of our civilian research facilities in the Murian Ocean."

Kemen maintained a Poker face, but he couldn't hide the eager gleam in his eyes. Finally, he relented and agreed. "Let us call it a night, Levi. This negotiation session has been a tough one. You always wear me out." Kemen removed a dusty wine bottle and two glasses from his wine cabinet. He filled the glasses and handed one to Levi.

Levi sipped it. "Excellent. Does this come from your own vineyards, Eminence?"

"I have no vineyards on my estate, Levi," admitted Kemen. "It comes from my brother's estate. His wines are highly prized throughout Atlantis."

"Have you ever visited Lemuria?"

"Once with my father when I was a small boy," recalled Kemen wistfully. "The memories still burn brightly. Then our people visited each other freely. Suminar has magnificent architecture and art that even a child like me could appreciate. Your waterfalls are just as breathtaking as ours. King Bakri's Crystal Palace is more beautiful than King Adeil's palace. At sunrise, the rainbow of light dazzles your eyes. Lemurian gardens are as fine as anything we have in Atlantis."

"Travel between the oceans is so long and tiresome," complained Levi. "It is regrettable that there is no waterway connecting the Atlantic and Murian Oceans. Think of all the sea travel time that would save!"

"Very true," agreed Kemen. "Unfortunately, there is none."

"Together our countries could build one," observed Levi. "Royal engineers have been studying the possibility for years."

Kemen laughed. "Build a waterway between the two oceans. What a silly—" Kemen stopped laughing. "We can build such a waterway!" he realized. "Once a treaty is signed, I will urge King Adeil to discuss the idea with King Bakri. A good proposal skillfully made should get serious consideration. Joint construction and joint operation are workable. That is a good selling point."

"Kemen, we have heard rumors that Atlantis is building a spaceship," said Levi changing the subject. "Is it true or is it just someone's conspiracy fantasy?"

The question took Kemen by surprise. Kemen's expression gave Levi his answer. Kemen seemed to debate within himself whether to brush off the inquiry or tell the truth. "It is true," he finally admitted.

Levi pretended to be concerned. "Lemuria has no similar project although we have the capability. The Sun Lords have forbidden space travel until a new Emissary is sent by Father Sun. Is it true that the penalty for violating the ban in Atlantis is death, even for the king himself?"

"It is," said Kemen firmly and without hesitation. Levi doubted that it could happen.

"I am deeply troubled that your military can keep such a thing secret even from King Adeil," said Levi. "No doubt General Garai is behind it. Who knows what other secret projects he has."

"In this matter, our mutual interests coincide," noted Kemen. "Whoever acquires the knowledge I seek and shares it with me, will have my gratitude."

Levi smiled. "I understand."

"Bringing back the Atlantean spaceship would get us the Artifact of the Year Award!" said Lisa excitedly after they got in the floater.

Levi grinned. "You can bet your life on that. I know just the man who can find it for us."

The historians found Dark sitting alone at a table drinking some wine. Except for two barmaids and a handful of customers, the bar and dining room were empty. "Why are you so glum, Jer?" asked Levi. Did your lady cancel on you tonight?"

Dark shook his head. "I can't forget that this wonderful land and most of its people will soon perish. No place on Telmieria has ever experienced a cataclysm like the one that will destroy Atlantis.

Reading about it thousands of years after the fact is much different than seeing it happen to people you have experienced personally."

"That is the regrettable downside of interaction missions," acknowledged Levi. "Jer, I have a new assignment for you. Kemen told me that General Garai is building a spaceship. According to Kemen, an Emissary from heaven forbade Atlantis to explore space until a new Emissary was sent. We will find that spaceship, but only to take it home with us. You are the right man for the job."

Dark could barely contain his glee. He could bring Kanya back in the spaceship and avoid a possible problem with the pilot of the timeship. Now that he and Kanya were joined, he couldn't bear to live without her. Dark knew she felt the same. "I will get to work on locating that spaceship first thing tomorrow. One way or another, I will find it and before we go home. I guarantee it."

A palace shuttle dropped off Seren at the royal beach. Only the royal family and palace personnel were permitted to use it. Seren regularly went swimming in the ocean. She always went alone after twilight had passed. The driver watched over Seren from the beach. She went to her usual spot and spread out her towel on the sand. The pleasantly cool breeze stirred her dress and hair. Seren teasingly removed her clothes for the benefit of the driver. She was naked except for the Brotherhood of Father Sun pendant containing her radio.

Seren walked slowly into the water until it reached her waist. Then she dived in and swam out fifty yards. Seren activated the waterproof radio. "Nightingale to Seagull, do you copy?" When she received no response she called again.

"Nightingale, this is Seagull," responded a pleasantly familiar manly voice. "Your transmission is loud and clear. Report."

Seren gave her weekly report on palace intrigues, gossip and useful information gleaned from overheard conversations of the King and his advisors. "You do not seem as close to Princess Nura as you once were," observed Seagull. "Why is this?"

"Princess Nura has become enamored with the storyteller," explained Seren. "Sometimes she includes me with her activities with him. Her feelings for him are much more than friendly."

"What have you learned about him?"

"Not much," admitted Seren. "He does not reveal much about himself, his life, or his background. The princess does not press him about it. Most people who know of him think he is from Lemuria. The storyteller is not a barbarian. I cannot begin to imagine what country or civilization could have produced a man like him."

"Levi is most certainly not Lemurian, Nightingale. Neither I nor my superiors know what to make of him. It does not appear that he is a threat to you or Lemuria. If he was not under the protection of the crown, I would have him picked up and taken to Suminar. Why did you not try to become his bedroom companion? A good pleasuring often loosens a man's tongue."

"I let jealousy overcome my professionalism," confessed Seren. "Had I controlled my emotion, I think Levi might have chosen me as his bedroom companion. Then I could get a better idea about his designs on Princess Nura. I did manage to get a night with him. I learned that he is very cultured, educated, intelligent and as comfortable with our technology as we are. It is like he was stolen at birth and raised in Atlantis or Lemuria."

"Maybe I should have one of our male agents approach Levi," considered Seagull. "Of course, they do not have your special advantages."

"A man who has been named Friend of The Crown is not likely to be turned," observed Seren. "His affinity for Atlantis goes far beyond Princess Nura. On a lighter note, I conned Maric into paying me to spy on Princess Nura and Levi. For stringing him along, I get paid three hundred gold sovereigns a week."

Seagull laughed heartily. "Your job has its perks, Nightingale. Your back pay has grown to a tidy sum over the years. The interest is substantial. Maybe when you return home, I can help you spend some of it. Are you as beautiful as you sound?"

"Are you as handsome as you sound?" countered Seren.

"Someday we must get together and see. Seagull out."

Seren smiled. Seagull was probably the Special Passenger of a fast runner. His ship might even be trading with General Garai. That would be extremely ironic. Seren suddenly realized that Nura was not sharing her bed with Levi. She would keep him entirely for herself. Seren could tell that Maric found her very attractive. If she played her cards right, she might become his mistress after he married Nura.

When she began her assignment in Atlantis, she had not expected it to continue for so many years. Someday, she wanted to marry and have children. She was already twenty-five and not getting any younger. Duty required her to try to become Maric's mistress if she could. If that did not work out, Seren decided to ask to go home.

Chapter Twelve

Nura and Levi returned to the palace after completing their run. At first, Levi hated getting so tired and winded. As he developed stamina, he began to enjoy it. His improvement pleased Nura. When they arrived at Nura's apartments, they found their towels and change of clothes waiting for them by the bathing pool. They cleaned off the dust and sweat from the run, then slipped into the pool.

"Levi, these apartments have seen few visitors," said Nura. "Most of them were silly, vain female cousins and my few friends, all of whom are now married. It has been very lonely here. Often I envied commoner women to whom marriage to men they loved was a right and not a privilege."

"My father agreed to let me marry a man agreeable to me. My brother was heir to the throne, so it did not matter greatly who I married. Ironically, my brother would have had to marry a suitable lady he most likely would not have loved. At least not at first. I never told Lord Kal, but I decided to marry him. We have been friends since childhood. I could not hope to find another man who would have been as concerned with my happiness as him."

"My hope and opportunity died with my brother in a sailing accident. One month after Akil's funeral, General Garai proposed a marriage between me and Maric. My father resisted it for years, but in time Garai gathered enough support in the army leadership and government to make a marriage between Maric and me unavoidable. My unhappy fate is to be the wife of a man I despise, a man who is unfit and unworthy to be king of Atlantis."

Nura put her arms around Levi. "A woman who follows the Sun Path should not surrender herself to a man outside of marriage. It is a great sin for me being a princess of Atlantis. I will not surrender my virginity to Maric. He would treat the gift with indifference or contempt. Levi, I care much for you. I know you also care much for me. Please share my bed until my betrothal."

Nura's plaintive plea didn't surprise him. He already knew her past and her future. Nura would never marry Maric. Levi knew she would not desert her country and her post to save her life when the end came. Being Nura's lover for a season wouldn't change history at all. No Time Control regulation expressly forbade it. It hadn't occurred to the Time Council to make one. Infuriating Maric was a bonus for Levi and Nura."

"Your father has entrusted your virtue to me," noted Levi. "I do not want to betray his trust."

Nura laughed. "You are a wonderful, noble fool! My father has given you permission to share my bed. Did he not tell you that I could enjoy you as I please?"

"Yes."

Nura smiled. "It is my pleasure that you share my bed, Levi. Until my betrothal to Maric, you will have no bedroom companion but me. Do not worry. I have taken precautions."

Levi chuckled. "Your will, princess."

They left the pool and dried themselves. Nura led Levi to her bed. At first, she was shy about her inexperience. Quickly she put aside her shyness. Levi experienced a rising tide of pleasure and joy that continually increased. Nura seemed to be experiencing it too. It differed greatly from the pleasure he experienced with Zira and Seren. It seemed to Levi that he and Nura were touching every part of each other's being.

Levi felt that he and Nura were touching each other's hearts, minds, and spirits. Suddenly he realized that what they were experiencing was The Joining. The Joining magnified their shared pleasure in a wonderful, inexplicable synergy. Levi also felt spiritually healed as well. Levi heard that joined couples remained faithful to each other for life. After experiencing the Joining, no ordinary lovemaking with someone else could satisfy them.

After they reached the height of their pleasure, it gradually decreased until just a warm satisfaction and afterglow remained. They felt both happy and sad. Nura sighed. "I never suspected that I had the gift of The Joining, Levi. If I had, I might have chosen not to share my bed with you. No, that is not true. This is the kind of memory that will sustain me throughout all my years with Maric. Nevertheless, we are joined together, heart, mind, and spirit, in life and in death."

Levi sighed. "The price of joining for me is great, almost too much to bear. I can still love and enjoy a woman again. Nevertheless, it will always be in the shadow of our Joining. Thank you for giving me the greatest gift a person to give to another."

Nura kissed him. "You are a worthy recipient, love. The Joining only happens to people who are meant to be joined. I never heard of a joined couple who did not marry. Our circumstances are unique." Nura smiled. "Perhaps Maric will suffer an unfortunate and timely death before our wedding."

Levi smiled. "Father Sun willing."

Levi and Nura spent the rest of the day in the palace library. Levi wished a had a year to just explore its historical treasures. Levi rejoiced that he and Nura shared a love of history. He felt that she would have made a good Temporal Historian. Levi had hoped to marry a fellow Temporal Historian. Until he met Lisa Stern, he thought it might never happen. At their first meeting, they felt a strong connection.

They also felt physically attracted to each other. Even after getting acquainted with Nura, he still planned to explore his possibilities with Lisa after they returned home from the mission. He hadn't expected his relationship with Nura to get serious. Levi never imagined that they would become joined. He could still love and enjoy Lisa. But could she be happy and content with a man who was joined with another woman?

At the end of the day, Zira returned to Nura's apartments for Levi. "Zira, you are no longer Levi's bedroom companion," announced Nura regretfully.

The unexpected news took her by surprise. "Have I done something to displease or offend you or Levi?" asked Zira plaintively.

"No, my good servant and friend," Nura reassured Zira.

For a moment, Zira was puzzled and confused. She smiled as the truth dawned on her. Levi and Nura had that special glow that only people who had experienced the Joining possessed. "I happily surrender the privilege to one who is more worthy than I. Thank you, Levi, for what you have given my lady."

Early the next morning Levi returned to the inn. He saw Dark sitting alone at a table, apparently lost in thought. Levi checked the clock over the bar. It was 0700. Lisa and the soldiers were probably up and preparing for the start of their day. Levi joined Dark at his table.

"You look unusually pensive, Jer," commented Levi. "Has your relationship with Kanya taken a turn for the worse?"

Dark smiled wanly. "Things are going too well with us. Kanya is pressing me to meet her parents. She wants to marry me."

Levi looked closely at Var. He noticed something about the man that he hadn't noticed earlier. "It's not strange or unreasonable that she wants to marry the man she has joined with."

Dark stared at Levi in amazement. "How do you know that?" he demanded. A moment later, Dark understood. "You have experienced the Joining with Princess Nura! Yesterday was more eventful than you could have imagined when it began. What a tangled web this mission has woven around us. Will you order or counsel me to break off my relationship with Kanya?"

"Not at all, Jer! How could I ask or order you to leave behind the woman you have joined with? I know what leaving behind half of your heart and soul would be like. Officially, I am informing you that removing anyone from the past without the express permission of the Time Council is forbidden. Unofficially, I wouldn't know that she stowed away on the Atlantean spaceship until after we returned home."

A rush of relief and euphoria flowed through Dark. It was quickly replaced by a deep guilt. Instead of showing his gratitude for the tremendous favor, duty required Dark to reward his friend with death. In time, Kanya would know, understand, and forgive. Dark doubted that he could ever forgive himself. Never had his duty been so distasteful.

"I do not know how to thank you, Levi."

Levi smiled. "Just continue to do a good job for me and don't ever tell anyone, especially the Time Council, that I looked the other way so you could bring Kanya to the present. How is the search for the spaceship progressing?"

"Slowly," admitted Dark. "The project is so secret; I have not been able to learn much. It is called Project Sky Bridge. Hacking military computers has been challenging. It's like there are not any computer records of it. Do not worry, boss. I will not let you down. I will not see you until late in the evening. After my day's work is done, Kanya and I will have dinner. Then we will attend the opera you and Lisa enjoyed."

"I want to hear all about it."

As usual, Dark picked up Kanya at the Grand Hotel entrance. He thought it odd that she wanted him to meet her parents yet never wanted to be picked up at home. Kanya gazed appreciatively at Levi's floater.

"It belongs to Levi," explained Dark quickly. "I have no royal connections. If it is all right with you, we can eat at Zelek's Grill before we attend the opera."

Kanya smiled. "Strangely enough, I am also in the mood for ribs."

Dark liked that Kanya enjoyed the peasant fare of the marketplace as well as aristocratic cuisine. One of the perks of his job was the opportunity to enjoy a wide variety of food from many worlds. Terran and Telmierian food pleased him most. Soon enough, he could share it all with Kanya. She didn't object when Dark suggested a walk in Market Square. Dark stopped at Ager's Fine Jewelry.

Ager hurried to serve Dark when he noticed that he was with a beautiful highborn lady. "You greatly honor this unworthy commoner businessman," gushed Ager. "Would you like a pendant, ring or bracelet, lady?"

Kanya smiled slyly. "I would like a ring. You pick it out, Jerrel."

Dark carefully looked over the rings. Did she like diamonds, emeralds, rubies, or sapphires? Dark noticed that Kanya was eyeing the sapphire rings. He spotted the best-looking one and picked it up. Dark slipped the ring onto Kanya's left ring finger. "What do you think, Kanya?"

Kanya studied the ring and smiled. "It is as fair a jewel as a lady could desire. The ring looks like it belongs on my finger."

"Congratulations, sir!" declared Ager enthusiastically. "You are one of the luckiest men in Atlantis!"

Kanya grinned. "He knows."

Dark found the conversation incomprehensible. The only thing that mattered was that he gave his lady a fine gift, and she greatly appreciated it. He had learned much about the Atlanteans and their culture. Dark figured he had missed something significant. He haggled down the price of the ring by thirty percent, leaving both buyer and seller happy.

Dark and Kanya hurried back to the floater. They didn't want to be late for the first act of the opera. No one outside of the opera or anyone seated near them seemed to know Kanya. They did glance curiously at her occasionally since she was with a white skinned man. After the performance began, Dark soon became caught up in the story. He was enjoying the opera as Levi had predicted. Kanya seemed very happy that he shared her enjoyment.

"This is the first opera I ever saw," revealed Dark as he and Kanya made their way through the crowd flowing out of the opera house. "I look forward to seeing another one."

"I have a surprise for you, Jerrel," announced Kanya.

Kanya refused to reveal the surprise. When they got into the floater, she programmed the navigation computer. Dark activated the autopilot. After a few minutes, it became clear to them which section of Aurelin they were headed for. He looked at Kanya in puzzlement. "I know no one in Sun City."

Kanya smiled mischievously. "But you do."

"We are going to your family's estate," realized Dark.

"Yesterday my parents told me that it is time for them to meet you," explained Kanya. "A family friend saw us together last week and informed them."

Dark chuckled. "Maybe you should let me put all of my affairs in order first and buy a grave," he joked. He didn't fear her father or brothers. Dark feared having to hurt them in self-defense. As soon as they reached the main house, Kanya's parents walked out the door. They looked concerned rather than angry. Kanya favored her mother, but she was a combination of the best of both parents. Although well designed and constructed with high quality materials, the house was sensible and practical. Dark wasn't a parent, but he could easily imagine their anxiety about him.

Kanya's parents gazed wide eyed and disapprovingly at her sapphire ring. Their reaction to the ring mystified Dark. "Kanya, does he understand the significance of your ring?" demanded her father.

Kanya laughed. "I must have forgotten to mention it to Jerrel. I am sorry for playing this trick on him and you."

"You do not look sorry to me," said her mother with a knowing smile.

"Father, mother, this is Jerrel Dark, the man I told you about."

Dark bowed to her parents. "Honor to your house."

Dark's use of the proper greeting to an aristocrat made a good impression on Kanya's parents. "Welcome to my estate, Jerrel Dark. I am Keril, this is my wife Aldora. Kanya, go inside with your mother." To Dark's surprise, she obeyed without question. "Come, let us walk," requested Keril.

Keril told Dark to walk by his side despite the differences in their classes, contrary to social convention. "Lord, you, and your wife are displeased by the ring I gave Kanya. I do not understand. The stone and setting are of high quality."

Keril smiled. "Kanya has rarely been impulsive in action even as a child. The trick she played on us is well conceived. An Atlantean man offers a lady a sapphire ring as a proposal of marriage. If she permits him to place it on her finger, she accepts the proposal."

"I had no idea, lord," Dark hastily assured him. "I never presumed worthiness to become your son-in-law. I understand that Kanya must marry a man of her class, not a foreign commoner like me."

"A person can be of noble worth without being a noble," observed Keril. "I just met you but already I can see that you are an exceptional man. You have strength and determination. Kanya has made it clear that she wants to marry you. The way you look at my daughter tells me that you are not averse to marrying her."

"That is so," admitted Dark. "But I accept that it cannot be. The social gap between Kanya and me is too wide."

Keril smiled. "Most commoners think we Children of The Sun marry exclusively among ourselves. That is not even true of the royal family. Infusions of good commoner blood keep our bloodlines strong. Kanya told me that you are the son of a king although unacknowledged. When I look at you, I can believe it. Would you marry Kanya if my wife and I consented?"

"I would," said Dark without hesitation. "Unfortunately, your religion forbids marriage with non-believers."

"It is true," acknowledged Keril. But the Brotherhood of Father Sun is open to all men, not just people of Atlantis. The Sun Path is forbidden to no one."

Dark had thought much about the Telmierian religion since his indoctrination in it during his mission preparation. He had never believed in Eikor the Terrible or even the kinder moon goddess.

Dark's experience of the Joining convinced him that there was a God. Quite possibly it was the one worshiped by Telmieria and Atlantis.

"I will study your religion and Book of Commandments and become a member of the Brotherhood of The Sun if I can do so sincerely," promised Dark. "Until then, 1 think we should put all other considerations on the back burner."

"Very sensible," approved Keril. "We will continue this discussion with my wife. During the past year, Kanya regularly disappeared at night. She refused to tell my wife and I where she went. Now we know."

Dark smiled. They knew nothing of Kanya's service in the Palace of Celestial Delights. Dark knew she would never reveal that part of her life to her family or anyone else. Neither would he. Through the Joining, Dark understood that neither pleasure nor rebellion had moved her to become a courtesan. She only felt that for some reason the Palace was where she needed to be. They knew that their Joining was ordained by Father Sun. Neither Dark nor Kanya ever imagined it would happen where it did.

Aldora took Kanya into the library and shut the door behind them. Now they could talk freely without being overheard by any of the servants. Aldora sensed that something strange had happened to Kanya. It both puzzled and frightened her.

"You have a special glow about you, Kanya," observed Aldora. "Something has happened to you."

"Maybe I am pregnant," parried Kanya.

Aldora frowned. "Please do not joke about this. I am very worried about you!" She took Kanya's hands. Seconds later Aldora received a strong impression. "You have experienced the joining with Jerrel!"

"How did you know that?" asked Kanya in astonishment.

Aldora smiled wanly. "My mother had the gift of The Joining. Unfortunately, she did not pass it on to me. I did receive the ability to sense the emotions of people. This changes everything. We need to inform your father."

As if on cue, the door opened revealing Keril and Dark. Keril closed the door behind them. "Kanya and Jerrel have experienced the Joining," announced Aldora.

The news shocked Keril. "That settles the matter of their marriage. What is done cannot be undone. In a situation like this, we can get a Special Dispensation from the Chief High Priest."

"Kemen is a good friend of my parents so that will not be a problem, Jerrel," Kanya reassured Dark.

"I happily accept my fate, Kanya. Lord Keril, I will keep my promise to you. I am a man of my word."

Kanya smiled. "I bear witness of that."

Chapter Thirteen

Dark sat in his stolen shuttle. He waited patiently for Maric across the street from the Palace of Celestial Delights. He had been following Maric's movements looking for the right moment to approach him. For too long he had procrastinated eliminating Levi and Lisa. The longer he waited, the harder it would be to do it. Dark couldn't bear to kill the historians by his own hand. He decided to hire an assassin to do it for him.

Being a sensible Rigellian, Dark decided to make some money out of it. Scamming the money from Maric made it even more enjoyable and satisfying. Dark checked the time. Maric had been in the high-class pleasure house for two hours. The arrogant lordling apparently had extraordinary libido and endurance. Maric probably spent more time amusing himself and indulging in pleasures of the flesh than he did performing his duties.

Dark wished he could teach Maric what power and strength were. Men who received power as a gift rather than earning in deadly struggle where no quarter was requested or given, didn't develop the strength and wit to hold on to it. Without the power and strength of better men backing them up, the Marics of the galaxy were nothing.

Finally, Maric and his bodyguards came out of the Palace of Celestial Delights. His shuttle pulled over to the entrance and picked them up. Dark drove to the spot he had chosen for an ambush. Maric's men never varied their route. Dark drove normally so he didn't get stopped by a policeman. When he reached the ambush point, he stopped and waited. As expected, Maric's shuttle turned the corner and headed toward him.

Dark had been monitoring the police channels. No police shuttles were within a five-block radius. Dark drove his shuttle into Maric's. The force of the collision spun the army shuttle around, It looked like it had been coming from the opposite direction. Dark jumped out of his shuttle and hurried over to pretend to help. Maric and his bodyguards had been shaken up. Dark assisted them out of the shuttle.

"Please forgive my poor driving, sir!" entreated Dark. Before the guards could gather their wits, Dark shot them with tranquilizer darts.

"An assassin!" exclaimed Maric fearfully. He reached for his sidearm, but Dark snatched it away before Maric's hand could touch it.

"I am no assassin, Lord Maric," said Dark reassuringly. "I have a proposition that I think will interest you."

Maric relaxed a little, but he eyed Dark warily. "You killed my men. That is a crime punishable by death!"

"Your men are just tranquilized," explained Maric. "What I have to say is for your ears only, great lord." Dark noted the greedy calculating look on Maric's face.

"What is your proposition?"

"We have a common enemy, Lord Maric," began Dark. "Princess Nura's barbarian lover."

Maric growled at the word lover.

"For a price, I can eliminate him for you."

Maric sneered. "Why should I pay you to kill your enemy?"

Dark smiled smugly. "You cannot touch him, lord. The storyteller is protected from you by the king. He is not protected from me."

Maric's eyes lit up with excitement. It was an offer he couldn't refuse. Along with delight, Maric felt fear. Any man who calmly and coolly discussed the killing of a Friend of The Crown, knowing the consequences of such a great crime, was a very dangerous man. Ego and jealousy helped him to make his decision. "What is your price?" whispered Maric.

"Ten thousand gold sovereigns," decided Dark. "I will accept whatever you have in your purse as a down payment. The balance is payable when the storyteller is dead."

"Done!" decided Maric. He took out his purse and tossed it to Dark.

Dark counted the money. "Two hundred thirty-five gold sovereigns." Dark chuckled. "You travel light, lord. When it is time for me to collect the rest, I will contact you. To ensure that you are not tempted to stiff or betray me, I have recorded our conversation. It will find its way into the king's hands." Maric's eyes grew wide as Dark played back their conversation. "You can be certain that I will not betray you. This job is off the books. Neither Gotzon nor his guild will get a cut."

Maric laughed. "It takes a lot of nerve to stiff the Assassins Guild. I can use a man like you in my service. Name your price."

"The pay would be better than working for the Assassins Guild," considered Dark. "I will let you know when our present business is finished."

Dark bowed, then got in his shuttle and drove off. He ditched it six blocks later and stole another one. Five blocks from the Assassins Guild headquarters he abandoned it. Dark walked slowly down the street continually scanning buildings, streets and alleys for criminals who haunted the night. Twice he saw men lurking in the shadows. Neither chose to trouble him. Up close, the building housing the Assassins Guild looked drab and ordinary.

Dark's keen eyes spotted a man with a rifle on a rooftop on the other side of the street. He thought that the guild had an interesting way to screen visitors. Dark suspected the guild guardian knew who a desired visitor was and who wasn't. Dark walked up to the front door with his hands raised. A man came out to meet him.

"I need the services of an assassin," announced Dark. He allowed the man to frisk him and take his weapons. The man gazed appreciatively at the dart gun and dagger. "I will keep your weapons. You can have them when you leave." He escorted Dark to an office at the end of the hall and rapped twice on the heavy steel door.

Gotzon's secretary opened the door. An ordinary looking middle-aged man sat behind an ornate teak desk. A large hardbound book with a picture of crossed daggers on the cover lay on the desk. Gotzon ordered the secretary to leave the office. He noted the look of confusion on Dark's face. "I am Gotzon, Master of The Assassins Guild. What is your need?"

"You are not what I expected the Master of the Assassins Guild to look like," confessed Dark.

Gotzon laughed heartily. "The best assassin is one that no one would ever imagine is an assassin. My unprepossessing appearance is a gift from Father Sun. When a job is exceptionally challenging, I assist with both planning and execution."

"I want two people dealt with," said Dark. "The storyteller Levi and his sister."

Gotzon looked shocked. "I thought that no job request could surprise me, but I was wrong. Never has anyone ever asked the guild to kill someone under the protection of the crown."

"You will not do the job?" asked Dark in disappointment.

"The job has great risk," observed Gotzon. "If the storyteller's death was connected to the guild, the king would deal harshly with us. Still, I am confident that we can avoid that. The guild will accept the job if the price is right."

"Are twenty thousand gold sovereigns enough?" asked Dark.

Gotzon gazed curiously at Dark. "Twenty thousand gold sovereigns are a lot of money for a peasant storyteller. Is he so important or dangerous?"

"I have my reasons," replied Dark mysteriously.

"Your reasons are your own business, friend," acknowledged Gotzon. "The job will cost you twenty-five thousand gold sovereigns. Five thousand down, the balance due upon completion of the job."

"Done!" said Dark.

He and Gotzon shook hands to seal the deal. "Killing a woman is a job without honor. Inek is the only man who will do it. His talent is second only to mine. Regularly, the guild gets requests from husbands seeking to dispose of their wives to inherit their fortunes or to marry their mistresses."

"Or to dispose of exceptionally shrewish wives," added Dark mischievously.

Gotzon laughed heartily. "That too. If you ever need our services again, you know where to find us."

Dark tossed a purse with the down payment onto Gotzon's desk. Gotzon slowly counted out the five thousand gold sovereigns. Then he placed it in his safe. Dark smiled. Maric didn't know that his money was paying for the deaths of the historians. He never would. The knowledge was a slight comfort to Dark.

Inek felt some trepidation when he received his latest assignment from Gotzon. The guild had never killed anyone under the protection of crown before. This was the first time anyone had even dared to request it. No doubt the customer was a foreigner. Inek had never refused an assignment or failed to carry it out successfully. This job would be no exception. The job also presented a unique opportunity to increase the profits.

Besides courtesans of the Palace of Celestial Delights, Maric entertained commoner women at his family's estate. The 'volunteers' were acquired by his men from poor neighborhoods at night. After Maric tired of them, he tossed them onto the street. Inek decided to 'volunteer' the storyteller's sister. Maric paid well for his playmates. Then Inek would put the poor woman out of her misery when Maric discarded her. Maric would pay a lot for the opportunity to cause the storyteller a lot of pain. He knew the best man for the job.

The historians arrived back at the inn ahead of Dark and the soldiers. Levi glanced at the clock. Dark and the soldiers were usually home by 2200. Levi ordered wine for himself and Lisa. They took their drinks to their favorite table.

"We have reached the halfway point of the mission, yet we still haven't figured out the Telmierian connection to Atlantis," mused Levi. "One would think that the answer is here in Aurelin. We have searched all the histories in the libraries and computer archives, yet we found nothing!"

"I'm as baffled and confounded as you are, boss," admitted Lisa. "Has the past been erased or hidden?"

"I lean toward hidden," said Levi. "The histories and records indicate that the Atlanteans are very meticulous in their record keeping. Maybe the answers lie in the hinterland. But how do we get the chance to search there?" wondered Levi. "I doubt that Nura will give me the opportunity. We must figure out something."

Lisa yawned. "Let's sleep on that. I'm too tired to think."

"Sounds good to me."

The historians didn't notice a pair of watchful eyes following them as they walked up the stairs to the second floor. When they reached the door, Levi checked to make sure it was still secure. "Be careful Levi," warned Lisa. "I sense someone close by with unfriendly thoughts." They drew their dart guns before entering their room. Levi switched on the lights. They searched everywhere but found nothing.

Lisa went to the refrigerator and took out a pitcher of mango juice. She poured juice into two glasses, then handed one to Levi. "My favorite Terran fruit. I'm glad that mango trees thrive on Telmieria." They drank their juice savoring each mouthful. The historians unexpectedly began to feel very groggy.

"Time Control, we have a problem," mumbled Levi before he and Lisa lost consciousness and fell on the floor.

Inek and his two helpers entered the room. "You two take care of the storyteller," ordered Inek. "I will take care of his sister. Report back to me as soon as you make the delivery. Meet me at the usual place to collect your pay. Handle him gently. He is Friend of The Crown."

Lisa woke up with a headache. Her throat was parched like she hadn't had anything to drink for a day. She struggled to focus her thoughts. It took her eyes time to adjust to the bright ceiling light. Lisa checked out her surroundings. The bed she was lying on was very comfortable. Lisa's commoner dress seemed out of place in her luxurious surroundings. Good God! She thought in alarm. Have I been sold to a pleasure house? Lisa tried to get up, but a wave of dizziness hit her. A few minutes later, she slipped off the bed and slowly stood up.

She poured some water from the pitcher on the nightstand. It took three glasses to quench her thirst. Lisa looked for her watch, but it was gone. Fortunately, her medallion com-link hadn't been taken. She tried to contact Dark but just got static. Something was blocking the signal. Lisa's heart sank when it hit her that she was completely cut off from the rest of the world. She couldn't contact Dark or the soldiers telepathically. They had to be out of range.

Lisa started in surprise when the door suddenly opened. She watched unbelieving as Lord Maric entered the room. He seemed much more mellow than when he had been at the marketplace. Lisa reached out to his mind. Providently, he didn't recognize her. Apparently, Maric's attention had been totally focused on Levi.

"Please do not be afraid, my lady," said Maric soothingly. "You are my special guest."

Lisa bowed. "I am unworthy of the honor," she simpered.

Lisa realized that seduction, not rape was Maric's game. His oversized ego couldn't accept having to take a woman by force. He probably used flattery, false claims of love and a promise of marriage to persuade women to surrender their bodies to him. This was just the opening gambit.

"My estate has beautiful paintings and sculptures by the greatest masters of Atlantis," boasted Maric. "All of them pale in comparison with you. Tomorrow when you are fully rested, I will give you a tour of the estate. If you are ready to eat, I will order dinner for you."

"Please!"

Maric bowed. "Until tomorrow."

Lisa watched Maric as he left the room. It all seemed like a crazy dream. She knew that everything was obnoxiously real. The presence of an armed guard outside of her door didn't surprise her. She checked the door. It was not locked, but it didn't need to be. She laughed at the absurd twist of fate that dropped her into Maric's hands. Aurelin had countless attractive women, but Maric's procurers had to choose her.

On the plus side, seduction took time. Maric didn't appear to be in a hurry. She touched the mind of the guard. His thoughts were mostly about army business and drinking with his buddies when he was off duty. Lisa could overpower the guard with a brain spike, but she could only deal with one man at a time. Her helplessness irritated her more than it worried her. Lisa doubted that any of the servants would risk their jobs or heads to help her. She decided to just enjoy the luxury for the time being and bide her time.

Levi slowly realized that he was awake. He opened his eyes to strange surroundings. A dusty ceiling lamp cast a feeble light throughout the room. The blackened windowless walls depressed him. A heavy layer of dust covered everything in the room. It hadn't been used or cleaned in a long time. Levi got the impression that the room was underground. His grumbling stomach and parched throat suggested that he hadn't eaten or drunk anything for a day.

Shackles bound Levi's limbs to a long five-foot-high wooden table. His former cell in the palace dungeon was much cleaner and more comfortable. He hoped that Lisa hadn't been abducted as well. Although she had no weapons to defend herself, she wasn't defenseless. To his relief, he still had his dragon medallion com-link. Unfortunately, he couldn't reach the emergency signal.

Levi noticed that a camera had been recently installed on the opposite wall. It seemed that he was going to be the star of someone's show. Levi figured his captor planned to kill him eventually. Only Maric had any animus toward him. He probably desired to prolong Levi's misery before putting him out of it. The thought of Lisa being in Maric's unclean hands greatly disturbed Levi.

Levi refused to surrender to despair. Until the cold embrace of death ended all hope and possibilities, he might yet prevail. He took heart from the example of Eric Morgan. Levi read his memoir of the Marauder War. Despite being in many challenging and dangerous situations, he never gave up or despaired. Levi refused to concede the game to Maric.

The door slowly creaked open. A serious looking, white haired man entered the room accompanied by a grinning boy about thirteen. The man's helper placed a large, handled case onto a metal table and moved the table near Levi's head. Levi had a very bad feeling. The man wiped the ceiling light clean. It doubled the illumination. While Levi watched, the man checked the function of several strange devices.

"Forgive me," apologized the old man. "I have been a poor host. Tani, bring my guest some food and water."

When Tani returned, he fed Levi a generous amount of beef and cheese.

"You feed your prisoners well," commented Levi.

"My client and I want you to keep up your strength. We do not want you to be weakened by hunger or thirst. Excuse me, sir. I am forgetting my manners. My name is Ison. The boy is my grandson, Tani. For my client's pleasure, I will introduce you to pain and discomfort you never imagined possible," Ison spoke the words with pride.

"Is your grandson the torturer's apprentice?"

Ison chuckled. "Occasionally I let Tani accompany me on a job. He dearly loves to watch me practice my art. I would be pleased and proud if Tani chose to follow in my footsteps."

Ison's cheerful, pleasant tone of voice chilled Levi. Tani's adoration of his grandfather's "art" appalled Levi.

"No knives or hot irons?" asked Levi.

Ison shook his head. "Much too crude. The torturer's art consists of inflicting maximum pain with the least physical injury. All too soon, physical abuse breaks down and kills the subject. Torture sessions with my tools could conceivably last for months without causing death. The subject would probably be driven insane by then. Do not fear. My client will not let you live that long."

"Thank Father Sun for little things," commented Levi sourly.

Ison chuckled. "Let me demonstrate show you my most important and useful tool." Ison removed a device from his toolbox the size of a small loaf of bread. Several wires hung down from it. He connected the wires to Levi's head, then switched it on. A red haze of searing pain flooded Levi's senses. After a few seconds, Ison stopped the pain. An afterglow of agony slowly faded.

"The neural stimulator is not my invention," Ison informed Levi. "I have made some improvements. Now the stimulator can cause an equal amount of pleasure. In time, I will introduce you to it. Is it not marvelous that I can cause you unbearable pain without hurting you at all physically?"

"Monstrous is the word," whispered Levi. "You are no better than a barbarian."

Ison took umbrage at the accusation. "A torturer delights in the excellence of his work, not the pain. It is merely the fruit of his labor."

"Ah, that is different."

Ison sighed. "It deeply pains me that you will die, storyteller. I feel like I am destroying a precious work of art. Regrettably, a customer sought my services to torture you. I was bound by honor to provide my service to him. In appreciation of your art, when the time comes I will make your death quick and painless."

"I wish I could return the favor."

Levi couldn't decide who was more reprehensible: the torturer who unemotionally caused great pain for gain or his customers who hired them. Levi felt sorry for the boy who had become so desensitized to the pain of others.

"I usually finish with the stimulator, but I might as well begin with it since it is already connected," decided Ison. "It is a great honor to be your torturer."

Levi felt very grateful that Dark had been chosen to go on the Atlantis mission. If anyone could find and rescue him, it would be the crafty, resourceful Karani adventurer.

Chapter Fourteen

Dark and the soldiers went to the dining room to have breakfast. To their surprise, Levi and Lisa were not there. "Usually, Levi and Lisa are here before us," noted Dark. "They must have gotten in very late last night."

Kinsey frowned. "If I learned nothing from in my Earthfleet experience, I learned that when people as regular in their habits as the historians break their routine, something might be wrong. Sergeant McNeil, see if Levi and Lisa are in their room."

McNeil saluted and hurried off to carry out his order. Five minutes later McNeil returned looking very worried. "Major, the door to their room was unlocked. Their bed hasn't been slept in. I searched everywhere but didn't find either Levi or Lisa."

Dark called Levi but he only got static. He tried several times more without success. Dark attempted to call Lisa several times. All he heard was static.

"The historians' com-links are being jammed," figured Kinsey.

"A serenium barrier might be blocking their reception and transmission," speculated Kelly.

"Maric must be behind the disappearance of Levi and Lisa," said Kinsey. "For all we know, the historians are dead. Hopefully, they are still alive. Alive or dead, they are most likely here in Aurelin. We need help to find them."

Dark nodded. "King Adeil will help us. Abducting and killing someone under his protection is an insufferable offense. I will go to the palace and see the king."

Dark took a taxi to the palace. Along the way, he realized that something was wrong. Inek had taken the historians prisoner. He should have just killed them at the inn. Why move them to another location to kill them and risk getting caught? By the time Dark reached the palace, he understood what had happened. Inek had sold them to Maric, Levi to torture, then kill, Lisa to use for his pleasure, then maybe kill. Maric dared not let her live. All bets were off now.

Dark figured that the responsibility for killing the historians had passed to Inek. As far as he was concerned, he had done his duty. It was a rationalization, but one Dark could live with.

The two guards at the main gate watched warily as Dark exited the taxi and approached the gate. "I must see the king," said Dark. "The storyteller Levi has been abducted! His life is in great danger!"

The guards looked at each other uncertainly. Their first thought was to dismiss the importunate stranger. Then they reconsidered. If the man spoke truly and the Friend of The Crown suffered serious injury or death because they failed to act, the king would imprison or execute them. One of the guards contacted Etor. Minutes later he arrived at the gate.

"Who are you?" demanded Etor. "What is your business here?"

"I am Levi's friend, Jerrel Dark. Usually, he visits with me and our other friends when he returns to the inn at night. We waited until midnight, but he still hadn't arrived, so we went to bed. We checked his room this morning. The door was unlocked, and the bed had not been slept in. Levi always notifies us when he will not be back until the next day."

"I dare not disbelieve you," decided Etor. "I will take you to the king immediately."

Nura rose earlier than usual. A strong feeling of foreboding roused her from her sleep. Whenever she had such feelings, someone close to her suffered injury, sickness, or death. Nura knew that Maric hated Levi because of his relationship with her. She felt that he might dare to strike at Levi despite his being under the Crown's protection. Nura quickly showered and dressed. She hurried to the king's Private Audience Chamber. When she arrived there, the guard immediately announced her arrival to the king.

King Adeil knew that Nura never interrupted a private audience without good cause. He dismissed the courtier, promising to see him later in the day. Adeil saw the concerned look on her face. "What troubles you, daughter?"

"A strong feeling of foreboding woke me this morning, father," began Nura. "As I pondered it, my thoughts turned to Levi. I feel that something bad has happened to him or will soon happen to him."

"I have learned to trust those feelings of yours," said Adeil. "If you wish, I will send Etor to check on him."

"Please send him now."

A knock on the door startled Nura and Adeil. The door opened and Etor walked in. "Your majesty, Levi's friend Jerrel Dark has come to the palace. He informed me that Levi has been abducted from the Inn of The Seventh Ecstasy."

"Bring him before Us!" ordered Adeil. Dark entered the chamber and knelt before the king. "Why do you think the storyteller has been abducted?" Dark told Adeil and Nura what he had told Etor and the guards at the main gate. He added that Lisa had also disappeared.

"I agree with your assessment," decided Adeil.

"Who took them and why?" wondered Etor. "Are they even alive? I can think of only one man who has the motivation and poor judgment to commit such a serious crime: Lord Maric."

"That greatly complicates matters," reflected Adeil soberly. "We cannot use palace agents, guards, or soldiers to search for Levi and Lisa. Maric and Garai would soon learn about it. We have no assets that they would not recognize."

"May I make a suggestion, Your Majesty?" asked Dark.

"Speak!" ordered Adeil.

"You can use the guilds, except for the Assassins Guild, to search for Levi and his sister," said Dark. "Their members can move freely and unobtrusively throughout Aurelin. The guilds have no love for Maric. If Levi and his sister were still alive, I would bet my last sovereign that they are still in the city. They are too hot to move."

"The guilds are our only hope, Your Majesty," agreed Etor. "The guild masters will not help us out of patriotism or love for their king. A significant reduction of guild taxes should get their cooperation."

Adeil smiled despite his anger at Maric's crime against him and Levi. "I can always count on you for good counsel, captain. I am confident that you will be sufficiently persuasive."

Etor had never set foot in the Night Kingdom or any guild's headquarters. His duties and responsibilities never required it. He got the location of the headquarters of the Thieves Guild. Etor hoped that he didn't need to look all over the Night Kingdom to find Zaki. To avoid attracting attention to himself, he took an unmarked palace shuttle used by palace servants. The few people Etor drove past seemed to be indifferent and unconcerned about his presence.

Night Kingdom residents were mostly nocturnal. Occasionally Etor saw people peeping out the windows. He slowed down as he approached the Thieves Guild headquarters. Two men stood outside the front door. They carefully observed the shuttle as it pulled up to the front door and stopped. Etor got out and approached the men.

They stared at him in astonishment. The men recognized his uniform and stepped aside. They looked displeased but said nothing. Etor stopped a man in the hallway and asked to be taken to Zaki. Reluctantly, the man did as Etor asked. The man knocked on the door, then opened it and ushered Etor inside.

Zaki rose from his chair. He stepped closer to Etor as if he thought he was hallucinating. He made a mocking bow. "I am humbled and honored by your presence, Captain of the Palace Guard. Are you thinking of trying a new line of work? I am willing to consider your application to the Thieves Guild."

Etor ignored the insult and insolence. "A Friend of The Crown has been kidnapped by Maric. The king needs the help of the guilds to find him."

"Maric!" spat Zaki. "Your plea and the king's friend do not move me, captain. You blue skins treat the people of the Night Kingdom like dirt. We have no interest in your problems."

"In exchange for the guilds help, the king will reduce the guilds' taxes."

Zaki's eyes shone with interest, but his expression gave away nothing. "How much?"

"Fifteen percent for the next three years."

"Very tempting," said Zaki. "The guild members will not like doing favors for blue skins."

"The man Maric abducted is the storyteller Levi," revealed Etor. "He abducted his sister Lisa as well."

Zaki cursed. "That misbegotten jackal kidnapped my friends! We will do all we can to help, captain. Before we proceed further, we need to sign a contract." Zaki took out a contract from one of his desk drawers. He filled it out, then signed it. Zaki smiled as he handed the paper and pen to Etor. The captain carefully read every word, then signed the contract as the king's authorized agent. "Simple, clear and unambiguous," commented Etor approvingly.

"We will proceed on the assumption that Levi and Lisa are still alive," decided Zaki. "Maric is not likely to give Levi a quick death. No doubt, he has already begun to torture Levi. Maric will not fail to take pleasure with a nice, lovely lady like Lisa. Most likely, she is being held at Garai's estate. That will be hard to confirm. Transporting Levi out of the Night Kingdom is much too risky. There are plenty of places in the Night Kingdom a man can stash a hot prisoner. Fear not, captain, we will search every likely possibility as quickly as possible."

Etor unhooked a com-link from his belt. He handed it to Zaki. "This is a secure com-link. The star button is my private frequency. I want updates on the searches every four hours." Etor handed Zaki photos of Levi and Lisa to copy.

"You will get them," promised Zaki. "Father Sun is cruel to curse Atlantis with a king like Maric."

After Etor left, Zaki called an emergency meeting of all the guild masters. He explained that Maric had kidnapped Levi the storyteller and his sister. Zaki informed them of the contract he had made with the king. They ratified the decision unanimously without dissent. The Guild masters ordered their people to begin the search for Levi and Lisa. Zaki summoned all his people. He explained the situation and ordered them to hit the streets and begin the search.

Dark returned to the inn to get his invisibility cloak after leaving the palace. Kinsey and the sergeants wanted to help with the search for the historians. Dark persuaded them to let the guilds search for Levi in the Night Kingdom while he checked for Lisa at Garai's estate. They wanted to accompany Dark, but he insisted that he go alone. Kinsey had read Dark's dossier. He grudgingly accepted that the Telmierian was right.

On their first day in Aurelin, all the team members bought shoes that let them move around almost soundlessly while they used their invisibility cloaks. Dark activated his cloak, then slipped out of his room. He left by the less frequently used back door. Garai's estate was five miles up the coast from Aurelin. Providence provided Dark with the ride he needed. He stole an illegally parked shuttle a few spaces from the inn.

When he determined that he was not being observed by anyone inside or outside the inn, Dark expanded the field to cover the shuttle. No one saw it abruptly vanish from sight. Dark had never driven a vehicle under cloak before. The challenge didn't frighten or worry him. He moved skillfully through the light traffic in a direct line with the Coast Highway that circled the island. Dark checked continually for tailgaters. Three times he had to pull completely out of his lane to avoid being rear ended.

Dark felt great relief when he finally turned onto the Coast Highway. In minutes, he reached the turnoff to Garai's estate. A large sign by the road said Authorized Personnel Only. He followed the road leading to the main house. Lanes leading to other areas of the estate branched off it. The estate sat on a plain with no bushes, trees, or other obstructions to cloak anyone trying to approach undetected to the estate. A ten feet high electrified fence surrounded the house.

Although his shuttle was very quiet, Dark pulled off the road and parked five hundred feet away from the main gate. He tried calling Lisa, but still got static. Once he was inside the fence, Dark expected to be able to contact Lisa. He scanned the guard booth. One guard was inside. Dark opened the door. Immediately, the guard turned his head away from his computer screen. To his great surprise, he saw no one. Before the guard could make a move, Dark hit him with a strong stun blast. The guard fell out of his chair onto the floor. He would be unconscious long enough for Dark to take care of business.

Dark found the control for the electric fence, then turned off the power. He manually opened the gate just far enough for him to slip by, then closed it. Luckily, the two-man roving patrol between Dark and the main house didn't notice it as they passed. He decided not to contact Lisa unless he had to. Dark didn't want to risk contacting her when she was not alone. When he reached the front door, he found it unsecured. Dark opened it just far enough to slip past it. No one was in sight.

He scanned the walls and windows for alarms, heat sensors and motion detectors. There were none. Dark's electronic lock pick easily circumvented the lock. Dark had obtained and studied the layout of the main house. The larger bedrooms had to be those of Garai and Maric. He moved quietly through the house passing servants as they went about their business.

Not surprisingly, Garai had many attractive female servants. He took time to listen to their conversations to learn something useful. Two female servants discussed Maric's latest lady 'guest.' They expressed surprise that Maric had treated her with unprecedented courtesy and respect. The servants hated that so many women were ill used by Maric. They figured that she might become his long-term mistress. Dark scanned each bedroom for Karani life signs.

He went to the room indicated by the scanner. Dark found that a guard had been posted at one of the bedrooms. Dark stunned the guard. He threw the man over his shoulder and took him to an empty bedroom. Carelessly, Darak dumped him on the bed. It amused Dark to contemplate the trouble the guard would be in if Maric found him there. He returned to Lisa's bedroom. Dark knocked lightly on the door and waited.

Lisa slipped into the bright yellow dress provided by her maid servant. The soft material felt very comfortable against her skin. Maric had many faults, but he had excellent taste in clothes. Her maid servant had expressed surprise that Maric had treated Lisa so well. She told Lisa that Maric was more impressed with her than any other women he had ever brought to the estate. The servant warned her not to expect Maric to marry her. He would someday marry Princess Nura. The maid servant enthusiastically assured Lisa that Maric just might choose her as his mistress.

Lisa put on the pearl necklace he gave her the day before. So far, he had given Lisa the pearl necklace, a gold bracelet, and a ruby ring. Maric showed great generosity to women who pleased him. Lisa tried to find a balance between encouraging Maric and rejecting him. So far, it seemed to be working. Lisa lightly touched his thoughts. Strangely enough, there were no strings attached to his gifts.

Lisa heard a knock on the door. It was an unfamiliar knock. She went to the door and opened it. To her surprise, no one was there. Suddenly she felt a hand over her mouth. An unseen arm dragged her inside. The door flew shut by itself.

Dark deactivated his invisibility cloak. Lisa hugged him in relief. "I thought you guys would never rescue me!"

"I am not here to rescue you, Lisa," confessed Dark. "I only came here to confirm your presence on the estate."

Lisa's relief turned to confusion and annoyance. "Why can't you take me out now?"

"You cannot just come in and kick down the door of the most powerful military leader in Atlantis and its future king," Dark reminded her. "Your 'host' is the Commander of the Atlantean Army. None of us like it, but we need to go through official channels."

"King Adeil," realized Lisa. "Have you or the king's men found Levi yet?"

"Regrettably not," said Dark. "Zaki and the guilds are scouring the Night Kingdom for Levi even as we speak. Zaki believes Levi is being held somewhere in the Night Kingdom. I agree. Right now, Levi is the hottest commodity in Aurelin. Trying to get him out of the city would be very dangerous for Maric. I must leave now. Hold off Maric a while longer. You will be sprung before the end of the day."

Dark activated his invisibility cloak and vanished from sight. Lisa watched as the door opened and shut by the unseen Dark. Lisa sat down on a chair and picked up the book she had been reading the day before. She hadn't expected to find a copy of the Book of Commandments in General Garai's library. Neither the general nor his son had patterned their lives after it. Levi told her that Princess Nura strove to live according to the Book of Commandments.

A half hour later, Lisa heard a knock on the door. It was Maric. She opened the door and let him in. He looked over Lisa with approval and smiled. "Your beauty graces my home."

Lisa sighed. "Princess Nura is much fairer than me."

Maric stiffened at the mention of Princess Nura. "That is not true," disagreed Maric strongly. "With blue skin, you would be as fair as any lady descended from the Sun Lords. Come, my lady. Today I will show you all the estate has to offer you."

Lisa felt like a liberated prisoner as she walked out of the room. Maric gave her a tour of the house. The general hadn't stinted on the furniture. The sergeants had learned that Garai had a source of secondary income: illegal trade with Lemurian smugglers. The highly profitable operation flourished under his protection. Possibly, King Adeil winked at it. Maybe the king didn't know about it.

The rooms and hallways were decorated with marble statues, paintings, and tapestries. Lisa found it strange that all the statues were athletes and soldiers, while the paintings had beautiful natural scenes. Maric took her outside and led her to the garden. She delighted in the songs of birds. Lisa sighed as pleasant breezes cooled her. A sundial by the rose arbor showed the time to be about noon. She figured that it was her second day on Garai's estate.

They moved on to the fountain at the center of the garden. Lisa inhaled deeply of the roses and star flowers. For a moment, she forgot who her hosts were. Maric gazed somberly at the fountain.

"When my mother was in the final stages of her illness, she spent as much time in the garden as her strength permitted," recalled Maric. "It always lifted her spirits. Sometimes her pain was great. Nevertheless, she endured it courageously. Despite our advanced medicine, some diseases even our physicians cannot cure. I was only eight when she died."

Lisa placed her hand on Maric's and closed her eyes. She reached out to his emotions. Lisa winced as a flood of anger and pain swept through her. She sensed a frightened little boy deep inside him that had never resolved the loss of his loving mother. Anger at his cold, insensitive father burned strongly in Maric. Garai's cruelty and indifference exacerbated it. Lisa felt evil in Maric's soul.

Had his mother lived longer, the evil in Maric might have been kept at bay. He vainly sought emotional peace and satisfaction in sensual indulgence. Like a mirage, satisfaction continually retreated from him.

Maric started when Lisa severed the psychic link. He gazed at her in wonder and delight. The mind to mind, heart to heart link was a two-way street. Telepaths unavoidably communicated part of themselves in the link.

"My father never remarried although my grandfather and I urged him to," said Maric bitterly. "He preferred to enjoy the charms of unchaste aristocrat women who were young enough to be his daughter. At least his present mistress, Kalara, is only seventeen years his junior." Maric took Lisa's right hand and held it tight. "This estate cries out for a woman's touch. It needs a woman like you."

Lisa couldn't believe her ears. Maric was inviting her to be his mistress and live on the estate. Lisa knew he meant every word. Maric had mistaken her physical attraction and compassion for love. For a commoner woman, being the mistress of the future king was the chance of a lifetime.

"But you will marry Princess Nura," replied Lisa ingenuously.

Maric grimaced at the prospect. "That is a marriage of state, not love. All she will do is bear my children and play the part of queen of Atlantis. The princess has made that abundantly clear. But you and your bed will be the refuge I return to for refreshment of my soul."

Lisa tried to look sympathetic. "Surely your father will be offended if you keep a barbarian lover in his house."

Maric laughed. "The general suggested it. He also recognized your quality."

The news about Garai didn't surprise Lisa. She sensed his lustful feelings about her. He no doubt intended to share her bed when Maric was absent. "This is all so sudden and overwhelming," responded Lisa truthfully. "I never dared to dream of receiving such an honor."

Maric pulled her close and kissed her. "Do not doubt your worthiness. You said you wanted to see my library. It is my great pleasure to share it with you."

Chapter Fifteen

The guards at the main gate of the palace gazed warily at the unprepossessing poor peasant who approached them. He eyed the guards nervously. The man bowed. "I have a message for Captain Etor. It is very important."

The senior guard regarded the man disdainfully. "I will be the judge of that, peasant. Give me the message."

Slowly the man pulled out a folded-up piece of paper and handed it to the guard. His eyes grew wide as he read it. "Who gave this to you?"

The man shrugged. "I never saw him before. A hood covered most of his face. He paid me five gold sovereigns to deliver the message to the palace."

The guard holding the paper called Etor and informed him about the message. Etor ordered the guard to bring it to him. Etor unfolded the paper. It contained just seven words: the storyteller's sister is at Garai's estate. Etor informed Adeil about the message. Adeil ordered him to go to Garai's estate immediately and pick up Lisa. Etor decided to use the king's floater to make the proper impression on Garai's guards.

Etor flew over the streets of Aurelin as fast as safety permitted. He increased speed once he got on the Coast Highway. The more he thought about Maric's seizure of Levi and Lisa the angrier he became. Ordering palace guards to imprison Levi in the palace dungeon was bad enough. Abducting a Friend of The Crown and his sister greatly exceeded that offense. If he learned that Maric had had Levi killed, he vowed that one way, or another Maric would never sit on the throne. Etor hoped that Garai would refuse to cooperate. Then he would embarrass the general by searching every inch of his estate. He had guards ready just in case a search had to be made.

When Etor pulled up to the front gate of Garai's estate, the guard saluted him. He let Etor pass without question. "Do not let anyone leave the estate until I return, by the king's command," ordered Etor.

He parked his floater and walked up to the front door of the main house. Shortly after Etor knocked on the door a male servant opened the door.

"I have important business with General Garai. I know the way to his office."

The female servants smiled at Etor as he passed. Male servants averted their eyes. When Etor arrived at the office door, he knocked firmly on it. Garai said, "Come!"

Etor entered the room and walked up to Garai. Etor saluted him.

"Is this visit social or business, Captain?" asked Garai.

"A foreign woman named Lisa is staying with you, general. She failed to notify her brother that she was staying with him. He has been very concerned about her. The king commands her presence at the palace immediately!"

Garai's only reaction was a slightly raised eyebrow. His eyes and expression gave away nothing. Garai appreciated the play. He quickly sized up the tactical situation. Etor knew Lisa was on the estate. If Garai refused to acknowledge her presence, Etor would bring in guards to search the estate from one end to the other. He would lose face with his men, the army, and the people. Garai took the opening the king gave him. He ordered Lisa to be brought to his study immediately. Five minutes later, a guard delivered Lisa to him.

Garai gazed disapprovingly at Lisa. "Lisa, you should have notified your brother that you were visiting Maric. He has been very concerned about you."

Lisa looked at Etor. She didn't need to read his thoughts. Etor made no attempt to hide his disgust at Garai's charade and the need to go along with it.

"The king has sent me to escort you to the palace," Etor informed Lisa.

Garai smiled slyly. "Maric and I hope you visit us again soon. You are always welcome here, Lisa."

Servants gazed in wonder and delight as Etor and Lisa passed by. She was the first woman brought the state who was not taken out and dumped on the street. When they exited the house, Lisa threw her arms around Etor and kissed him. "I am sorry that I cannot do more unless you marry me."

Etor blushed and cleared his throat. "I, uh, appreciate the thought."

Etor informed Adeil he was returning to the palace with Lisa. On the way to the palace, Etor informed Lisa of the efforts to find Levi. So far, Levi hadn't turned up alive or dead. Lisa smiled knowingly when Etor told her that someone had tipped him off that she was being held on Garai's estate. Etor regretted that Maric was absent at the time of her rescue. Rubbing Maric's loss in his face would have been very enjoyable and satisfying.

King Adeil and Nura met with Etor and Lisa in the Private Audience Chamber. "Thank Father Sun that you are all right, Lisa," said Nura with relief.

"Tell me everything that happened to you while you were at General Garai's estate," ordered Adeil.

"Levi and I had just returned to the inn after a long day," began Lisa. "After retiring to our room, we drank some mango juice to pleasantly quench our thirst. When we began to get groggy, we realized that it had been drugged. It knocked us out so fast; we did not have time to think. When I woke up an unknown time later, I was lying on a luxurious bed in a strange house. I have no idea who took me there. Levi had been taken somewhere else. Shortly after I woke up, Lord Maric visited me."

"Did Maric beat or rape you, Lisa?" demanded Nura.

Lisa shook her head. "Lord Maric treated me like an honored guest. He showed me great courtesy. To my surprise, he invited me to remain permanently at the estate as his mistress, although he did not put it that bluntly."

"Maric is very welcome to keep ten mistresses at his estate after we are married," said Nura. "I hope that you did not accept his offer, Lisa."

"Not to save my life!" Lisa assured her. "I have more respect for myself and my family than that."

Adeil frowned. "The fact remains that Maric kidnapped a respectable woman from her residence and held her captive at Garai's estate. That crime cannot go unpunished even if he is an Atlantean lord and general."

"Your Majesty, strictly speaking I was not held captive," noted Lisa. "No one told me that I could not leave. The guard outside of my bedroom door strongly suggested that I could not. He might have been stationed there to protect me rather than keep me from leaving.

Maric told me that his guards found me lying at the side of the road near Garai's estate. My time at the estate was very pleasant."

Nura examined Lisa's pearl necklace, ruby ring, and gold bracelet. "You really did make a powerful impression on Maric."

"That settles the matter with Lisa," decided Adeil. "The matter of Levi remains. We will continue the search for him until we find him alive or dead, preferably alive. I want to tie Maric's crime against the Crown like a millstone around his neck. We have one big advantage: Maric does not know that the guilds are searching for Levi. If we can catch Maric with Levi, his dream of ruling Atlantis will be dead. Lisa, you may remain here at the palace or return to the inn. If you return to the inn, I will assign guards to protect you."

"That will not be necessary, Your Majesty," said Lisa. "The friends who are traveling with Levi and me are former soldiers. I will be fine."

"As you wish," granted Adeil. "Etor will notify you when Levi is found."

Zaki sat at his desk waiting and hoping to hear soon that Levi had been found. He felt happy and relieved to hear that Lisa had been located and rescued. Zaki was pleased that the searchers had quickly covered more ground than he expected. One thing puzzled him. None of the people the searchers questioned had seen or heard anything. That confirmed that Maric had helpers from the Night Kingdom. People would pay little attention to them. Zaki was determined to learn who they were and enforce guild justice on them.

Neither Etor nor the king knew that the guilds would have happily searched for Levi for nothing. He was an honored member of the Storytellers Guild. The guilds took care of their own. King Adeil offered the guilds a reduction of the Guild Tax rate for their help. It would be very bad manners to refuse the king's gift. Zaki convinced the other guild masters to give much of the money saved to the guild members. The guild masters would still get a large share.

When two days had passed with no progress with the search for Levi, Zaki decided to take a different approach. Looking for all the torturers would considerably decrease the amount of ground to be covered. Unfortunately, the torturers had no guild. All of them operated independently. Torturers didn't care what their competitors were doing. The best ones had more offers than they could accept.

No doubt, Maric would choose the best. Zaki sent word to all the searchers to focus their attention on torturers.

The searchers approached people known to have used the services of torturers. They soon got lucky. A thief encountered a man who had used torturers occasionally. The man told the thief the names of men whose services he had used. He wanted to hire Ison, but he only served the rich, aristocrats and on occasion, the Army. The thief passed the information to Zaki. Zaki informed Etor. Etor got Ison's address and gave it to Zaki.

Levi sighed with relief when the agony of the neural stimulator finally ended. Ison then gave him a heavy dose of pleasure. Levi had come to hate the pleasure as much as the pain. It made the pain much worse when it returned. Ison unfailingly provided Levi with enough food and water to maintain his strength. Each torture session seemed like a moment for the customer, an eternity for the sufferer. Ison's pleasantness and politeness stood in strange juxtaposition to his actions. Had Levi not known the Atlantean character and mindset, he would have thought Ison psychotic.

Ison checked his watch. "Time for a refreshment break. Tani, bring wine for us."

A few minutes later, Tani returned with the wine. Levi enjoyed the taste of the wine, but he wished it had been water.

Ison looked over his tools. "Each torture session is unique," Ison explained to Levi as if to an apprentice. "I let inspiration guide me. Torture is as much art as science."

"Has your client wearied of my suffering yet," asked Levi.

Ison smiled. "On the contrary, he remains very enthusiastic. He is in no hurry to end your discomfort. You have suffered greatly already. If I was the customer, I would be merciful and end your misery now. I would like to suggest that to him, but that would be unethical. Time to get back to work and earn my pay." Levi grimaced as he watched Ison pick up the neural stimulator. This time it would be pain.

Levi, Ison, and Tani were startled when someone kicked in the door. Two men with guns drawn entered the room. One of them pointed his gun at Ison. "Release the storyteller before my gun goes off accidentally!"

Ison and Tani quickly unshackled Levi. One of the men helped him to his feet "Are you all right, Master Levi?" he asked.

"I am now. Thank you for crashing this party."

One of the thieves helped Levi out of the building to a waiting shuttle. The other took Ison and Tani into custody. He glared at Ison. "Master Levi is Friend of The Crown. If the king is merciful, he will grant you a quick death."

"I did not know he was friend of the crown!" wailed Ison. "How could I know?"

Before the thief could ask Ison who his client was, a shuttle screeched around the corner. As it slowed down, the front passenger side window opened. A man dressed in black shot Ison and Tani from just six feet away. Then the shuttle sped off and disappeared into the night.

One of the thieves checked Ison and Tani. Both were dead. The hit on Ison also killed two of the thieves. The thieves knew Maric had hired Ison. Maric wasn't going to confess. Now it could never be proved that he hired Ison. All that was left to do was report to Zaki and get Levi to the palace as quickly as possible.

When the shuttle with Levi arrived at the palace, medical personnel, awaited him. They rushed him to the palace infirmary. Adeil, Nura and Lisa watched as the king's personal physician, Doctor Kerson, examined him. "No broken bones, no damage to any organs, no burns, no physical injury whatsoever!" marveled the physician.

"The torturer Ison used devices that caused me intense pain but did not injure me," explained Levi. "The worst torture session was the neural stimulator. Unspeakable agony, then great pleasure, followed by agony again. The pleasure part made the pain worse when it returned."

"The torturer and his child assistant were shot and killed in a drive by shooting before they could reveal their client," reported Etor. "Maric planned his crime well. I ordered the torturer's tools to be destroyed."

"My patient needs to rest, Your Majesty," Dr. Kerson reminded Adeil. "I will run some tests, but he should be all right with a few days' rest."

"Very well," said Adeil. "I can assign bodyguards to you and your sister for the remainder of your stay in Atlantis, Levi."

"No thank you, Your Majesty," replied Levi quickly. "I think Lord Maric will not trouble me again."

Dark felt greatly relieved when Lisa reported that Levi had been found and rescued. He immediately shared the news with the soldiers. Lisa told him that she would stay at the palace for a few days. She requested that he and the soldiers continue with their recording. Dark had some business to take care of before returning to work. He drove to the Assassins Guild Headquarters to see Gotzon.

Since Dark was now a recognized customer of the guild, he was allowed to enter the building without question. He figured that the chances were good that Gotzon would be his office. Unlike during his first visit, Dark saw no one inside the building. He made it to Gotzon's office without encountering anyone. Dark knocked on the door. He entered the office when Gotzon said, "Come."

Gotzon smiled when he saw Dark. He got up and shook his visitor's hand. "Welcome, my generous friend! Do you have a new job for the guild already?"

Dark shook his head. "I paid to have Master Levi and his sister taken care of. Inek not only failed to do the job, but he also sold them to Maric."

The news shocked and displeased Gotzon. "That is a very serious offense. I cannot believe that any assassin would be foolish enough to try to cheat the guild or me that way."

"Inek is that foolish and greedy," insisted Dark. "My sources have confirmed it."

Gotzon smiled unpleasantly. "I have sources too, friend." Gotzon made several calls. After the last call, he cursed and ended the call. He shook his head in disbelief. "Inek was the last man I would have expected to commit this offense. As you said, he was greedy and foolish. I apologize for this shameful act. Your payment will be returned in full." Gotzon called Inek's com-link and ordered him to come to his office.

Gotzon and Dark waited patiently for Inek to arrive. Twenty minutes later, they heard a knock on the door. Inek opened the door and entered the office. The look on Inek's face told Dark that the man realized that he was in trouble.

"Have you completed the job on schedule as we all agreed, Inek?" asked Gotzon mildly.

Inek seemed to be debating within himself whether to lie and deny or tell the truth. "No, Guild Master," he confessed. "I sold the storyteller and his sister to Maric to enjoy before I killed them. He paid me fifteen thousand gold sovereigns."

Gotzon sighed. "Thank you for not insulting me with a cowardly lie. Because you respected me, I will be merciful." Gotzon swiftly pulled out his gun and shot Inek between the eyes.

"A strange kind of mercy," observed Dark with amusement.

"I could have made his death slow and very painful," explained Gotzon. "Tomorrow, I probably will probably regret that I did not. Nevertheless, Inek will be a very motivating object lesson to the rest of the guild."

Gotzon summoned men to remove Inek's body.

Dark felt a twinge of concern and uncertainty about causing Inek's death. Did it negatively impact the time continuum? It wasn't like he had killed the assassin himself. He most likely had not survived the destruction of Atlantis. Dark figured that the world of this day was not diminished one whit by Inek's loss. Levi, Lisa, and the Time Council believed that the past could be changed. Dark had come to agree. Killing an evil tyrant might end up creating an even worse one. Dark knew that neither he nor anyone else would do a good job playing God.

Chapter Sixteen

Levi needed three days to recover his strength from Ison's torture. Doctor Kerson insisted on complete bed rest during that time. Levi happily obeyed. He felt as exhausted as if he had marched sixty miles carrying a sixty-pound load. Levi hoped the torture hadn't knocked a few years off his lifespan. The Karani rejuvenation treatments made him feel his age again. Levi greatly appreciated all the time Nura and Lisa spent with him.

He woke to the pleasing sight of Nura sleeping peacefully beside him. It was probably the first time in days that she had a peaceful look on her face. Just being close to someone and touching them gave joined couples much delight. Last night, he experienced renewal as well pleasure from Nura. Levi felt very annoyed that he had lost three days of work because of Maric. At the same time, he felt grateful for having survived the torture mentally and emotionally.

Levi studied Nura's medallion. She never took it off even when showering, bathing, or making love. It had to be more than mere adornment. The platinum medallion was circular with a variety of precious gems in an unusual pattern. A diamond, ruby, sapphire, emerald, amethyst and peridot circled a citrine. A scan revealed that the medallion had electronic circuits. What they did, Levi couldn't determine. Was the medallion's significance political or religious? Levi had wondered about it for weeks but didn't want to risk offending Nura by asking about it.

Nura opened her eyes and smiled. "Good morning, Levi. I am happy that you are now fully recovered from the torture. In time, the memories of your suffering will seem like a distant bad dream. I see that my medallion interests you."

Nura can sense thoughts, realized Levi uncomfortably. He had to guard his thoughts about his mission carefully. "Your medallion interests me because you never take it off. Something tells me it is not just jewelry."

"This medallion is worn by the heir to the throne of Atlantis," declared Nura proudly. "My brother Akil wore it until he died. Then it came to me. The Sun Lord Maren gave it to his son and heir Nald. It was passed down from generation to generation until it came to me. It will be passed on to the next heir to the throne."

"Do the gems on the throne have some significance?"

"None that I am aware of," admitted Nura. "Levi, I have a special treat. Today we will sail on the royal yacht Sun King. Lisa may join us if she desires."

"She will be happy to come, Nura," Levi assured her. "For weeks, people have been excited about a sailing competition called Master of The Sea. Who competes in it?"

Levi listened with great interest as Nura told him the history of the competition. Fifty years ago, an idle boast by an Atlantean prince led to the competition. He claimed that Atlantean sailboats could beat any sailboat in the world. The heir to the Lemurian throne challenged him to prove it. That led to the first Master of The Sea Competition. The best Atlantean ship and the best Lemurian ship competed in a series of nine races for bragging rights.

Atlantis won most of the competitions. It currently enjoyed a five-year winning streak. This year the Lemurians were the consensus pick to win. During wartime, truces were declared so the Master of the Sea competition could take place. The law required visiting Lemurians to travel in groups of ten accompanied by 'guide protectors.' Aristocrats were permitted to flout the law, visiting their Atlantean friends without an escort. During the competition, people exchanged gossip and brought each other up to date about events in their friends' countries.

Levi and Nura quickly showered and dressed. After they had breakfast with Lisa, the three of them went to Nura's floater. They found Etor and four guards waiting for them. "After what happened to Levi, you and he will go nowhere outside of the castle without me, princess," Etor informed them."

"I have no objections, captain," Levi assured him.

Levi and Lisa hadn't returned to the harbor since visiting Captain Badrik. They weren't permitted to enter the section reserved exclusively for the aristocracy and the rich. When the floater reached the harbor, Levi noticed a circle of small two-story buildings to the left. "Those buildings are stores reserved for royalty and aristocrats," explained Nura. "And the rich."

"Except aristocrats who squandered their fortunes," noted Etor with amusement.

The day could not have been better for sailing: sunny with a pleasant cool breeze. Levi inhaled deeply of the salt air. It reminded him of sailing in his catamaran in Hawaii. Etor followed the serpentine road until he came to the dock where the Sun King awaited Nura and her guests. He parked the floater near the gangplank. The captain welcomed Nura and her party aboard. First the guards boarded the yacht. Nura, Levi, Lisa and Etor followed. The crew cast off and the Sun King got underway.

The yacht had a beautiful, long-haired woman on the prow. She was practically naked. The Sun King's decks and hull were wood reinforced by steel plates. For this trip, it used sail rather than engines because of the stiff breeze. Levi, Nura, and Lisa leaned against the railing watching ships entering the harbor.

"There she is!" exclaimed Etor excitedly. "The Star of Suminar!" He pointed to a yacht passing by the Sun King to port.

"The Star of Suminar is the Lemurian challenger in the Master of the Sea competition," explained Nura. "It will compete against our Aura's Glory. If she sails as well in the races as she has in her practice runs, I fear we will lose."

All the passengers and crewmen of the two ships on deck waved to each other. Sailors ribbed each other and made conflicting predictions about which ship would win the competition.

Etor joined his charges. "Follow your head, not your heart, when you bet," he counseled. "I bet five hundred gold sovereigns on the Star of Suminar. I have not lost a bet in the last five competitions."

"Father and I also bet on the Lemurian," confessed Nura. "We like to win too."

A yacht flying the Lemurian flag approached the Sun King from the north. Etor borrowed a pair of binoculars to get a closer look. "The Satara."

"Prince Adar's ship!" exclaimed Nura in delight. "He missed the last competition. It will be nice to see him again."

The Satara changed course and headed toward the Sun King. As the Lemurian ship drew closer, the frigates watched it warily. They permitted it to come within hailing distance. A handsome man wearing a black silk robe appeared on deck. He smiled and waved to Nura.

"Greetings to the divinely fair and incomparable Princess Nura of Atlantis! In the name of King Bakri, I invite you and your guests to join me for lunch. Captain Etor, you may bring as many guards as you need to protect the princess from us evil Lemurians!"

Nura laughed gaily. "Flatterer! I accept your thoughtful invitation. We will be over directly."

"Captain, can he be trusted?" asked Levi uncertainly.

Etor placed his hand reassuringly on Levi's shoulder. "Prince Adar has pledged the honor of the royal family. No king or prince has ever violated it. Only one guard will accompany you, Nura and Lisa as a matter of form. Myself."

Levi regretted that he couldn't work on both the Atlantis missions and the Lemurian missions to come. He had to choose one. Atlantis had captured his heart and imagination. Perhaps he could squeeze in an off the record visit to Suminar during Atlantis II. Levi and Lisa could only visit Lemuria as tourists.

Prince Adar welcomed his guests and personally escorted them to his private dining room. The correct number of places had been set. Already the first hot courses had been placed on the table. Glasses of Adar's best wine filled the crystal goblets. Adar placed Nura to his right and Lisa to his left. Etor sat beside Nura. "How provident for me that you came along when you did," observed Adar with a sly smile.

"Fortunate, ha!" snorted Nura. "There is no more chance to our meeting here than your presence at this year's Master of the Sea competition."

Adar chuckled. "Only fools try to deceive the judicious. When I got word that you would soon be betrothed to that jackal Maric, I decided to offer my condolences in person. This is the last time I will have to enjoy your company and conversation." Adar sighed. "Being the son most distant from the throne, I am free to marry whom I will. What a pity that you do not have the same privilege and opportunity. It is a cruel God who permits a man like Maric to marry a woman like you. Father Sun willing, Maric will experience an untimely death and you will be free to accept a better offer."

Levi understood that one of the offers would be Prince Adar's. The Lemurian prince was in love with Nura. Adar would be a far better husband than Maric. Nura seemed to find the prince agreeable to her. Levi knew the death of Nura would hit Adar very hard.

Nura smiled. "Father Sun willing. Will you stay for the entire competition?"

"Certainly! I want to be present when the Star of Suminar receives the crown of victory."

"What if the Star of Suminar loses, Prince Adar?" asked Lisa mischievously.

Adar chuckled. "Then I will console her crew." He turned his attention fully to Nura. "I did not just come here to see you and enjoy the competition. This is also an unofficial state visit. My father thinks this is the right time for Lemuria and Atlantis to finally make peace."

Levi looked inquiringly at Lisa. She reached out to Adar's mind. A moment later, she contacted Levi's mind. "It's all right, Levi. King Bakri's negotiators are not due to arrive until after Atlantis perishes."

"I bring a gift as a token of peace," announced Adar. He ordered one of his servants to fetch the gift. The servant rolled in a cart with a three-foot-high replica of King Bakri's Crystal Palace. It even had a Lemurian flag at the top.

Nura gazed at the replica in wonder and delight. "King Bakri's gift is well chosen. We will reciprocate with an appropriate gift for King Bakri. I hope someday that I will have the opportunity to see Suminar and the real Crystal Palace. No doubt, my future husband will happily endure my absence when I visit you. I hope the official lines of communication will soon be open between Aurelin and Suminar."

"King Adeil might not be in a mood to talk if the Star of Suminar wins the competition," joked Levi.

A mischievous gleam appeared in Adar' eye. "Perhaps I should command my captain to lose."

Nura laughed. "That would make us angrier than if we lost honestly."

"I see that Princess Amaia did not accompany you this time," noted Etor casually.

Adar smiled. "Princess Amaia asked to me convey her regrets that royal duties prevent her from attending this year's competition. She expects to attend the next one." Levi detected disappointment in Etor's voice.

Nura's eyes twinkled with merriment. "Whenever Princess Amaia attends the competition, she insists that Etor be her personal escort," she explained to Levi and Lisa. "She seems to like him."

"Perhaps you should command Etor to marry Amaia," suggested Adar waggishly. "I fear she may become an old maid otherwise."

Etor reddened with embarrassment. Levi suspected that Etor was not averse to marrying Princess Amaia. It seemed that he and the Lemurian princess had become more than casually acquainted. No doubt, King Adeil had to approve of the woman Etor married. He could hardly object to a princess even if she was a Lemurian one. Such a marriage would have great political and diplomatic value.

Adar summoned a female servant. He ordered her to bring him the gift he brought for Princess Nura. She left and returned with a nine inch by twelve-inch book. The servant bowed, then presented the book to Nura. "I thought you might like to see what the highborn women of Lemuria are wearing this year. Happily, hemlines are up, and necklines are down."

Nura paged through the book with delight. "I really missed these fashion books the last two years. Thank you very much, Adar."

"Choose what pleases you most and it will be shipped before the end of the day," promised Adar.

"The importation of Lemurian goods into Atlantis is strictly prohibited," Nura reminded him.

"Etor can arrange to be waiting at a certain cove not too distant from Aurelin where he can intercept and confiscate the shipment," suggested Adar.

Etor cleared his throat. "The law only prohibits the importation of Lemurian goods for sale. Personal gifts are not mentioned in the statute."

Nura gazed in mock disapproval at Etor. "Captain, you have the mind of a lawyer and the soul of a smuggler."

"I saw many personal gifts for sale in the marketplaces of Aurelin," commented Lisa.

"It is an amusing game that our countries play," agreed Adar. "Luckily for us, businessmen are more sensible about these things than kings. The amount of unofficial, unacknowledged trade between Atlantis and Lemuria would shock the commoners if they knew."

Adar brought Nura and Etor up to date with the latest gossip of Lemuria. They listened very closely to the palace intrigues. Levi thought Atlanteans had much more in common than not with

Lemurians, religiously and socially. It greatly puzzled him how the two countries had evolved so far ahead of the rest of the world. Something had given them a leg up, but what could it have been?

Despite Adar's drollery, Levi realized that something was troubling the man. When Adar's expression turned serious, Levi's suspicions were confirmed.

Adar dismissed all his servants. "Nura, I need to speak to you and Etor in private."

"You can speak freely in front of Levi and Lisa," Nura assured him. "Levi is Friend of The Crown. Lisa has been entrusted with important state secrets." Nura told Adar of the abduction of Levi and Lisa by Maric. They had both sworn by Father Sun not to reveal what had happened to anyone unless authorized by the king or herself.

"Nura, some factions in our countries do not want peace," warned Adar. "One of the king's special agents on General Jencir's staff heard whispers of a plot against you. The general has an agent in Aurelin who has access to you. Most likely, it is a courtier or high-ranking army officer. The agent learned one more thing. The operation is supposed to take place on or near the Feast of Maren."

"That would surely cause King Adeil to declare war on Lemuria," said Etor. "This must not happen! I am very grateful that you shared this information with Nura and me. We must find the agent and neutralize him as soon as possible."

"The danger to Nura is in Aurelin," reflected Adar. "Etor, I think it would be wise to quietly move her to an isolated secure location guarded by men you trust most."

Nura placed her hand on Adar's. "Thank you for warning us. You are a courageous and honorable man. I appreciate your friendship and your efforts to maintain peace between Atlantis and Lemuria. Thanks to you, we should be able to foil the plot. Father Sun willing, between us we can unmask and defeat the conspirators."

Levi had expected the Atlantis mission to be mostly uneventful. A simple, innocent activity like telling stories in the marketplace had caused an unanticipated chain of events complicating the mission. Joining with Nura had personal complications that he had to live with for the rest of his life. Levi expected Nura to keep him with her wherever she hid out. If he had to, Levi decided to spend the rest of the mission under cloak. For the moment, all he could do was wait and see how things played out.

Chapter Seventeen

Levi and Nura remained at the palace while Etor consulted with Adeil. Lisa returned to the inn. Etor and Adeil decided that the greatest danger to her was being around Nura and Levi. Levi chafed at being stuck in the palace when there was so much more recording to do. The team also needed to look outside of Aurelin for the answers to the team's biggest questions. If the team had to finish its mission under cloak, so be it.

Lisa kept Levi up to date with the team's activities. Dark figured Maric wouldn't try anything again, at least not until he became king. He would most likely just bide his time until he could kill Levi and make Lisa his mistress. Dark suggested that he and the soldiers be wary but not paranoid. Levi had come to depend a lot on Dark and his useful abilities. Such a man almost seemed like a necessity on an interaction mission. Levi hoped he could convince Dark to participate in the next Atlantis mission. He expected the Time Council to see Dark's value.

Nura asked Adeil to be permitted to visit her friend Galina in Gal-Rian rather than be confined to some isolated army base. She presented her case for traveling incognito as commoner tourists. If she covered up her blue skin and used no makeup, she would be hidden in plain sight. Adeil and Etor discussed it at length. Nura fretted that the king might deny her request. After two days, the jury was still out.

While Nura and Levi were eating breakfast, they heard a familiar knock on the door. "It seems that the jury has returned a verdict," commented Levi. Zira opened the door and let in Etor. "Would you like something to drink, Captain?" asked Zira.

"No, thank you, Zira," decided Etor. "You may leave us. The king has granted your request to visit Gal-Rian, Nura. I and four of my men will provide security. Lisa may go with us if you like."

"Thank Father Sun!" exclaimed Nura with delight. "An excellent idea. I can get to know her much better during our travels. May we stop and see some sights along the way?"

Etor smiled. "Certainly. That is what tourists do. We will both have an unexpected vacation. I am confident that the itinerary will be satisfactory to you. We will need to travel light. That will be a new experience for you."

"When do we leave, Etor?" asked Nura eagerly.

Etor made a quick mental calculation. "We should be ready to leave before dawn the day after tomorrow. Zira can obtain the commoner clothes you need. She can also get Levi's clothes from the inn."

"A good idea," agreed Levi. "I will arrange for Lisa to give the clothes to Zira." Levi glanced at Nura. The idea of wearing commoner clothes clearly displeased her. No doubt covering up her beautiful blue skin pleased her even less. He could see that it didn't dampen her joy at going on her first real vacation since the death of her brother.

Nura and Levi looked over their itinerary. First, they would drive to Arvalon. From there, a boat would take them on a ten-day cruise to Castle Rock. A shuttle waited for them for the drive to Skymount. The other stops were places unfamiliar to Levi. Their final stop would be the mountain village of Gal-Rian. It contained the sacred Shrine of Alaya. Each member of the Brotherhood of the Sun was required to make a pilgrimage to the shrine once during their lifetime. Nura could accomplish hers. Waste not, want not, seemed to be an unofficial Atlantean motto. Levi was very unhappy when he learned that the final part of the journey would be on horseback.

Neither Levi nor Nura slept deeply the night before their departure. They were excited about their imminent freedom. Both woke up before the alarm. They wasted no time showering, dressing, and eating breakfast. Nura sighed. "The only thing I will miss is my bathing pool. We will not have another civilized bath until we reach Gal-Rian. For the first time in my adult life, I can go somewhere without drawing a crowd."

Zira and Seren came in to say good-bye. They gave Nura and Levi a good-bye hug. "Good journey and fair weather," wished Zira. "Seren and I wish we could go with you."

"Enjoy your time off, ladies," suggested Nura. "You need and deserve a break."

Zira smiled. "I will have to console myself in Lord Kal's arms."

"I will never forget you or the night we shared," whispered Seren in Levi's ear. She kissed him and left with Zira.

Etor entered the room with Lisa. He saluted Nura. "All the provisions and clothes have been loaded into the shuttle, princess."

"From this moment until we return to the palace, do not call me princess or Nura in public," she reminded Etor. "Please do not salute me. When you address me or refer to me around other people, call me Manera."

"It will be difficult at first, but the guards and I will manage," promised Etor. "I told my men to just act like overprotective older brothers."

The royal party and its security boarded the shuttle. It was a civilian family shuttle with room for ten people used by middle class families. Etor had the windows and windshield replaced with bulletproof glass. Metal plates capable of stopping any bullet reinforced the roof, hood, doors, and gate. Etor and his men only carried sidearms concealed in their clothes.

Etor arranged for all the power in a five-block radius to be turned off at his signal. The shuttle drove out the side gate where deliveries were made. Nura's driver wore night vision goggles to safely navigate the dark streets. When the lights came on, the driver removed his goggles and turned on the headlights.

The shuttle took the long way to the Coast Highway. Soon it reached the King Tarkon Highway which led directly to Alvaron. Only a few vehicles traveled on the highway as the sun peered over the horizon. Dawn revealed the full beauty of the land that had been mostly hidden during the moonless night. Leaf bearing trees and evergreens appeared sporadically by the sides of the road. Verdant fields of grass beyond the trees flowed like waves in the wind.

Gradually the terrain became much less interesting. Levi, Nura, and Lisa decided to rest their eyes for the rest of the way to Alvaron. Three hours later, Etor roused them. The Shanya River had come into view. The flat land gave the impression that the river was closer than it was. All the major rivers of Atlantis flowed from the central mountains to the sea. The Shanya River flowed leisurely through Maranor Province in which Aurelin lay.

Atlantis scrupulously maintained the pristine quality of their rivers, lakes, and streams. The government's approach to business was lassez faire. They worked cooperatively to keep the environment clean while making business productive and profitable. The people wanted to protect the land, but at an acceptable financial cost. Fines for littering and pollution were high.

"Nura, you and your guests are in for a real treat," announced Etor. "I have chosen the Azara to take us to Skymount. It is the best passenger boat cruising the Shanya River. The cabins are very nice and affordable. You have a wide variety of food to choose from."

"You sound like you have had personal experience," commented Lisa.

Etor smiled in pleasant recollection. "I used the ship on a couple of assignments. One of the Azara's specialties is their fish. They drop lines and soon the main course is ready to prepare! Normally I do not care for fish. The cook's special sauce and Lemurian spices change a palatable meal to a delightful treat."

The shuttle finally reached Alvaron. The docks were on the outskirts of the city. None of the boats tied up there looked very impressive. Etor warned everyone not to judge those books by their covers. The shuttle exited the highway onto a two-lane road leading to a small building near the docks. After the shuttle was parked, Etor went out to get the tickets.

To Etor's relief, the line was short and moved fast. Soon he reached the head of the line.

"Good day, sir!" greeted the ticket agent with a smile. "Do you have reservations?"

"Reservation for eight for the Azara's 0900 cruise. The name is Ezar."

"An excellent choice, sir!" approved the ticket agent. "You made a deposit of six hundred fifty gold sovereigns. The balance due is one thousand nine hundred fifty gold sovereigns."

Etor counted out the money while the ticket agent watched carefully. The small coin was one hundred gold sovereigns. When Etor finished, the ticket agent gathered up the coins with one swipe of his meaty right hand.

"The Azara is the first boat," said the ticket agent. "Boarding has already begun."

"Could someone help us to get our bags to the Azara?" asked Etor.

"Certainly, sir!" The ticket agent summoned two men to assist Etor.

"I am glad that my employer is picking up the entire tab for our vacation," commented Etor while the men loaded their bags onto wheeled carts. He gave them a good tip.

When Nura, Levi, Lisa, and their security arrived at the Azara, the captain awaited them. "Welcome to the Azara! I am Captain Forton." The disappointed looks on the faces of everyone except Etor didn't faze the captain. "I see that this is the first time that you have sailed with me. I guarantee that you will be completely satisfied with your experience on the Azara. Allow me to take you on a brief tour."

A raised platform on top of the barge provided tables and comfortable chairs for the people to eat and drink while enjoying the scenery. The security fence around the ship was high enough to see over but not low enough for someone to fall over. No one would go over the side unless they tried to. The law made everyone responsible for their stupidity and bad judgment.

Levi gaped at the interior of the ship when he stepped inside. Beautiful bright crystal lights illuminated the passageways. Breath taking ocean and mountain scenes had been painted on the walls. The plush sky-blue carpet seemed brand new. Captain Forton proudly showed everyone the elegant dining room. He took great pride in his spotlessly clean kitchen. Forton informed them that lunch would be served as soon as the Azara got underway. Three lovely young women passed in front of Captain as a crewman guided them to their cabin. Their clothes suggested to Levi that they were pleasure ladies. The ship had plenty of potential customers.

After their bags had been taken to their cabins, Levi, Nura, and Lisa went to the dining room, discreetly watched over by the guards. The passenger lounge at the stern had tables, cards, and chips for people to gamble if they desired. Roving musicians came into the lounge and serenaded the passengers with violin and a lyre kind of instrument. They played classical and popular tunes. Three men wearing business suits sat at a corner table discussing politics. They didn't seem to care if anyone overheard them.

"We must have unforgivably offended Father Sun to be cursed with a king like Maric," grumbled the first man.

The second man nodded agreement. "I wish General Garai had only had daughters. We have not had a bad king in two centuries. Why did Maric have to be born in our lifetime?"

"It would have been best if Garai's wife had been barren," commented the third man. "May the Evil One soon call him and Maric home!"

"Those gentlemen have good taste and good judgment," decided Nura. "Etor, buy them a round of drinks on me."

A crewman came and guided Levi, Nura and Lisa to the Captain's Table. Captain Forton welcomed them warmly. He seemed very impressed with them. Forton told them how he had come to be owner and captain of the Azara. He had served in the Atlantean Navy for twenty-five years. When he retired, he took all his pension in a lump sum and bought the Azara. With the help of family and a Veteran's loan, he bought and fixed it up. It had been a big gamble, but it paid off handsomely.

Forton treated his guests like family. He did all that he could to please them. That along with good prices, helped him to achieve great and enduring success. Etor had to use all his connections to get tickets at short notice. Forton set very high standards of service and crew conduct. He insisted that every guest be treated like he was the most important one. Forton paid and treated his people well.

At night, Levi, Nura, and Lisa went up to the Observation Deck to enjoy the stars. The Azara soon left all the city lights far behind. The ocean of stars of the Milky Way filled the cloudless sky. Atlantean sound suppression technology minimized the noise of the engines. The galaxy of the twenty-third century and the world of Time Control seemed more like a dream than reality to Levi. The pleasant night breeze completed the perfection of the moment.

Nura gazed wistfully at the stars. "Are there people on other worlds or are we alone in the universe?"

I pray that we are not," said Levi. "I believe there are worlds with glorious civilizations. You and I may never see them, but they exist."

Nura looked at Levi in wonder. "You speak like someone that has actually seen them."

"Levi has insight into the future," interjected Lisa. "It is a gift he received from Father Sun."

"What do you see in the future, Levi?" asked Nura.

"I see our world exploring the stars and colonizing other worlds," replied Levi. "I see the people of the world united in peace, striving to improve themselves instead of seeking wealth, power and control over others."

Nura smiled wanly. "That is more than I dare to hope. It would take a miracle of Father Sun to bring it to pass."

The promise of Terra's glorious future pleased and comforted Nura. Levi couldn't tell her that neither Atlantis nor Lemuria had any place in it. He wanted badly to make her a part of that future. Although he wanted that as much as life itself, he couldn't do it. Levi would die rather than break his Time Control oath. He felt a little comfort that Dark could fulfill his heart's desire. With great difficulty, Levi put aside the depressing thought.

At 0000, Captain Forton apologetically announced that the Observation Deck was closed for the night. It would open again at dawn. The bar and Passenger Lounge were also closed. Levi and Nura returned to their cabin. They went to bed after a quick shower.

"Tomorrow we will be in the mood, Levi," whispered Nura. One minute later she fell asleep.

"How does she do that?" wondered Levi enviously.

Chapter Eighteen

The next day at noon the Azara reached its first stop, Port Makal. It was well known as a shopping stop for exotic Atlantean and foreign merchandise. The prices were the lowest in all of Atlantis. After breakfast, Nura told Etor that she and Lisa wanted to go shopping. As Levi expected, Etor didn't like the idea.

"Etor, I may never have another shopping opportunity like this," pleaded Nura.

Etor frowned. "I do not want you to go to any place that I cannot properly secure."

"It would look very strange and might attract attention if two normal women passed up a prime shopping opportunity like this," said Lisa half in jest.

"All right," agreed Etor reluctantly. "I want you two back in two hours. Keep out of crowds and try to leave yourself an out. Please do not buy anything bulky."

"Are you coming with us, Levi?" asked Nura.

"I will pass," decided Levi. "I am a man who has everything he wants. I would only get in the way of your enjoyment."

"We will only buy jewelry and clothes," promised Nura. "Just one bag apiece."

Etor's men accompanied Nura and Lisa while Etor remained with Levi.

"That was a surprise," commented Etor. Levi looked at Etor in puzzlement. "Whenever Nura goes shopping in Aurelin, she always insists that I be her escort. Now that is torture!"

Levi laughed. "Nothing says love like a lady not forcing her man to go shopping with her."

"To be honest, I really do not mind going shopping with Nura," confessed Etor. "She is more than the princess I am sworn to defend to my death. Nura is a good friend. We grew up together in the palace. She is the sister I never had. I am continually tempted to kill

Maric to save her from him. Only my soldier's oath prevents me from ridding the world of him."

"Does anyone like Maric?" wondered Levi.

"Only people who can get some favor or advantage from him," figured Etor. "Levi, I wish that Nura was as unknown as you in the heartland. I hope that no one ever realizes who she is."

"Having your image on silver coins makes it much harder not to be noticed," observed Levi.

With troubling regularity, people came up to Nura and told her that she looked a lot like Princess Nura. Invariably she responded, "You are very sweet to say that. How I wish I had her lovely blue skin!" Etor and the guards were not amused.

When Levi, Nura and Lisa had dinner with Captain Forton on the second day, he stared at Nura like someone he knew but couldn't quite remember. "You look very much like Princess Nura," swore Forton. "For many years, I wanted to meet her but I am sure that she would not even deign to acknowledge my existence or say hello to me."

Nura placed her hand on Forton's. "I had the honor and pleasure of meeting Princess Nura. I assure you that she is not proud or snobbish."

After dinner, Nura and Lisa played Pyramid with three other passengers. Levi took the opportunity to sneak in some reading. He borrowed The Riddle of Time from Nura's personal library. The scientist-philosopher who wrote it had much insight. His speculations were mostly on the mark. Had Atlantis discovered the temporal rift first, the Atlanteans might have created the Time Door. Levi wondered how they would have used it. Maric would not have used it for good.

It puzzled Levi that the so-called Sun Lords had cultivated disbelief in time travel. Possibly, they wanted to keep the people from seeking and maybe finding a means of traveling through time. If the Sun Lords knew that time travelers could change the past, they would understandably want to prevent it. Levi had learned that both government and the priests had cooperated in the effort. Levi wondered what Adeil and Etor thought about time travel if anything.

It fascinated Levi that the Karani had so quickly and easily converted the native Atlanteans to their worship of the Universal Father. To make it easier, everyone referred to God as Father Sun.

The former Atlantis had much more sophisticated religious beliefs than the rest of the world.

The last generation of old Atlantis needed many years to fully overcome their fears and suspicions about advanced technology. Once people embraced it, they found that they didn't want to live without it. Few of the people Levi talked to in Aurelin remembered much about the old days. Levi and Lisa got the impression that the people didn't think much about that time or care to.

The old Atlanteans had converted quickly to the Telmierians' religion. Christianity had taken centuries to gain that degree of widespread acceptance in the Roman Empire. Of course, blue skinned beings who came down from the sky couldn't fail to powerfully impress the superstitious masses. Levi suspected that something had changed the people themselves so they could comprehend advanced technology. He and Lisa still didn't have the answer.

Each night while they watched the stars, Nura shared her experiences with the people of Gal-Rian. She got acquainted with a lady named Galina from the mountain village during her visit to Aurelin. Nura had been so impressed and pleased with Galina that she visited her in Gal-Rian. The mountain people opened their hearts and homes to the princess. They respected her station, but treated her like a member of their tight-knit family. Nura could let down her defenses and be herself. Nura visited Galina for two weeks every year since the death of her brother. Since Nura became the heir to the throne, she rarely had opportunities to travel.

The Shrine of Alaya was in Gal-Rian. It greatly interested Levi and Lisa. They felt and hoped that it contained an important piece of the puzzle of Atlantis. The shrine was the holiest place in Atlantis. Religion had a huge place in Atlantean life and history. As far as Levi could tell, the priests persuaded and motivated their flocks through love rather than force or fear. Every land had its non-believers. Atlantis was no exception. Their non-believers wisely didn't persecute believers or mock their religion, so the king tolerated them. One tenth of the population worshiped the moon goddess. They kept completely to themselves.

Levi figured that he and Lisa wouldn't be allowed to enter the Shrine of Alaya. It had a guardian who prevented all non-believers from entering it. Levi doubted that the guardian had ever matched wills with Nura. She treated her social inferiors with kindness and respect. At the same time, Nura didn't like anyone opposing her royal will.

The Atlanteans old religion didn't forbid or hinder exploration. Atlanteans had a bold and adventurous spirit. They sailed to the Americas, Europe, and Africa. Until Atlantis had advanced technology, the people didn't venture much into Asian waters. Atlantis and Lemuria had not encountered each other or known of the other's existence until two centuries before the coming of the Sun Lords. After their uplift, they became military and economic rivals. Atlantis and Lemuria strove to minimize civilian casualties in wartime. Levi considered that a touchstone of true civilization.

Levi had mixed feelings when the Azara docked at Castle Rock. The voyage had been so pleasant, peaceful, and refreshing. Nura greatly enjoyed living freely as the common people did. They wouldn't have the pleasure of a return trip on the Azara. To save time and increase security, Etor decided they would fly back to Aurelin from Gal-Rian. Levi had mixed feelings about that.

Captain Forton stood by the gangplank as the passengers disembarked from the Azara. The captain thanked each of them by name for choosing Azara. He didn't need to ask them to recommend the Azara to other people. They would gladly do so. Captain Forton's eyes lit up with delight when Nura and Lisa approached him. "You are the loveliest ladies to grace the Azara in a long time. I hope that I will see you again."

Nura sighed. "I will always remember this cruise. It has been one of the happiest times of my life. Father Sun bless you always."

"If we get the chance to take another cruise on the Azara, we surely will," promised Lisa.

Etor checked all the bags before removing them from the Azara. The locks and seals had not been broken. He had arranged for another suitable shuttle to be delivered for the next leg of the journey. Etor efficiently loaded everyone and the bags aboard it. They drove all day trying to make the most of the remaining light. Supper consisted of army rations chosen by Etor. Levi, Nura, and Lisa couldn't believe how good they tasted.

The driver took the Erigu Highway which led to the mountains. Near sunset they crossed into Kimmaren Province. The green hills gave way to the mountains with their spectacular lookouts. They stopped at one of the lookouts and gazed at the ocean of stars free of all man-made light. For two hours, they couldn't tear themselves away from the sight. They had the pleasure of viewing the mountain flowers near the highway. Levi expected a botanical team to be sent to catalog flowers and plants unique to Atlantis. They would bring back seeds of extinct species.

Etor decided to stay overnight at the village of Galgold. They couldn't reach the next village until at least 0300. In any case, Etor didn't want to travel at night. At 2200, the driver stopped at the village inn. Fortunately, it was the off season, so the inn had enough rooms for Nura's party. While the innkeeper checked them in and took care of their bags, he kept glancing at Etor as if trying to place a familiar face. The scrutiny made Etor uneasy.

"You seem very familiar, sir," said the innkeeper. "Have you stayed here before?"

"I have a brother that looks a lot like me," parried Etor. "He stayed here before." The explanation seemed to satisfy the innkeeper.

Levi, Nura, and Lisa decided to visit the Common Room for a while before going to bed. The guards placed themselves strategically throughout the room trying to look as natural as possible. The newcomers sat near the fireplace. Farmers, artisans, traveling salesmen and businessmen socialized and chatted with each other. They spoke of their businesses, families, and the latest happenings in Aurelin. A businessman from the capital told them of an amazing foreign storyteller named Levi. Nura found herself to be the hottest topic of discussion.

"Neither Princess Nura nor Master Levi have been seen in Aurelin for nine days," announced the businessman.

"I hope nothing has happened to them," fretted a tanned middle-aged farmer.

A grizzled old man shuffled over to the fireplace to warm himself. He sighed. "If only we had a storyteller. They rarely travel to the mountains."

"I am a storyteller," blurted out Levi without thinking. All conversations in the room immediately ceased. Everyone gathered around him expectantly. Nura, Lisa and Etor glowered at him. Levi had learned half of Mikel's repertoire. Using the holo-thought imagizer or telling tales of Chin would be dumb and dangerous.

Levi launched into one of his favorite Atlantean tales. He used one of Mikel's tricks. When performing for small groups of people he lowered his voice. The people had to be quiet to hear his words. No one recognized him or suspected that he was anything but an Atlantean storyteller. The people applauded enthusiastically when Levi finished his performance.

An alluring young woman pressed a silver coin with a star flower inscribed on it against the palm of Levi's hand. "A token of appreciation from one professional to another," she whispered in a sultry voice.

"Uh, thank you."

Nura and Etor laughed as the woman walked away. Levi didn't understand what they found so amusing. "That entitles you to a free night of pleasure with her," explained Etor. "You have been greatly honored."

Levi placed the coin in Etor's hand with an evil grin. "I pass on this choice gift to you, my friend. I am confident that you will be a more than satisfactory substitute." He had overheard Etor reminding his men that neither he nor they were permitted to enjoy that pleasure of the flesh for the duration of their assignment.

"I will get you for this!" promised Etor.

Etor roused everyone at dawn. Within thirty minutes, everyone had eaten, cleaned up, dressed, and boarded the shuttle. It had rained during the night, but the sky had cleared by dawn. Levi considered it a good omen. They traveled nonstop until 1100. Etor unexpectedly ordered the driver to turn onto a narrow dirt road.

"I have a surprise for you and your guests, Nura," announced Etor. "This road leads to the moon goddess temple dig Professor Ziram has been studying."

"I had completely forgotten about it!" exclaimed Nura. "Two years ago, the professor found an ancient pre-Sun Lord temple here. It had been heavily overgrown with vegetation for centuries. A lightning strike started a fire that burned away most of it. The moon goddess worshipers abandoned the temple after the coming of the Sun Lords. They moved to their present home in Teyron."

"May we visit the moon goddess temple in Teyron?" asked Lisa eagerly.

"That is not possible, Lisa," replied Nura regretfully. "Teyron is an isolated community that allows no non-believers to enter their city.

The Sun Lords granted them complete autonomy to make and enforce their own laws. Moon goddess priests have complete control of their temple. Teyron and other moon worshiper cities are also exempt from taxation. They trade only with each other. For centuries, archaeologists and adventurers went to Teyron to study the moon goddess worshipers. All of them disappeared without a trace.”

Two hours down the road, the moon goddess temple appeared. They saw several men clearing dirt from artifacts. Two armed soldiers stood between the shuttle and the temple.

The shuttle stopped at the checkpoint. Etor got out and approached the soldiers.

“Until Professor Ziram and his men finish their work on the temple, only authorized visitors are permitted to visit the temple dig at this time,” explained one of the soldiers.

“I am a captain in the Sun Legion,” said Etor. “My friends and I would be very grateful if you permitted us to visit the temple before I begin a special assignment.”

The soldier came to attention and saluted Etor. “It is an honor to meet you, sir. I hope that you and your friends enjoy your visit.”

“Luckily for you that the soldier didn’t ask you for your army ID,” observed Nura when the soldiers were out of earshot.

“Etor has an honest face, even if he does not always have an honest tongue,” needled Lisa.

“I told the entire truth,” claimed Etor piously. “Technically, my men and I belong to the Sun Legion. We are stationed at the palace. No other soldiers are permitted to guard the royal family.”

The temple turned out to be smaller than Levi had expected for such an important religious structure. Nevertheless, a scan showed that it could accommodate at least one hundred fifty people. The temple stood a mere fifteen meters high. Curiously, it had a domed roof. A series of windows two meters below the roof provided ventilation.

The professor and his men were so engrossed in their work, they didn’t notice their unauthorized visitors until they were just six feet away. Ziram was an aging blue skinned man. His workers were all white skinned. Levi had heard of Ziram. He was a professor of Archeology at Aurelin University as well as the foremost expert on pre-Sun Lord Atlantis. Ziram looked very annoyed to have unexpected and unwanted visitors.

Before the man could speak, Etor said, "Professor Ziram, foremost authority on pre-Sun Lord history. I have read all your books with great interest and pleasure."

Ziram looked pleased by the recognition and sincere tribute. "You must be a soldier, or the guards would not have allowed you to pass. I am flattered that a soldier has read my books. Which one did you like best?"

"Without doubt, Religious Structures of The Magon Dynasty," replied Etor without hesitation. "I agree with your theory that the religions of Atlantis and Lemuria have a common origin."

"Atlantis and Lemuria have too many similarities to be coincidental," agreed Ziram. "Since you and your friends are here, you might as well see the temple. It is a smaller version of the Great Temple of the moon goddess in Teyron, except for the dome. Until now, only army and navy brass and important government officials have visited the dig. In six to eight months, it will be open to the public. We need to be continually on guard against artifact robbers. If it was my decision, all of them would be summarily shot. Follow me, please."

Etor ordered his men to secure the entrance to the temple. Ziram led Levi, Nura, Lisa and Etor inside. Cold fire lamps hung from stone torch holders. They cast a brilliant but eerie light. For the historians, it was a glimpse of religious life from many centuries ago. Ziram launched into a lecture on the ancient religion of Atlantis as he guided his guests through the temple. He explained the significance of the temple's architecture.

One half of the temple served as a hall of worship. Rows of stone benches lined the hall. A black crystal altar was at the front of the hall. Levi detected no traces of blood, so it hadn't been used for animal or human sacrifices. Light from the moon came through a triangular opening. It shone on the altar during a full moon. Ziram had found no evidence that the moon goddess ever practiced human sacrifice. Two rooms behind the altar contained the remains of beds where worshipers experienced the joining with the moon goddess. Ziram believed the practice was still taking place. Without access to present moon goddess temples, it couldn't be confirmed.

Levi gazed in wonder and appreciation at the six-foot-tall statue of the moon goddess behind the altar. She stood regal, proud and aloof. Her arms were outstretched as if to receive the sacrifices due her.

The sculptor had carved a flawlessly formed long haired nude beauty. She projected a powerful sensuality but without wantonness.

According to Ziram, on the holy days the priests and priestesses chose people to receive the joining with the goddess in an erotic spiritual union. Levi commented that beauty probably played a part in the cleric's choices. Priests and priestesses who had sexual union with devotees outside of the temple were burned alive. It greatly surprised the historians to learn that all the temple priests and priestesses are married.

Ziram sighed. "Sometimes I am almost tempted to consecrate myself to the moon goddess to learn about the present-day worship of the moon goddess." Ziram smiled. "No doubt the eyes of the goddess can penetrate any deception."

For an hour, Ziram shared the history of the moon temple dig with his now welcome guests. He spoke more like a storyteller than a lecturer. None of his listeners were bored by the information or the delivery. Levi dutifully recorded everything the professor said. He wished that they could stay longer.

Ziram shook hands with his guests after they exited the temple. "It has been a pleasure to have visitors who truly enjoy and appreciate history. I hope that you will catch my lecture about the discoveries my people and I made during the excavation. I do not have time to share all of it with you now."

The trip to the interior turned out to be much more educational than Levi had expected. He couldn't imagine a better combination of work and play. After his experiences on an interaction mission, he could never be content with mere recording of records and gathering of artifacts like the Alexandria I mission.

Before the driver could get the shuttle back on the road, a long army convoy consisting mostly of tank carriers passed by heading south toward Aurelin. Etor found the movement of armor curious and disquieting. He had heard nothing about it. Etor figured that General Garai was up to something. He decided that he would check into the matter when he returned to Aurelin. The sooner that happened the better.

An hour before sunset, the shuttle reached Kiral Pass. Two forts overlooking the pass guarded it against invaders. It provided an effective choke point for an invading force trying to advance to the interior from the south and east. With Atlantis' advanced technology, the forts were no longer necessary. They now served as popular tourist attractions. Occasionally, the Army put on mock battles that were wildly popular with both the Atlanteans and foreign visitors.

After Levi, Nura and Lisa explored one of the forts, the driver drove through the pass to High View. First they had to stop at a Custom's station at the mouth of the pass. All civilian vehicles and transports had to pay a small toll. It helped to maintain the Erigu Highway. High Point was a tale of two cities. Half the village looked as modern as Aurelin. The other half looked like the outdoor set used to make movies set in ancient times. Its residents disdained modern technology except for electricity and refrigeration.

High View, like most of its mountain neighbors, traded their crafts with the big cities. Demand for their tapestries often exceeded supply. Craftsmen produced pottery like their pre-Sun Lord ancestors had. It had become very clear to Levi that Atlantis was very diverse geographically, socially and culturally. Religion more than anything else created and sustained social unity. The opportunity for upward mobility by the lower classes minimized social stress.

Etor decided to push on so the royal party could reach Skymount by the end of the day. Even at a distance, they could see the magnificence and beauty of the holy mountain, sacred to the moon goddess worshipers as well as the Brotherhood of Father Sun. The Sun Lords had closed it to the moon goddess. Skymount was the second highest mountain in Atlantis. Clouds hid the peak from sight.

"Skymount!" whispered Nura in awe. "Where earth and heaven meet."

Etor pointed to a building that was barely discernible. "The moon goddess worshipers had a shrine where that monastery now sits. A rockslide destroyed it just before the arrival of the Sun Lords. Everyone suspected that the Sun Lords had caused the rockslide. Possibly Father Sun had His hand in it. We cleared the site and built the monastery."

"The moon goddess worshipers probably had a moment of existential doubt about what had happened," suspected Nura. "I wonder how their clerics explained it away."

"We will stay at the monastery tonight," announced Etor. "Since one of the reasons you are going to Gal-Rian is to make your pilgrimage, we will be permitted to stay overnight."

Nura had never been to the monastery, so she wanted to go on a tour. The three-story building had a sloped roof to protect it from rocks that occasionally broke loose and fell onto the roof. Half of the monastery served as an inn for pilgrims traveling to Gal-Rian to make their pilgrimage. The first level housed the religious library and the scholar priests who maintained it. They studied and interpreted the Atlantean scriptures, chief of which was the Book of Commandments.

When the royal party arrived at the front door of the monastery, an elderly priest wearing a scarlet robe came out to meet them. He held up his hand in greeting. "Peace be with you, my children. Are you pilgrims?"

"I am making my pilgrimage, grandfather," responded Nura. "My friends are accompanying me on my journey. May we have a tour of the monastery?"

"Certainly, my daughter," agreed the priest readily. "I am Reverend Neron. You may call me Neron. I oversee the monastery and the work of its religious scholars."

"I am not familiar with this place," confessed Etor. "Perhaps if I was a more religious man, I would be."

Neron sighed. "In the past, we struggled to accommodate all the pilgrims who desired to stay for the night. Now, few pilgrims stop by. I hope this decrease in piety is only temporary. You may leave your shuttle where you parked it. No one else will be coming today." Neron studied Etor and his men. He seemed to think there was more to them than met his eye. Fortunately, he asked no questions.

Neron clearly enjoyed playing host and guide to his guests. He explained that a group of scholars continually studied and interpreted scripture and writings of the Patriarchs and Chief High Priests. They also reviewed ordinances and traditions. The Council of Scholars rarely made big changes. The Sun Lords had ordered the creation of the Council of Scholars. Scholars served for five years, then returned to the congregations they came from.

Throughout the halls of the monastery, portraits of past great holy men and priests hung on the walls. None of them had a halo of light over their heads. Nevertheless, the painters managed to capture the spirituality of the men. Stylistically, the monastery seemed like a living religious museum. At the same time, it contained indoor plumbing, heating, and electricity. The priests enjoyed every modern comfort.

"In the past, a pilgrim had to reserve a room for months in advance of their pilgrimage," recalled Neron glumly. "It has been months since a pilgrim stayed with us. All of you may stay for the night as my personal guests."

Neron had the royal party sign the guest register. He personally took them to their rooms. Neron gave everyone separate rooms. He seemed to know that neither Nura nor Lisa was married. After Neron left them, Nura explained that all married people wore wedding rings. She felt very annoyed with herself for forgetting to take wedding rings for herself and Levi. After Nura retired for the night, Levi and Lisa went to the library and began to speed record the most important books and documents. They knew that the Religion Specialist historians would be ecstatic about what the team had learned about the Atlantean religions.

Chapter Nineteen

A palace shuttle dropped off Seren at her usual spot on the royal beach just as the last of the twilight disappeared. She spread out her towel on the sand and sat down. Seren watched as the stars appeared in the sky one by one. It had been many years since she had seen the stars of home. Seren had greatly missed her family and friends. She understood the importance of her service in Atlantis.

A deep curiosity and dissatisfaction filled her mind. A galaxy of worlds and wonders awaited mankind. It only had to reach out and touch them. Self-seeking clerics in Atlantis and Lemuria continued to chain humanity to the mother world. Did the Sun Lords truly institute the ban on space travel? The priests were like possessive mothers could not accept that their children had grown up.

Lately, some minor Atlantean and Lemurian clerics had begun to warm to the idea of rescinding the ban. The Chief High Priests of Aurelin and Suminar would not budge from their anti-space travel position: no space travel until the Sun Lords end the ban. Did anyone really believe that would happen? In any case, the ways of Father Sun and the Sun Lords were a mystery to her.

Seren smiled. Things might change when Maric became king. If he chose to end the ban, Lemuria had to follow suit. Neither Garai nor Maric had made a secret of their desire for an end to the ban. Seren wondered if the Chief High Priest knew the danger he faced. For all his wisdom, he seemed oblivious to the coming earthquake. She wouldn't be surprised if Kemen experienced an untimely death.

She checked the time. Her musing had made her late for her report to Seagull. Seren rose and removed her clothes. She ran into the surf and dived in. When she was one hundred meters away from shore, she activated her pendant com-link. Seren hoped that Seagull wouldn't be very annoyed by her tardiness.

"Nightingale to Seagull. Do you copy?"

"I copy Nightingale. You are a bit late," noted Seagull. Seren thought he sounded more concerned than displeased. "Proceed with your report."

The report took half the time it usually did. Since Nura and Levi left for Gal-Rian, little of interest or significance had happened in the palace. Everyone serving the princess but herself had gone on vacation. Many of her best sources were courtiers who had been absent from the palace lately.

"Be assured that your gleanings from the palace have had great value. Nightingale, your assignment is over. Repeat your assignment is over. You will leave Atlantis tonight. The arrangements have already been made."

The news stunned Seren. "Have I been compromised?"

"If you had been, we would not be having this conversation."

"I will be hard if not impossible to replace," Seren reminded him. "My close friendship with Princess Nura took years of diligent cultivation. She will never again trust any servant as much as she has come to trust me. Must we throw it away?"

"This is an order from the General himself," Seagull informed her. "You can be certain that the reason for your recall is a compelling one."

Seren had mixed feelings, but it would be wonderful to see home again. "What must I do, Seagull?"

"Take nothing with you except what you can fit into one large bag," ordered Seagull. "An agent will meet you at midnight in the Common Area of the Inn of The Seventh Ecstasy. He will proposition you using your code name. Follow his lead. He will take you to a smuggler's cove where a boat will take you to a fast runner. It will rendezvous with a submarine that has just finished its Atlantic patrol. Within a month, you will be in Suminar. Very well done, Nightingale! Seagull out."

Seren finished her swim and returned to the palace. After showering, she put on her favorite dress. She packed her next favorite dress. Fortunately, all her jewelry fit into the bag. Seren's assigned driver took her to the Inn of The Seventh Ecstasy. She told him that she would let him know when she was ready to be picked up. Seren sat down at the bar and ordered some wine.

Seren realized that something she had told Seagull resulted in the termination of her assignment. She couldn't think of anything that she had reported of such great interest and consequence.

Seren casually looked around the bar and dining room for her contact. Was he any of the men around her? She didn't even have a description of her contact. No doubt he had a good description of her. Seren tried to remain calm despite the possibility that security agents might suddenly appear and arrest her. So far, none of the men tried to pick her up. She almost felt insulted. An intoxicated man a couple tables away smiled at Seren. He got unsteadily to his feet, then he weaved unsteadily and plopped back on his chair.

Out of the corner of her eye, Seren noticed a man entering the inn. He was dressed like a barbarian sailor. His well-trimmed mustache and beard mitigated his barbarian appearance. The powerful arms, deep chest and scars suggested a man who had fought men and the sea and had won. Seren's pulse quickened as he approached her.

The stranger bowed. "You are far from your usual haunts, lovely nightingale."

Seren moved closer to him. "A friend of mine told me that I might find a diamond in this dung heap. It appears that he is right." The man sitting to the right of Seren gave her a dirty look.

The stranger caressed her hand. "A fine jewel deserves a worthy setting."

Seren smiled. Never had she been so elegantly propositioned. "You are a man of taste as well as discernment, sir."

The man took her hand and guided her to the back door. "What is your real name, nightingale?" he whispered.

"Seren," she whispered. "What is your name?"

"My name is Feran, humble sailor and guide to lovely ladies."

Seren laughed. "There is nothing humble about you, Feran. You are a pleasant rascal. When a gentleman suggests pleasure to a lady, he should deliver."

Feran chuckled. "The night is not yet over." Then he became serious. "We have no time to waste. The submarine risks detection by the Atlantean navy every minute it remains in Atlantean territorial waters."

They casually walked out the door to avoid drawing attention to themselves. A black shuttle waited for them. The driver, a man with a shaved head and stumpy body, got out and helped Seren get in.

Feran sat down beside her. He looked over the immaculate interior. "Very nice."

"This shuttle is worthy of me and my lady friend. I hope you did not steal it, Sentzio."

Sentzio laughed. "I bought it yesterday. Between my day job driving for guild masters and my night work for Seagull, I do very well. Time to get moving."

Sentzio started the engine and turned on the headlights. He drove several blocks then abruptly turned right. Sentzio took a circuitous route to the Coast Highway. He turned south and headed toward the secluded cove where boats from fast runners dropped off and picked up agents and contacts.

"Why do you use the barbarian persona, Feran?" asked Seren.

"I have many barbarian contacts," explained Feran. "They feel a lot more comfortable dealing with someone who looks like them. Civilized clothes and a shaved face make them less accepting and trusting." Feran scratched his beard. "I like the look but not the itch. On the bright side, I do not need to shave."

Twenty minutes later, Seren and Feran arrived at their destination. "Time to say good-bye, friends. It has been a pleasure to serve you. I am not philosophically opposed to receiving gratuities."

Feran playfully cuffed Sentzio's head. "Seagull pays you more than you are worth. See you next trip."

Sentzio dropped them off just a short distance from the pickup point. They scanned the horizon but didn't see anything "Do you know who I am, Feran?" asked Seren.

Feran smiled slyly. "I know who Seagull is. He does not deal with minor players. All I need to know is that you are a priority package I am supposed to pick up and deliver to him."

"Smuggling is just your cover," realized Seren. "You are one of Seagull's agents."

"You are as smart and perceptive as you are beautiful," noted Feran appreciatively. "It was Seagull's brilliant idea to combine the smuggling operation with our intelligence gathering. The General rewards him well for it. Smuggling pays for our operations in Atlantis. The General also pays everyone else well. I suspect that you have a lot of backpay waiting for you. Is there a man waiting for you?"

Seren sighed. "No one. I do not think it will take me long to find a good husband."

The fast runner came into view. It stopped and lowered a speedboat into the water. Two men dressed in black wearing black face paint got in. The speedboat made good time over the smooth water. It stopped at the edge of the surf. Seren took off her dress and put in her waterproof bag. She and Feran swam out to the speedboat. The sailors quickly helped their passengers aboard and headed back to the fast runner.

The sailor who was not steering the speedboat looked over Seren. "Very nice. Captain, you should have brought along a couple of her cute friends."

"Captain?" echoed Seren in surprise.

Feran grinned. "Packages as lovely and valuable as you I pick up myself."

Seren smiled. "I am lucky to be in such strong, capable hands." She noticed a man standing on the deck of the fast runner observing the progress of the speedboat with binoculars.

"That is Seagull," Feran informed Seren, "He has looked forward to meeting you for a long time, nightingale."

The speedboat pulled up beside the fast runner. A deck hand hung a ladder over the side. Quickly and efficiently, Seren, Feran, and his crewmen climbed aboard. The crewmen then hauled up the speedboat and secured it. Seagull welcomed Seren aboard. Unlike Feran, Seagull was clean shaven and dressed in a business suit.

Seagull bowed to Seren. "You are even more lovely than your voice suggested, nightingale. Happily, I will have the pleasure of your company and conversation all the way to Suminar. We can wait until tomorrow to begin your debriefing."

Seren smiled. "The pleasure will be mutual. Do you know why my assignment in Atlantis was terminated?"

Seagull smiled slyly. "I do. Regrettably, I may not share that information with you. I can tell you this much. What we have gained is far greater than what we lose by bringing you home now." Seagull sighed. "You would have become our most precious asset in Atlantis if you could have become King Maric's mistress. That was a gamble. The opportunity you have given us is a sure thing."

Feran laughed, "You will not get him to say more even if you employ truth drugs, torture, or seduction. He will not object if you try the latter method."

"I have some important work to attend to now," said Seagull. "If you will excuse me."

"How long have you known him?" asked Seren after Seagull went below.

"Almost six years." Feran smiled in pleasant recollection of his time with Seagull. "Smuggling and intelligence work are an exciting and hazardous mix. I could tell you stories...but I would be shot if I did."

"Perhaps you can share some non-classified experiences with me," suggested Seren. "How long will it be until we rendezvous with the submarine?"

"About an hour and a half," estimated Feran.

Seren smiled. "If you provide dinner, I will provide the dessert."

Feran grinned. "You have a deal. Seagull left some clothes for you in my cabin. They came from the store Princess Amaia herself shops at. They are a token of appreciation from the General."

Seren smiled. "As soon as we get cleaned up, I will try on all the dresses Seagull gave me. I will reserve them for special occasions. Like now."

Chapter Twenty

Etor got everyone moving early. They had a four-hour drive to the stables at Alveron where they would get their horses for the journey to Gal-Rian. Etor had made the arrangements before they left Aurelin. After they had breakfast, they said goodbye to Neron. Levi and Lisa wished they had enough time to record everything in the monastery library. They only had time to record a fraction of its treasures. Finishing the job had to wait until Atlantis II or III.

Levi and Lisa both had the feeling that they were on track to find the big answers they were looking for. At present, they had no idea where those answers might be found. Levi wondered how many missions it would take to get the complete history of Atlantis. Perhaps a couple of missions could be devoted just to recording Atlantean life.

The royal party arrived at Alveron at 1200. They had a quick lunch at the local inn. The innkeeper owned the stable as well. A cheerful young man named Lippo rented Etor eight horses for the five-day ride journey to Gal-Rian. Unlike the infamous Hobson, he allowed the customers to choose the horses they wanted. Etor carefully examined all the horses before he chose the best eight available. Lippo commended Etor for his knowledge of good horseflesh.

Levi and Etor watched with amusement and appreciation as Nura haggled for the best price. Levi rated her effort and the result an eight. By necessity, the royal party had to travel light. They only took rations, water, clothes, sleeping bags, night vision googles, weapons and enough ammunition for the journey.

Levi gingerly mounted his horse. The horse seemed to sense that it had an inexperienced rider. Nura laughed. "Relax, Levi. He will not bite or buck."

Levi laughed nervously. "I just hope he knows that."

The royal party followed the road into the mountains for a few miles. It narrowed into a trail that was only wide enough for two horses to ride abreast. The trail wound up and around. Occasionally, small rocks fell down the slope on the trail. Etor took the lead followed by two guards. Levi, Nura, and Lisa preceded the last two guards. The trees and grass became sparser. Regularly they encountered beautiful flowers found only in the mountains.

Etor had no concern about bandits. A nearby garrison had swept the trails between Alveron and Gal-Rian. Levi stopped often to pick up interesting rocks and quartz like crystals. He figured that the geological mission would be as delighted as the Temporal History teams. An hour before sunset, the royal party found a suitable spot to camp out for the night. After eating their rations, everyone spread out their sleeping bags.

At night, they saw the vast ocean of stars as they had during the cruise on the Azara. Nura sighed with contentment. "I hope that I will not soon wake up and find this has all just been a wonderful dream."

"Who could have imagined that a chance meeting with me in market square would lead to this?" mused Levi.

Nura smiled. "It was not chance, Levi. Etor never allows me to enjoy the performance of storytellers away from the palace. He asks the master of the Storytellers Guild to choose people to perform for me at the palace. The day I met you, I was entertaining Maric. A great restlessness came over me. Something drew me irresistibly to Market Square. Maric was more puzzled than annoyed. The day you visited me at the palace, I knew our meeting was ordained by Father Sun."

Etor cleared his throat. "Etor, you are worse than an old maid chaperone!" chided him affectionately. "As soon as I begin to enjoy myself, you want me to stop."

"We should sleep now so we can get up at dawn," suggested Etor. Before Nura could object he added, "We will arrive at Gal-Rian sooner if we use all the daylight hours."

Nura sighed. "Very well. Good night Levi, Lisa, Etor."

Etor divided up the watches and took the first one. Levi soon fell asleep. Before he knew it, Etor was gently shaking him awake. By the time he and Nura shook off the stupor of sleep Lisa, Etor and the guards had eaten breakfast and were ready to move out. Levi and

Nura ate as they rode to save time. The trail widened five miles down the road so three horses could ride abreast. Levi noticed that Etor looked concerned.

Levi left Nura and rode up to Etor. "Expecting trouble, Etor?"

"Always," replied Etor. He looked all around but spotted nothing and no one. "In the mountains, trouble has too many places to hide in. A company of soldiers went before us and checked the trail all the way to Gal-Rian. They encountered no one. It would not be too hard for someone who knows these mountains to slip through the cordon. Trouble could be sneaking up on us even as we speak."

"I hope you will not be too disappointed if trouble never arrives."

Etor chuckled. "That is a disappointment I do not mind."

Suddenly ropes flew down from above, catching Levi and Etor in their loops. Sharp yanks jerked them off their horses. Four men wearing face paint and camouflage uniforms dropped down from above. They shot all the guards. One guard killed an attacker before he too was taken out. A moment later, the commander of the Strike Force slid down the slope and joined his men.

"All enemy soldiers neutralized, and all prisoners secured, sir" called out one of the enemy soldiers. "We lost one man."

"Etor futilely struggled against the rope that bound him. The enemy captain relieved Etor of his com-link and weapons. Etor watched helplessly as the enemy captain smashed the com-link with his foot.

"Failure is very bitter," he commiserated. "Losing all your men compounds the bitterness."

"Lemurians!" spat Etor. "This means war!"

The Lemurian captain laughed. "With Princess Nura in our hands, I think not." After securing the hands of his prisoners, he cut the other ropes. The Lemurians covered up the bodies of the dead guards. They were going to throw away everything Nura and Lisa had purchased. Nura persuaded the Lemurian captain to let them keep the dresses and jewelry.

Etor chafed at his helplessness. He chose not to waste his strength trying to break the strong rope that bound his hands. For the present, all he could do was bide his time. "Why have you spared the rest of us?"

The Lemurian captain smiled unpleasantly. "You and your friend have value to us as well as the princess." He leered at Lisa. "You will have your uses on the long trip home."

Neither Etor nor Levi liked the sound of that. "Forgive me for failing you, princess," apologized Etor.

"Etor, is it not a remarkable coincidence that a Lemurian Strike Force should intercept us at this particular spot?" asked Levi.

"Coincidence?" repeated Etor. "Or betrayal."

"It had to be someone at the palace," said Lisa. "Etor, who knew about our planned trip and our itinerary?"

"The king, myself, you, Levi, Nura and the four men I chose to guard the three of you. Once I chose the men, they were not permitted to talk to anyone about it."

Nura looked pained and guilty. "There were two others, Etor. Zira and Seren. Zira practically grew up in the palace. I cannot believe she is a traitor. Seren was the last handmaid to enter my service. Now that I think about it, she never said very much about her family and background. I did not wish to invade her privacy, so I did not press her about it."

"I would not be surprised to find that Seren is a Lemurian spy," said Etor. "I hope we all live long enough to find out."

"Before we left, Seren told me that she would not forget me or the night we shared," recalled Levi. "I wish that it had occurred to me that she was saying a final goodbye."

The Lemurians remained silent and aloof as they hurried their prisoners along. They spoke only when necessary. Whenever Nura requested time to rest, it was granted without hesitation or question. The Lemurians unbound Levi, Lisa and Etor when it was time to eat. A soldier held a knife to Nura's throat to discourage any rash moves by Etor or Levi. Twice Nura deliberately slowed her pace to irritate her captors.

The Lemurian captain dropped back to her the third time she slowed down. "Please do not delay me any further, princess" he warned.

"I am doing the best I can," insisted Nura.

The captain pulled out his pistol and placed the barrel against Levi's head. "Do better! I know all about your barbarian lover. Keep pace or our number will be reduced by one."

Near sunset, they reached a suitable spot and made camp. The Lemurian captain roused everyone at dawn. They resumed their journey at a quicker pace. Nura no longer attempted to slow up the Lemurians. The Lemurian captain kept Nura at his side. Levi and Etor realized that they, not Nura, were in immediate danger. The Lemurians treated her with all the respect due to a princess. If they got her to Suminar, she would be a well-treated hostage. At worst, she might be wed to Adar. That was hardly an outrageous fate for someone destined for a marriage of state.

"I can understand why they did not kill you, Etor," whispered Levi. "They can pick your brain for valuable information. I do not see what possible use the Lemurians could have for me or Lisa."

The Lemurians shepherded their prisoners down a steep path to the bottom of a canyon. Two hours later, they took a trail veering sharply west. Etor had seen the trail before but had never taken it. They headed roughly southwest.

Etor became alarmed. "I know what is in store for us. If we continue along this trail for three days, we will end up in Teyron!"

"Then we better become moon goddess worshipers if we are given the chance," suggested Levi without humor.

"That is unlikely," replied Etor. "Many people have long suspected that the moon goddess worshipers of Teyron practice human sacrifice. The people who disappeared while trying to learn Teyron's secrets are the only ones who would talk. Their voices have been silenced forever."

"Why do your priests tolerate the moon goddess worshipers?" wondered Levi.

"They are no threat to anyone outside of their cities" said Etor. "They do not proselyte. Kemen feels even to acknowledge their existence is to take them more seriously than they deserve. It seems that only Father Sun can save us."

Major Kinsey and his men continued their recording chores while Levi and Lisa toured the interior with Princess Nura. Earthfleet Command had ordered them to assist the Temporal Historians when they requested it. McNeil and Kelly cheerfully accepted their historian duty. Kinsey felt annoyed and put out at first. As he researched and recorded military history, Kinsey became enthusiastic.

Before the mission, he had considered history a subject of little value. At the Academy, he had been an indifferent student of history.

The living history of Atlantis dispelled his former notion about the subject. Kinsey wouldn't admit to the rest of the team that he was now very grateful to have been chosen as a Special Observer on the Atlantis I mission. He had been displeased about being with the mission because he had expected to have no useful part in it. Kinsey and his men would be a part of Earthfleet history. The Commanding Admiral himself planned to meet with them when they returned home.

Kinsey had been gathering information and records to write a biography of General Garai. He struck the major as a more urbane and sophisticated George Patton. They were both warriors who loved war for its own sake. The two men would have enjoyed talking to each other and sharing their thoughts on tactics and strategy.

Kinsey decided to give his brain a break. He left his room and went to the bar for some wine. When he was on and off duty during the mission was not perfectly clear to him. While clearly on duty, alcohol was forbidden to him and the sergeants. What Earthfleet Command didn't know, wouldn't trouble it. Kinsey made it clear to them that if he ever caught his men drunk, they would be busted down to private.

As Kinsey ordered his wine, McNeil and Kelly returned to the inn. They joined him at the bar. Kinsey ordered a bottle of wine for the sergeants. "The wine is on me tonight. I trust that your day was productive and enjoyable."

The sergeants thanked Kinsey for the wine. "Recording can be tiresome at times, but sometimes it's fascinating," said Kelly. "Has Jerrel returned yet?"

Kinsey shook his head. "He has been getting back later each day since Levi and Lisa left for their trip to the interior. Heaven knows when Dark will turn up. If I had a lady like his, I would be in no hurry to get home either."

"If there ever was a man who burned the candle at both ends, it's Mr. Dark," commented McNeil. "I think he has gone native."

"Dark is a man of many talents who is adding to his legend in Atlantis almost daily," said Kinsey. "If he ever writes his memoirs, I will buy a copy whatever the price. I wonder why he is so reluctant to talk about his adventures in our time. No one can rightly accuse him of blowing his own horn.”

“Major, just how much of what we have experienced in Atlantis may we share with family and friends?” asked Kelly.

Kinsey smiled. “I am certain that Earthfleet Command will make that very clear when we are debriefed. If either of you gentleman have known any Atlantean ladies in the Biblical sense, I suggest you zip your lips about that.”

“We may not be officers, but we are gentlemen, sir,” said McNeil piously.

An out of breath Dark burst into the room. “I found the Atlantean spaceship! Anyone interested in seeing it?”

“We would like to see it now!” said Kinsey eagerly. “If you weren’t planning to go to bed.”

“Go to bed at midnight?” asked Dark incredulously. “Follow me, gentlemen.”

Chapter Twenty-One

"Teyron lies just beyond the hill ahead of us," announced Etor. "In less than an hour, we will have the opportunity to learn what Professor Ziram has been very anxious to know about Teyron and the moon goddess worshipers. If by the grace of Father Sun, we survive and return home, I will be certain to share our knowledge with him."

"The Sun Lords' religious tolerance may be the death of us," observed Nura with annoyance.

"The irony is not lost on me, Nura," said Etor sourly.

"The living always have possibilities, Etor," Levi reminded him as well as himself. "As one of my country's greatest warriors said, 'never give up! And as another great warrior said,' only he is lost who gives himself up for lost."

"I refuse to go quietly," vowed Etor. "If I must die, I will die on my feet fighting!"

"What is the connection between the Lemurians and the moon worshipers?" wondered Lisa. "I cannot think of a more unlikely alliance."

"I cannot either," admitted Etor. "The Lemurians no doubt made this arrangement to help them pull off the abduction of Nura. It gives them a safe base of operations. No one pays any attention to Teyron."

"We can be certain that the moon worshipers are getting something for their help and cooperation," figured Lisa.

"With me in their hands, the Lemurians will have great leverage over Atlantis," fretted Nura. "I cannot believe that Adar had any part in this. It is harder still for me to believe that King Bakri was planning my abduction while pretending to be seeking peace."

"Prince Adar did recommend that you get out of Aurelin," recalled Lisa. "Seren knew you would go Gal-Rian."

When the Lemurians and their prisoners reached the last hill, a warrior on the hill spotted them. Immediately, he left to announce their arrival. Minutes later, the Lemurians and their prisoners rode past the hill and Teyron came into view. A small village of square log houses spread out before them as far as they could see. Levi figured that the houses were spacious to comfortable house eight to ten people. Loud horn blasts announced the arrival of the visitors.

People streamed out of the houses and gathered around them. The adults appeared more curious than hostile. Children gazed at the visitors in wide eyed wonder. At the center of the village stood an impressive ziggurat-like structure. It had three levels with the top being a broad-based pyramid. The top layer had two lions that guarded the entrance. Levi figured that sacrifices were made on the top level.

A path suddenly formed in the crowd. Two men walked up to the Lemurian captain, one tall and the other five inches shorter. The taller man wore a shaman-like headdress and white robe. Most likely, he was the High Priest. His shorter companion wore a gold medallion with a bear emblem around his neck. Levi figured that he was the chief.

The Lemurian captain gazed sadly at Etor. "We could gain so much useful information from you, captain. Regrettably, you are too dangerous to keep alive. I will leave you to the not so tender mercies of the moon worshipers."

The Lemurian captain held up his hand in greeting. "The peace of the moon goddess be with you, son of the Great Bear. I have brought three gifts for the goddess." He seized Nura's arm. "This woman is a gift for my king."

The chief and High Priest smiled unpleasantly. The High Priest scrutinized Levi, Lisa, and Etor. "They are acceptable," he solemnly declared.

"I regret that we cannot stay for the sacrifices," said the Lemurian captain. "My king wants his gift delivered to him as soon as possible. The journey to Lemuria is a very long one."

"We are Princess Nura!" declared Nura imperiously. "Release Us and Our friends at once or the king will burn your village to the ground!"

All the villagers laughed heartily at her claim. "Be silent, woman!" commanded the chief. He slapped Nura hard across her mouth. Etor lunged at the chief. A warrior knocked him down. He pinned Etor to the ground with his foot.

"No more foolishness from you!" warned the chief. "Take this madwoman away, captain!"

The Lemurian captain seized the reins of Nura's horse. He and his men rode off with her while Levi and Etor watched helplessly. "The messengers to the moon goddess will be sent tomorrow," announced the High Priest.

"Is it not written that the goddess knows true hearts from false?" demanded Etor.

The High Priest nodded. "It is written."

"Then let us prove that our hearts are true!" demanded Etor boldly.

The High Priest and chief moved off and privately conferred. A minute later, they returned to the prisoners. "The three of you will face the Three Challenges," declared the High Priest. "The woman will first face the Test of Fire." The High Priest looked at Etor. "Then you will face the Test of Steel." The High Priest smiled smugly "You will face the Test of Wisdom," he informed Levi. "Tonight, all of you will rest and make your peace with your god."

Levi's heart sank when he heard the dread pronouncement. He was heartened that Etor had a literal fighting chance. Levi suspected that Lisa's fate was entirely out of her hands. He hoped that he had sufficient wisdom to successfully meet his challenge. If Earthfleet had given them the personal shields that Gideon Warner requested, neither he, Lisa or Etor would be in danger now.

Levi, Lisa and Etor were confined in an unused cabin. It had a table and chairs but no beds. Fortunately, it had a tub large enough for everyone to bathe in at the same time. It seemed that the moon worshipers didn't want to offend their goddess by sending dirty messengers to her. They received a meal of boiled vegetables and water. Levi felt that the bland, meatless meal was the final insult added to their injury. Levi, Lisa and Etor all slept fitfully.

The High Priest roused the prisoners at dawn. Apparently, the moon worshipers wouldn't be giving the condemned a last meal. The High Priest and chief led the prisoners to a circle of yellow flame at the center of the village. Flames shot up seven feet high. The High Priest halted the prisoners six feet away from the fire. He ordered a lesser priest to prepare Lisa. The priest returned with a white robe. He removed all of Lisa's clothes and placed the robe on her.

"The Keeper of the Divine Flame brings this woman before you to be tested," declared the High Priest solemnly. "Judge her heart, lady of the night, and reveal to us whether it is true or false. We await your judgment."

Lisa hugged Levi and Etor. "When I am weighed in the balances, I hope that I will not be found wanting."

Levi cursed the moon worshipers in English. "Pigs will fly on their own power before we get any justice in this place. "

A murmur of approval rippled through the crowd as Lisa walked voluntarily toward the fire. They waited expectantly to see what the judgment of the goddess would be. Levi thought that the High Priest and chief looked confident that the verdict would be guilty. Just before Lisa stepped into the fire, a startling change came over it. To the astonishment of everyone, the fire turned blue.

Lisa stepped into the flame without hesitation. The flames didn't scorch or consume her.

She faced the High Priest and chief and laughed. "The fire is cool!"

The totally unexpected turn of events elicited cries of fear and dismay from the crowd. Clearly few people had ever received a favorable judgment from the goddess. Levi couldn't believe that the Divine Flame had any intelligence. He had no idea why Lisa had been found not guilty. Neither he nor Lisa were going to question the decision of the goddess.

After spending a minute in the fire, Lisa stepped out. Immediately the flames turned yellow and hot. The High Priest and chief turned to the astounded villagers. "The prisoner has passed the test!" stammered the High Priest.

"How did it happen?" demanded the chief in consternation.

The High Priest shrugged. He hastily cut the ropes binding Levi and Etor. Two warriors took Etor to an eighteen foot wide roped off circle followed by the chief, High Priest, prisoners, and the villagers. They outfitted Etor with a sword and shield. Etor tested the weight and balance of the sword. He judged it more than satisfactory. Etor frowned at the chief's son who kept Lisa close to him.

No one stopped Levi when he approached Etor. "Father Sun be with you."

"Father Sun help us all," agreed Etor. "I am a fair swordsman, but I have not used my sword for a long time. I have never been in any situation that required using it."

"Are the sword and shield as good as they look?" asked Levi.

"They are, but my opponent has a helmet and armor. I do not," noted Etor.

The High Priest held up his hand. Immediately all talk ceased. "The next prisoner will face the Test of Steel!" He ordered Etor and the Champion into the ring.

Etor sized up his opponent. The Champion stood seven feet tall, heavily muscled with minimal fat. He looked very confident. To Etor's surprise, the Champion saluted him with his sword. Etor returned the courtesy.

"The contest has only three rules," declared the High Priest. "Neither fighter may leave the circle during the contest. There are no rest periods. The contest ends when one of the fighters is dead. Let the contest begin!"

Etor took the offensive. He peppered the Champion with a flurry of furious blows. Had any of them got through, the contest would have ended. The Champion parried all the blows. He went on the offensive and drove Etor back with heavy blows that were just barely fought off. Etor lunged at the Champion with his shield and knocked him down. He swung his sword as fast as he could. It struck the ground instead of the Champion who rolled away in time.

With surprising agility and quickness, the Champion got back on his feet before Etor could take advantage of it.

Etor began to tire from the unaccustomed exertion of a fast-paced fight to the death. The Champion looked as fresh as when the contest began. Etor continually found himself on the defensive. His shield arm was getting tired. The Champion began to get past Etor's guard. He scored several small cuts on Etor's arms and a superficial cut on his left thigh. The Champion pressed Etor against the rope.

The Champion stepped back as if to savor the moment. Etor welcomed the respite. He sank gratefully to one knee and caught his breath. The Champion renewed this attack. Etor scored a cut on the Champion's left arm. It drew blood but it didn't slow him down at all. The Champion scored a deep cut on Etor's left arm. It bled badly.

The Champion sensed victory and prepared to end the contest. He slipped unexpectedly while making a thrust. The Champion momentarily lost his balance. Etor gathered his remaining will and strength. He thrust his sword deep into the Champion through the joint between his chest and lower body armor. Etor released his sword and fell to his knees.

The Champion gazed at him in amazement and disbelief. He staggered back a couple of steps. His eyes glazed over. He fell hard onto the ground and didn't move. Levi helped Etor over the rope. The chief ordered a healer to tend to Etor. With alacrity, the healer bound Etor's wounds.

"The goddess makes slippery the paths of all who oppose her will," declared the High Priest in fearful awe. "The prisoner has passed the Test of Steel. Take the remaining prisoner to the Divine Flame where he will face the Test of Wisdom."

The High Priest and the chief led Levi to the Divine Flame, followed by the other priests. The chief's son dragged Lisa along. The High Priest ordered Levi to step up to the Divine Flame. "Goddess mother, we bring this man before you to face the Test of Wisdom. Enlighten his mind or dull his wit, according to your holy will."

The chief prodded Levi forward to the High Priest with his knife. The chief's son stood three feet behind Levi. Levi suspected that he was brought to judgment by the Divine Flame so the moon worshipers could more quickly consign him to the fire if he failed the test. Levi feared that Lisa's experience with the Divine Flame was a fluke.

"Answer me now, outsider," demanded the High Priest. "What are the greatest treasures in the world?"

Levi pondered the question. He turned his thoughts to one of the greatest wise men in Terran history. Happy is the man that findeth wisdom, and the man that getteth understanding. For the merchandise of it is better than the merchandise of silver, and the gain thereof of gold. Live joyfully with the wife whom thou lovest all the days of your life. Love, family and health.

"Wisdom, love, family and health are the greatest treasures," answered Levi. "There are none greater."

Everyone but Lisa looked very disappointed by Levi's response. "It is even so," acknowledged the High Priest sourly. "What things should a man fear most?"

Levi considered his response in terms of the Atlantean culture and mindset. Certainly, a man should fear God. As Solomon the Wise observed, the wrath of the king is as messengers of death. Levi recalled the words of Diogenes. The most dangerous wild animal was the slanderer, and the most dangerous tame animal was the flatterer.

"The things that a man should fear most are the wrath of the goddess, the wrath of the king, flatterers and liars."

The High Priest grimaced. "It is so," he acknowledged. The High Priest smiled. "The final test of wisdom is discernment." He clapped his hands. The chief brought two lovely young women before Levi. He thought that the ladies didn't look happy about their part in the test.

"Which one of these women is my daughter?" demanded the chief. "If you answer correctly, you many choose either one of them for your wife."

Levi scrutinized the women. Each of them resembled the chief. Levi cursed inwardly. He hadn't expected a test like that. Levi hated the thought of being stopped just short of the goal line by a shoestring tackle.

"How long do I have to decide?" asked Levi nervously.

The chief smiled smugly. "Consider well, but not all day."

Levi studied the chief. He impressed Levi as a man who would deal from the bottom of the deck. The moon worshipers had stacked the deck against their prisoners. Fifty-fifty odds were great when gambling at a casino. They weren't so great when a person's life was on the line. Then the answer hit him: the shell game!

"Neither of these women are your daughter, chief," declared Levi confidently.

The Chief's mouth fell open. "How did you know?"

Levi laughed. "The last thing you want is a non-believer son-in-law. You would not have offered me the choice of either woman as my wife if one of them had been your daughter."

"The goddess mother has truly granted you wisdom," acknowledged the High Priest. "You and your friends may depart Teyron in peace."

"No!" shouted the chief's son. Levi turned around. He shoved Levi toward the Divine Flame. "Sacrilege!" screamed the High Priest.

For a moment, Levi felt the heat of the Divine Flame. Just before he entered it, the flame turned blue and cool. Levi felt peace and joy. He basked in the pleasing coolness of the fire. Reluctantly he left it.

The High Priest seized the chief's son. He dragged him to the edge of the Divine Flame. It immediately turned yellow and hot. "Were you not the son of the chief, I would consign you to the fire!"

The chief's son fell to his knees. "Forgive me, holy one!" he implored.

The High Priest raised him up. "You are banished from the Valley of the Moon for one year. During that time, you will be as dead to the people of the goddess mother. Return here before the end of the year, and your body will feed the fire!"

Two priests seized the chief's son and led him away. The High Priest gazed fearfully at Levi. "The woman our Lemurian brothers took away truly was Princess Nura. King Adeil will raze the valley and kill all my people!"

"Not if you help us help us to rescue her," promised Levi.

"What can we do to help?" asked the High Priest eagerly.

"Do you have a com-link?" asked Etor.

The High Priest looked confused for a moment, "Ah, the communication device our Lemurian brothers gave us. Our brothers gave it to us so we can contact each other. If they return to Teyron, they will become messengers to the goddess!" The High Priest ordered a priest to get the com-link from his home.

"Excellent! I can adjust it to use one of our frequencies. How do the Lemurians plan to get Princess Nura out of the country?" demanded Etor.

"I overheard the captain speak of a floater waiting to take them from Kalorn to a waiting submarine," recalled the High Priest. "It is a day's journey through the mountain to the trail that leads to Kalorn."

"Did you say through the mountain?" asked Levi in puzzlement.

The High Priest smiled. "Neither rock nor stone can bar the passage of the faithful."

"We have a good chance to catch the Lemurians if they are not in a hurry," figured Levi. "They think you and I are dead, Etor, so they might travel a little slower. If only something could delay the Lemurians!"

Chapter Twenty-Two

Nura glanced back at Levi, Lisa and Etor as the Lemurians led her away from Teyron. She felt overwhelmed with guilt at their plight. Trusting Seren had given the Lemurians an opportunity to capture her and threatened to throw the succession into chaos. Her father wouldn't name Maric his successor without her to ride herd on him. Nura also felt guilty for placing so much trust in Seren who turned out to be a Lemurian spy.

The Lemurians rode at a moderate pace. With the deaths of Etor, the storyteller, and his sister, they felt no need to hurry. Soon Teyron disappeared from their sight. In an hour, they arrived at the mountain tunnel built specially for operations in Atlantis. The Atlanteans had no idea that it existed. Nura smiled as a nasty idea occurred to her. The Lemurians had permitted her to keep the saddlebag with the rocks Levi had collected. Time to make good use of them.

Nura slipped her hand into the pocket containing the largest rock picked up by Levi.

"Captain," she called pleasantly.

When the captain turned his head, Nura hurled the rock at his head with all her strength. It struck him above his right eye. Nura spurred her horse forward before the surprised Lemurians could grab the reins of her horse. She didn't look back. The shouts of the soldiers grew steadily fainter. Minutes later the sun set making Nura's trail hard to follow. She slowed her pace after the sun set. Nura rode a few minutes away from the trail.

Nura couldn't accept that Levi, Lisa and Etor were dead. If they had somehow managed to obtain their freedom and horses, she had to delay the Lemurians long enough for them to catch up with her. Nura had enough food and water for a day. A day's delay might be all that Levi, Etor and Lisa needed. Unfortunately, the Lemurians had night vision goggles. They might even have heat sensors. Just because they hadn't used them didn't mean they didn't have them.

Until the encounter with the Lemurians, Nura's 'vacation' had been as delightful as she had hoped. At times, she couldn't believe that it wasn't just a wonderful dream. The Lemurians rudely reminded her that she wasn't dreaming. The hours passed slowly for her. After what seemed like days, the new day dawned. As soon as the sun rose above the horizon, Nura rode further away from the mountain tunnel the Lemurians planned to use.

Nura looked around but didn't see the Lemurians. She hoped that they weren't good trackers. Most likely they were. At noon, Nura decided to stop and wait for the Lemurians. Her canteen was almost empty. She had bought her friends a day to help them catch up with her. Hopefully, it was enough. Minutes later, the Lemurians appeared in the distance. They caught up with Nura fifteen minutes later.

The captain had a bandage where Nura's stone had struck him. He glared at Nura. "What did you expect to gain from this escapade, princess?"

Nura threw back her head and laughed. "Satisfaction!"

"Royalty," muttered the captain in annoyance.

The Lemurians rode at a slightly quicker pace than they had the previous day. It didn't take long to reach the mountain tunnel. The captain dismounted and walked over to a rock formation ten feet from the tunnel. He opened the top revealing a control to the door. The outline could only be discerned close. After the captain threw a switch, the door to the tunnel slowly swung open. It revealed a large cavern that stretched out as far as they could see. Two parallel rows of bright lights over them suddenly came on. Once everyone was inside, the captain closed the door.

"How did your people make this tunnel without being detected?" asked Nura.

The captain laughed. "Your soldiers almost never patrol this area. Understandably, there is no need. We studied this area for many months. Air patrols over this part of the province are very rare. During this time, we saw no ground patrols. It still was a gamble. Unfortunately for you, it paid off for us. Most of the cavern is natural. We just had to enlarge it at spots."

The Lemurians and their prisoner kept to the center of the cavern. Occasionally, they had to ride around large rocks. The thought of Lemurian soldiers operating so freely in the heart of Atlantis, unknown to everyone, angered and troubled Nura. It puzzled her that the Lemurian captain answered all her questions honestly and without reservation.

"Do you and your men actually worship the moon goddess, captain?" asked Nura. He and his soldiers laughed at the question. "Yes, but without sincerity," confessed the captain merrily. "When we join with the goddess, it is with very sincere intent. You were wise to hide your blue skin. If you hadn't, I could not have said or done anything to save you from the Divine Flame."

"My captain and my friends were to be burned alive?" asked Nura in horror.

The captain reflected for a moment. "If they were lucky, the High Priest permitted them to face the three challenges. According to the chief, no one has ever passed them."

Time passed with agonizing slowness for Nura. Visions of Levi, Lisa and Etor being consumed by the Divine Flame continually tormented her. Something deep inside Nura refused to accept that they were dead. If King Bakri found that he didn't have the leverage over Atlantis that he expected, she expected to be married to one of his sons.

For Nura, the journey through the mountain seemed endless. She felt great relief when they arrived at the end of the tunnel. Nura had struggled with feelings of claustrophobia during the ride through the mountain. She managed to tough it out. Nura had looked forward to seeing the sun again. She would never take sunlight and fresh air for granted ever again. Nura figured it was another two days to Kalorn. Once the Lemurians reached Kalorn, nothing could stop the Lemurians from escaping with her.

The Lemurian captain uncovered and opened the door. As soon as everyone was outside, he closed the door. "The ride to Kalorn will be much smoother," promised the captain. "Princess Nura, you will be the first member of the Atlantean royal family to visit Suminar in forty-five years. We deeply regret that you are not coming under better circumstances."

"Be assured that We are not thrilled, delighted or charmed," Nura angrily informed him.

The news of the flagship Pendaran's destruction shocked General Jencir out of his smug complacence. All his well-laid plans were now blowing up in his face. He had received the glorious news of the capture of Princess Nura. The news about the loss of Pendaran to an unknown Atlantean super weapon dumped ice cold water on his celebration. Jencir ordered all civilian and army agents in Atlantis to locate the weapon and learn what they could about it.

The Lemurian agents ranged farther into the heart of Atlantis than they had previously done. They had to find, and if possible, destroy the super weapon. The agents' contacts could tell them nothing. To the dismay of the agents who sought the help of the most potentially useful guilds, the guild masters flatly refused to help them. The Lemurians hurriedly left the Night Kingdom pursued by guild guards. All the agents left Aurelin. The weapon was nowhere near the city.

The Lemurian agents visited many villages and small cities in the interior. They discreetly questioned people if they had seen or heard of any unusual army installations near them. Finally, their hard work and persistence paid off. An agent overheard a man telling a friend at an inn about a strange experience he had had recently. The man had taken the wrong road on a foggy night and suddenly found himself surrounded by five soldiers.

They grilled him for six hours. He finally convinced the soldiers that he had taken the road by mistake. The soldiers warned him not to make the same mistake again. Lemurian agents scoured the area and found a secret installation. They watched the local inn carefully. Every weekend, soldiers came to the inn to enjoy drinking, gambling, and pleasure women. An attractive female agent took a room at the inn. She lured soldiers into her bed. The agent loosened their tongues with a truth drug slipped into their wine.

She confirmed that the super weapon was at the installation near the village. The soldiers couldn't tell her anything about the technology or operation of the weapon. She learned that security was much too tight for all her fellow agents in Atlantis combined to breach. After the agents had learned all that they could, they sent their reports to Lemuria. The alarming reports moved swiftly up the chain of command until it reached General Gelas, the head of Army Intelligence.

Gelas read the reports with alarm. As soon as he finished reading them, he took them hastily to Jencir's office. Jencir's face turned ashen when he read the reports. "Damn that accursed Garai!" shouted Jencir. "He managed to keep the weapon's existence secret even from King Adeil. If Princess Nura is killed, the very least Adeil will do is level Suminar! Get word to the Strike Force leader to surrender himself, his men, and the princess to the nearest civil or military authority. It may not fully appease Adeil. Hopefully, it will cause him to remove his finger from the super weapon's trigger."

Gelas saluted and rushed off to carry out Jencir's order. Jencir slumped back against his chair. All his carefully conceived and executed plans had completely fallen apart. The capture of Princess Nura had gone down perfectly. Only Garai's secret weapon ruined everything. Jencir regretted that he would never have the chance to share experiences with Garai over some of Lemuria's finest wines. Jencir smiled at the sublime irony of it all. Garai's secret scheme had unwittingly derailed his own secret scheme.

Jencir ordered his driver to prepare his floater. For the final time, he left his headquarters as the Supreme Commander of the Lemurian army. Twenty minutes later Jencir arrived at the crystal palace. Jencir walked tall and proud to the throne room. He approached the throne and knelt before King Bakri.

The king smiled and lifted up Jencir. "It is always good to see you, general. What can I do for you?"

Jencir explained fully about his secret plan to capture Princess Nura. He informed the king of the super weapon and its destruction of Pendaran. Bakri listened impassively at first. Gradually his expression grew very dark. "What other secrets have you kept from me, general?" asked Bakri with deceptive mildness. "A scheme to place yourself on my throne?"

"Nothing else!" swore Jencir.

"Because of you, I must humble myself before Adeil!" shouted Bakri. "I will look like an incompetent who cannot keep his generals under control. Pray that my apology and explanation of your treachery will turn aside Adeil's wrath. Atlantis now possesses a weapon against which we have no defense. It will hang like a sword over our heads from now on!"

Bakri summoned the Captain of the Guard. "Captain, you will place former General Jencir under arrest and confine him in the dungeon."

The captain grinned. "I obey with pleasure, Your Majesty."

Levi, Lisa and Etor waited outside of the tunnel for the Lemurians and Nura to exit. The High Priest had given them the exact location of the door. A company of Kimman base's best men had arrived hours earlier. Adeil told Etor about Jencir's plot and the former secret solar gun.

"King Bakri must be telling the truth," said Levi. "Otherwise, he would not have told King Adeil about it. I hope the Strike Force captain got the word to stand down and surrender."

"Maybe they did not get the word from King Bakri," said Etor in alarm. "If the Lemurians were inside the mountain when Bakri tried to contact them, the radio signal would not have gotten through. Jencir gave orders for the Strike Force to kill Nura if they were caught!"

"Let us hope that the Lemurians do not want to be dead heroes," commented Levi without humor.

A soldier near the tunnel door shouted, "The door is opening, captain!"

As soon as the gate was completely open, the Lemurians rode out of the tunnel. They gazed in surprise and dismay at the armed soldiers waiting for them. The captain turned to Nura. "It appears that Captain Etor and your friends passed the three tests," he noted ruefully. "I had hoped to see my wife, children, and homeland again. It has been almost a year… My bones will rest in a foreign land."

The captain dismounted and pulled Nura off her horse. He held his knife against her throat as he considered the tactical situation.

"You will not be harmed if you surrender, captain," pleaded Nura. "I promise you and your men a royal pardon if you spare me."

The captain smiled wanly. "You do not understand. My orders were very clear. If we cannot get you to Lemuria, we must kill you."

"I cannot believe that King Bakri could give you such an order. My father and I believe him to be an honorable man."

"The order came from General Jencir, not King Bakri," revealed the captain.

"If you obey Jencir's order to kill me, you dishonor your king and your people," said Nura.

The captain's com-link suddenly beeped. He answered it without delay. "Strike Force Gold leader, do you copy?"

"I copy," responded the captain.

"Thank Father Sun, we finally reached you. By order of King Bakri, you are to stand down and surrender to the Atlanteans. Repeat, stand down and surrender to the Atlanteans. Do not, I repeat, do not harm Princess Nura. Project Sun Lord is over. Do you copy?"

The captain sighed with relief. "I copy. Strike Force Leader out."

"Would you have killed me if you had not been ordered to stand down, captain?" asked Nura.

The captain smiled. "I am not a murderer or an assassin, Princess Nura. Let us not keep your countrymen waiting."

The Atlantean soldiers cheered when they saw Nura leading the unarmed Lemurian soldiers over to them. The Lemurians acted more like they were her honor guard than her former captors. The Atlanteans quickly bound the Lemurian prisoners. Nura ran over to Levi and hugged him. "Thank Father Sun that you, Etor and Lisa passed the three challenges."

"How did you know about that, Nura?" asked Lisa.

"The Lemurian captain told me that you could only have survived in Teyron if you passed the three challenges. You are the first people to pass them."

"Are you all right, Nura?" asked Etor anxiously.

She hugged him carefully, seeing his wounds. "The only injury I suffered was to my royal dignity. Your injury was much more serious."

The commander of the rescue force came to Etor. He handed him a com-link. "The king wishes to speak to Princess Nura."

Chapter Twenty-Three

Nura walked a short distance away from everyone so she could speak privately to her father. They talked for almost thirty minutes. Levi wished he could listen in on that conversation. Lisa could eavesdrop telepathically, but she wouldn't intrude on anyone's thoughts without great need. Finally, the conversation ended. The triumphant look on Nura's face told Levi that she had won the argument.

"Etor, the king wishes to speak with you!" called Nura. She handed him the com-link and rejoined Levi and Lisa. "We have permission to continue on to Gal-Rian," announced Nura. "Now that the Lemurian threat has ended, there is no need to return to Aurelin."

Levi smiled. "It looked to me like you did some serious arm twisting."

"I did," admitted Nura. "For a while, I feared that my father would say no."

Levi, Lisa, and Nura watched Etor while he spoke with Adeil. After five minutes, the conversation ended. Etor rejoined them. The look on his face was not triumphant.

Etor gazed disapprovingly at Nura. "If it was my choice, we would return immediately to the palace. The choice is not mine. We will travel to Gal-Rian by floater with six soldiers and myself to protect you. A company of soldiers from Kimman Base will secure Gal-Rian for the duration of your visit. The floater should arrive in about ten minutes."

"That is acceptable to me," decided Nura.

Etor sent the soldiers away. "Nura, the king received a remarkable and very unexpected call from King Bakri. He informed King Adeil that Garai's Lemurian counterpart, General Jencir, had organized an operation to kidnap you and bring you to Suminar. Bakri declared it to be a rogue operation done without his knowledge or authorization."

"Wow!" commented Levi. "Do you and King Adeil believe him?"

"We do. Our agents in Lemuria had heard nothing about Jencir's plot. Bakri informed King Adeil that his flagship Pendaran had been destroyed by a mysterious weapon. Their agents learned that the shot that destroyed Pendaran came from the sky."

"That would require a space-based weapon," realized Nura. "Neither I nor my father are aware that we had one. Garai must have built the weapon and launched it into orbit. The thought of Garai or Maric being in control of such a weapon frightens me. I do not trust anyone to have it."

"The king's loyal intelligence people are seeking the facility controlling the gun as we speak," revealed Etor. "Lemuria has no similar weapon. Jencir would have used it if he had had one. I recommended that we immediately destroy the weapon, control facility and the technology. The king agreed."

Levi had expected to discover many fascinating things about Atlantis. He never imagined that Atlantis had rocket technology. Until now, these technologies were thought to be just theoretical by the commoners. The weapon must have been eliminated before the end. The space mirrors were gone by the Terran space age.

The royal party wasted no time boarding the floater when it arrived. Unlike its first escort, the second one was armed with rifles, sidearms and grenades. They no longer needed to use stealth. No one had much to say during the flight to Gal-Rian. The royal party had been mentally and emotionally drained by its experience with the moon goddess worshipers and the Lemurian soldiers. Levi hoped that the Atlantis II mission would turn out to be less eventful.

During the flight, Levi pondered the striking contrast between the people of the plains and the people of the mountains. In some ways Atlantis was truly two countries. It astonished Levi that the two groups of people managed to co-exist so peacefully and cooperatively considering their very different lifestyles and mindsets. The Brotherhood of Father Sun held Atlantean society together.

The less accessible places like Gal-Rian were out of the government's sight and mostly out of mind. According to Nura, most mountain people had never visited Aurelin. They rarely traveled more than a week's journey from their villages. People lived much like their pre-Sun Lord ancestors did. They didn't care to see the ocean or the 'Golden City.' Levi found that difficult to comprehend.

He gazed in delight when Mount Helia came into view. Even in deep twilight, its beauty and majestic could be seen. The snowcapped mountain rose 12,000 feet above the surrounding hills. Gal-Rian was the only village on the mountain. It was built many centuries ago to serve people making their pilgrimages after the coming of the Sun Lords. Only the Temple of the Sun in Aurelin was a holier place than Mount Helia and the Shrine of Alaya.

Levi got a good look at the Shrine of Alaya as the floater descended toward the village. The pyramid-like structure looked out of place with the rustic wooden buildings and houses. Hundreds of steps cut into the side of the mountain led from the village to the shrine. They might have been cut with a laser drill. Levi felt tired just thinking about the climb. He knew Etor could never make the climb with his wounds.

"Every pilgrim must climb all 854 steps to the shrine unaided," explained Nura. "A person who is physically unable to make the climb by themselves may be assisted by one family member or friend."

"Fortunately, I have already made my pilgrimage," said Etor. "It will be weeks before I will be able to climb those steps again."

"Are there certain times that people can make their pilgrimages, or can they go anytime?" asked Lisa.

"People can make their pilgrimages all year round," said Nura. "Most people come during late spring through early autumn."

The floater landed at the edge of the village. Gal-Rian's log cabins reminded Levi unpleasantly of Teyron. Its log houses were twice as large as those of Teyron. Levi suspected that extended families lived in them. Except for soldiers on patrol, the village was deserted.

"Where is everyone?" wondered Nura with concern. "Etor informed the chief when we were coming."

Everyone disembarked from the floater. As if on cue, people carrying torches streamed out of the houses and converged around the royal party. The people greeted her but didn't touch her. A venerable looking elderly man slowly made his way to Nura. His gold medallion with the wolf head indicated that he was the chief. Levi couldn't believe that Gal-Rian had so many attractive men and women. Even the older people looked good.

The chief bowed. "You honor and delight us with your presence, Princess Nura. We hope your stay with us will not be short."

Nura kissed him on the cheek. "I am very happy to be back, grandfather."

A petite raven hair young woman ran up to Nura and hugged her. "It is wonderful to see you again, princess."

Nura laughed. "Do not dare to call me princess, Galina! Levi, Lisa, this is my dear friend Galina. We met during her first visit to Aurelin. We were both much younger then."

Galina hugged Levi and Lisa. "It is a great pleasure to meet friends of Nura." Galina noted Nura's disheveled appearance with curiosity and concern. "Your journey seems to have been an adventure."

"It is an adventure I may not share with you, Galina," replied Nura regretfully.

"Share with me what you can. First you, Etor and your friends need to refresh yourselves." Galina led the royal party to the Guest House that had been prepared for them. After Levi, Nura, Lisa and Etor had showered they relaxed in the communal bath. After the others went to bed, Nura visited Galina at her house. They sat down on a wolf skin rug by the fire.

"I am glad that you brought your fiancé with you, Nura," said Galina. "He looks like a fine man. You obviously love each other. I prayed that you would marry a man of your choice."

Nura sighed. "Levi is not my fiancé. If only he was. Levi is not of noble birth, but he is of noble worth. On the Feast of Maren, my father will announce my betrothal to Maric."

The news hit Galina like a punch in the stomach. "Then the rumors are true. For now, you can forget about your unhappy fate. Will you make your pilgrimage this time?"

Nura nodded. "I procrastinated it long enough. Tomorrow or the day after, I want to show Levi and Lisa the shrine."

"The shrine is forbidden to non-believers," Galina reminded her.

"I am a princess and Levi is Friend of The Crown. The Guardian will not gainsay me," predicted Nura confidently.

Galina looked dubious. "I hope the Guardian will make an exception for you."

"I am sorry that I could not let you know earlier that I will visit," apologized Nura. "By necessity, my friends and I had to leave in secret and travel in disguise."

"I thought that was why you covered up your true color. It seems that someone penetrated your disguise."

"Only my father, Lord Kal and the people who traveled with me will ever know what happened on the way to Gal-Rian. Sometimes I get so weary of all the fawning and fussing over me. If I could marry Levi and live here the rest of our days, I would be the happiest woman in Atlantis."

"At least you are sharing love with a good man for a season," commiserated Galina. "How did you and Levi get acquainted?"

Nura told Galina how she was drawn to the main marketplace during a visit from Maric. She encountered Levi while he was performing his stories of Chin. Nura noted with delight how incensed Maric had been. She enjoyed the stories so much that she invited Levi to the palace for a private performance. Over time, they became friends, then more than friends.

"Levi must perform for us!" insisted Galina. "Stories from another country are an unexpected treat! Few storytellers come to Gal-Rian. When they do, they are usually just passing through on the way to a city."

"Levi has never scorned an opportunity to perform," noted Nura ruefully. "Knowing him, he will perform as a gift to the village." Nura yawned. "It has been a long day, Galina. I will see you in the morning."

Nura returned to the guest house. She found Levi sleeping deeply. Nura removed all her clothes and slipped under the covers. "You will be in the mood tomorrow night, love," she whispered in Levi's ear.

Nura laughed when Levi mumbled in his sleep. "Your will, princess."

The next day, Nura took Levi and Lisa on a tour of Gal-Rian. It surprised the historians to find that the village was not as primitive as it appeared at first glance. The houses and buildings had indoor plumbing. They managed to supply the houses with running water without modern technology. Nura explained that this had been done before the coming of the Sun Lords. She couldn't explain how the people kept so fit or why most people were so attractive.

Levi gave three performances for the villagers in the Council Hall. It had a stage for local and visitor performances. He wanted to give everyone a chance to experience his performances. Levi limited the performances to an hour because of giving three performances instead of his usual two. The mountain people loved the stories as much as the city slickers of Aurelin.

In between Levi's second and third performances, the villagers surprised him and Lisa with a special performance of their own. The young people performed traditional dances from ancient times. The dances were based on the myths of the old religion. An exceptionally lovely woman performed the Dance of The Moon Goddess. Originally, the dancer only wore garlands of flowers that covered little of her body. Now the garlands of flowers were artificial. Levi felt relieved that the Sun Dance had no relation to the American Indian Sun Dance.

The priests' tolerance of the ancient dances surprised Levi. After broaching the subject with Galina after the performance, she explained that the mountain people no longer believed in or worshiped the moon goddess. To them, the dances were simply their tradition and history. Levi was glad the village priests saw things the same way. He learned that the followers of the Sun Path lived sober but happy lives. People laughed and smiled often. The Sun Path promised happiness in this world as well as the next for the righteous and faithful.

At 2100, Nura and Etor accompanied the historians to the shrine. The floater dropped Etor at the top of the steps. The stone stairway had handrails on both sides. He waited patiently as Levi and Lisa slowly climbed to the shrine one weary step after another. After one hundred steps, Levi began to get winded. Nura and Lisa didn't seem winded yet. They allowed him a moment of rest every hundred steps.

Levi looked back at regular intervals to see how much progress they were making. When he reached the eight hundredth step, he got his second wind. After reaching the level of the shrine, he felt like he had just run a marathon. "Now I know why you put off your pilgrimage so long, Nura," commented Levi after catching his breath.

"Waiting until you are old to make your pilgrimage is a bad idea," said Etor.

The four of them approached the Guardian of the Shrine of Alaya. He regarded them warily. The Guardian was a deceptively frail looking man of average height. Levi saw the power of the man in his eyes. The guardian wore an unadorned white robe. He bowed to Nura.

"Welcome to the Shrine of Alaya, Princess Nura. I see that you have come to make your pilgrimage. Do your friends belong to the Brotherhood of the Sun?"

Nura pointed to Etor. "He does. My other friends are visitors to Atlantis."

The Guardian frowned. "Heathens and foreigners," he muttered. "I am sorry, princess, but they may not enter."

"Levi is Friend of the Crown," warned Etor. "This lady is his sister."

That fact didn't impress the Guardian. "Even the king knows that I cannot set aside spiritual rules and tradition for the convenience of his friends."

Nura's face grew dark. Refusing her was one thing. By extension, refusing the king was quite another. Levi took Lisa aside. "Read the Guardian's mind and see if there is a way to satisfy him and accomplish our purpose here."

Lisa reached out to the Guardian's mind. She smiled as she found the answer to their dilemma. Levi listened in confusion to the words she whispered in his ear. "What good will that do?" asked Levi impatiently.

"Just do it!" insisted Lisa.

Levi shrugged. He bowed down before the priest touching his forehead to the ground. "I acknowledge before heaven and earth that there is no God, but Father Sun. Blessed be His holy name forever!" Lisa did the same.

The Guardian smiled and raised them up. He anointed their heads with consecrated oil. "Father Sun rejoices in your passage from ignorance to knowledge, from darkness to light," he solemnly intoned. "Be faithful to the Sun Path unto death and be received into eternal bliss with Father Sun."

Nura hugged Levi and gave him a congratulatory kiss. "You and Lisa are no longer strangers but brother and sister to all who follow the Sun Path," Etor informed the historians.

"Nothing else is needed?" asked Levi in confusion.

Nura laughed. "You have just taken the first step. You will have a special ceremony in the Temple of The Sun. Galina's priest will give you and Lisa your own copy of the Book of Commandments. You must learn the commandments and live according to them."

The guardian stepped aside. "All of you may now enter." Nura led everyone into the shrine. A circle of torches on the walls illuminated the room. At the center of the shrine lay a marble altar. To the right was a life size statue of a tall, powerful looking man. The statue stood like a protector of the holy place.

"It is Lord Maren, the greatest of the Sun Lords!" whispered Nura.

Lisa established a link to Levi's mind. "Levi, Prince Maren's Colony Ship was not lost. Somehow it arrived here instead of Telmieria!"

Levi scanned the altar. It was hollow except for some circuits and mechanisms. He studied the altar closely. The odd shaped opening on the top of the altar intrigued him. Something clicked in Levi's mind. "Nura, may I have your medallion for a moment?" She disconnected the medallion from the chain. Nura it to him without hesitation. Levi eased it into the opening. It fit the opening almost perfectly. A second later they heard the hum of machinery. They gazed in wonder and astonishment as the altar rolled forward. It revealed a passageway.

"I never imagined…" murmured Etor. He removed two torches from their holders. Etor handed one to Levi. He stepped into the passageway. Bright ceiling lights came on automatically. Etor led everyone down the stairway to a door at the bottom. He opened it with a control on the wall. Ceiling lights came on automatically when he entered the room. They all stared in amazement at the huge computer in front of them.

"I have never seen or heard of a computer like this," swore Etor. "Who put it here and why?"

Nura hesitantly walked over to the computer. She sat down on the chair at the control panel. Nura looked over the unfamiliar controls. Before she could decide what to do, a hologram of a blue skinned scholar appeared.

"I am the Keeper of the archives," declared the hologram. "Who seeks to enter?"

For a few seconds, Nura was too stunned to speak. "I, Princess Nura, descendant of King Maren, seek to enter the archives."

"Place your right hand on the blue panel," directed the hologram. Nura placed her hand on the panel. Her hand was bathed in a bright blue light. Levi figured the computer was scanning her DNA. The blue light disappeared abruptly. "Enter, Princess Nura, descendant of King Maren!"

"What knowledge does the archives contain?" asked Nura diffidently.

"My data banks contain the science, art and history of your progenitors and their world."

Both Nura and Etor gasped at the shocking revelation. "Their world?" repeated Nura in disbelief. "We were taught that the Sun Lords came down from heaven."

The computer screen lit up, A yellow star and four planets appeared. "Your progenitors came from the Karani system, ten thousand light years from this world. Six hundred Atlantis years ago, the Karani sun went supernova. The Karani people constructed Colony Ships and evacuated as many people as they could. Most of the survivors fled to other worlds of the Karani Republic. The flower of the Karani people traveled to the Promised Planet of Telmieria to start over again and preserve their civilization."

Levi wanted to laugh. The answers to Atlantis had been staring him and Lisa in the face all along, but they had looked right past it. Despite the clues, the answers eluded them. For millennia, the Karani on Telmieria thought Prince Maren's ship had been lost or destroyed on the way to Telmieria. By the strangest twist of fate, he had ended up on Terra. Finally, the Karani would have closure. Now he and Lisa had another Holy Grail quest: finding the Colony Ship if it still existed.

"How did Prince Maren and his people come to rule Atlantis," asked Nura.

In response, the Keeper began to play a video recording from the colony ship.

Prince Maren opened his eyes after the completion of his revival. He gazed at the anxious face of Lord Akil. Akil helped Maren out of his hibernation freeze tube. "I see that we have survived the long journey to Telmieria.

"What is troubling you, Akil?" asked Maren with concern. "Is the ship damaged?"

Akil hesitated. "The ship is fine, Highness, but we are not where we belong."

Akil explained what he had learned with Maren on the way to the bridge. Maren stared at the image of Terra filling the main viewscreen.

"This beautiful blue world even outshines Telmieria," murmured Maren. "How did we end up here?"

"Instead of braking and making the final approach to Telmieria, the computer let us fly right by it," replied Akil guiltily as if it had somehow been his fault.

"Sabotage?" speculated Maren.

Akil shook his head. "A defective circuit gave a false reading that threw us off course. No one was awake to take us the rest of the way manually. Had this world not been here, we would have soon been stranded in space waiting for our food, fuel, and air to run out."

"What is this world like, Akil?"

"It has all the minerals we need to recreate our technology and civilization," replied Akil enthusiastically. "This planet also has twenty percent less gravity than the Karani Home World. That will be an advantage for us. The humanoid life is genetically compatible with us."

"We need to wake up the Council of the Six and discuss our options," decided Maren. "It seems like I have spent most of my adult life in service to the Republic, preparing to lead the people after my father was gathered to his ancestors. I can scarcely remember a time when I was not serving on a diplomatic or trade mission. It seemed like I had plenty of time to choose a consort. I continually procrastinated it."

Akil chuckled. "At least you had beautiful women to ease your loneliness."

Maren smiled. "I closed a few deals with lady ministers and lady ambassadors through bedroom diplomacy. I fear that my future holds more work than pleasure."

"Does that mean we will not even try to get to Telmieria?" asked Akil in surprise.

Maren smiled wanly. "We do not have enough fuel to reach even the nearest star system. We have no idea where we are in relation to Telmieria. Our communications are limited to this star system. This world is now our home."

Maren stared at the world that would be his permanent new home. "My brother Sandor will become king of Telmieria after I am officially declared dead. He is a good and capable man. Despite his inexperience, he will serve the people well as king. I will miss his company and counsel very much."

"We must marry native women to continue our family lines," mused Akil. "I will need time to adjust myself to that reality."

Maren sighed. "As will I, old friend. As will I. Revive the Council of the Six. After we have dinner, we will discuss how to deal with the native population. Until we determine our future course, the rest of our people will remain in hibernation freeze."

Prince Maren and his people debated where they would live and how they would deal with the native population. The council narrowed down the choices for their home to Atlantis and Lemuria. In the end, they chose Atlantis. Ideas ranged from conquering Atlantis and imposing their rule on the people to exterminating the native population. In the end, Maren and the council agreed that he would pretend to be the Emissary from Lord Sun the Atlanteans were expecting. Karani technology would convince the natives to accept Karani rule. When the rest of the world was ready, Atlantis could share its science and technology. Maren declared himself king of Atlantis. His marriage to the eldest daughter of the old king cemented his power.

The playback of the Colony Ship records ceased. "Do you have any more questions, Princess Nura?" asked the Keeper.

"No, Keeper," replied Nura in a small voice. The hologram disappeared and the computer screen became dark.

Nura trembled. "The ancestors of the Children of The Sun came from the stars, not heaven as we have been taught."

Levi held Nura reassuringly. "The Karani are children of Father Sun just as we are. You and Etor are greatly blessed to share their blood and heritage. Nura, you have the blood of royal lines from two worlds. Father Sun has given you a wonderful gift."

Levi's words calmed Nura. "Learning about the Karani was a big shock," she admitted. "It is good to know who and what I am. By the grace of Father Sun, I know what only one other person in the world knows: my father. The key to this knowledge was meant for my brother Akil. I believe Father Sun brought me here so the archives can be kept secret from Maric and Garai. I swear by Father Sun that only my firstborn son will know about our Karani heritage."

Etor checked his watch. "We have been here an hour. The Guardian must be wondering why we have been here so long. We must leave now!"

They left the computer room and shut the door behind them. When Levi removed the medallion from the altar, it moved back to its former place. He handed it to Nura. She placed it back on the chain. When they left the shrine, the Guardian was waiting for them.

"No one has ever stayed in the shrine as you and your friends have, Princess Nura," the Guardian informed her.

"The spirit of Father Sun was so great we hated to leave," replied Nura. "My friends and I will always remember this day."

Chapter Twenty-Four

Levi lay on his back watching the shadows from the fire flickering on the walls and ceiling. He was too excited about the knowledge he had gained from the Karani computer archives to sleep. Levi glanced at Nura. She lay curled up beside him apparently asleep. It was a wonder that she could sleep at all after having her world turned upside down. Even for himself and Lisa, the revelations were a bit of a jolt.

Without interacting with the people of the past, the historians wouldn't have learned about the Karani archives hidden in the Shrine of Alaya. Even had they known about the shrine, only Nura possessed the key to it. Sharing this year's Historian of The Year with Lisa made the success of the mission even sweeter. It would be his fifth and Lisa's first. His joining with Nura overshadowed everything else for Levi.

Levi recalled with amusement all the so-called UFO sightings before the beginning of the Alliance. People thought some of them were spaceships from other worlds. Paranoid people thought that they were gathering intelligence for an invasion or seeking human specimens to study and experiment on. No serious scientist believed that. The truth turned out to be less sinister and dramatic.

The first ambassador from the Empire revealed the truth of the UFOs to President Harrison. Waggish Rigellians messed with the Terrans' heads by flying their ships where they could be seen by humans. Sometimes they dressed in weird alien costumes to frighten and confuse people. The Rigellians occasionally captured humans and pretended to experiment on them before releasing them.

The Alliance had become the foremost ally of the Telmierian Empire. Through shared values and hundreds of thousands of intermarriages, the Alliance and Telmieria had become joined at the hip. Levi had long desired to marry a Karani lady. He didn't have the chance to get acquainted with any because of his busy career. Fate and interstellar politics brought Lisa Stern into his life. Unlike Nura, he could marry Lisa. Levi wanted to explore that possibility when they returned home. His telepathic links with her revealed she felt the same way. Levi greatly respected her for not being jealous of Nura.

"Levi are you awake?" asked Nura softly.

Levi started. "Yes. I have been thinking about what we learned from the archives. Everything I believed about my world has been turned upside down."

Nura sighed. "I tried to sleep but I cannot quiet my thoughts. The words of the Keeper continue to run through my mind."

"Do you regret knowing the truth?"

Nura reflected for a moment then shook her head. "Truth is the foundation of a meaningful life. Some truths shake you to the depths of your being. They require you to make big adjustments to your thinking. What troubles me most is that the priests have lied to the people for centuries."

Levi put his arm around Nura. "The priests of Maren's day knew they taught untruths about the Karani. In later generations, the truth had been forgotten. Maren and his people wanted the people of Atlantis to learn the truth someday. The following generations decided that they liked things just the way they were."

"Are the people ready for the truth even now?" wondered Nura. "I do not know. If they are not ready, the truth would tear Atlantis apart. The Karani also shared their technology with Lemuria. They did not share their blood with the Lemurians. It is good that we have Lemuria to counterbalance unrighteous Atlantean ambition."

A soft rap on the door interested their reflection. "Come in," invited Nura. She and Levi covered themselves with their bearskin blanket. To Levi's surprise, it was Lisa and Etor.

"Sleep seems to have eluded all of us," observed Levi. "We need to visit the archives again. Our visit gave us more questions than answers. I do not think that any of us will be satisfied until we learn more."

"That is not the issue, Levi," said Etor. "The knowledge of the archives is reserved for the king and his chosen successor. By unfortunate chance, we learned of it. We cannot unring the bell. What we can do is let matters remain as they are."

"No one has actually forbidden us to enter the archive," pointed out Nura. "I have custody of the key. How can it be wrong for me to use it?"

Etor snorted. "That is legalistic hair splitting and you know it! Only the king's officially designated heir has the right to access the archives, and at the proper time. If the king knew what has happened, he would forbid us to access the archives again and for our own good."

"We could ask the king for permission," suggested Lisa in apparent seriousness. Levi noticed the twinkle in her eye.

Etor seemed torn between his curiosity and the unwritten law. "I, uh, think it best not to trouble the king. I fear that we will learn even more disquieting things. The decision to enter the archives again is not mine. It belongs to the princess."

Levi smiled. Etor passed the buck to Nura. If she chose to return to the archives, he could satisfy his curiosity but without incurring any consequences. "I wonder what happened to the Colony Ship."

Nura and Etor stared at Levi. The thought hadn't occurred to them. "Perhaps I can shed some light on the matter," offered Etor. "During the reign of King Maren an enormous fiery object crashed in the mountains north of Gal-Rian. Mountain people call it the night the sky fell. It might have been a huge meteorite. It could also have been the destruction of the Colony Ship."

"The explosion created an enormous crater in an isolated valley. Few people visit the sight." Etor chuckled. "Even sophisticated, educated city people think of the location as a cursed place."

"I do not think the Karani would have destroyed the Colony Ship," said Lisa. "It had both practical and sentimental value. The ship was their only connection to their past and the other Karani people. Maren and his people also needed the Colony Ship's machinery and production facilities to recreate their technological base."

"Of course!" exclaimed Nura. "Most Atlanteans do not like to remember that we were not much more advanced than the rest of the world when the Karani arrived here. We can take credit for nothing that we received from them."

"Kemen has some access to the archives too!" realized Etor. "How else could the Chief High Priests have gotten the technology they bestow although in small amounts?"

"Kemen claimed he received it through revelations from Father Sun," noted Nura sourly.

"I almost forgot to mention the accounts of strange sightings by mountain people," interjected Etor. "Over the centuries hundreds of people claimed to have seen ghostly images of mounted warriors with flaming swords. When they got too close to the warriors, they warned the people to leave the area because it was sacred to the Sun Lords. The warriors fired what the mountain people call silent lightning at them. That would be an appropriate name for lasers."

"Superstitious nonsense!" scoffed Nura. "Still, mountain people are sober, sensible and down to earth."

"The accounts were all very consistent," said Etor. "That makes them very credible to me."

"When was the last ghost warrior sighting, Etor?" asked Levi.

"More than fifty years ago, I believe," recalled Etor. "I guess people have learned to avoid the places where the ghost warriors have been sighted."

"Then we will go to the archives again," decided Nura. "It will be the last time, Etor. I promise." Nura yawned. "I think that I am finally ready to sleep."

Lisa and Etor took the hint and left.

"I am descended from people who came from the stars," murmured Nura dreamily. "Levi, I did not expect you to handle the knowledge of the Karani as well as you have."

Levi laughed. "I am not certain that this is real. It seems more like a crazy dream."

Nura kissed him. "I think we are in the mood after all."

"Your will, princess."

After Levi finished showering and dressing the following morning, Galina arrived with breakfast. Etor and Lisa arrived seconds later. "Did you have a confrontation with the Guardian?"

"He refused to allow Levi and Lisa to enter the shrine as you predicted," admitted Nura. "Not even the possibility of incurring the wrath of the king would move him. Being defied by the Guardian greatly displeased me. Levi and Lisa solved the problem by accepting the Sun Path."

Galina hugged Lisa, then kissed Levi. "Is this some kind of holy kiss?" asked Levi.

Galina laughed. "That was personal. What are your plans for today, Nura?"

"Levi, Lisa, Etor and I have some important business to take care of first. Then I will get you caught up with all the palace gossip and the news of Aurelin."

Nura brought two guards along when she, Levi, Lisa and Etor returned to the shrine. When they arrived at the shrine, the Guardian raised an eyebrow at the sight of the soldiers. "I did not expect you and your friends to return so soon or with guards."

Nura ordered the soldiers to allow no one to enter the shrine until she and her friends left. "We are sorry to impose upon you, Guardian, but this is a matter of great importance."

The Guardian clearly heard the royal we. "As you wish, Princess Nura. I hope this visit will also be uplifting and memorable for you and your friends."

Levi smiled. "I have no doubt that it will be memorable, Guardian."

The royal party made its way to the archives as they had the previous night. This time they knew what to expect. Nura sat down in front of the computer and waited for the Keeper. The hologram of the Keeper appeared. "I am the Keeper of the archives. Who seeks to enter?"

"I, Princess Nura, descendant of King Maren, seek to enter," declared Nura boldly. She placed her hand on the blue panel.

The Keeper again scanned her DNA. "Enter Princess Nura, descendant of King Maren!"

"Show me a visual overview of the Karani Home World and its capital," ordered Nura. "I want to see how the Karani lived."

The computer screen lit up. An image of the Karani Home World appeared. It filled the entire screen. The blue oceans and continents looked much like Terra. Unlike Terra, water covered just over half of the Home World's surface. The largest three continents had lakes like the Great Lakes of North America. Great rivers connected all points of the compass like they had been made to order.

The Keeper informed them that the Home World had gravity 1.2 times that of Terra. Its gravity would have been endurable to humans, The Home World had twice the arable land of Terra. It exported much food to other worlds. Like Telmieria, it had a wide variety of flowers. Zurine, the star flower, was the favorite of the Karani. It had a powerful fragrance as well as beauty. The Home World had many Edenic places.

Everyone gasped in amazement when the capital appeared on the screen. Levi had not seen anything like it even on Telmieria. Houses, apartment complexes businesses and public buildings stretched out as far as he could see. No structure rose higher than fifteen stories. Abundant space separated the buildings. Despite the urban development, there was plenty of grass, trees gardens and parks. Transparent transport tubes crisscrossed the city. They whisked citizens swiftly and safely to their destinations.

Pedestrians and bicycle riders leisurely traveled along bike paths and sidewalks. City streets appeared to be used almost exclusively by civilian transports and military vehicles. Floaters flew over the ground traffic. Levi noted the complete lack of production facilities in the capital. When questioned about it, the Keeper explained that all factories had been built away from the cities.

The capital had been built in a sub-tropical zone. People wore light colorful clothes. They preferred blue, red, and yellow. Females dressed as revealingly as Atlantean and Telmierian women. Blue, brown and red skinned people lived in all the large cities and the capital. Most of the people were Karani.

At the end of the overview of the capital, the Keeper took everyone on a quick tour of the beauty and wonders of the Karani Home World. It had giant redwood forests, snow-capped mountains, volcanoes, white sand beaches and grass covered plains just like Terra and Telmieria. The original Karani Home World had more breathtaking waterfalls than either Terra or Telmieria.

"Keeper, I would like to see the end," whispered Nura.

Immediately the scene changed to an enormous hall that looked like a legislative chamber. It seemed to Levi that it seated at least one thousand people. Every seat was filled. Somber looking men and women who looked like scientists and high-ranking government officials representing every racial group. A venerable looking Karani scientist described in harrowing detail the imminent fate of the Home World.

The scientist spoke of the coming supernova that would obliterate the Karani system. The scientific teams couldn't determine what had started their sun on the path of extinction. They only knew that destruction would surely come. The king spoke after the scientist finished his address. He didn't question God or complain about his world's fate. The king thanked everyone for their efforts to send as many people as possible to safety on other worlds to preserve the Karani civilization and heritage.

From the time they learned of the coming supernova, all the people worked together to build Colony Ships as fast as possible. All people who had their own personal ships took as many people with them as they could to other worlds of the Karani Alliance. In time, those people would be absorbed into the society and culture of their new worlds. To preserve the fullness of the Karani civilization and history, the flower of the Karani were sent to the chosen world of Telmieria. The previous day, Prince Maren, the heir to the Karani throne, departed in the last ship chosen for Telmieria.

The king concluded his address with words that Levi would never forget.

"What we are about to experience is not an end but a beginning. For those of us who must remain on the Home World, it will be a swift transition from time to eternity, from mortality to immortality. This life is just a prelude to the joys of the heavenly realm reserved for the righteous and faithful. That is no cause to weep or wail. For the people who go to Telmieria, it is an opportunity to plant our seed and civilization in a distant part of the galaxy where the Karani civilization will continue."

"I will remain at my post until the end doing my duty as befits a king. I honor everyone who has worked so hard to help the people they will not join. Never have I been more proud of you. The qualities that have produced our civilization are the same ones that will ensure that it will survive. Your nobility and sacrifice will be honored and remembered long after the Karani System is gone. Peace be with all of you. May we all be together again in the heavenly realm with the Father."

The scene dissolved and the capital reappeared on the screen. People lined the streets, men women and children. The king and queen stood in their midst. They all looked up into the sky. Levi couldn't tell if he saw peaceful resignation to their doom or the peace of assurance that some part of them would live on after the destruction of their bodies. The end came quickly. In a moment blinding light filled the screen, then it went dark.

For a long moment no one could speak. Hearing or reading about some terrible happening didn't have nearly the impact of seeing it happen before your eyes. Levi recorded everything played by the Keeper. In time, a team would return just to download all the information of the computer. Levi glanced at Lisa. She looked shocked and stunned as if she had just witnessed all her family members being murdered. The Karani were her people.

"Keeper, what happened to King Maren's Colony Ship?" asked Nura.

To everyone's surprise, the Keeper didn't respond. Levi wondered if the file with that information had been corrupted. "Keeper, what happened to King Maren's Colony Ship?" repeated Nura. "Was it destroyed?"

"King Maren buried the Colony Ship in Atlantis before his death," responded the Keeper.

"Where?!" demanded Nura.

"That information is not in the archives."

Everyone felt deflated and disappointed to know that the Colony Ship existed but not where it lay. Atlantis covered a lot of ground. They didn't have the time or means to search the country one square mile at a time. Levi couldn't believe that Maren would preserve the ship but keep its location secret from everyone. It didn't make sense.

"I think we would be making a mistake in assuming that Maren did not want anyone to find the Colony Ship," said Lisa. "Why preserve something of great practical and emotional value only to prevent everyone from seeing it?"

"Maren should have left a map or at least some clues if he wanted someone to find the Colony Ship," figured Nura.

"Maren did leave clues," realized Etor. "Mount Helia and the Shrine of Alaya are just a few days away from the places where the ghost warriors were sighted. Those are the first clues."

"The Ghost Warriors tried to kill the people who encountered them," noted Levi. "They clearly want to discourage everyone from proceeding farther in that section of the mountains."

"No one was ever killed by the ghost warriors," countered Etor. "I think Maren was using reverse psychology to encourage the right kind of person or people to seek out the Colony Ship."

"You could be right, Etor," allowed Nura. "I think we should look for it. Everything we know strongly suggests that it is not terribly far from Gal-Rian. If my keeper permits us, I say that we go."

Etor smiled. "Nura, you not only have the right to find the Colony Ship. You also have a duty to do so now that you know about it. If we do not do it find the Colony Ship, who will?"

Nura gazed at Etor in wonder. "I thought I would have to pull rank on you to participate in the expedition. That will be all, Keeper." The hologram bowed then vanished. Nura rose from the chair.

"There is only one reason bring you on the expedition," revealed Etor. "The Colony Ship may only grant access to a direct descendant of King Maren. I am not. It will take a couple of days to acquire the equipment we need for our journey. Army rations will be space and weight efficient."

Chapter Twenty-Five

Levi, Nura and Lisa waited impatiently for their equipment and rations to arrive from Kimman army base. Nura expedited the delivery by making it a royal command. In less than half a day, everything had been delivered. Etor's men had everything packed and ready for departure by dawn the following day. They questioned why they would not be escorting Princess Nura. Etor declined to explain. He ordered the soldiers from Kimman base to see that no one left or entered the village until the royal party returned. The villagers didn't like it, but they could do nothing about it.

Galina came to say good-bye. She watched in curiosity and concern when she saw Levi with his rifle. Despite her closeness to Nura, she understood that the purpose of the royal party's trip was need to know. When Galina asked Nura about it the previous night, Nura replied in all seriousness that if she told Galina about it, Etor would have to shoot her.

Galina hugged Nura, Levi, and Lisa. "Good journey and Father Sun protect you. See that nothing happens to Nura, Levi and Lisa, captain."

"The purpose of our journey is secret, but it should not be dangerous," Etor assured her. "Princess Nura is in very good hands."

Galina watched in silence as the royal party rode off. She didn't have any sense of foreboding. Nevertheless, she would be very happy and relieved when everyone returned safe and sound. Usually when Nura visited her, they both forgot that their stations were far apart. Nura's secret journey reminded Galina powerfully that although they were friends, they were not social equals. She greatly appreciated that Nura had always treated her as if they were.

The royal party rode to the path leading out of the village to the north. Five soldiers guarded the pass leading out of Gal-Rian. The royal party watched as the soldiers denied entry to a group of confused and annoyed mountain people. The people were more confused than annoyed that entering and leaving Gal-Rian was restricted until further notice. After the royal party left the pass, they soon reached the neighboring hills.

Everyone felt a bit uneasy whenever they passed large rocks and patches of forest that could hide people shadowing them or lying in ambush. They all felt spooked after the ambush by the Lemurian soldiers. As time passed and they encountered no one, they gradually relaxed a little. It appeared that the soldiers had done a good job in clearing the area this time.

"How far it is to the closest locations of ghost warrior sightings?" asked Levi.

"Two days as the hawk flies, three for us," estimated Etor.

"And there you and Levi will do battle with the Ghost Warriors," murmured Nura. "That is our first obstacle and test. I wish I could be a participant rather than an observer."

"Your role in the expedition is smaller than mine, but still very important, Nura," Etor reminded her.

They rode most of the day, only stopping for lunch, supper, and brief rest breaks. Near sundown, they found a suitable place to camp. The land was flat with nothing that dangerous people could hide behind. Soon the last minutes of twilight passed. Levi gazed at the vast ocean of stars above them. He regretted that he and Lisa had to keep the truth about Atlantis and Telmieria from Nura and Etor. They deserved the truth, but the Time Control oath forbade Levi and Lisa from sharing it with them.

"It is strange that no one from Telmieria ever visited our world," reflected Levi "Perhaps Telmieria is much farther away than we suspect."

"For now, all we can do is wait and hope that Telmieria will contact or visit us," said Nura resignedly. "Hopefully, not while Maric is king."

"It is sad that Maren's family, friends and people never knew what happened to him," said Lisa. "I wonder if the Karani still remember him." Lisa knew well that Telmieria had not forgotten Maren.

After sharing their thoughts about what they might find on the Colony Ship, everyone went to bed. Etor had chosen a six-man thermal tent for them to sleep in. He wanted everyone to be together for greater security. It provided warmth in the winter, coolness in the summer. The tent also provided enough room for everyone to stretch out. Etor, Lisa and Levi each took a watch.

In the morning, they resumed their journey. They stopped at a spring along the way to refresh themselves. The path disappeared so Etor used his compass to keep them on track. Late in the day, they came to a hill that commanded the area for miles. Etor scanned the hill with his binoculars. "There is a man on horseback at the top of the hill. He does not appear to be moving. I think we have found a Ghost Warrior. We will see if he is in the mood for company and conversation."

Etor ordered everyone to stop when they reached the bottom of the hill. "Nura, you and Lisa wait here while Levi and I get acquainted with our friend."

"We must not be close enough to trigger a response," figured Levi.

Levi and Etor dismounted. They slowly climbed the hill. Etor expected a response from the Ghost Warrior at any moment. When reached the halfway point, the Ghost Warrior abruptly came to life. He held up a shield in one hand and a fiery sword in the other.

"Leave the sacred land of the Sun Lords!" commanded the warrior. Its amplified voice hurt Levi's ears. "It is forbidden to all mortals. Persist in your sacrilege and you will die!"

The warrior aimed his flaming sword at Etor. It fired a laser blast that struck the ground six feet in front of him. When Etor failed to retreat, the Ghost Warrior first a second blast that struck the ground three feet to Etor's right. The eyes of the Ghost Warrior glowed brightly. Etor dropped to the ground just before a laser blast passed the spot formerly occupied by his head. Levi dived behind a large rock.

"Fall back!" ordered Etor. He and Levi retreated down the hill dodging laser blasts that came uncomfortably close. When Levi and Etor were just one quarter of the way up the hill, the Ghost Warrior stopped firing. Etor studied the Ghost Warrior with his binoculars. "Our friend seems to have shut down. It must be programmed to respond to people when they get within a certain range. The Ghost Warrior warns intruders to leave. If they do not, it fires two warning shots. The third shot is a kill shot. All the people who encountered the Ghost Warriors survived the encounter with it. Apparently, they heeded the ghost warrior's warnings."

"I cannot believe that the Ghost Warrior has maintained enough power to function after all these centuries," marveled Levi. "We need to take it out to ensure that we have safe passage past the hill."

"Wait until tomorrow," suggested Lisa. "There is not much light left."

"You were wise to bring those grenades, Etor," commented Nura. "The rifles are useless against the Ghost Warrior."

Etor took the first watch. Everyone else went to bed. Morning came around much too early for Levi. He needed until after breakfast to completely shake off the stupor of sleep. Nura prayed for Levi's and Etor's success and safety. Levi thought he and Etor had more than a prayer of success and survival. Levi had pleasantly surprised Etor with his unexpected, good marksmanship. He felt very glad that target shooting was his hobby although not with projectile weapons.

"Do not take any foolish chances, Levi," ordered Nura. "You are not a trained, experienced soldier like Etor."

Levi chuckled. "I am painfully aware of that."

"Are you ready for your first taste of combat, Levi?" asked Etor.

"Not quite as ready for battle as you, captain. I hope that I do not embarrass myself or endanger you."

"I think you will do fine, Levi," predicted Etor. "You go up on the right and I will go up on the left. Good luck! Remember what we discussed last night."

Levi and Etor slowly made their way up the hill. Before they had gone two hundred feet, the Ghost Warrior came to life. "Land of the sacred Sun Lords!" it shouted at a deafening volume. "Forbidden to die in your sacrilege!" The Ghost Warrior began to fire wildly in all directions.

Etor cursed. "We would arrive here when the computer controlling the Ghost Warrior deteriorated to this degree. Levi, you occupy our friend while I get close enough to toss a couple of grenades. Keep firing at it. I suspect that it will prioritize the greatest immediate threat."

The Ghost Warrior stopped firing. Levi and Etor took advantage of the lull to get much closer. There were a few large rocks they could hide behind along the way. As Etor had expected, Levi's firing occupied the Ghost Warrior's complete attention. His bullets bounced harmlessly off it. Etor only needed to get thirty feet closer to toss his grenades. He hoped that two would be enough.

Despite Levi's continual firing at the Ghost Warrior, it abruptly turned its attention to Etor. Etor barely managed to drop to the ground before a laser blast could cut him down. He hadn't gotten as close to the Ghost Warrior as he desired. Levi decided to take matters into his own hands. To Etor's astonishment and consternation, Levi got up and charged the Ghost Warrior letting out a Rebel yell. When the Ghost Warrior turned to fire at Levi, he hit the ground.

That was all the distraction Etor needed. He charged the Ghost Warrior and tossed two grenades when he was fifteen feet away, then dived behind the last rock before his target. Seconds later, the grenades exploded one after the other. They toppled the Ghost Warrior. The lights in its eyes winked out. Etor and Levi warily approached the fallen Ghost Warrior.

Etor looked over his handiwork and smiled. "I knocked out the power source. Our friend is quite dead."

"Those grenades pack a powerful punch, Etor," commented Levi after surveying the remains of the Ghost Warrior.

Etor gazed at Levi with pride and respect. "Levi, I do not know if you are brave or just crazy. Were you not scared?"

" Every second!" confessed Levi. "Courage is the mastery of fear, not the absence of it. Not bad for someone who is untrained and inexperienced in combat. Everything seemed so unreal." Levi could now say that he had looked the Great Death in the eye. He hadn't blinked.

Etor and Levi fired off a victory round before heading down the hill. Nura and Lisa praised and hugged Levi and Etor. Etor slapped Levi on the back. "Levi has courage. I would fight at his side anytime, after he gets some army training."

Nura beamed with pride. "That is high praise coming from Etor.

"You are a credit to the family," declared Lisa proudly. "Papa Gideon and mama Amara will be so proud."

"Appalled is more like it," muttered Levi under his breath. Maybe that detail would be best left out of the mission report.

Etor took Nura aside and whispered something into her ear. She smiled and nodded her head. Nura rejoined Levi and ordered him to kneel before her. "For valor in service to the crown I, Princess Nura, bestow upon you, Levi Thurman, a commission as Sub Lieutenant in the army of Atlantis."

"The king must ratify it, but I am sure that he will," interjected Etor.

"We assign you permanently to the Palace Guard," continued Nura. "You will take orders only from the king, myself, and the Captain of the Guard during your service. Congratulations, Sub Lieutenant Thurman!"

Etor grinned. "Before you begin your service, you must go through all the training required of a member of the Sun Legion. I will train you myself. Your training will begin after the Feast of Maren. Your rank is honorary until you successfully complete your training. A member of the Palace Guard serves until the age of retirement. He can only be released by order of the king or queen. Neither King Maric nor Queen Nura will grant you that release, although for very different reasons. You can be honorably discharged in case of severe permanent injury or loss of limb."

Levi chuckled. "I do not plan to shoot off my foot to get a discharge from King Maric's service."

Lisa saluted Levi. "Any orders, Sub Lieutenant Thurman, sir?"

Levi thought for a moment. "Scratch my back. I have an itch I cannot reach."

Chapter Twenty-Six

Etor got the map printout of the area from his saddlebag. He spread it out over the ground. "I marked all the locations of the Ghost Warrior sightings. Coincidentally or maybe not coincidentally, all of them point to the access points of that valley in the middle."

"Has anyone ever visited that valley?" asked Nura.

"The valley has nothing of interest or value that I am aware of," replied Etor. "I do know that it is uninhabited. It has no mines or other human activity."

"How far away is the valley?" asked Lisa.

"About five or six days by horse," estimated Etor. "The trails ahead are narrow and rocky. Maren has surely placed other challenges in our path. According to the latest weather report, we can expect rain in two days. It should not be very heavy and just last one day. Our rain gear will keep us dry as well as our tent. Time to get moving. I want to cover as much ground as possible before it rains."

Etor led the royal party at a brisk pace, but without taxing his charges or the horses. The first day passed quickly and uneventfully. They encountered no humans or animals. The level ground helped them to make good time. Near sunset, the sky began to cloud up. By the time they went to bed, clouds filled the sky. The next day they woke up to a steady rain. After eating their rations, the royal party resumed their journey.

At the end of the day, the rain continued. When they woke up the following day, they found to their annoyance that the rain fell steadily. When Nura complained about the rain lasting longer than predicted, Etor reminded her that weather forecasting was an educated guess at best. After two straight days of rain, only Etor didn't complain about it. Everyone felt relief when the sky was completely clear when the new day dawned.

Etor detoured to a stream two hours away. They discovered to their delight that it had enough water for them to bathe in. Etor checked and found that it was safe to drink. After filling their canteens, everyone bathed. It felt good to be clean and fresh again. Etor reminded his charges that it would be the last time they would be bathing before they returned to Gal-Rian.

On the morning of the sixth day, the royal party reached the western approach to the valley. He took out his binoculars and studied the trail ahead. "The trail looks clear as far as I can see," announced Etor. "I wonder what else Maren has in store for us."

As the royal party proceeded up the mountain trail, Etor slowed their pace. The trail was wide enough for two horses, but Etor ordered everyone to follow him in single file. Levi followed six feet behind him. Nura and Lisa also maintained a six feet separation.

Etor became alert when he heard a metallic click. He immediately spurred his horse forward. Two seconds later, four-foot-high sharp spikes shot up from the ground. Then they slowly withdrew into the ground. Levi rode slowly to the spot near where the trap had been triggered. He and Etor figured how to get by the trap safely, then one by one Levi, Nura and Lisa safely passed by it.

"I think I prefer traps like the Ghost Warrior," decided Levi. "The danger is visible rather than hidden."

"That makes two of us," agreed Etor. "We must proceed even slower now. I am glad that we still have plenty of daylight left."

The higher they went, the more anxious they became. It was not a question of if they would face another trap but when. On the bright side, the first trap confirmed that they were on the right track. Before the royal party left Gal-Rian, Etor made certain that no overflights to the area had been scheduled for the next month.

Despite the dangers and tension, Levi thought Nura was enjoying the adventure. For the first time in her life, she faced danger and risk. Levi expected that Nura would have some difficulty adjusting to her golden cage at the palace after experiencing the freedom commoners took for granted. Levi realized that his life in Time Control had shielded him from all risk to life and limb just as Nura's palace life had also shielded her.

Without warning, a spear suddenly shot past Etor's horse missing it by six inches. Etor spurred his horse past the spot where the spear had come from. He stopped six feet away.

"That was even closer than the spike trap," noted Levi with concern.

"There must be an electric eye that triggered the spear," figured Etor. He dismounted and took his rifle. Step by step he moved toward the spot where the spear had been fired. He held out the rifle to see where the eye was. Suddenly the spear shot out striking the barrel of the rifle. The force almost knocked the rifle out of Etor's hands. After a close examination of the rock face, he spotted the eye. He took out his knife and jammed it into the eye. Etor backed up, then moved over the eye. Three times he held the rifle over the eye. Nothing happened.

Etor returned to his horse and mounted it. He placed his rifle back in its scabbard. "It is safe to pass now," said Etor. One by one, Levi, Nura and Lisa passed safely past the eye.

"I doubt that we are the first people to seek the Colony Ship," said Nura. "We might be the first people who ever got this far."

"When the knowledge of the Karani is fully made known, there will be a big technological leap forward," said Lisa.

"Are the non-Karani people of the world ready to handle our science and technology?" reflected Etor. "It does not appear that they are more ready for the truth of the Karani than the people of Maren's time were. Will it take another six centuries for them to be able to endure the truth?"

"Will you tell the king about the dangers we faced during our quest to find the Colony Ship?" asked Levi.

Etor chuckled. "I have a bad habit of telling the whole truth even when it might be better for me if I did not."

Everyone felt greatly relieved when they reached the end of the mountain trail where it overlooked the valley. It stretched out a mile in all directions. Levi and Lisa knew that was much more than enough to hold the colony ship. From their vantage point, they saw nothing to suggest that there was anything unnatural about the valley.

Etor took out his binoculars and studied the natural trail leading to the floor of the valley. "The trail is about as wide as this one. If we take our time we should be all right." Just before Etor stepped onto the trail leading into the valley, a hologram of a smiling blue skinned man appeared before him. "King Maren!" gasped Etor.

"Peace be with you, my children. I speak in the plural. A man could not have reached this point alone. I regret that I cannot welcome you personally. By the time you see this image and hear my voice, my generation and I will have passed away. We Karani did not come from the heavenly realm. Our lost Home World was like heaven to us. I regret the necessity for the Sun Lord charade. The people of my day were not ready for the truth. Hopefully, your generation can endure it. You must make that judgment for yourselves."

"The time has come for the people of Atlantis to reach out to the stars. Regrettably, the good ship that brought ten thousand Karani survivors here after a supernova destroyed their world will sail among the stars no more. With the knowledge contained in the main computer, you can build your own spaceships. I wish I could see you take your first steps into the galaxy beginning with this star system. Seek out our people on Telmieria that both you and they can become one people. Please give my personal greetings and good wishes to the descendants of my brothers and sisters. Our robots will service and preserve the Colony Ship until you arrive."

"I am confident that you will keep my charge to spread the light of the Karani throughout the world. That is the Karani way. There are many races of beings in the galaxy. Many are civilized and friendly, many are not. All the people of the world must unite to defend the world from the enemies who will surely come someday. I hope Atlantis and Lemuria worked together to raise up the rest of the world."

"My children, the tests we placed before you were to prove your courage and resolve, not to injure or kill you. Nevertheless, there was the possibility of death. Only he who is willing to risk all deserves to gain all. From this point on, you are on your own. The Colony Ship rests in the valley, waiting for you to find it." Maren smiled enigmatically. "Look unto heaven for the illumination that will guide you. Farewell!"

It took a while for Maren's words to fully sink in. Etor sighed. "Maren greatly overestimated his descendants. None of them made the slightest attempt to share the Karani light with the rest of the world. Neither the clerics nor the kings wanted to surrender the superior position of Atlantis."

"Did the kings and Chief High Priests work together to keep us earthbound?" wondered Nura. "Dare I demand the truth from my father? Dare I not?"

They reached the floor of the valley safely and without incident. Etor carefully scanned the entire valley with his binoculars. He sighed. "I see nothing that indicates where the entrance to the Colony Ship is. It seems that Maren has left us without a clue to help us find it."

Levi and Lisa tried to scan the valley for the entrance. To their surprise and disappointment, their scanners didn't work. They realized that there had to be an energy dampening field in the valley. Levi and Lisa checked their scanners for damage when Etor and Nura weren't watching them. Lisa linked with Levi's mind.

"Maren must have anticipated that the person or people who found this place would try to find the entrance to the Colony Ship the easy way, boss. Maren is forcing us to depend on our wits and imagination."

"We forgot to have supper," realized Etor. "Let us pitch our tent here. We only have a couple of hours of daylight left so we might as well relax until bedtime. We will maintain our watches until we call for our ride home. I think is best not to make a fire. If some plane or floater flies over us unexpectedly, it may attract attention. My friends, I do not look forward to returning to the palace."

Chapter Twenty-Seven

The royal party wasted no time beginning their search for access to the Colony Ship the next day. Etor decided to begin with a perimeter search. They split up to complete it more quickly. It took most of the day to complete the perimeter search. After splitting up the valley into quadrants, they continued their search. Day after day, they found nothing. By the end of the fourth day, everyone had become discouraged. They began to doubt that they would ever find the entrance to the Colony Ship.

Everyone became frustrated and irritable. Although no one had suggested giving up the search, they learned nothing to encourage them or give them the slightest hope for success. For the last two days, Maren's words had nagged at Levi. He felt that Maren had given them a clue, but they just weren't seeing it. The Karani prince wanted to make them earn their success, not keep it from them. As they ate their evening rations, something stirred in Levi's mind.

"I think Maren might have given us the clue we need," announced Levi. "Do you remember the last words he spoke to us?"

"Look unto heaven for the illumination that will guide you," responded Lisa.

Levi smiled. "That is correct. What light comes from heaven?"

"Figuratively, the light of the Holy Spirit of Father Sun," offered Etor. "Literally, sunlight."

"Exactly!" said Levi. He pointed to a stone tower that looked like a giant finger. "For the last three days, I have watched the sun set over that rock. The shadow pointed to a certain spot in the valley."

"Yes!" exclaimed Etor excitedly. "The entrance may be where the shadow first falls! Thank Father Sun, for finally illuminating our minds. Tonight, we will know whether we are right or not."

Levi, Nura, Lisa and Etor waited impatiently for the sun to set. They fixed their eyes on the finger rock. To everyone's dismay, a large cloud began to move across the sky toward the spot where the shadow of the rock would fall. With agonizing slowness, the cloud crossed the sky. Just in time, it moved out of the way of the shadow.

Etor watched carefully where the shadow first fell. After lining up the spot with a tree he shouted, "Marked!"

Levi, Nura, and Lisa followed Etor to the spot indicated by the shadow. "If the rock is indeed the clue Maren gave us, the entrance should be within a fifteen-meter radius." Except for one large rock, the entire area was flat without any indication of an entrance to the Colony Ship. Etor and Levi eagerly checked the rock for some kind of control.

Etor sighed. "The entire rock is solid. There is no hatch control in it. I do not understand."

"Could the control be under the rock?" wondered Nura.

Although the rock was heavy, Etor and Levi managed to push it several feet. They saw the outline of a small circle. Etor cleared around the edge revealing a circular metal panel about eight inches wide. He cleared the dirt from the top. Etor pulled on the handle he had uncovered. Beneath the cover was a panel like the blue one on the computer in the shrine archives.

"Now it is my turn," said Nura. She placed her hand on the panel. It scanned her DNA as the Keeper of the Archives had done. Seconds later an access hatch opened. A ladder led down to the deck. Levi began to record.

"I will go first to make certain that it is safe," said Etor. "How did Maren dig a grave for a giant spaceship?" he muttered.

Etor drew his pistol and started down the ladder. Levi, Nura, and Lisa looked down at Etor. When he reached the deck, he looked around. He then moved out of their sight. For five minutes, they waited anxiously for Etor to reappear. To their relief, he finally came back into view, apparently unharmed and unconcerned.

"All of you can come down," shouted Etor. "The air is good to breathe. There does not appear to be anyone aboard. I did not encounter any of the robots."

Levi, Nura, and Lisa quickly climbed down the ladder. "We are actually in a spaceship that traveled thousands of light years to our world," noted Etor in awe.

"The ship looks great considering it is over six centuries old," said Nura.

Levi looked around the square room. The lack of an airlock suggested that the crew only used the hatch when the ship was not yet in space. One large sun dome illuminated the room. When Etor opened the door at the far end, it revealed a long corridor. A line of sun domes brightly illuminated it.

Levi had expected the Colony Ship to feel more like a library or tomb. He sensed that the spirit of the Karani still lingered. If the spirits of any of the departed Karani remained, they were peaceful ones. Levi felt that somehow he belonged there. Lisa linked with his mind.

"Levi, even if I were blind I would know that I was in a Karani ship. I feel like I belong here."

"Oddly enough, I feel the same way, Lisa. Through my Joining with Nura, I am in some way joined to the Karani through her. It's pleasantly strange. I now understand at least in part what it is like for you with your dual Karani-Terran heritage."

Etor led the others in a single file down the long corridor. They were wary, but no one felt like they were in danger. Etor ordered everyone to halt. "We need to get to the bridge. Without knowing the ship's layout, we could wander around for hours."

A strange looking machine appeared around the corner at the next intersection. It stopped and scanned each member of the royal party one by one. The box shaped machine began to move slowly toward them. It had several flexible arms that appeared to be capable of performing several different functions. The machine had eyes that could rotate three hundred sixty degrees. It rode on two sets of wheels.

"This may be one of the robots King Maren spoke of," said Levi.

"All Karani descendants and their native friends are honored guests of Colony Ship One," announced the robot in a monotonous mechanical tone. "Your weapons will not be needed here. We caretakers are programmed to defend all guests from intruders. In the name of King Maren, I welcome you to Colony Ship One."

"Are you a robot?" asked Nura.

"I am Maintenance Robot 44. My function is checking and servicing computer control panels and all electrical systems in this section."

"Are the lifts still functional?" asked Etor.

"All lifts on the ship are fully functional," reported the robot.

"We desire to go to the bridge," said Nura. "Can you guide us, robot?"

"There are currently no problems, checks or diagnostics requiring my immediate attention," replied the robot. "Follow me, please."

The robot led the royal party to the nearest lift two hundred feet down the corridor. It touched the door with one of its arms. The door opened automatically. They followed the robot into the lift. "The lift is voice controlled," the robot informed them.

"Take us to the bridge," ordered Nura.

The lift car shot forward toward the other side of the ship. Automatically the car slowed gradually to a stop until it arrived at the bridge. The door opened and the robot and the royal party entered the bridge. Automatically the door shut behind them.

"For the duration of the journey, the ten thousand Karani passengers slept in hibernation freeze," explained the robot. "Most ship functions are autonomic. The ship ran on autopilot until the caretaker Lord Akil was revived. Manual control automatically activated when Lord Akil left Hibernation Freeze. You are the first visitors to come here since the final visit of King Maren."

Levi hadn't expected such a small bridge for so large a ship. Six workstations with chairs spread out in a half circle behind the captain's chair. The six feet by five feet main viewscreen was blank. Nura walked over to the captain's chair and sat down. She noticed a blue panel like the one on the shrine's computer. Nura placed her hand on it.

The computer scanned her DNA. "Descendant of King Maren recognized," pronounced the computer.

"Computer, show me the Karani star system and all the star systems allied with it."

Four Terra size planets orbited the Karani sun. The third planet was the former Karani Home World. Each star system associated with the Karani system had a rising sun on it. Levi noticed that the Karani system lay almost in the center of the map. That would make it easier to respond to an attack on a Karani ally.

"Did the Karani have an empire?" asked Nura.

"The Karani Republic consisted of the original Karani System and thirty star systems colonized by the Karani over four hundred Terran years," responded the computer. "Forty-one allied star systems maintained close economic and military ties with the Karani Republic."

"Why did the Karani choose to relocate to a world thousands of light years away from their original home?" asked Nura.

"King Kalan and the High Council wanted to recreate the Karani civilization on a suitable world far from the Republic's enemies. Long range probes discovered the planet they called Telmieria five years before their sun went supernova. It had abundant water and an atmosphere comparable to the Home World. Telmieria was too distant for colonization. When the Home World learned of the coming supernova, King Kalan chose Telmieria to be the new Home World. He sent the strongest and most intelligent people there."

"Did King Maren leave any messages for us?" asked Nura.

The star map faded out. The smiling face of Maren replaced it. "Welcome to Colony Ship One!" greeted Maren. "I commend you for discerning the clue I gave you. The main computer contains a file with all the knowledge you need to build your own star drive spaceships. Ask the computer to open the file called spaceship. Our construction robots helped us quickly build the technological base of the new Atlantis. We retired them once they had fulfilled their purpose. I have programmed them to assist you in building the fleets of warships that I could only dream of. Good luck and Father Sun bless you as you move out into the galaxy. Honor your heritage always."

Etor sighed. "The Children of the Sun have strayed far from the principles that guided King Maren and the other Karani. They would be very disappointed with us for holding tight to the light and technology of the Karani. None of us have failed King Maren more than Garai, Maric, and their ilk. They built the solar gun without the king's knowledge or approval. They planned to force Lemuria's surrender. Then nothing could have stopped Garai and Maric from creating a world empire controlled by Atlantis. Garai knew the king would never agree to his plan. Now we know why those tanks were heading toward the capital. There is a bright spot to Garai's treachery, Nura."

Nura raised an eyebrow. "I cannot imagine what that might be, Captain," said Nura dryly.

Etor grinned. "Garai gambled that we would not discover the solar gun before he made his move against the king. The delightful irony of it all is, the Lemurians learned about the solar gun before we did. They informed King Adeil about it. He cannot allow a weapon like that to be controlled by the Garai faction. It would be suicide. Maric will not become king."

"Thank Father Sun!" exclaimed Nura with great delight and relief. "I feel like a condemned prisoner who received a pardon from the king just before being executed."

"We need to get back to Aurelin as soon as possible," said Etor. "We do not know how soon Garai will make his move against the king. Let us complete our tour of Colony Ship One quickly."

Everyone marveled at the ingenuity of Maren's people in making the most efficient use of space in the colony ship. From the Observation Dome at the top of the ship to the water recycling system at the lowest level, not one cubic inch of space had been wasted. Thin serenium bulkheads allowed the Karani to transport more people.

The Colony Ship had seven sections: hibernation freeze compartments, living quarters for one hundred people, engineering, maintenance, production facilities, food supplies preserved in hibernation freeze compartments, and water and waste treatment and recycling. It had an ion drive rather than the hyperdrive used by twenty-third century Telmierians. The spherical ship was an ark intended for a one-way trip. The Karani adjusted the ship so the robots could access any part of the ship to perform their maintenance and repair function.

At the end of the tour, the robot escorted the royal party to the compartment with the hatch they had used to access the Colony Ship. "Currently, only a direct descendant of King Maren may enter Colony Ship One along with accompanying guests," the robot informed Nura. "If you wish to grant access to more people, you can authorize it through the main computer." With that pronouncement, the robot returned to its duties.

Etor tried to call Gal-Rian for their ride home. To everyone's dismay, the com-link wouldn't work. "I am not certain if the problem is our location or interference from the Colony Ship. I will ride to the top of the trail and see if my com-link works there. If it does not, we will need to use the radio of the Colony ship."

To Etor's relief, his com-link worked when he was completely out of the valley. He contacted the king and requested a transport to bring the royal party back to Aurelin. Adeil told him that he would send Lord Kal to pick them up. He ordered Etor to return directly to Aurelin. Etor informed the officer in charge of Nura's security detail in Gal-Rian that the royal party would be returning to the palace.

After Etor returned to his friends, he had very mixed feelings. He deeply regretted that Nura and Levi couldn't marry. It was unthinkable to him that a joined couple would not be permitted to marry. It had never happened before. The king would have permitted their marriage if Prince Akil hadn't died. Etor decided that he needed to discuss the matter with the king. He didn't look forward to that discussion.

Etor thought of his own situation. The king had to approve the prospective bride of the Captain of the Palace Guard. Etor smiled. The king had already decided who he would marry. Etor had no objections. He thanked Father Sun that he didn't have to marry a female equivalent of Maric. All of Atlantis would be surprised when the king formally announced his betrothal.

Etor returned to Nura, Levi, and Lisa to await the arrival of Lord Kal. "The com-link worked once I was clear of the valley," he informed them. "Lord Kal should arrive in two hours. By order of the king, we will be returning directly to Aurelin."

Nura sighed. "It would have been nice to spend a few more days in Gal-Rian, but we have pressing business at home. Has Kal been informed about Garai's plot and super weapon?"

"Not yet but he will be," said Etor. "He is our most loyal and trustworthy general. Kal will be of great help in dealing with Garai and his faction."

Exactly two hours from the time Etor called for a ride home, Lord Kal arrived. The sound of the transport announced its arrival before it came into view. A minute later, it appeared over the valley. Slowly Kal set down his transport at a safe distance from the royal party. Everyone greeted him warmly and enthusiastically. Nura ran over to Kal and hugged him.

"King Adeil told me that you continued your journey after you were rescued from the Lemurian soldiers. It surprised me that the king permitted it. I must confess that I did not expect to find you in this isolated and ignored valley."

"All will become very clear once we speak with my father," Nura assured Kal.

"I have some interesting news," announced Kal. "Your handmaid Seren disappeared two days after you left Aurelin. She went to the Inn of the Seventh Ecstasy. Seren left with a strange man and has not been seen since that time. Neither Seren nor her corpse have turned up as of the time I left Aurelin."

"That is because she was a Lemurian spy!" growled Etor.

Kal chuckled. "Police and security forces sought Seren like a mother desperately searching for her lost child. No wonder the Lemurians managed to capture you. And to think I once considered marrying Seren."

"The king must be furious that the Lemurians managed to place an agent in the palace itself," said Etor. "I hate to think of all the useful intelligence that Seren picked up in palace gossip alone."

"Urian has been fired and will face a court martial for his intelligence failure," announced Kal. "He may even receive time in prison. Let us get moving. We can talk on the flight to Aurelin. I asked Zira to marry me, and she said yes. I want all of you to attend our wedding."

"Lisa and I would be honored, Lord Kal," said Levi.

Kal smiled. "Levi, Zira told me that you were one of the nicest and most enjoyable men she ever served as a bedroom companion, second only to me."

Levi reddened. "I appreciate her high regard for me. Who won the Master of The Sea competition?"

Kal frowned. "The Lemurians. We only won two races. On the bright side, I bet on the Star of Suminar at five to one. The payout greatly comforted me."

Chapter Twenty-Eight

Nura and Etor gave Kal a detailed account of their journey from the time they left Aurelin until the time that they arrived in Gal-Rian. Kal noted the dearth of details about their time in Gal-Rian. He also noticed the complete lack of information about what happened after they left Gal-Rian.

Nura promised that they would tell him everything once the king authorized them to share the information with him. Kal seemed very interested in their adventures in Teyron. He was very displeased when Nura told him how the chief struck her.

"The Chief of Teyron should be executed for that offense," commented Kal.

"My true skin color was covered by the pigment," Nura reminded him. "No one in Teyron had ever seen me. They had no way of knowing who I was."

Kal listened with great interest to Etor's account of the three challenges. He was amused that Levi had seen through the chief's scam with the two women. Kal admitted that with a fifty-fifty chance, he would have made a choice, not realizing he was being scammed. After Nura and Etor finished their account of their pre-Gal-Rian experiences, Kal brought them up to date with the latest palace gossip and news from the capital.

As soon as Kal and the royal party arrived at the palace, a guard informed them that the king wanted to see them in his Private Audience Chamber immediately. It suddenly occurred to Levi that discovering the archives beneath the Shrine of Alaya and finding Colony Ship One had changed Atlantean history. His interactions with Nura and his storytelling changed the past. Fortunately, they were changes that would have no negative impact on the timeline. Everything else remained the same.

The guards at the door of the Private Audience Chamber immediately permitted Levi, Nura, Lisa, Etor and Kal to enter. They all bowed to the king. Levi thought Adeil looked both pleased and annoyed with them.

"Nura, you, Kal, Etor and I have serious matters to discuss," began Adeil. "First, we all need to discuss your journey to that valley. You left Gal-Rian without notifying me. I thought you were still there. I checked with your security detail. The officer in charge informed me that Etor had left Gal-Rian with the royal party for an unknown destination. He and his men had been ordered not to say anything about it to anyone including me. Then a week and a half later, Etor called me requesting transportation back to the palace from an isolated uninhabited valley northeast of Gal-Rian. What was your interest in that valley, Nura?"

"We found the archives at the Shrine of Alaya," replied Nura hesitantly.

"How could you have possibly discovered the archives?" demanded Adeil in consternation.

Nura smiled. "I cannot take the credit for that. When Levi, Lisa, Etor and I visited the shrine, Levi noticed that my medallion fit the opening in the altar. When he placed the medallion in the opening, the door to the archives was revealed. I accessed the archives and learned the truth about King Maren and the Karani people."

Adeil frowned. "The Keeper permitted non-believers to enter the shrine?"

"Levi and Lisa embraced the Sun Path, so they had the right to be there," said Nura.

Adeil sighed. "Levi, I cannot decide whether you are a blessing or curse to Atlantis. I do not doubt that Father Sun has sent you here for a purpose. I only hope that we survive it. Like every heir to the throne of Atlantis, I received a medallion like the one Nura wears. My father took me to the archives. He told me that when I became king I had to decide if my generation was ready to learn the truth about the Karani. You can see that I judged that it was not. Perhaps unconsciously I did not want Atlantis to lose its superior position in the world."

"When we learned that the Colony Ship still existed, we had to find it," interjected Etor.

"The archives do not contain its location," noted Adeil.

"Levi got me to thinking about the sightings of the Ghost Warriors over the centuries," explained Etor. "I took a map and marked all the locations where people claimed to have seen them. At the center lay the valley where we ultimately found the Colony Ship. The traps we encountered told us that we were on the right track. When we came to the trail leading down into the valley, a hologram of King Maren appeared to us. He told us that the ship was in the valley, underground as it turned out. Maren gave us a clue that we fortunately figured out. The shadow of a natural rock tower revealed a hatch we used to access the ship. A robot gave us a tour of it. Maren told us to find the rest of the Karani who lived on the planet of Telmieria. He gave us access to the knowledge of how to build spaceships. Maren expressed confidence that we would share the light and technology with the rest of the world."

"And we Children of the Sun failed to do so," acknowledged Adeil guiltily. "Maybe the time has come to begin the process. I think King Bakri and his people should have some say in the matter. It concerns Lemuria as well as Atlantis."

"Your Majesty, I take full responsibility for the journey to find the Colony Ship as well as the risk to Princess Nura, Levi and Lisa," said Etor.

Adeil gazed approvingly at Etor. "Nura has never experienced real danger in her life. A king or queen who has never taken risks or faced danger, is ill prepared to rule. You also figured out the significance of the Ghost Warriors and connected the dots. We thank you for that great service. Levi, if my son Akil still lived, I would have permitted you and Nura to wed. The man she marries will be the next king of Atlantis. Maric, through his treachery, has forfeited his chance to succeed me on the throne. There is only one man who is not only capable of being king, but he also has my complete trust. That man is you, Kal. Nura, is Kal acceptable to you to be your husband?"

"He is," acknowledged Nura. She gazed sorrowfully at Kal. "I know that you love Zira and you want to marry her. It is a great sacrifice that the king and I ask of you. The survival of the kingdom depends on it."

Kal sighed. "Your will, Your Majesty. We need to arrest Maric, Garai, and their fellow conspirators immediately."

"No!" disagreed Adeil strongly. "Garai no doubt plans to make his move on the Feast of Maren. We will arrest them before then with my most trusted men. It is clear to me that the death of my son Akil was a well disguised assassination to open the way for Maric to become my heir. Knowing Garai, he contracted with the Assassins Guild to kill Akil. No doubt, he has contracted with the guild to assassinate me as well. Gotzon would not entrust the job or the knowledge of it to anyone else. Captain, it is time for Gotzon to face justice."

"Assassinate the King of Assassins," reflected Etor. "Very appropriate, Your Majesty. It is my honor and pleasure."

"We feel that the time has also come to end the Assassins Guild," decided Adeil. "I fault King Maren and our line for not doing so by now. Captain, I leave that task in your very capable hands. Levi, Lisa, do you swear by Father Sun that you will keep secret everything that you know of the archives, the Colony Ship and everything you have heard in this room today?"

"I do," swore Levi.

"I do," swore Lisa.

"Now the two of you must leave," ordered Adeil. "Nura, Etor, Lord Kal and I have affairs of state to discuss. Go to Nura's apartments. She will join you when we are finished."

"There is one smaller matter to take care of first," interjected Nura. "For his valor in service to me and the kingdom during our quest, I awarded Levi a commission as Sub Lieutenant in the army. At the good Captain's suggestion, I assigned him to the Palace Guard."

Adeil gazed with approval at Levi. "We decline to confirm the appointments. We have a job for Levi that he is better qualified to do. Levi will serve the kingdom, but as a Royal Counselor. Who better than he to assist Us and the kingdom to begin the uplifting the rest of the world?"

"An intriguing idea," murmured Kal.

"A Royal Counselor must be a citizen of Atlantis," pointed out Etor. "Levi is unfortunately a foreigner."

"A non-citizen named Friend of The Crown automatically becomes an Atlantean citizen," Nura reminded him.

"Will you accept the office of Royal Counselor, Levi?" asked Adeil.

For a moment, Levi couldn't wrap his brain around it. "If you feel that I am worthy and able to serve you as Royal Counselor, I accept, Your Majesty. May I still perform as a storyteller occasionally?"

Adeil chuckled. "We will see. Lord Kal, I strongly urge you to retain Levi as a Royal Counselor when you become king."

Kal smiled. "I would not think of wasting such a valuable resource."

"Until you are approved by the Council of Ministers, you may not attend state meetings and briefings," said Adeil regretfully.

Levi bowed. "I understand, Your Majesty." He and Lisa left the Private Audience Chamber.

"You have a new addition to your already impressive resume, Levi," noted Lisa. "Advisor to the king of Atlantis."

Levi smiled smugly. "No other Temporal Historian will ever equal or top that. I hope that I don't wake up and find that this was just a dream."

When they arrived at Nura's apartments, they found Zira and a handmaid they had never seen before. Levi figured that the new servant was Seren's replacement. Zira greeted Levi and Lisa warmly. Levi was happy that he and Lisa didn't have the responsibility of delivering the bad news about Lord Kal to her.

Etor parked his floater in front of the headquarters of the Assassins Guild. His men had already taken care of all the guards watching the building. Wearing civilian clothes, they quietly eliminated the guild guards with knives. Etor walked into the building unchallenged by the assassins who observed him after he entered. The unexpected and unprecedented visit of the king's chief protector astonished and puzzled them.

When Etor reached Gotzon's office, he knocked gently on the door. "Come!" responded Gotzon. The Master of the Assassins Guild stared wide eyed at his unexpected visitor. "The Captain of the Palace Guard," marveled Gotzon. "This is historic. Does the king desire the guild to do a job for him? If so, you should have been more discreet, captain."

Etor smiled unpleasantly. "You are considered the greatest assassin of the last five centuries, and rightly so. Who else could assassinate the heir to the throne of Atlantis, yet make it look convincingly like an accident, and get away with it?"

Gotzon's eyes narrowed in suspicion. "That is both compliment and slander, captain. I thank you for the compliment, but I warn you not to express that opinion publicly."

Etor struggled to keep his anger under control. "Should I take that as a threat, Gotzon?"

"You think that the guild fears you, captain?" sneered Gotzon. "Adeil, like all past kings, is too scrupulous about the law to accuse and try me with no evidence. There is none."

Without realizing it, Gotzon had admitted the truth of Etor's charge. When someone said there was no evidence for the alleged crime rather than simply declaring their innocence, they acknowledged that they were guilty. Gotzon's ego and professional pride wouldn't let him totally deny credit for a perfect murder. Trying Gotzon and justly convicting him would be impossible without evidence. In the end, the survival of the king and the kingdom trumped all other considerations.

"The assassination of Prince Akil is both murder and treason. You made a contract with Garai to kill King Adeil. That ties you to his treason."

Gotzon laughed. "You missed your true calling as a storyteller, captain. I enjoyed your visit, but I must bring it to an end. I have a lot of work to do. You can see yourself out."

Gotzon watched in astonishment as Etor drew his pistol. "Gotzon, I arrest you in the name of the king for the murder of Prince Akil and conspiracy to murder King Adeil."

"You are serious," realized Gotzon. Slowly he took out his knife and pistol, then tossed them onto his desk. "I will not give you an excuse to shoot me while claiming I was resisting arrest. My lawyer will quickly spring me."

"After you, Gotzon," ordered Etor.

"No binders?"

"Professional courtesy."

Gotzon's men watched in astonishment as Etor took him out of the building. When they moved to stop Etor, Gotzon ordered them to stand down. After Etor and Gotzon left the Assassins Guild headquarters, a shot rang out. Gotzon fell dead on the ground with a bullet hole in his forehead.

A civilian shuttle drove up behind Etor's floater. Two men dressed in civilian clothes got out. "Dispose of this trash," ordered Etor. The men loaded Gotzon's body into the shuttle. Etor watched the shuttle drive off with dark satisfaction. For many years people would wonder and speculate about the death and disappearance of Gotzon. Only the members of the Assassins Guild would miss or mourn him. They didn't know that they would soon join their deceased master.

Chapter Twenty-Nine

After spending the night at the palace, Levi and Lisa returned to the inn. They decided to surprise Dark and the soldiers. After a palace floater dropped off Levi and Lisa, Dark and the soldiers drove up in Levi's floater. Dark jumped out and hugged Levi and Lisa. "Glad to see you guys back safe and sound. I hope it wasn not too dull for you, boss."

"Boredom was not a problem," Lisa assured Dark.

"Tell us everything and don't leave out a single detail," begged Dark.

Levi examined his floater carefully before they went inside. "Not a single scratch, ding or dent, Jer. Your floater privileges will continue."

They gathered around their usual table. Levi narrated the story of their journey as if he were telling a story in the main marketplace. Lisa jumped in when he forgot an important detail. Dark and the soldiers listened intently occasionally asking a question or seeking clarification. They congratulated Levi and Lisa for passing their tests in Teyron. Their discovery of the archives with the heritage of the Karani particularly interested Dark.

"Maren actually buried the Colony Ship," marveled Dark. "Will anyone in the Empire believe it? The truth was staring us in the face, but we did not see it. Prince Maren and his people, not Karani of our time, came to Atlantis. No one has ever transformed a country the way Maren transformed Atlantis. Levi, I am very happy and proud that you proved yourself to be much more than a Time Control bookworm. I must confess some surprise."

"I surprised myself," admitted Levi. "On the way back, I decided that we will focus our recording efforts on people and our relationships with them. That more than anything will show the humanity of the Atlantean people. We don't have the time or manpower to record all the written history and records of this age, let alone the complete history and records from Maren's time until the destruction of Atlantis."

"You won't get any argument from me," declared Kelly.

"I have a surprise for you and Lisa, Levi," announced Dark. "While you were gallivanting about the interior enjoying yourselves, I found the Atlantean spaceship."

"How did you accomplish that?" asked Levi.

"After a week of nosing through government and army computers, I learned absolutely nothing," said Dark. "That greatly annoyed me. It puzzled me even more. At first, I thought the computer defenses had stumped me. Finally, I realized that the project was completely off the books. For a couple of days, I pondered the problem. Then I realized that if you cannot get through the door, try a window instead."

"Meaning what?" asked Lisa.

"I attacked the problem logistically," replied Dark. "The base containing the project had to be large. Soldiers must eat and the base needs supplies and building materials. I discovered enormous amounts of food and materiel going to localities with no military or scientific installations."

"No official ones," noted Kinsey.

Dark grinned. "Exactly, my friend. I checked out each locality where the food and supplies went, one at a time. It took days to check them all out. As you can imagine, the last place I checked was the right one."

"What does the spaceship look like?" asked Levi.

"Why not see for yourself?" suggested Dark. "I can take you and Lisa to see it now if you have no other plans."

"We don't," said Lisa.

Levi let Dark serve as chauffeur. He knew how much Dark enjoyed driving the floater. "I must get one of these when we get home," decided Dark as he buckled up. "The Telmierian floaters have more goodies than the Terran ones."

"Your floater has something that no other floater in Atlantis has: an invisibility cloak," announced Dark proudly. "I installed mine in it while you gone. I took the liberty of storing your cloaks in the floater in anticipation of this moment."

"Sweet," commented Levi. "I will take my floater with me when we go home."

"Will the Time Council let you keep it?" wondered Lisa. "It was a personal gift so it should. We can load a lot of artifacts in it. We can't backpack them."

Dark took the floater to two thousand feet above the city, then headed northwest. He detected no other airborne vehicles in radar range. When Dark thought no one was looking, he activated the invisibility cloak. The floater faded from sight.

"We are only invisible from the outside as you can see," noted Dark. "It takes getting used to."

"How tight is the base security?" asked Lisa.

"Not tight enough to keep me out, visible or invisible," boasted Dark. "I must confess that the lack of high-tech security measures puzzles me. The military could have used motion detectors and heat sensors, but no one seemed to think that they were necessary. If Garai wants to make our trespassing easier, why fight it?"

In slightly under two hours, the secret base with the spaceship came into view. Dark checked the southern side of the base for stationary guards and roving patrols. Fortunately, the floaters made little noise. Dark moved the floater thirty feet over the security fence. He drove past buildings and facilities until he came to the hanger housing the Atlantean spaceship. Dark set down the floater where it seemed less likely for anyone to bump into it.

"Follow me," said Dark.

"If you installed your cloak in the floater, you will be visible once you leave the floater," pointed out Levi.

Dark grinned. "While you were gone, Time Control sent a message informing us that Timeship One is now in service. I requested another cloak to replace the one I installed in the floater. I said that mine had malfunctioned. Before I knew it, my special order arrived."

Dark led everyone to the hanger containing the spaceship. After making certain that no one saw them, Dark effortlessly picked the lock of a side door. Levi studied the spaceship. The saucer shaped craft was a lot smaller than he expected. Then he remembered that the Atlanteans didn't need a bigger one to develop the technology. Once they worked all the bugs out of the spaceship, they would increase the size of succeeding generations until they were large enough to haul passengers and freight.

"The ship has a two-man crew," began Dark. "Its graviton drive is not as sophisticated as ours, but just as serviceable. The designers didn't waste one cubic inch of space like true Karani. Next week the spaceship will make its first flight, just a few orbits around the world. If that flight goes well, the next flight will be a trip to the moon."

"Graviton power is fine for interplanetary travel but not interstellar," noted Lisa. "I wonder if Atlantis would have developed hyperspace drive if it hadn't been destroyed."

"I heard some interesting conversations between some scientists and General Garai," continued Dark. "The General wants to build a space station and orbital shipyard. I do not think he appreciates the challenges of working in zero gee."

"We are definitely taking the spaceship with us when we leave," decided Levi. "It will be hard for any future missions to equal or top that. Flying the spaceship home will be your job, Jer. Your dossier says you can pilot just about anything."

"The ship is not bad for a first try," granted Dark "It is very advanced compared to Terra's manned rockets and space shuttles of the twentieth century."

Levi gazed at Dark in wonder. "I never imagined that you were a space travel history buff. One of the sergeants can drive my floater. I will take back all the coins we didn't need for our expenses. Since all the Atlantean currency will soon end up in Davy Jones locker, we, meaning you Jer, will acquire enough coins and paper money to fill the floater."

Dark laughed. "Thank you for giving me the best jobs, Boss. Will the Time Council mind if I dedicated a bag or two for my retirement."

"Why not?" figured Levi. "You have earned it. We need to know if the spaceship will be available when we leave. If it won't be, you will need to steal it and stash it someplace handy. Emperor Marcellus did Time Control a huge favor when he chose you as the Telmierian Special Observer for the mission."

Dark smiled slyly. "I have no doubt that my part in this mission will surprise him when he learns of it. Can we head back to Aurelin now, Levi? I am having dinner with Kanya and her parents. I do not want to be late."

"We really have written ourselves into the story of Atlantis, haven't we Jer," mused Levi. "All right. I guess we are done here. It's strange. We have just three more weeks left, yet nothing indicates the destruction of Atlantis is imminent. It's a sad end to a great story."

As soon as Dark dropped off Levi and Lisa at the inn, he drove leisurely to Kanya's parents' estate. He had enough time to arrive early so he had no need to rush. Dark greatly appreciated and respected Kanya's parents for being practical and sensible about his relationship and Joining with her. Strangely enough, they liked and respected him. Dark hoped that Kanya's family escaped the destruction.

When Dark arrived at the estate, Kanya was outside waiting for him. She smiled. "You are always where you need to be when you need to be there. To me, a gentleman's punctuality shows that he values his lady and her time. You never take me for granted."

"I only return your courtesy and respect," said Dark.

Dark and Kanya went inside. They went to the dining room where Keril and Aldora awaited them. After they sat down, servants began to bring in the food. "The time has come for us to discuss your wedding to Kanya, Jerrel," announced Keril.

"Before we do, I have an announcement to make," interjected Dark. "I have decided that I can honestly embrace the Sun Path. After reading the Book of Commandments and pondering its teachings, I acknowledge that there is no God but Father Sun."

"That means we can get married in the Temple of The Sun!" exclaimed Kanya in delight. Then she gazed searchingly at Dark. "Are you doing this just for me?"

Dark shook his head. "I am doing it for me. When I was a child, I received no religious instruction of any kind. I grew up to be a man without character, integrity, or concern about anyone. People were just tools to be used for my benefit. By the grace and mercy of Father Sun, my friends Levi and Lisa came into my life. Their lives showed me how empty mine was. Their friendship has made me a much better man. When I experienced the Joining with Kanya, it healed my spirit and revealed the divine to me."

Aldora smiled. "Your spirit confirms the truthfulness of your words. All her life, Kanya dreamed of a big wedding. Now she just wants a smaller wedding feast with only family and our closest friends. Instead of taking months to organize and prepare the wedding feast, it will only take a few weeks. Everything can be ready four weeks from today."

"The Chief High Priest Kemen himself will perform the wedding ceremony, Jerrel," announced Kanya happily. "It is a rare honor."

"May my friends Levi and Lisa attend our wedding?" asked Dark.

"Certainly," said Keril. "You have no family here so it is only right that some friends can share the most important day of your life."

"Are there any dishes from your home country that you would like us to prepare as part of the wedding feast?" asked Aldora.

Dark didn't think that Atlanteans would enjoy any of the unique Rigellian dishes of the Home World. After being away from the Home World for years, he lost his taste for many of them. Dark hoped Kanya could cook or learn if she couldn't. Lisa could teach her if necessary.

"I am content to enjoy the many Atlantean dishes that I have tried and liked," said Dark. "Some ribs Zelek style would be a welcome addition to any wedding feast."

"They are very delicious," agreed Kanya.

"I want to join the Brotherhood of the Sun as soon as possible, Keril," said Dark. "I think your priest should perform the ceremony."

The suggestion pleased Kanya and her parents. "I will call Reverend Zarek after dinner. I am certain that he will be delighted to participate in bringing a heathen into the fold."

Dark chuckled. "Thank you for not saying barbarian, Keril."

Kanya smiled. "There is nothing barbaric about you, love."

"Thanks to Father Sun and you," agreed Dark. And his preparation for his mission.

Dark considered the man he was with the man he had become because of Kanya. Rigellian men would say he had been neutered. When the mission began, Dark would have agreed. Manhood was not defined by rudeness, cruelty, selfishness and indulgence in sensual pleasure. The Karani had real iron Rigellians missed by only looking at their civilized ways and manners. No wonder the Home World never made much progress. Dark resolved to raise his sons Karani.

Chapter Thirty

General Zarian arrived alone without an escort at the main gate of General Garai's estate. Only his driver knew of his presence there. He was sworn to secrecy. The guards allowed the general to pass without question. When Zarian reached the front door of the main house, the guard at the door ushered him inside and notified Garai of Zarian's arrival. An escort took him to the door of Garai's office.

The escort knocked on the door, then opened it. "General Zarian to see you, sir."

"Come in, Zarian," invited Garai. He dismissed the guard and ordered that no one disturb them. Garai gazed in puzzlement and curiosity at his unexpected guest. "What are you doing here, Zarian. Why are you not at Project Sun Lord where you belong?"

"Because there is no more Project Sun Lord!" growled Zarian.

"What do you mean?" demanded Garai.

Zarian lowered his voice as if fearing that someone might overhear him. "Three hours ago, fighters came out of nowhere and descended on the base. They destroyed everything above ground. Four companies of soldiers followed the air attack. One of the survivors informed me that all the scientists and techs had been shot. The attackers destroyed all the computers and hard copy files. Had I been at the base during the attack, I am certain that I would now be dead."

Garai cursed. "Somehow the king learned about the solar gun. I cannot imagine how. I knew Adeil would not approve of it. That is why I kept all knowledge of it from him. If someone's wagging tongue tipped him off, I will find him and make certain that his tongue will wag no more. By a strange coincidence, Gotzon disappeared two days ago. No one has any idea where he is."

"Could Adeil have gotten wind of our plan to take him out?" wondered Zarian. "That would explain Gotzon's disappearance."

Garai grimaced. "If the king had any evidence of our scheme, we would now be in prison or dead. Killing Adeil is no longer an option. The only assassin we could trust with the job is Gotzon. If Maric marries Nura, our plans will still work out in the end."

"Project Sky Bridge is still secret and safe," Zarian reminded Garai. "If it remains secret, we will still have space-based weapons. It will just take longer than we desired or expected."

"I wonder..." murmured Garai. "One thing has been bothering me for weeks: that foreign storyteller, Levi. He comes to Atlantis from some unknown country. While he performed in Market Square, Nura providently passes by in her floater, escorted by Maric no less. Princess Nura takes a fancy to him and invites him to the palace. Since that time, he has been a fixture there. Levi and Nura are like best friends. I would not be surprised if they were also lovers. Adeil permits this and shows no indication that he had a problem with it."

"A strange thing considering that Maric will soon become heir to his throne," reflected Zarian. "What is behind this calculated insult and disrespect to him, and by extension you? Could it be that Adeil plans to declare Levi his heir instead of Maric?"

Garai laughed off the idea. Then he stopped laughing. "No, it is too crazy. The people would not accept a foreigner peasant as king."

"You think so? Levi is very popular with the commoners. He has charm, a quality Maric lacks. Levi does not look, speak, or act like a peasant. I wonder if he is one. Through being named Friend of the Crown, Levi gained Atlantean citizenship. If he joined the Brotherhood of Father Sun, there would be no legal impediment to him marrying Princess Nura or assuming the throne."

"True," acknowledged Garai uneasily. "But let us be realistic. It is far more likely that Adeil would replace Maric with Lord Kal. He is completely loyal to Adeil and an excellent leader, popular with the army and the people. If the people could choose their king, they would surely choose Kal. We must wait until the Feast of Maren when Adeil declares his heir. I fear that we underestimated Adeil."

Chapter Thirty-One

Just days after Levi and the team returned to Aurelin, King Adeil officially nominated Levi as a Royal Advisor. Within an hour, Adeil sent the nomination to the Council of Ministers. The nomination and the speed at which it had been sent for confirmation astonished the ministers. They understood clearly that the king wanted the storyteller to be confirmed and quickly. They also understood the king expected a thorough consideration of the nominee, not a rubber-stamped confirmation.

A few ministers seemed to understand the king's thinking. The others thought the king might be losing his mind. As the Council discussed Levi, they began to view him with a more open mind. The members were impressed by his command of the Atlantean language and his civilized ways. They all agreed that Levi was not a barbarian. The more the Council members thought about him, the more difficult it was for them to believe that Levi had come from a barbarian country.

A good advisor was not a yes man. He challenged conventional thinking and provided a different perspective. A king who punished rather than rewarded independent thinkers, received bad or useless counsel. King Adeil, unlike most previous kings, understood that wisdom and probity were not the exclusive possession of the aristocracy. The Council acknowledged that Adeil was the greatest king since Maren. After hours of deliberation, the Council of Ministers made their decision about Levi's nomination. Without delay, it informed the king of its decision.

Nura watched with pride and appreciation as she listened to Levi as he performed his stories for the servants of the royal family. Adeil allowed Levi to use the Hall of Audiences. The servants' work schedule hadn't allowed any of them to attend Levi's performances in the marketplace. Levi no longer performed in public. Nura suspected that Levi came from an aristocrat family, but pretended to be a commoner. His kindness to the servants endeared them to him.

Her Joining with Levi revealed a truly kingly soul. Levi had leadership ability, but sought no government office. That didn't surprise her. Service to the country demanded much of an office holder's time. Nura saw how much of her father's time and energy ruling the country had cost him. A king or a high office holder who truly served the country and the people ended up being married to his job. Nura broached the idea of naming Levi as successor to the king. He didn't dismiss the idea. That spoke volumes to her. Nura decided that she would be willing to accept being, in effect, the mistress in the marriage of King Levi and Atlantis.

All the servants thanked Levi profusely after he finished his performance. Everyone returned to work except for Zira. Levi felt glad that the performance had lifted her spirits. The news of Kal's marriage of state with Nura had hit her hard. Slowly she was coming to terms with the dashing of her dream.

Zira hugged Levi. "Your performance means much to me and my fellow servants." She gazed sympathetically at Nura. "Doing our duty sometimes wrenches our heartstrings. Giving up the woman you are joined with is a much greater sacrifice than losing Kal is for me. Thank you for your example of strength and courage."

Nura sighed. "At least I knew even when I was a child that I might have to marry for the good of the kingdom rather than my own happiness. Until Akil's death, I had real hope to marry for love. We must trust in Father Sun's perfect knowledge, wisdom and love, Zira.

The arrival of Etor ended the musings of Nura and Zira. Etor saluted them. "Princess, the king desires you to see you and Levi in his Private Audience Chamber immediately."

Etor escorted Levi and Nura to the Private Audience Chamber. "Do you know why the king summoned us, Etor?" asked Levi.

"Maybe he decided to name you his heir instead of Lord Kal," joked Etor. "The king looked serious but not angry." Etor knocked on the door, then ushered in Levi and Nura. They prepared themselves for the worst.

"Sit down, Levi," invited Adeil. For a moment, Levi couldn't wrap his brain around the rare and unexpected honor he had been given. Levi hesitantly sat down. "I nominated you to be a Royal Advisor. Minutes ago, the Council of Ministers informed me that it unanimously confirmed your appointment. I do not expect to regret my decision. Nura completely trusts you. Anyone who can earn her complete trust, has my complete confidence.”

“One more thing,” added Adeil. “You need to become a member of the Brotherhood of Father Sun before you can serve as my advisor. Kemen will perform the ceremony tomorrow.”

“I fully understand and accept what that requires of me, Your Majesty,” replied Levi.

Etor gazed in wonder at Levi. “You have come a long way since the day you met Princess Nura in Market Square, Levi. Was it chance, or was it the will of Father Sun?”

“Maybe both. Uh, I have a problem, Your Majesty,” said Levi hesitantly. “It concerns the Chief High Priest.” He quickly explained how Kemen had mistaken him for a secret Lemurian envoy. Levi told him of the negotiations they conducted ostensibly for a peace treaty and trade agreement between Atlantis and Lemuria. Kemen had signed off on the treaty and agreement.

Levi could tell that Adeil was struggling not to laugh. He couldn’t quite suppress a smile.

“Why do you not just tell him the truth?”

“It was very enjoyable conducting those negotiations as if they were real,” confessed Levi. “I had to do a great deal of homework to pull it off. I would be very grateful if you would smooth things over with Kemen.”

Adeil chuckled. “I will deal with Kemen. More likely than not, he will be more impressed than angry. I will ask for copies of the treaty and trade agreement. If they impress me as much as they impress Kemen, he will present them to the real Lemurian negotiator when he arrives. Levi, I have a question that I want an honest answer to: are you a prince or aristocrat masquerading as a commoner?”

Levi looked Adeil in the eye. “To my knowledge, I am not, Your Majesty. Ability is not exclusive to royalty or the aristocracy.”

“Obviously,” murmured Adeil. “Levi, it is not appropriate for a Royal Advisor to reside in a common inn. Until you purchase a house or estate, you will reside in the palace.”

Etor grinned. “The office of Royal Advisor is a lifetime appointment, unless the king finds your service unsatisfactory and fires you.”

Adeil smiled. “That detail slipped my mind. I hope that Lisa and your friends will also make their home in Atlantis.”

"All of us would be very happy to remain in Atlantis until we die," Levi assured Adeil. Levi couldn't remain in Atlantis even if it had a future. A ticket to the past was always round trip.

Levi and Nura spent the rest of the day discussing his new post. Nura told him that he was the first Royal Advisor to reside in the palace. Levi asked Nura what the salary of a Royal Advisor was. It amazed him that its equivalent was half of President Harrison's salary. She promised to do all that she could to get him up to speed. Levi knew that their pillow talk would not be the same for the rest of his sojourn in Atlantis. As soon as Nura was asleep, Levi left the bedroom and called Lisa.

"What did your scans of the fault lines reveal, Lisa?" whispered Levi.

"Nothing has changed since we first arrived in Atlantis," replied Lisa. "The end is days away, but there are no signs of an imminent earthquake or any other kind of natural disaster. Certainly, nothing catastrophic enough to destroy the island. We can't escape the conclusion that the destruction was caused by some human action or actions."

"By accident or design, Atlantis will die," reflected Levi. "From what we and the soldiers learned, the Atlanteans are very careful with their technology. No barbarian would have the knowledge to cause the catastrophe. No Atlantean would have the desire. I feel like a detective who ruled out the last suspect of a murder. All we can do now is wait and see. We will have Dan Preston here early enough to pick up all the artifacts and coins we have accumulated. That will take at least a couple of trips. It will be a tight fit, but there should be room for the team as well. I will be with Nura when the end comes. Be sure to pick me up on time. Coordinate everything with Dark and the soldiers."

"Will do, boss."

Kemen permitted Lisa, Dark and the soldiers to attend Levi's ceremony in the Temple of the Sun. To Levi's surprise, non-believers were permitted in the temple if they were invited by members of the Brotherhood of Father Sun. They could be guests for important events like membership ceremonies and weddings. Nura, Etor and Adeil himself served as witnesses.

The ceremony was much like the ones in the Telmierian temples. Levi felt a strong spirit in the temple. Everyone else seemed to sense it too. Levi accepted the responsibilities of membership without reservation. He believed in the Karani conception of God, the Father of the Universe. Fortunately, he read and remembered most of the Book of Commandments. The presiding priest tested his knowledge and understanding of it before the ceremony began.

At the end of the ceremony, Kemen placed a gold rising sun pendant around Levi's neck. He instructed Levi to always wear it as the Sun Path required. After the ceremony, Kemen and the attendees had a celebratory dinner at the palace. Levi decided to wear his Brotherhood pendant and Friend of the Crown medallion for the rest of his life. Someday, they would either become treasured family heirlooms or exhibits in the Atlantis section of the Time Control Museum.

Etor had important information that he had been keeping from the king. It weighed heavily on his heart and mind. Nura had told him weeks ago that she and Levi had experienced the Joining. He knew that he should have immediately informed the king about that important development. King Adeil needed to be aware of it. Then Nura was destined to marry Maric, so it hadn't mattered.

Maric forfeited his chance to marry Nura through his treason. The king decided that Lord Kal would marry her instead, being a more than acceptable alternative to Maric. Etor had only known Levi for a few months, yet he had learned much about the man. Although Levi continually insisted he was just a commoner, Etor didn't believe it. Neither could he believe that the Joining with a noble lady like Princess Nura could happen with someone lesser than she.

It astonished Etor, yet at the same time, he thought that it should not have surprised him when the king appointed Levi a Royal Advisor. Father Sun worked in mysterious ways, sometimes using unusual instruments. After much thought, Etor decided that Levi was the best man to help Atlantis to begin to share the Karani light and knowledge with the rest of the world.

A week after Levi became a member of the Brotherhood of Father Sun, Etor requested a private audience with the king. Adeil readily granted it.

Adeil directed Etor to sit down. He waited expectantly to hear what was on the captain's mind. It had been a long time since they last had such a conversation. Etor never came to him with unimportant or minor things.

Etor sighed. "Forgive my dereliction of duty, father. I have been withholding important information about Nura from you. You know that Levi and Nura have been lovers. What you do not know, they have experienced the Joining."

The news shocked Adeil. "Nura never spoke of this to me. I forgot that my mother had the gift of the Joining. It usually skips a generation, sometimes two. Even so, how could I possibly have imagined that Levi was the man she was meant to join with?"

"It was a very unlikely possibility," agreed Etor. "Father, I think it is the will of Father Sun for Nura and Levi to wed."

"Nura's husband will be the next king of Atlantis," Adeil reminded Etor. "The king must be of the line of Maren."

"By law, a worthy man or woman can be adopted into the royal line," noted Etor.

"A fascinating idea," mused Adeil. "But would the people accept Levi as their king?"

Etor smiled. "It would be the love story of the ages, the Princess, and the Storyteller. The people value and respect Levi as a man, not just a storyteller. They also love Nura. Her relationship with Levi is no secret, although they may not know it is more than friendship. No one has expressed any anger or displeasure about it. They probably suspect it. If Nura herself made the public announcement of her betrothal to Levi, the response would most likely be positive."

"This is a time of great changes," said Adeil. "Who better to guide us and the world into this new age than Levi?" Adeil chuckled. "Nura and I envied his freedom to live a simple, free life. Now I will condemn him to our golden cage. I hope that he will forgive me someday. Before the Feast of Maren, I will inform Nura and Levi of my decision. You will say nothing of this to them. I am certain that they will enjoy the pleasant surprise."

Etor smiled. "As well as Lord Kal and Zira."

Levi's historical work ended when he became Adeil's Royal Advisor. He spent two evenings a week with the king and his fellow advisors discussing the most important state affairs. Levi hadn't appreciated how much work the king did ruling Atlantis. The advisors didn't just give advice. They also served as overseers of the executive branch.

They had great power to act in the king's name. Regularly, Adeil demanded an accounting from all his advisors.

Having such power was a heady experience for Levi. Nevertheless, he felt no temptation to misuse it. His fellow advisors appreciated his hard work and quick progress. His advisory work proved to be enjoyable as well as illuminating. Nura surprised Levi with her knowledge of statecraft. They hadn't discussed it earlier, their focus being on history. Levi recorded every minute of his sessions with the king.

For the first time since he had joined with Nura, Levi had to close off part of his thoughts to Nura. He hoped that she didn't notice. It amazed him how seamlessly he had blended into the tapestry of Atlantis. Whether it was the will of heaven or not, it had happened. The same was true for Jerrel Dark.

Levi excused Dark from all historical work after he informed Levi that Kanya's parents had approved of his marriage to her. Dark had already provided tremendous service to Levi and the mission. Lisa and the soldiers carried on diligently and without complaint. Levi, Nura, Lisa, and the soldiers joined Dark, Kanya, and his future in laws at Dark's Membership ceremony. Not surprisingly, Kanya's priest, Reverend Zarek, officiated. Kemen would attend the ceremony as an honored guest. For a moment, Levi and his people forgot about Atlantis' impending doom.

A week after Levi joined the Brotherhood of Father Sun, Dark had his own ceremony. Before coming to Atlantis, Dark had never truly experienced happiness or contentment. He deeply regretted that Atlantis had no future that he and Kanya could share.

Dark knew that the man he had replaced was being held in New Washington just in case he was outed. The first thing he decided to do after returning to the present was to work out a deal with Solar Alliance authorities to remain with Kanya in the Alliance. He would use the real Jerrel Dark as leverage.

Now that he had completed his mission to his satisfaction, he would renounce his Rigellian citizenship and allegiance. He planned to offer his services to the Solar government and Time Control. Dark hoped that he could spend much time working with Levi on his future interaction missions.

Before he began his mission, Dark had planned to kill his father for his crimes against his mother and the mothers of his fellow bastards. His burning desire for revenge had finally overcome his strong survival instinct. Dark still desired to make his father pay. He would foil his father's schemes and embarrass him as much as possible. Nothing could be more embarrassing than revealing the truth about his other half-brothers. For the moment, Dark would just enjoy his lady and her world to the fullest.

The scientists who monitored the activity of Atlantis three volcanoes considered their jobs to be a punishment. King Maren ordered that they be watched continually so that no more eruptions caught the people by surprise. None of the volcanoes had erupted since the coming of the Sun Lords. Before the coming of the Sun Lords, the volcanoes erupted once a century. Now most Atlanteans consider them to extinct. Volcanologists knew volcanoes may sleep for thousands of years, but they could someday awaken from their slumber.

Despite the chilly relations between Atlantis and Lemuria, scientists from both countries maintained close contact with their scientific counterparts. Lemuria's two volcanoes had not erupted for more than one thousand years. The Lemurians also monitored their own volcanoes, not wishing to be taken by surprise either. Their scientists shared the boredom of their Atlantean colleagues. The last volcanic eruption had caused death and devastation that still burned brightly in collective memory of Lemuria.

Atlantean volcano watchers became alert when a tremor began near Mount Shacor on the Windward coast. At first, it seemed harmless. Instead of dying out, the tremors gradually increased. The scientists became alarmed when they heard that the same thing was happening at Mount Darkfire and Mount Starock. Soon the tremors became an earthquake that was felt throughout the entire kingdom. Small cracks appeared in the ground and city streets of Aurelin. Gradually, they grew wider and deeper.

Sergeant Kelly had dropped Dark off at Project Sky Bridge hours before the expected destruction of the island. Dark waited anxiously for the hour of Atlantis' doom to strike. He slipped into the spaceship when the tremors began. While everyone in the base was preoccupied with the earthquake, he started up the engines. He activated the invisibility cloak. Seconds later, it vanished from sight.

Dark took the spaceship up to two thousand feet and headed for Aurelin as fast as safety permitted at that low altitude.

Levi was at the palace with Nura. By now, Lisa and the soldiers should have taken the floater to the pickup point. When Levi was ready, the timeship would pick him up at the palace. He knew how much time he had left. Dark knew very well how hard it would be for Levi to tear himself away from Nura. He hoped that his friend didn't wait too long and get literally swallowed up by the destruction.

By the time Dark reached Aurelin, Mount Shacor had begun to erupt. It sent lava flowing toward the city. Many buildings had experienced much damage. None had completely collapsed due to the sturdiness of Karani engineering and building materials. Soon the cracks in the roads would make it impossible for vehicles to drive on them. To Dark's great surprise, most of the people headed to the harbor in a mostly orderly manner.

Dark somberly contemplated the destruction of a land and people he had come to love. He had found love, healing and the first constructive purpose of his life. If he could have, he would retreat into Atlantis' past and live out the remainder of his days with Kanya. Dark had a feeling Kanya's family would be all right. He planned to ask Levi to determine their fate for his and Kanya's peace of mind.

Carefully, Dark made his way through the crowd of floaters over Aurelin heading to the harbor. Soon Keril's estate came into view. Dark turned off the invisibility cloak. He observed the family servants loading food and water. A couple of servants carried the portable family treasures. All the servants looked up at the spaceship when they noticed it.

Dark landed the spaceship on a clear spot near the shuttles. Kanya and her parents came out to see what had attracted the attention of the servants. They gazed in wonder at the spaceship. Their astonishment increased when Dark opened the hatch and stepped out. Kanya rushed over and hugged him. "Thank Father Sun you are safe! What is this ship? How did you get it?"

"This is Atlantis' first spaceship," replied Dark. "I stole it from General Garai's secret base in the north."

Keril and Aldora hesitantly approached the spaceship. "This is truly a spaceship?" asked Keril. "Space travel is forbidden by the Sun Lords."

"Neither commandments nor law ever stopped Garai from doing what he wanted to do," noted Kanya dryly.

"How I got this ship is irrelevant," Dark reminded them. "Kanya, Keril, Aldora, I do not belong to this time. This day is a distant yesterday to me. Levi, Lisa, and our friends journeyed to this time and place on an important mission. The mission is over. Now I must return home. Kanya, I want you to come with me."

Kanya looked at her parents, then Dark. "You have never lied to me, Jerrel. I know that you would not be joking at a time like this. This is too much for me to process all at once."

Keril gazed in wonder at Dark. "Have you really come from another time, Jerrel?"

"I have," confirmed Dark. "My friends are historians who have come to Atlantis on a mission to learn about its history. Thousands of years from now your country is just a myth and legend."

"Then this really is the end," realized Aldora in horror.

"Keril, most likely you, your wife and other children will escape the destruction," said Dark. "I would stay with you and see that we all get to Lemuria if I could. The people who control the Time Door would send people to bring me back if I did." And even if they didn't, Dark knew that he would get desynchronization psychosis, then die.

Dark turned to Kanya. "Kanya, we are united in the Joining. Both of us would be unhappy and miserable for the rest of our lives if I leave without you."

"Will I be permitted to stay in your time, Jerrel?" asked Kanya.

"I cannot say for certain," admitted Dark, "but most likely you would be. Kanya, it is our only chance! If we do not take it, our separation and misery are assured."

"Go with Jerrel, Kanya," counseled Keril. "He is right. We will miss you and regret not seeing your children."

"I think it is Father Sun's will," decided Aldora. She hugged Kanya. "You and Jerrel visit us at least once, so we know you are alive, well and happy."

"If we are permitted, we will," promised Dark.

After saying good-bye, Dark and Kanya boarded the spaceship. Dark activated the invisibility cloak. Keril and Aldora watched in astonishment as the spaceship vanished from sight. Dark headed straight to the rendezvous point.

As soon as word came about the eruption, Etor began the evacuation of the palace. The palace guard regularly conducted evacuation drills. Just as they had rehearsed many times, the guards quickly and efficiently gathered everyone and moved them out of the palace. All off duty personnel had been ordered back to duty. Once everyone had been escorted out of the palace, they would help to evacuate the aristocrats living in Aurelin.

Etor knew that the terrain would guide the lava flow straight into the city. Fortunately, that would take a while. He took the lift to the Observation Tower. Etor watched in disbelief as Mount Shacor shot molten rock and smoke into the sky. Much of the city had already been devastated. The destruction increased as he watched. Etor's first duty was getting the king, Nura, and Levi to safety. He found the king sitting calmly on the throne.

"Your Majesty, Mount Shacor has erupted!" said Etor "Eventually, the lava flow will reach the city. Nothing is safe including the palace. Please come with me!"

"No, my son," replied Adeil sadly. "Atlantis is dying. I can feel it. I will die with it."

Etor stared at Adeil in bewilderment. His indifference to his survival alarmed Etor. He realized that no argument would persuade the king. "You must live for the people. They need you now like they never needed you before. Willingly or not, you will come with me!"

Adeil sighed. "My son, I prefer to die a king in Atlantis than live out the rest of my days as a refugee in a strange land. Go to the palace archives. Get the history of Atlantis since the coming of the Karani and the genealogy of the Children of The Sun. The glory and memory of Atlantis must not be lost. Then get Nura and Levi to safety."

Tears welled up in Etor's eyes. He couldn't bear to desert his king and father. "Go!" commanded Adeil sternly. "It is your duty and responsibility to preserve the line of Maren!"

Adeil was Etor's king first and his father second. "As you command, Your Majesty."

As Etor was about to leave the throne room, he stopped and looked back. The roof above the throne fell and crushed Adeil. Without warning, the lights went out as Etor reached the historical archives. Seconds later, the emergency lights kicked in. Etor summoned two guards and ordered them to take the box of records to the king's floater. He questioned several guards, but none could tell him where Princess Nura and Levi were.

Etor remembered that they usually went to the royal garden at this time of day. Surely they had already been escorted from the palace by other guards. Etor couldn't assume that. His heart sank when he saw a large fissure bisecting the garden. Etor spotted a handkerchief lying by the fissure. He picked it up and looked closely at it. It had Princess Nura's personal crest. Etor grudgingly accepted that his sister and Levi were dead. He would never leave the woman he had joined with. Before Etor could investigate the fissure, it doubled in size.

He ran to the floater, passing and seeing no one. Apparently, everyone else had gotten safely away. For a moment, Etor felt overwhelmed by a wave of grief and sadness. He had lost his father, sister, and the man he wanted to become his brother-in-law. Etor got in the king's floater and headed toward the harbor. Smoke and fire covered much of the city. Whole sections had already sunk deep into the ground. He called Kal and informed him of the deaths of Nura and Levi.

Etor watched helplessly as fire and destruction killed hundreds of people. A two-block wide fissure knifed through the center of the city. He saw no foreign ships in the harbor. Etor figured that they must have started to leave when Mount Shacor began to erupt. He noticed a man and a woman standing on the roof of a building just ahead. They watched the destruction around them with apparent calmness. The man seemed familiar. Curiosity moved Etor to take a closer look.

The man noticed the floater and waved. "Do you have room for a couple of passengers, captain!" he shouted.

"Zaki!" marveled Etor. He set down the floater on the roof.

The woman stirred from her catatonic state when she saw Etor. "Help us!" she begged.

"Care for some congenial company on the way to Lemuria?" inquired Zaki insouciantly. "My dear love, Alita, will show her gratitude to you every night."

Etor couldn't help smiling. Even staring death in the face, the master of the Thieves Guild had courage and style. He quickly got Zaki and Alita aboard the floater. Seconds after the floater cleared the building, it collapsed completely. Alita thanked Etor profusely and kissed him. Despite her disheveled appearance, Etor found her attractive.

Zaki patted his waist. "At least I saved my money belt. I have nothing less than five hundred gold sovereign coins. Wherever we end up, I can buy us a new start. Thank you for saving this miserable thief and his lover."

"I owed you that much for what you did for Princess Nura and Levi," said Etor.

Zaki had been so wrapped up in his concern for himself and Alita, he hadn't noticed the absence of Nura and Levi. "Captain, did Levi and Princess Nura leave with other guards?"

Etor shook his head. "A fissure swallowed them before I could rescue them. The king is also gone. He refused to leave."

Zaki sighed. "In his place, I would have done the same. Alita and I will start a new Golden Palace in Suminar. Stealing will not be the same as in Aurelin. Captain, you will have free unlimited pleasure at the new Golden Palace for the rest of your life, or at long as your libido lasts."

Etor laughed. "Zaki, let no man call you ingrate."

The news of Nura's death hit Lord Kal hard. She had been one of his closest and most trusted friends. At the same time, he felt guilty about his relief at not having to marry her. Kal checked around until he found where Zira had been taken. He loaded as many people as he could and took them to the ship where the palace servants had been assigned. As soon as he landed, he learned which cabin she was staying in.

He hurried to the cabin and knocked on the door. When Zira opened the door, she stared at him in disbelief. "Thank Father Sun you are alive, Kal!" She hugged him in joy and relief. "Where are Nura and Levi?"

"They are dead," announced Kal sadly. "Etor told me they perished when a fissure in the palace garden opened beneath them. I still cannot believe that they are gone."

Zira sighed. "Nura and I were more than friends. We were like sisters. Having you as my husband will make her loss easier to bear. Kal, if we have a son and daughter let us name them after Nura and Levi."

Kal considered the idea. "I can think of no better memorial or tribute."

Garai quickly received reports of the volcano eruptions and the powerful earthquake shaking the very foundations of the island. Although he had no science background, he understood that three volcanoes erupting almost simultaneously was not just unprecedented, it shouldn't even have happened. As the destruction increased, the entire ruin of Atlantis seemed possible.

Both Garai and Maric had been feverishly organizing the evacuation of the most important members of the government and the military. Garai hoped to save at least a few divisions and their equipment. He didn't mind serving under King Bakri in Lemuria. Garai felt confident that he could convince the king that the solar gun had been created by a rogue group in the Atlantean army. The Atlantean flagship would be a more than satisfactory substitute for the destroyed flagship Pendaran.

Garai began to formulate a plan to get Bakri to marry his daughter Princess Amaia to Maric. The fact that the princess found Maric distasteful was irrelevant. Maric had almost no chance of inheriting the Lemurian throne. He could become a significant power, nevertheless. Garai put aside those thoughts. Job number one was surviving. Garai's servants informed him that all his most cherished books, paintings and crystals had been loaded aboard his floater, along with all the gold and silver it could hold.

As Garai walked out the front door of the main house, Maric's floater landed beside his. Maric's servants had already left the house carrying his money and clothes. Maric had no sentimental attachment to his other possessions.

"We have done all that we can do, father," said Maric. "The thing I will miss most of Atlantis is our estate. Few Children of The Sun have estates as rich and fine as ours. If our new estate in Lemuria is even half as fine, I will be content. I had a company of my best men searching for Lisa. Unfortunately, no one was left in the palace when they arrived. She might well have been buried under the rubble. Having no further opportunity to marry Princess Nura, I would have found comfort in Lisa's arms."

"She was exceptionally fine as well as beautiful," acknowledged Garai. "Your floater is fully loaded. It is time to close the door to our past life and embark upon the new. A long time ago, I read about an old forgotten account of an Emissary who had been sent to Atlantis to call the people to repentance. He gave the people a year to repent, or they would be destroyed. Nothing happened at the end of the year. People concluded that the execution had been canceled permanently. If the account is true, Atlantis only received a stay of execution. The jury must have been still out. The verdict finally came in: guilty."

Lisa, Dark and the soldiers waited anxiously for the arrival of the timeship. They watched in horror as fire and earthquake consumed Aurelin. Seeing it with historical detachment would have been hard enough to bear. Seeing it with an emotional attachment to the people and the land wrenched their heartstrings. Lisa recorded everything from the time the destruction began.

It required all her emotional strength and professionalism to endure it.The unnatural end of Atlantis made Lisa think of the destruction of the Karani System millennia ago. Nothing natural had caused the Karani sun to go supernova. The destruction of Atlantis was equally unnatural. Lightning had struck the Karani twice. Lisa wondered if anyone would ever learn what had caused the obliteration of two Karani civilizations. Neither the Karani System nor Atlantis deserved to die.

Everyone felt great relief when the temporal field began to form in front of them. Seconds later, Timeship One passed through the door. The door closed behind the timeship. Dan Preston opened the hatch. "Timeship One is now ready for boarding. First Class passengers and privileged characters may now board." He gazed in wonder at the floater and spaceship. "Where is Levi?" asked Preston in alarm.

Lisa sighed. "He's saying good-bye to Princess Nura. Go get Levi, Dan. The rest of us will wait here."

Levi and Nura relaxed in the palace garden sitting on a bench near the star flowers. Levi felt glad that Nura had been very happy and at peace since King Adeil told her she would not have to marry Maric after all. She had entertained a small hope of convincing her father to make Levi his heir instead of Lord Kal. Levi knew that Nura would have enjoyed some happiness with Lord Kal. It couldn't compare with the happiness he and Nura enjoyed through the Joining.

"Thinking of home, Levi?" asked Nura.

Levi smiled. "And other things."

"Levi, will you forgive me?" asked Nura unexpectedly.

Levi gazed at Nura in confusion. "Forgive you for what?"

"For keeping you here in Atlantis and the palace with me, even knowing that you will be close to me and unable to share my life and bed. At times, it will be like torture for us."

Levi held her close. "Having you completely out of my life would be a worse torture." It was the bitter truth.

A mild tremor suddenly began. It gradually increased in intensity. The end of Atlantis had begun. Despite the distance from Mount Shacor, Levi and Nura could hear it rumbling. "Father Sun preserve us!" whispered Nura. "Mount Shacor has wakened from its centuries long sleep!"

Levi signaled Preston that it was time to pick him up. When he entered the timeship, the mission was officially over. More than anything, he wanted to take Nura with him. He was truly leaving a part of himself behind. Like the king and queen of the Karani Republic, Nura would not leave the vast majority of Atlanteans behind who could not escape the destruction of their country. Neither would King Adeil. Levi figured that the king would order Etor to save himself to ensure the future of his family line.

The ground beneath the palace and garden began to tremble. The shaking grew in intensity until Levi feared the entire palace would collapse. The ground in front of Levi and Nura began to crack. A fissure stretched from one end of the garden to the other. They backed away, struggling to keep from falling. The wall facing the garden buckled. The upper levels of the palace collapsed on each other.

"Atlantis is dying," realized Nura. "I can sense its life slipping away." She gazed in wonder at Levi. "You do not seem surprised about what is happening."

Before Levi could respond, Nura saw the timeship rushing toward the palace. It flew above all the floater traffic until it reached the garden. It stopped, then descended vertically until it landed six feet away from Levi and Nura. Preston opened the hatch and stepped out. "We don't have time to waste, Levi. Please make it a quick good-bye!"

Nura gazed fearfully at Levi. "Who are you?"

The Temporal Prime Directive forbade him to reveal his identity or mission to anyone else in Atlantis. In this instance, it would not matter. "Lisa and I are historians from the distant future," confessed Levi. "We came to Atlantis to begin the recovery of its lost history."

Nura didn't deny or dispute his claim. "It is unimaginable, but the Joining tells me you are speaking the truth. You and Lisa are like Atlanteans, yet you are neither Atlantean nor Lemurian. No barbarian land could have produced people like you. Levi, I can scarcely imagine what it was like for you to be here and a part of Atlantis, all the time knowing what would ultimately happen. I could feel your emotion, but I could not understand what was behind it. Please take me with you, Levi! Let Atlantis and the line of Maren live on through me!"

"I swore an oath to obey all Time Control regulations even at the cost of my life. Bringing people from the past to the present permanently is forbidden."

Nura did not weep or reproach him. She understood perfectly the demands of duty and honor. Nura kissed him good-bye. "Remember me, and everyone you came to know and love."

Levi had no need to say, 'I love you.' The Joining made that unnecessary. Levi boarded Timeship One. He closed the hatch behind him. "I hope you tell me all about that someday, Levi," said Preston. He wasted no time getting back to the floater and spaceship. The swirling colors announced the opening of the Time Door. Preston moved the timeship through the door. The floater and spaceship quickly followed. In the confusion and chaos, no one noticed the opening and closing of the temporal doorway.

Levi didn't say much to Preston on the journey home. He had no desire to speak about anything that he had experienced. After what seemed like hours to Levi, the timeship synchronized with the present. The timeship maneuvered around the rift and set down on the open area before the Time Door. As soon as Levi and Preston disembarked, the Chief Artifacts inspector rushed past them into the timeship.

Preston chuckled. "Russ will drool when he sees what you brought back, Levi. Wait until he notices that spaceship and floater. Did you bring back anything just for yourself?"

Levi felt the Friend of The Crown medallion and the gold pendant under his shirt. "A few gifts from friends."

The spaceship and floater landed on the other side of the platform. Lisa, Dark, Kanya and the soldiers disembarked. They joined Levi and Preston. Levi smiled. "It looks like you brought home a souvenir of your own, Jerrel."

Everyone's eyes widened in astonishment when they saw another Jerrel Dark flanked by two Time Control security men approaching them. Levi looked at one Dark, then the other. He didn't think that Dark had a twin brother the Empire hadn't told Time Control about.

The real Jerrel Dark walked up to the pseudo-Dark and grinned. "It is a great pleasure to meet you, Mr. Dark." Dark gazed appreciatively at Kanya. "This is one story I got to hear."

Chapter Thirty-Two

News of the destruction of Atlantis spread slowly throughout the world. Survivors and witnesses of the sad end of Terra's most advanced and glorious civilization could scarcely comprehend the enormity of it. Friends of Atlantis wept, its enemies rejoiced. King Bakri declared a thirty-day period of mourning. He welcomed all Atlanteans who managed to reach Lemuria.

The central mountain regions of Atlantis survived the first phase of the cataclysm. They sank slowly enough to allow most mountain people to construct boats and escape their country's destruction. For a month, the highest mountains remained above water. Then they too slipped beneath the waves, lost to history.

Many Atlanteans made their way to Egypt. The Egyptians found their advanced science and technology beyond their ken. Out of respect to the lost civilization, they preserved the knowledge of the Atlanteans in their archives. They never learned the language bequeathed to Atlantis by the Karani. When the Atlanteans died, both their descendants and the Egyptians completely forgot the power and majesty of the former ruler of the Atlantic world.

Priests and Shamans, jealous and afraid of Atlantean science and technology, commanded their peoples to bury or destroy the products and gifts of Atlantis. They commanded that the name of those people who the gods had condemned and destroyed should be forgotten for all time.

After completing and turning in his Mission Report, Levi decided to visit Aran Var. Despite Var's attempt to have him and Lisa killed, he didn't hold it against the Rigellian. Duty to his king, not personal animosity, motivated it. After being healed through the Joining, Var's heart was not in his mission. The Alliance and the Empire might well have done the same as the Rigellians if the shoe had been on the other foot. Levi couldn't blame the Rigellians for being very concerned about the Time Door.

Security took Var to the Detention Center and confined him in a holding cell. Currently he was security's sole guest. On the way to visit Var, Levi received a call a call from Lisa. "Levi, Kanya wants to see Var, but the SBI and Earthfleet guards won't allow her to. Is there anything we can do to help her?"

"Lisa, they think Aran is a dangerous enemy agent," Levi reminded her. "Until his change of heart, he was the greatest and most dangerous Confederacy agent. Escort Kanya to Aran's cell. I'll meet you there. There is something that I can do."

Levi, Lisa, and Kanya arrived at Var's cell. They found two men arguing about who had jurisdiction over the prisoner. One of the men was a Marine colonel. Levi figured that the other man was an SBI official. Neither man would give an inch. They turned their attention and displeasure to Levi.

"Gentlemen, your men have refused to allow Gideon Warner's special guest, Lady Kanya, to visit Mr. Var," said Levi. "I and my fellow Temporal Historian, Lisa Stern, also wish to visit him."

"Only the colonel and I are authorized to visit Var," declared the SBI man emphatically. "You and Miss Stern know very well how dangerous he is."

Levi smiled. "That was once true, but no longer. I demand that you grant us access to your prisoner."

"Totally out of the question!" insisted the SBI man. "As soon as we receive authorization from the President, Var will be removed from Time Control and taken to a maximum-security facility to be interrogated at length."

Levi smiled. "Let me remind you and the colonel that Time Control and Project Timestream are by law, an autonomous state wholly administered by the Time Council. It has its own court and a security force that performs police and investigative functions. Extradition of your prisoner requires written authorization from Gideon Warner who is President of the Time Council. President Harrison and the Commanding Admiral are aware of this. Dr. Warner plans to debrief Mr. Var personally. The debriefing hasn't been scheduled yet."

"Are you a security officer or official agent of the Time Council?" demanded the SBI man.

"I am not," admitted Levi freely.

The SBI man smiled triumphantly. "Then you may not visit the prisoner."

Levi took out his com-link and called Gideon Warner's office. "What can I do for you, Levi?" asked Warner's secretary.

"I, Lisa Stern, and Lady Kanya want to visit Aran Var. Our visitors from Earthfleet and the SBI won't let us. Please convey my request for access to Dr. Warner."

"Please give me a few minutes."

Levi was confident that Gideon Warner would grant him permission to visit Var. It would send a powerful message to the government and Earthfleet that the Time Council President was the boss of Time Control, not them. Ten minutes later, a Time Control Academy cadet delivered an official looking document to Levi. After handing the document to Levi, the cadet saluted Levi and left. Levi handed the document to the SBI man. He frowned as he read it. Without comment, he handed the document to the colonel. He read it with equal displeasure.

"You are a man of much influence in Time Control, Mr. Thurman," observed the SBI man ruefully, but with increased respect. "Guards, Mr. Thurman, Miss Stern and Lady Kanya are permitted to visit Mr. Var without limitation or restriction by order of Gideon Warner."

Reluctantly, the guards opened the cell and allowed the visitors to enter. Var had been lying on his bunk. He rose and bowed to the ladies.

Var smiled. "I thought I would never see you guys again." He hugged Kanya. "Ladies, please have a seat. Levi, I don't know how you did it but thanks. I suspect that the SBI and Earthfleet are arguing about who gets custody of me. Hopefully, they will not divide me with a sword. I officially requested asylum in the Solar Alliance. I offered to help the Alliance and the Empire to root out all the Rigellian spy networks operating inside them in exchange for a complete pardon. As a further incentive, I can help teach Alliance and Imperial agents how to work more effectively in the Confederacy and its allies."

"That is an offer I wouldn't refuse," commented Lisa. "President Harrison and Emperor Marcellus would be crazy to refuse it."

Levi chuckled. "I guarantee you that they will not. The Time Council will grant Aran asylum if the Alliance and Empire don't. We won't let a valuable resource like you be wasted."

"I am a certified telepath in the Alliance as well as the Empire," said Lisa. "If I declare Aran's intentions and word are good, President Harrison would have no reason not to pardon Aran."

Levi noticed that Kanya looked anxious. He knew exactly what was troubling her. "Kanya, you will not be sent back to your time unless you want to go. The Time Council will never give up a living historical treasure like you. The Telmierian Empire and the Karani would raise hell if we sent you back. Time Control has a machine that will prepare you to live in this time permanently. I know that you want to know what happened to your family. I promise that you will get that answer."

Kanya hugged Levi. "Thank you lifting that burden from my heart." She gazed at him in sadness. "When Aran came for me, I thought that you would bring Nura back with you."

Levi sighed. "I could not do so without violating my Time Control oath and forsaking my duty. Nura wanted to come with me, but she understands duty and oaths very well. Aran was able to bring you with us because of a loophole in the Time Control regulations. "Levi sighed. "Be assured that I am not left without comfort."

Levi gazed at Var and Kanya and sighed. He was happy that they would be together making a new life together in the Alliance. Var would have suffered even more than him had he left Kanya behind. According to a strict interpretation of Time Control regulations, Var could bring her to the present. Only Time Control personnel were forbidden to bring people from the past to the present. Var was not Time Control personnel. No doubt, the Time Council would move quickly to eliminate that loophole.

Levi left to say good-bye to the soldiers. At first, he had resented their presence on the Atlantis mission. After getting to know the soldiers and work with them, Levi had come to like and respect them. Kinsey had initially been stiff and aloof, but he loosened up a lot. The sergeants cheerfully helped with recording Atlantean history. Levi got over his resentment at their taking Bobby Bowen's anticipated place on the mission.

He found the soldiers waiting in the transporter room. They had changed back into their Earthfleet uniforms. Each soldier carried a large duffle containing their Atlantean clothes and souvenirs. They gave Levi a soldierly hug.

Kinsey sighed. "The sergeants and I regret that our historical adventure has come to an end. Thank you for getting permission for us to keep our Atlantean clothes, coins, and military artifacts."

"It was a bonny adventure, Levi," agreed McNeil. "If Time Control ever wants some soldiers on future missions, we hope you will call us."

"Levi, for a civilian who never served in Earthfleet, you are an all-right guy," declared Kelly.

Levi chuckled. "I think that's a compliment."

Kinsey smiled. "If it will help, the sergeants and I will be character witnesses for Aran at his trial."

"Don't worry, gentlemen. Mr. Var will be fine," Levi assured the soldiers. "Good luck and Godspeed."

One by one, the soldiers transported out. Levi left the transporter room and ran into Jerrel Dark. Dark sighed with relief. "I have been looking all over Time Control for you, Mr. Thurman. I tried to visit Aran Var, but the guards would not let me. They informed me that you were the man to see about obtaining permission to see him."

"They informed you correctly," confirmed Levi. "To save time and trouble, Gideon Warner gave me full authority to determine who would or would not have access to Aran." Levi studied Dark. "I hope you are the real Jerrel Dark and not another Rigellian agent in disguise."

Dark laughed. "I am, as you Terrans say, the real McCoy. It was so bizarre seeing my face on another man. The look on Var's face when he saw me was priceless. He and two Rigellian helpers jumped me at my hotel. They injected me with a drug. I woke up hours later in a reasonably comfortable cell. My Rigellian captors told me we were on a ship heading to the Rigel Home World. I had no reason to doubt them. As it turned out, I was being held in an unoccupied building in New Washington. The SBI with some Telmierian assistance finally tracked me down almost three months later. I arrived at Time Control just before Timeship One returned with your team. Levi, do you think that I will get a chance to be an observer on another mission?"

Levi shrugged. "I honestly don't know. If you do get another chance, I strongly suggest that you don't let another Rigellian double replace you."

"You can bet your life on that," promised Dark. "By the way, how do you decide at what point on the timeline Temporal History teams return?"

"An excellent question," acknowledged Levi. "I do not recall any visitor ever asking me that before. The time the teams spent in the past is added to the time of departure. My Atlantis team arrived at the point where we would have been at had we just lived through that time normally."

Levi took Dark to Var's cell. The guards admitted him without question. A moment later, Lisa left the cell. Lisa smiled. "Kanya thought she was seeing double when Jerrel Dark entered the cell. I wonder if Aran will change back to his own face."

"I never thought to ask him," admitted Levi. He probably will want his own face back. I'm sure that he will want to have blue skin."

"Let's take a walk, Levi," suggested Lisa.

"After every mission, I go to the Time Door and reflect on all of my past missions," revealed Levi. "I was about to go there."

"I do the same. So many thoughts have been running through my mind since we got back."

As they walked, they discussed the Karani connection to Atlantis. Gideon Warner informed the Empire about the fate of Prince Maren and his Colony Ship. For millennia, Telmieria had wondered about his fate. Finally, they knew that he reached Terra and established Karani civilization in Atlantis. Their joy would be tempered by the sorrow of Atlantis' destruction.

The Atlantis mission had been especially poignant and meaningful for Lisa. Her family was descended from one of Maren's sisters. She could trace her family lines back to the Karani Home World. Now that the Telmierians knew about their connection to Atlantis, they would want to be a part of all future Atlantis missions. How many of them would be interaction missions neither Levi nor Lisa could say. Levi wouldn't be surprised if the Time Council cancelled all future interaction missions after reading his Mission Report.

When Levi and Lisa reached the Time Door level, they didn't see or hear anyone. They could hear their own footsteps as they walked to the Time Door. They passed the many generators that powered it. Levi and Lisa stopped at the platform where the Time Door opened. Levi smiled as he recalled the story of the man who unwittingly discovered the temporal rift. He had been offered the opportunity to participate in a historical mission, but he understandably declined it.

"Fifty years ago today, Gideon Warner took the first journey to the past," reflected Levi. "The Alliance and the galaxy haven't been the same since that fateful day."

"Levi, did you know that the Time Council was initially reluctant to accept my application to the Time Control Academy?" revealed Lisa.

Levi shook his head in disbelief. "It's very hard to believe."

"But it is true," continued Lisa. "The Time Council back then felt uncomfortable about having a Temporal Historian who wasn't born and raised in the Alliance. Emperor Marcellus expressed his deep disappointment and displeasure to President Harrison. The emperor told him bluntly that after all the Empire had done for the Alliance, the least it could do was permit one person from the Empire to join Time Control. President Harrison and the Warners persuaded the Time Council to open Time Control to citizens of the Empire."

"I was not aware of that," confessed Levi.

Lisa smiled. "Only a few people know about that. It helped a lot that I was the granddaughter of Will and Dawn Stern. My application to the Time Control Academy was finally accepted. The rest is history, pun intended. Levi, there is something that I've wanted to do for months but couldn't." Lisa pulled Levi close and kissed him.

"After I graduated from the Academy, I decided that the most suitable and desirable wife for me would be a fellow Temporal Historian," revealed Levi. "When we met at the Warners' Golden Anniversary party, I thought you might be that lady."

Lisa sighed. "Then Princess Nura came between us. Although you are joined with her, I still love you and feel no jealousy about what you shared with her."

"I can feel her through the Joining even after thousands of years," revealed Levi. "That makes that makes it a little easier to endure Nura's physical absence. As she told me, we are joined together in life and in death. You are a comfort and a delight to me, Lisa, not a consolation prize. Never doubt that. If you can live with the ghost of Nura, marry me."

Lisa hugged him. "Yes! I am not jealous of her or her place in your life. If you are still determined to leave Time Control, I will go with you."

Levi smiled. "With you as my wife, I think I can bear to remain in Time Control."

Levi and Lisa almost jumped when a voice behind them said, "Gideon Warner wants to see you in his office, Mr. Thurman." The ASAP was understood.

They turned around to find a serious young Academy cadet standing at attention. His uniform was well pressed and immaculate. They smiled in recollection of the time when they were in the cadet's place.

"Very well," said Levi. "Wait for me in my quarters, Lisa. This might take a while."

When Levi arrived at Gideon Warner's office, his secretary immediately ushered Levi inside. Warner directed him to sit down.

"Amara and I read your Mission report with great pleasure," began Warner. "We couldn't put it down until we finished it. You made history truly and fully come alive just as we envisioned it when we organized Time Control. We aren't the stodgy old fogeys that we pretend to be because people expect it of us. All the members of the Time Council are delighted with the Atlantean spaceship and floater. The resignation that accompanied your report shocked us."

"Levi, we know all our Temporal Historians like we know our own children. Only Amara and I could read between the lines. We know that you came to love Princess Nura. Losing her has been a very painful loss for you. That's what prompted your resignation."

Levi smiled wanly. "I thought that only my mother would have discerned that. Nura and I have experienced the Joining. That makes it so much harder to live without her. Maybe it would be easier being away from Time Control. This place constantly reminds me of what I have lost."

Warner sighed. "If I had to leave Amara behind the way you left the princess behind, I would feel the same way. Levi, Amara, and I have long sought someone we feel has the character, wisdom, judgment, and humanity the President of the Time Council needs. As the decades passed, we began to despair that we would find that person. Levi, you are the man we want to succeed me. Although you would never ask, I know you would like to bring Princess Nura to our time. If that is the price we must pay to keep you in Time Control, Amara and I are willing to pay it."

Taking Gideon Warner's place in the Time Council! Never had he ever imagined himself as President of the Time Council. No greater honor or heavier responsibility existed in the Alliance. The job and its responsibilities frightened Levi. Nevertheless, he couldn't refuse the job if it was offered to him. He should have known that his inclusion in Time Council meetings was leading to something.

"You would do that for me, Dr. Warner?" asked Levi, not daring to believe.

"One of Time Control's Prime Directives is to never remove anyone permanently from their time," Warner gently reminded Levi. "But this is a unique case. No member of the original Time Council ever imagined a situation like yours. Until recently, we had never even considered an interaction mission. Interaction with the past can lead to unexpected and unforeseen complications as it did with you. Who could have imagined that something as innocuous as telling stories in the marketplace could lead to what it did during your mission."

Warner gazed wistfully at Levi. "To my and Amara's sorrow, none of our children chose to join Time Control. I have had a father's pride in your career and accomplishments. Bringing Princess Nura to our time would in no way change the past. The future if it exists is fluid. Levi, I will plead your case to the Time Council with all the energy and eloquence I possess. If the exemption is granted, the choice of Princess Nura coming to our time is entirely hers."

Levi felt that a great weight had been removed from him. "Nura will come. She begged me to bring her back with me."

"The exemption like all important decisions must be unanimous," Warner reminded Levi. "I can only guarantee you two votes: mine and Amara's. I honestly don't know how the rest of the Council will vote."

Levi found Lisa waiting anxiously for him. "Did Dr. Warner ask you to withdraw your resignation?"

"Not directly, but yes."

Lisa studied Levi. He seemed much more peaceful and relaxed than he was before he met Gideon Warner. Unconsciously, she lightly touched his mind. "He's going to ask the Time Council to allow you to bring Nura to the present." Lisa felt happy and sad at the same time. "I hope the Council grants you an exemption. If you get it, I won't hold you to your proposal."

Levi respected Lisa, but never as much as he did now. Her strength and character ran deep. In that moment, he realized how much both Nura and Lisa meant to him. Levi had the feeling that the three of them were meant to be together. Maybe it didn't have to be a zero-sum game for Nura and Lisa. They could both win if Nura agreed.

Levi looked into Lisa's eyes. "Lisa, could you be happy as my second wife if Nura agreed, assuming I am permitted to bring her here?"

The question greatly surprised her. Levi thought she seemed open to the possibility. He hoped that she was. Would Nura be open to the possibility? What Levi had learned about her gave him real hope that she could accept Lisa as part of their family.

"This is very unexpected, Levi," admitted Lisa. "I always expected to be the only wife of my husband. Imperial law permits a man to have two wives if both women consent. It is rare but it happens, usually when a wife can't bear children. I never imagined being in a situation like this. To have you as my husband, I think I can accept sharing you with a woman like Nura."

Levi and Lisa waited patiently while the Time Council met in Special Session to consider whether to allow Nura to be brought to the present or not. It had been years since the Council had last met in Special Session. Those sessions usually lasted many hours. Some had lasted for an entire day. Levi noted that on the bright side, they wouldn't have to wait for days or weeks for the Time Council to make its decision.

Like the Supreme Court, Time Council decisions served as precedents. Levi and Lisa knew that the Council's decision would speak to the future. The Time Council always thought long term. It made no important decisions without painstakingly considering every angle as well as possible consequences. Had the Council immediately just said no, it would have been much easier to accept. Now that his hopes had been raised, a no would be much harder for Levi to live with. Now he could only stay in Time Control if Nura was with him.

Levi had complete confidence in the Council's judgment and fairness. Levi witnessed it in the Council meetings that he had attended. If he was going to be the future President of the Time Council, he needed to learn how the Council made its decisions. The experience of sitting in on important Council sessions was very illuminating.

As the hours passed, Levi felt a growing confidence that the Council was going to decide in his favor. He had no reasonable or logical basis for that confidence. Levi hadn't been fully honest with Gideon Warner. He had already decided to stay in Time Control when he met with Warner. Having Lisa as his wife would make remaining in Time Control endurable. Levi never imagined that the Council would even consider letting him bring Nura to the present. For that reason, he had not asked.

Levi and Lisa were startled by a knock on the door. When he opened the door, he found a Time Control cadet standing at attention. "The Time Council requests your presence in the Council meeting room immediately, Mr. Thurman." With that pronouncement, he turned away and left.

Lisa hugged Levi. "Good luck."

Levi felt a twinge of uncertainty as he walked to the Council meeting room. He decided that he wanted Nura to participate in the Atlantis II mission if he was able to bring her to the present. Having an actual Atlantean on his team would be poetically appropriate and useful. He hoped that Lisa had the desire to be on the Atlantis II team if Nura denied him permission to have her as a second wife.

One of the guards at the Time Council meeting hall ushered Levi inside as soon as he arrived. The Council members sat silently and impassively around the table where they conducted all their business. Amara Warner was sitting in the President's Chair. That was a good sign. Gideon Warner would deliver bad news himself, not pass the buck to his wife. Levi braced himself for the worst.

"The Time Council has given your request to bring Princess Nura to the present very much thought and the utmost serious consideration," began Amara Warner. "Our decision will serve as a precedent. Therefore, we must look beyond the immediate issue. Occasionally, we have brought people from the past to learn more about them and their time. When we learned what we desired from those people, we returned them to their own times. Your situation is unique. It came to pass only because of your mission being interactive. You did not seek personal involvement with Princess Nura. She sought it and insisted on it. The Council accepts its share of the responsibility for what happened."

"All of us in the Council agree that bringing Princess Nura to the present would not change the past in any way. After debating our options, we were leaning toward granting an exemption. We were not yet ready to approve it. Your Joining with Princess Nura was the consideration that fully tipped the scales in your favor. None of us could live with ourselves if we denied you the opportunity to be with her, knowing that the two of you experienced the Joining. Your exemption is granted. You are authorized to bring Princess Nura to our time. We wish you and Princess Nura a lifetime of happiness together."

Levi let out an unprofessional whoop of delight. "I don't know how to thank you and the Council."

Gideon Warner smiled. "I think you do."

"Before I leave, I have a question that has been on my mind for months," said Levi. The Council waited expectantly. "Nura and I want to get married in the Temple of the Sun in Aurelin before her time. Would a marriage in the past be legal and recognized in the present?" The looks on the faces of the Council members told Levi that they hadn't ever considered the idea.

"I think I can answer that question," announced Clark Clements, the Time Council's resident legal expert. "All marriages performed legally in any locality of the Alliance are recognized. The fact that the country and authority no longer exist is irrelevant."

"We will permit you to marry in the past as you desire under one condition: have someone record the entire proceedings for the archives," decided Gideon Warner.

Levi grinned. "You have a deal, Dr. Warner."

Levi rushed back to his quarters to give Lisa the news. She listened quietly as he told her what the Council had told him. Levi knew that part of her rejoiced with him, part of her felt sad that she would lose him if Nura decided that Levi would only have one wife.

Lisa hugged him and sighed. "If I can't be your wife, I still want to be your friend. Hopefully, Nura can accept that much."

Levi smiled. "Nura shouldn't have a problem with that."

By noon the following day, all the arrangements had been made for Levi's brief return to Atlantis. Dan Preston, the pilot of Timeship One, had to be recalled temporarily from his vacation. The alternate pilot had just undergone a major operation and wasn't available. Levi appreciated the near absence of red tape in Time Control. The

Warners were almost obsessive about efficiency. Lisa came to see Levi off. They both had very mixed feelings about his journey to Atlantis. Silently they watched as Timeship One moved from the far end of the cavern to the open space in front of the platform where the Time Door formed. The pilot got out and joined the Temporal Historians.

"I had my vacation interrupted so you could take your Atlantean jaunt, Lev," Preston informed him. "Linda and I were packed and ready to leave when I got a call from Gideon Warner. He informed me that I was taking you back to Atlantis. Did you leave something important behind?"

Levi smiled. He had left someone very important behind. "Sorry about the inconvenience, Dan," apologized Levi. "This trip has a very important purpose. We are bringing Princess Nura to the present."

Preston stared unbelieving at Levi. "This isn't an elaborate gag?"

"It's no gag, Dan," Levi assured him.

"Why are we bringing the princess here?"

Levi smiled. "So she and I can get married and work together in Time Control."

Preston shook his head. "Levi, you really made history with your interaction mission. Marrying an Atlantean princess will get you a lot more than a historical footnote. Do you want to get Princess Nura some flowers or something first?"

Levi smiled and shook his head. "Fire up the generators!" he called out to the Doorkeeper. "Time for us to board Timeship One, Dan. We will be back shortly, Lisa."

Levi and Preston entered the timeship and sealed the hatch behind them. They watched the swirling waves of color heralding the opening of the Time Door on the main viewscreen. A moment later they entered the timestream. Preston listened in fascination as Levi told him about his relationship with Nura. It amused Preston that Levi's storytelling in the marketplace had led to a series of adventures and misadventures that no one could have anticipated.

Preston chuckled. "How will any other Temporal Historian be able to top or even equal that, Levi?"

Levi chuckled. "I suspect that the Time Council hopes and prays that no one ever does. The doctors will treat Nura so she can stay in our time permanently."

Before Preston could reply, a beep announced their imminent arrival at their destination. When the Timeship synchronized with Nura's present, Atlantis appeared on the viewscreen. They could see the smoke and fires of Aurelin in the distance. Seeing the destruction again pained Levi more than it had the first time. It dampened his joy of seeing Nura.

In minutes, the timeship reached the palace. Most of it had been destroyed by the earthquake. Levi spotted Nura standing at almost the exact spot in the palace garden where they said goodbye. As the timeship descended, it caught her attention. Her eyes grew wide as she watched it land beside her.

"Make it quick, Levi!" ordered Preston. "The ground might open up at any time and swallow us and the timeship."

Levi jumped out of the timeship and ran over to Nura. For a moment she couldn't accept that Levi was with her. She reached out hesitantly and touched him, then she hugged him. "You are real and not a hallucination, Levi. Thank Father Sun!"

"Nura, come with me to my time," entreated Levi. "I have been given permission to bring you to it. Sometimes there are exceptions to the rules. The Time Council made one for us. Be my wife and join me in Time Control. The line of Maren must endure."

"It is Father Sun's will," decided Nura. "And mine."

Levi hurried Nura into the timeship. As he closed the hatch behind him, the ground began to shake. As soon as the timeship cleared the palace, a huge crack in the ground opened and swallowed the entire palace garden. The Time Door opened in front of the timeship. Preston immediately took the ship through the door. The long journey to the twenty-third century began.

Preston gazed at Nura in appreciation and wonder. "Welcome to Timeship One, Princess Nura," said Preston in Telmierian. "It is a privilege and a pleasure to be your pilot."

Nura looked around the timeship. "Levi, did you and Lisa come to Atlantis in this ship?"

Levi smiled. "I wish that we had. Only the kindness of an Atlantean couple saved me and my team from a long walk to Aurelin. I only told stories in the marketplace to earn money for our expenses. If I had let Jerrel Dark steal money from rich people as he desired, I would have never met you."

"Levi was the destruction of Atlantis a punishment from Father Sun?" asked Nura plaintively.

"Legend painted your people as evil degenerates, condemned and destroyed by the gods," said Levi. "I never encountered a finer group of people anywhere."

"Thousands of years of lies and misconceptions about my country and people will soon be laid to rest," rejoiced Nura. "Levi, my mother would have liked you. My father came to have a very high regard for you. My brothers would have accepted you into the family."

"You only mentioned one brother, Akil, the one who died in the sailing accident," recalled Levi.

Nura looked uncomfortable. "Etor is my father's illegitimate son. He and my father did not know that I knew. I loved him as much as a full and acknowledged brother. None of the palace guards or servants would tell me who his mother was. It had to be a woman who had served in the palace. I hope Etor survived and made his way to Lemuria."

The revelation about Etor didn't surprise Levi. He and Nura sometimes scrapped like siblings. Etor regularly played jokes on her. Adeil showed him unusual forbearance and favor. Levi finally noticed how much Etor resembled the king.

"I will find out for you tomorrow," promised Levi. "We will visit Etor if he did."

Nura sighed. "Levi, all my life I dreamed of getting married in the Temple of the Sun in Aurelin. Now the temple and Atlantis are just a memory."

Levi smiled. "The Time Council approved my request to have our wedding and honeymoon in Atlantis. We can get married in the Temple of the Sun before your parents were born."

"It still seems so strange that you and Lisa are historians who travel through time," mused Nura. "I want to become a historian like you. Can I join the two of you on your next mission to Atlantis?"

"You would be a great asset to the mission, love," said Levi. "The Time Council will surely agree. I will twist their arms if necessary."

A beep indicated that the timeship would reach Time Control momentarily. Seconds later, the cavern housing the Time Door appeared on the viewscreen. Preston carefully maneuvered Timeship One around the temporal rift and set it down.

Preston smiled. "I hope that I get to transport you to your wedding and honeymoon in Atlantis. When you return from your honeymoon, Time Control will have a wedding celebration people will never forget."

Lisa ran over to Levi and Nura and hugged them. "Only fifteen minutes passed since Timeship One left for Atlantis. Dan cut it very close, but he is that good. Nura, I am truly happy to see you again."

"I am happy to see you too. Levi, Lisa, the three of us need to talk."

Levi took Nura and Lisa to his favorite lookout point near Time Control. They gazed in delight at the vast ocean of stars in the heavens above them. Fortunately, there was a new moon. For a long time, no one spoke. They watched as a graviton powered freighter lifted off from the Earthfleet base that serviced Time Control and Project Timestream. They followed it across the sky until it vanished from sight.

"When I was a little girl, the Chief High Priest Kemen gave me a special blessing," said Nura dreamily. "One of the things he predicted was that someday I would travel to the stars. He looked shocked by what he had said. Nevertheless, he did not take back his words or try to rationalize them. Kemen was truly inspired by Father Sun."

Nura smiled slyly. "Lisa, in Atlantis Levi claimed that you were his sister. At first, I accepted it unquestioningly. As time passed, I sensed that your feelings for Levi were not those a sister has for her brother. Your eyes occasionally revealed the truth. I realized that you were in love with him. This knowledge made me very happy. I rejoiced that he had a fine lady he could share his life with after I married Maric." Nura gazed at Levi and waited expectantly.

Levi realized that Nura had the same abilities as Lisa. What Nura thought were feelings, were unconscious contact with his mind and Lisa's. "After we returned to Time Control, I did not think that the Time Council would ever consider letting me bring you to my time. It would have been a tremendous personal favor I could not ask for. I asked Lisa to marry me because I love her too. Then without asking him for it, Gideon Warner, the President of the Time Council, suddenly told me that he would ask the Time Council to authorize me to bring you here. The Council unanimously said yes, so I brought you here."

"Levi, I knew how you felt about Lisa through our joining. Something like that cannot be hidden. You made no attempt to hide your emotion from me. There is abundant room in your heart for both me and Lisa. I do not feel at all crowded."

"Alliance law permits a man to have two wives if the first one consents," Lisa informed Nura. "I am content to be Levi's second wife, if you consent."

"It is clear to me that the three of us are meant to be together," said Nura. "This is Father Sun's will, not chance. Levi, I happily give my consent for you to take Lisa as your second wife. There is one condition. You must wait one year before you marry Lisa. During that year I want you all to myself."

Levi understood that he and Lisa were not permitted to know each other in the Biblical sense until after their wedding. "I accept your condition, Nura."

Lisa smiled. "As do I."

"I have long contemplated the mystery of time," revealed Nura. "I believe time is the first creation of Father Sun. I had believed that the past could not be changed. Our experiences have shown that it can be, at least to a point. I believe Father Sun has placed limits on the changes we can make to the time continuum. The Time Council and Time Control have become partners in creation with Father Sun. I do not think it would have happened unless Father Sun willed it."

Was my involvement in the past ordained by heaven, wondered Levi. Had God intended for Nura's life to span millennia and be joined with his? Was the Time Door contrary to His will? So far He had indicated no displeasure with him or Time Control. Heaven must have set certain bounds for mankind. When it exceeded them as it had with the Tower of Babel, He slapped mankind down hard. With the intelligence and wisdom of Nura and Lisa added to his own, Levi felt that someday he just might adequately fill the Warners' shoes.

Epilog

Kemen stood alone in the Holy of Holies in the Temple of The Sun. The spirit told him that the growing destruction around him heralded the end of Atlantis. Like all his fellow Atlanteans, he believed that their country and civilization would endure until the end of the world. Kemen didn't believe that Father Sun had weighed Atlantis in the balance and found it wanting. His people were proud and imperfect, but they hadn't committed sins worthy of their complete destruction.

From the early years of his life, Kemen felt that the majority of Atlanteans placed more faith in science and technology than Father Sun. That, not backward superstition, moved all the Chief High Priests to share the technology of the archives in the Shrine of Alaya sparingly. Kemen understood that Atlantis had slowly been moving toward creating a world empire. Spaceships would be used in accomplishing that unworthy end. To forestall that, Kemen continued the ban on space travel ordained by Maren. He underestimated the determination and imagination of the Army.

Kemen found the timing of Atlantis destruction ironic. The people had been generally righteous and faithful in their religious duties. King Adeil had begun the process of establishing peace with Lemuria. Garai, through his arrogance, ended up destroying his scheme to place Maric on the throne. Atlantis had so much to live and strive for. Kemen suspected that technology had something to do with what was happening. He would never know for certain.

Before leaving the temple, Kemen took a long last look at the sacred art. It grieved him that the temple would soon be just a memory. Temple worship was one of the Chief High Priests most important responsibilities. Until a new temple could be built in Suminar, Kemen felt like he was missing a spiritual arm. He realized that no matter how many Atlanteans reached Lemuria, eventually their descendants would be absorbed into Lemuria. Atlantis would eventually be forgotten.

Kemen had already sent his family with everything he wanted to save to the flagship of the Atlantean navy. He returned to his office to retrieve the greatest treasure bequeathed by the Karani. It was passed down from each Chief High Priest to his successor. Kemen removed the staff of power from its secret location. The device had been used by King Maren to move huge blocks of stone during the rebuilding of Aurelin. Since that time, the staff of Maren was only used on ceremonial occasions. Kemen regretted that he hadn't spent more time in the archives of the Karani. Soon the legacy from the Karani would be lost forever.

Unhurriedly, Kemen departed from the temple. His anxious driver breathed a sigh of relief when he boarded the floater. The driver took the floater to a safe height. It flew over the crowded streets of Aurelin. Kemen somberly observed the masses of pedestrians and vehicles as they fled the approaching destruction. All reason and order had fled.

Floaters filled the skies over the city and harbor. They moved in an orderly manner toward the ships that waited to take them to safety in Lemuria. Only along the waterfront did order prevail enforced by the Army. Tanks and personnel carriers controlled all access to the docks. All the foreign ships had already fled. Guards passed high government officials, scientists, and blue skinned people without question. Bags of gold from rich people bought them passage to safety. The guards also passed on extraordinarily beautiful commoner women.

Kemen's driver set down the floater on an open spot on the deck. Sailors unloaded the floater, then pushed it overboard. The captain came and welcomed Kemen aboard. He kissed the orb of the staff. Kemen inquired of the captain if Maric or Garai were aboard. When the captain said they were, Kemen requested that a seaman escort him to their quarters. Kemen and his escort took a while to reach Garai's quarters, pushing their way through the crowded passageways. When they reached their destination, Kemen's escort announced Kemen's arrival. After receiving permission to enter, the seaman ushered Kemen inside.

Maric smiled smugly. Garai bowed to Kemen who was his social equal. Kemen held out the staff. After a moment of hesitation, both Garai and Maric kissed it. "I am pleased that you escaped death,

Kemen," said Garai unctuously. "You will no doubt provide needed comfort and spiritual guidance to our fellow survivors."

"You are just saving your privileged skin like the rest of us," sneered Maric. He gazed disdainfully at Kemen's staff. "You should have left that useless relic of the peasants' religion back in the temple. Little good will it do you in Lemuria. I suggest that you learn a useful trade on the way to Suminar. You are not likely to gain much sympathy or help from the Lemurian clerics."

Kemen smiled. "I will manage well enough in my new home, Lord Maric. No doubt you and your excellent sire will thrive in Lemuria. If you can arrange enough fatal accidents to King Bakri's children, Maric might someday sit on the throne of Lemuria. It will not be easy as it was in Atlantis. You only needed to eliminate Prince Akil to clear your way to the throne."

Maric glared at Kemen and placed his hand on his pistol. For a moment Garai was taken aback, but he quickly recovered. Garai smiled. "Our ambitions in Lemuria are much more modest."

Kemen gazed impassively at Garai. "Maybe you can interest King Bakri in creating his own Project Sky Bridge," speculated Kemen.

Kemen felt a rising tide of anger and frustration rising within him. Both Garai and Maric had committed more than a few crimes that merited death. Their greatest crime was the murder of Prince Akil. Kemen knew that Garai and Maric would cause trouble for Lemuria and the Atlantean survivors once they reached Suminar.

The smug looks on the faces of Garai and Maric infuriated Kemen. All their lives they had broken laws, disobeyed Father Sun's commandments and trampled on the Code of The Kings in their pursuit of power. Their only redeeming aspect was honesty in their financial affairs. They had always evaded the consequences of their actions. That had to change.

Garai poured a glass of wine and offered it to Kemen. "The wine is excellent. It comes from your brother's vineyards. Your future in Lemuria could be a much brighter one. You have much influence with the clerics of Lemuria. I would not be ungrateful if you used it on my behalf."

Kemen studied Garai. Was the man serious or just giving him further offense? "Ingratitude is not one of your failings general," acknowledged Kemen. "But no, my lord general. I do no favors for blasphemers, traitors, and murderers."

Kemen stretched forth the staff. Blue fire glowed within the orb growing brighter by the second. A power beam erupted from the orb striking Garai and Maric. Too late they realized their danger. Before they could draw their guns, their legs buckled. Kemen watched with satisfaction as the power of the orb drove the proud lords to their knees. Seconds later the beam pinned them on the deck. They gazed up at Kemen in fear and wonder.

"I thought the power of the orb was just a myth," gasped Garai. "It appears that I was mistaken."

"You were always a man of style, general," noted Kemen with a touch of regret.

Garai tried to speak but a weight as heavy as the world bound his tongue. Finally, it crushed the life out of him. Maric resisted a few seconds longer before death claimed him too.

"No one is exempt from the law of Father Sun or the king, Garai," said Kemen softly. "Your punishment like Maric's has just begun."

The Door to Yesterday
Short Story

D r. Gideon Warner waited patiently at the security desk of the Solar Science Institute. The armed security guard painstakingly checked his ID and security clearance. The guard also required a retinal scan. Warner was not offended by it. With all the top-secret projects at the institute, less security would be foolish and dangerous. The guard looked offended by Warner's long hair, beard, and casual clothes.

"The Director's office is the third door on the right," the guard stiffly informed Warner. "He's expecting you."

Warner knew Director Ellison by reputation, but had never met him. He first arrived at the institute as a boy wonder of eighteen. Over three decades, he morphed into a middle-aged bureaucrat. Warner was something of a boy wonder himself. He had chosen a much different path than Ellison. When Warner arrived at the Director's office, he knocked on the door. The Director's secretary ushered him in, then left.

The Director got up and shook Warner's hand. "Thank you for coming here on such short notice, Dr. Warner. Please have a seat. Would you like something to drink?"

"No, thank you, Director Ellison," replied Warner. "I'm honored but surprised by your invitation. None of my research has any military applications."

Warner got the impression that Ellison felt uncomfortable around him. Maybe it was because Ellison had publicly trashed his speculations on time travel.

"Earthfleet has been looking for a suitable site for a new weapons R & D facility," began the Director. "We thought we had found it in a cavern we recently discovered in Colorado. The survey team encountered something very unexpected on the final day of its mission. This survey recording will explain everything."

The Director activated the viewscreen on the wall behind him. He pressed a button on his desk and the video record began to play. The man who was apparently the leader of the survey team, talked excitedly about the suitability of the cavern for the R & D facility. He felt confident that the Director would be very pleased. One of the men near the center of the cavern called the rest of the team to see something he had discovered.

When they were six feet away, the man beckoned them to follow him. He took four steps, then completely vanished. The men immediately halted. They called their boss and reported what had just happened. Ellison immediately ordered a scan of the area. The scan failed to detect the missing man. A scan of the entire planet didn't detect him either. The recording ended abruptly.

"Incredible," murmured Warner. "But why call me?"

Ellison hesitated a moment. "I called you because of your paper on the possibility of interdimensional and temporal rifts."

Warner smiled. "Theories you publicly dismissed as crackpot ranting, as I recall."

Ellison cleared his throat. "Sorry about that, Dr. Warner," he mumbled in feeble apology. "We can't even begin to explain that survey man's disappearance." Ellison gazed imploringly at Warner. "Do you have any idea what happened to him?"

"He was not transported out of the cavern," declared Warner confidently. "There was no transporter beam. Had he been vaporized by an energy weapon; the beam would also have been visible. Director, this may sound completely crazy, but I think the man may have passed through a temporal rift. I will need to visit the cavern with my special equipment to confirm it."

"Crazy indeed," agreed the Director. "But I can't think of a better explanation. If there is a temporal rift, we better seal off the cavern permanently so no one else accidentally passes through it."

"Why don't we use it to create a doorway through time instead?" countered Warner.

"Is that really possible?" asked the Director breathlessly.

"Indeed, it is, Director," Warner assured him.

Warner and Director Ellison went to the cavern. They confirmed that it did contain a temporal rift. They thoroughly discussed Warner's idea of creating a Time Door. Ellison called President Harrison and pitched his idea to him. At first, Harrison thought

Ellison was joking or crazy. Curiosity and the possibility of time travel moved him to meet with Ellison and Warner. Warner hoped that the forty-two year-old Alexander Harrison still possessed some of his youthful imagination and an open mind. Ellison and Warner pitched a proposal to create a time portal and the recovery of lost historical records and art to the President. Harrison listened intently but impassively.

"Where do you think that man is now, Dr. Warner?" asked Harrison at the end of the presentation.

Warner shrugged. "We have no idea where or when he is, Mr. President. He could be at the Alamo, the opening of the Parthenon or the Great Library of Alexandria in Egypt. We have no way of knowing. I fear that the poor man's trip is one way. President Harrison, just imagine the ancient science we could recover as well as history!"

President Harrison's eyes shone with interest. "I'm no history buff, but the idea of such a tremendous expansion of historical knowledge excites me. We could also recover the great art lost or destroyed during recorded history. I'd like to see what Venus De Milo looks like with her arms. The more lessons we learn from the past, the better. Dr. Warner, we will build your Time Door. I will write an Executive Order authorizing the creation of your project. I give you the honor of naming it."

Warner felt great relief. Had Harrison said no, the dream would have been dead. Warner didn't trust any other politician with the idea. "How about Project Timestream?" suggested Warner.

"Very appropriate," approved President Harrison. "Project Timestream it is. We will have to get the Solar Council to provide the funding. It will cost me a lot of political capital, but I am willing to spend it. What greater legacy could a President bequeath to future generations? I'm confident that I can persuade the council to fund Project Timestream. We must keep the true purpose of this project secret until the Time Door becomes fully operational. I'll have anyone shot who speaks one word about the Time Door before its unveiling."

Neither Warner nor Ellison doubted the President's word. He always meant what he said and never bluffed. Warner and the Director also understood the need for absolute secrecy. Although the Telmierian Empire was the best friend and ally of the Solar Alliance, it would not be happy about a doorway to the past over which it had no control or oversight. The Rigellian Confederacy, the greatest enemy of the Solar Alliance, might even go to war over it. Warner wondered if the citizens of the Solar Alliance could accept the reality of the Time Door without going off the deep end. He and the President decided that they would cross that bridge when they came to it. First, build the Time Door and make it work.

Warner quickly gathered and organized his team. He knew who he wanted and needed. None of the people he invited declined the invitation. Warner didn't have to twist anyone's arm after making his pitch. Had any of them declined to join the project, they would have been held incommunicado until the Time Door was announced.

The last person on Warner's list was Dr. Amara Taft. She was the only mainstream scientist who publicly expressed belief in the possibility of time travel. Taft received fewer invitations to big projects than her brilliance merited. She had difficulty working under bosses who were not even half as smart as she was. Warner sympathized with that. He knew that the best way to handle Taft was to put her to work and stay out of the way. More than anyone he knew; Taft could think outside of the box.

A knock on the door announced Taft's arrival. Warner's secretary ushered her inside, then left. "Please have a seat, Dr. Taft. Thank you for accepting my invitation." Warner felt a bit jealous of Taft. At twenty-eight she had achieved greater success than he had at thirty-five. Warner admitted to himself that he had hindered his own professional progress with his impatience with people who disagreed with his theories.

Contrary to Warner's expectation, Taft wore a modest blue knee length dress that was attractive yet professional. It was her way of saying I'm a scientist but also a woman. Warner liked her long wavy brown hair. He wished Taft was less attractive.

"Your invitation was a bit cryptic, Dr. Warner. I'm very curious to hear what it is that I promised not to disclose."

"Absolute secrecy is vital to this project," explained Warner. "The goal of Project Timestream is to create a stable doorway through time."

Taft looked stunned as if Warner just told her that he had found a cure for stupidity. All she could say was, "How?"

Warner showed her the video of the man who had unwittingly become the first person to travel through time. He explained that the survey man had passed through a stable temporal rift. Her initial skepticism turned to belief as she read the data gathered by Warner's temporal energy sensors.

"Where do think that man ended up, Dr. Warner?"

Warner shrugged. "Truly, God only knows. So far, He hasn't shared that knowledge with me."

"How can we make use of the rift?"

Warner smiled. Taft was hooked. "The same way we beat Einstein and Relativity: hyperspace."

"Yes!" exclaimed Taft with sudden understanding. "We can create and control the temporal doorway the same way we control hyperspace drive and travel. The power that will be needed just to open a temporal doorway would be enormous. The engine would have to be enormous too. Dr. Warner, sign me up! To be a part of a project like this, I would work for just room and board if necessary."

Warner smiled. "If that compensation is acceptable to you, we definitely have a deal."

Taft laughed. "I think you and I will get along fine, Dr. Warner."

"What are your salary requirements, Dr. Taft?" asked Warner.

"Money is not the important thing," replied Taft. "Whatever you think I'm worth is fine. I want two things from you personally."

Warner couldn't imagine what she could possibly want from him.

Taft smiled. "One: give me complete access to all your personal research. Two: call me Amara."

Warner pulled out a contract he had already signed. He added the conditions Taft required of him. After reading everything slowly and carefully, she signed the contract. "You will be Assistant Project Director, Amara. Your salary will be just forty thousand credits less than mine. I promise that you will earn every credit."

"I wouldn't have it any other way, Gideon."

Warner leaned back in his chair. "Amara, I didn't do you a favor by making you Assistant Project Director. You will have the unenviable responsibility of doing most of the grunt work of getting Project Timestream organized and up and running. Your headaches and aggravations will be comparable to mine. But I promise that you will get full credit for your part of the project."

Amara smiled. "I expect no less from Gideon Warner."

Amara quickly learned that Warner had not exaggerated in the least. Once the design of the base was completed, building materials, machinery and all the necessary electronic equipment were ordered. Things quickly became very chaotic. Amara soon put her finger on the problem: Warner's old friend Brion Gill. She traced all the mixed-up orders back to him. Without consulting Gill or Warner, Amara dived into the chaos. Within a short time, she imposed order on it.

Gill stormed into Amara's office without knocking and stalked over to her desk. "Come in," said Amara calmly. "What can I do for you, Brion?"

Gill leaned over the desk. "Procurement is my responsibility, Dr. Taft," he informed her through clenched teeth. "Your interference is not appreciated!"

"But apparently it's not your area of expertise," observed Amara correctly if undiplomatically. "You did well enough with small projects. A project this size requires greater organizational skills than you seem to possess, or are you putting all the blame on your subordinates? The ultimate responsibility for acquiring everything we need is mine."

"This is unacceptable!" shouted Gill. "Call Gideon now!"

Amara rang Warner. "Gideon, can you come over to my office now? Brion wants to speak with you."

"I'll be there in about five minutes," replied Warner. True to his word, Warner walked into Amara's office five minutes later. He looked at Gill, then Amara. Warner knew exactly what the problem was, but he asked, "What can I do for you, Brion?"

"Procurement is part of my job and my responsibility," Gill reminded Warner. "Dr. Taft made procurement decisions without even consulting me!"

Warner struggled not to smile. "Brion, procurement is not the best use of your time and talent. I'll assign someone else to take care of it. From now on, devote all your time and energy to the temporal spatial coordinate software. I'm not happy with the progress that your team has made so far."

At first, Gill seemed annoyed, then he seemed to change his mind after some thought. "You're right, Gideon. I have some ideas I should explore now. The sooner I get to work on them the better." Gill left the room without further comment or complaint.

"You handled that very well, Gideon!" declared Amara with admiration. "I never imagined that you had such good people skills."

Warner chuckled. "Neither did I. Seriously, Brion is the only person who can develop the time-space coordinate software. Without that software, the Time Door won't work. Thanks for straightening out his mess. Check on things occasionally, but don't let it distract you from your own work. Keeping everyone continually focused on their part of the project is a never-ending job."

"We need to keep the Time Door out of the hands of people who would use it to gain wealth and power," agreed Amara. "You have my complete confidence and trust to be the guardian of time. I was planning to call you when Brion rudely barged into my office. We both forgot one important member for our team: an Earthfleet Chief Engineer."

Warner looked at Amara in confusion. "Why do we need a military engineer, Amara?"

"Not just any Earthfleet engineer. The hyperdrive engine we are using for the Time Door is not just a larger version of a star cruiser engine," she explained. "It is significantly different from the engines the Alliance produces. Remember, we got ours from the Telmierians."

"That's right," replied Warner with sudden recollection. "None of our people have worked with it. I heard that some Earthfleet Chief Engineers have."

"Military engineers have to be especially resourceful and imaginative," pointed out Amara. "They must be able to repair severe battle damage under adverse conditions. I've already checked out all the star cruiser Chief Engineers in Earthfleet. The best one for our purposes is Bryan Casey, Chief Engineer of the star cruiser Atlantis. He is the only Chief Engineer with significant experience working on our engine."

Warner chuckled. "You are proactive to a fault, Amara. That's one of the reasons I chose you for my team. President Harrison and I really hated to mislead the Telmierians about our plans for the engine. I feel even worse because they gave us such a good price for it."

Amara smiled. "You two did a bit of tap dancing around the truth," she allowed. "Since Earthfleet Command is not in the loop, President Harrison needs to make the call to the Commanding Admiral."

Captain Reynolds summoned the Chief Engineer to the bridge. Minutes later, he stepped out of the lift. He saluted the captain and waited for the explanation for the summons. Captain Reynolds was a strict, by the book CO. Chief Casey wracked his brain to come up with a reason why the captain wanted to see him. He couldn't think of anything he had done or failed to do that might have displeased the captain.

The captain gazed at Casey with a puzzled look on his face. "Chief Casey, I've just received orders from the Commanding Admiral. He received a direct order from President Harrison transferring you indefinitely to a top-secret project on Terra. This project is so secret, even Admiral Wallace didn't know about it." The captain chuckled. "He was very unhappy about that. As soon as you pack your uniforms and personal effects, you will be transported to the project site."

For a moment, Casey couldn't speak. His brain struggled to process the information that had just been inputted. "An order from the President, sir? This does not compute."

"It's no joke or mistake, Mr. Casey," the captain assured him. "I contacted the Commanding Admiral himself to confirm the orders."

"What important project could possibly need the services of a humble star cruiser Chief Engineer?" wondered Casey.

The captain snorted. "Only Wayne Waldron of Supernova is a better Chief Engineer than you. Make certain that your performance and conduct reflect well upon me, Atlantis, and your shipmates. Especially me. I'm certain that you will do nothing to make me reconsider my recommendation for you to participate in the Engineer Exchange Program with the Telmierian Empire. Dismissed!"

The shuttle flight to Terra took five hours. Throughout the flight Casey tried to imagine what kind of project needed his skills and experience. He couldn't imagine a civilian project so secret that Earthfleet Command hadn't been told about it. Could the project have something to do with the Telmierians? Casey didn't relish working with civilians. To Casey's great surprise, the shuttle dropped him off at the Presidential Palace. A guard met him and escorted him to the President's personal transporter. A minute later, he materialized on a transporter pad at the mysterious project site.

An attractive brunette waiting by a corridor hopper came over to meet the newest member of the project team. "Welcome to Project Timestream, Chief Casey," greeted the woman. "I'm Amara Taft, Assistant Project Director. Please forgive us for all the mystery, but secrecy is vital. Only a handful of people outside of the project even know what it is. I will escort you to Dr. Warner, the project director."

Casey smiled. He figured that Warner expected him to be displeased about his transfer to the project. Taft's beauty succeeded in soothing his savage breast as Warner had hoped. Casey was beginning to like his new boss.

"You guys rolled out the red carpet like I'm a VIP," noted Casey. "First the Assistant Project Director, then the big man himself."

"You are a very important person, Chief," Amara assured him. "That's why you are here."

Casey gave Amara a discreet appraising look. "Are all the lady scientists here as pleasing to the eye as you, Doc?"

Amara smiled. "That you will have to decide for yourself."

After a short ride to Warner's office, Amara handed off Chief Casey like a baton to Gideon Warner. Casey came face to face with his new if temporary boss.

"Welcome to Project Timestream, Chief Casey," greeted Warner as he shook the newcomer's hand. "I'm Gideon Warner, Director of Project Timestream. The reason we requested your services will soon become very clear. Please follow me."

They walked through the many rows of computers and generators until they came to the heart of the complex. Casey immediately recognized the mammoth machine when he saw it. "This hyperspace engine could power a ship bigger than twenty star cruisers! What in the hell are you planning to do with it, doc: move the entire planet through hyperspace?"

Warner chuckled. "No, we plan to use it to move people and objects through time."

Casey shook his head in disbelief. "It's a little early for April Fools jokes, Mr. Warner."

Warner expression didn't suggest any humor. "It's no joke, Chief. And I'm not joking when I tell you that if you disclose anything to anyone outside of the project before President Harrison announces the Time Door to the galaxy, he will have you summarily shot."

Casey realized Warner was indeed very serious. "I can see why, Doc."

Warner gave Casey a brief overview of the project and its goals. Although not a history buff, Casey felt excited and exhilarated by the thought of the military history the Time Door could gather and record. He imagined seeing all the ships and navies of past centuries and millennia. Casey wanted to see the great naval battles that changed the course of history like Midway, Trafalgar and Salamis.

"When Captain Reynolds informed me that I was on loan to your project, frankly I was feeling kind of put out," confessed Casey. "Now I'm grateful and honored to be a part of it. I promise you that I will keep my lips zipped and earn my pay every day."

"Speaking of pay, you will not only be receiving your Earthfleet pay, but the project will also be paying you a senior civilian engineer's salary," Warner informed him. "I insisted on it."

"Doc, you just made a friend for life!"

Warner noticed Brion Gill standing by the open office door listening to his conversation with Casey. Gill walked over to Casey and glared at him. "You will address the Project Director as Dr. Warner or Director Warner, Mr. Casey!"

Warner smiled. "My title is not sacred to me or the government, Brion," he reminded Gill "Don't let it trouble you."

Gill gave Casey a sour look, then left the office without further comment.

"Don't trouble yourself with Brion, Chief," said Warner. "Although I am included in his very small circle of friends, he's sometimes very tiresome with me too. He has no authority over you or any of the people you work with. The only orders you need obey are mine and Dr. Taft's."

"Thanks for the heads up, Doc," said Casey gratefully.

"Come with me, Chief," said Warner. "I want to introduce you to the engineers you will be working with."

Roy Kern, the Chief of Project Security, decided to take a look at the new man Dr. Warner just added to the Project Timestream team. As he expected, he found Chief Casey at the hyperspace engine. Kern had no engineering talent or education, but appreciated and respected people who did. His talent was security. Few things escaped his notice. After reading the Earthfleet Intelligence file on Casey that Warner gave him, Kern felt comfortable about the Atlantis Chief Engineer.

Casey sensed Kern's presence and turned around. The man didn't seem to be a scientist, technician or construction worker. "We have something in common, Chief Casey. We are both chiefs. You are a

Chief Engineer, and I am Chief of Project Security. I was a bit surprised when I learned that Earthfleet lent you to us at Dr. Warner's request. How do like working with us civilians?"

"Doc Warner has a fine crew and I'm proud to be part of it, with a few exceptions like Mr. Gill," replied Casey. "He is a pompous, self-important sourpuss. Gill doesn't bother me, but he made it very clear that he doesn't appreciate my presence."

Kern chuckled. "Gill's a real charmer, isn't he? Just ignore him, Chief. Just about everyone else does. What are you working on?"

"Just straightening out a few things. I'm continually finding things wired wrong or installed improperly. I don't understand it. None of our civilian engineers should make mistakes like these. They are top notch professionals."

Kern felt uneasy about what he just learned from Casey. The SBI and Earthfleet Security had examined every member of the Project Timestream team and the construction people with a microscope. Everyone had passed with flying colors. Too many people working on Project Timestream had the knowledge to cause a lot of damage if they desired to. All Kern could do was stay alert and keep his eyes and ears continually open.

"You know what this place needs, Mr. Kern?" asked Casey. "A saloon or at least a bar. A pool room and a bowling alley would be nice too. Hell, I'd gladly pay for their use. I'm making a lot of money between my Earthfleet pay and project pay. Unfortunately, there is nothing to spend it on!"

"Those things would be very nice," agreed Kern. "I will put that recommendation in Dr. Warner's suggestion box. He has one in his office. Dr. Warner considers every suggestion."

The Speaker of the Solar Council materialized on Warner's private transporter pad. He found Warner, his shuttle, and his driver waiting for him. Warner shook the Speaker's hand. "Welcome to Project Timestream, Speaker Marshall, I didn't think it would take you this long to pay us a visit."

Warner noted that the Speaker just wore a suit without his Council robe. No doubt, he wanted to attract as little attention as possible.

"I've been very busy since you, Dr. Taft and President Harrison pitched your Time Door idea to me, Gideon," replied the Speaker wearily. "Grim necessity brings me here at this time."

Warner didn't like the sound of that. He and Speaker Marshall said nothing further until they arrived at Warner's office. Warner ushered his guest inside and they sat down. He secured the door. Warner waited for the Speaker to elaborate on his statement.

The Speaker looked over the books in Warner's bookcase. It contained time travel novels, books on temporal physics, and history classics like *The Decline* and *Fall of The Roman Empire*. "The Time Machine by H.G. Wells," murmured the Speaker. "How appropriate. I wonder what Mr. Wells would think if you showed him the Time Door."

"Now there's a thought," considered Warner. "Most likely, he would think he was dreaming or crazy as would I in that situation."

"Gideon, I'm honored far beyond my worthiness to be a part of this marvelous endeavor, even if indirectly," began the Speaker. "Even now, it still seems so strange being one of a handful of people outside of Project Timestream to know what it is. It's funny that despite the projects name, no one has figured out its purpose."

"I know it required a lot of arm twisting and horse trading to secure our funding," acknowledged Warner. "We could not have gotten it without your help."

"I came here for two reasons," continued the Speaker. "First, I wanted to be certain that our conversation was private. I accept your word that nothing we discuss here will be recorded. Second, I wanted to finally see this wonder that I helped to bring to pass."

"After we finish our talk, I will give you the grand tour of Project Timestream," promised Warner. "Scientists tend to be mildly political or apolitical. We don't follow politics and current events as much as we should. Working on the Time Door occupies most of our time and focus. I promise you that from now on, I will keep an eye on what's happening in the rest of the Alliance. Everyone here understands perfectly well that the Constitution Party is where our bread is buttered."

"Please maintain your focus on Project Timestream," counseled the Speaker. "President Harrison and I will take care of the politics."

"Gideon, members of both parties in the Finance Committee have been privately grumbling about the project's secrecy and high price tag. Soon they will be publicly expressing their dissatisfaction. Privately, they have warned me that they will make their complaints public if they remain out of the loop much longer. Some of them can be entrusted with the knowledge of Project Timestream, others cannot. I can keep them in line for the near future. Beyond that, I can guarantee nothing."

"If the cost is troubling the Solar Council, I assure you that I spend the taxpayers' money as carefully and frugally as I do my own money. My people continually kid me about my credit pinching."

The Speaker smiled. "The Finance Committee doesn't care about the cost of the project if it produces the desired results. In this instance, however, it doesn't know what the project is or what results should be expected. Earthfleet Command is also very unhappy about not being in the loop. Admiral Wallace regularly complains about it to me and President Harrison. What progress have you made since your last report?"

Warner smiled. "Let me show you."

Warner led the Speaker around the cavern showing him the machinery, generators, computers, and the equipment needed to make the Time Door work. They stopped for a moment at the Telmierian hyperspace engine. Chief Casey was running a diagnostic on it.

The Speaker frowned. "An Earthfleet Engineer here, Gideon?" he asked accusingly.

"We needed Chief Casey," explained Warner. "This special hyperspace engine came from the Telmierians. They use it in their Colony Ships. Chief Casey has more knowledge of it and experience working on it than all my civilian engineers combined. As you know, a star cruiser Chief Engineer must be able to make major repairs quickly and under adverse conditions. Casey's resourcefulness and imagination have served us well."

The explanation mollified Marshall.

Casey noticed Warner and Marshall and joined them. "Speaker Marshall, it's a pleasure to meet you! You're a damn good man for a politician. I would have voted for you if I lived in your district."

The Speaker chuckled and shook Casey's hand. "No greater tribute have I ever received from a citizen. Is the engine performing as well as we hoped and expected Chief?"

"This engine is a work of art," declared Casey enthusiastically. "The Telmierians make these large engines for their Colony Ships. I'm surprised that you got them to part with one."

"President Harrison and Dr. Warner can be very persuasive," noted the Speaker. "How close are you to sending someone through time?"

"Not as close as we would like to be," admitted Warner. "We finally have the temporal spatial coordinate software working perfectly. It took three months of hard work and aggravation to accomplish it. We have been testing the door and our temporal tracers this week. The tracers are for finding future time travelers who don't end up where or when they were supposed to be. Starting with a small dish, we worked our way up to a large barrel. The tracers have worked well so far."

"Have you sent anything living through the door, Gideon?" asked the Speaker hopefully.

Warner shook his head. "In a few days we will experiment with some plants. Then we will send back and retrieve some small animals. Our last non-human test will be a chimp. If it suffers no ill effects, we will send the first human back in time."

The news greatly relieved the Speaker. "Can you show me a test?"

Warner smiled. "I thought you would never ask." He led the Speaker to the Master Control Panel. He ordered Casey to activate the attractor beam projector and stand by. 'Speaker Marshall, observe the platform closely. One thing we will soon know is whether time is mutable or not. Amara and I both believe the past can be altered. We hope that we will be proven wrong. If the past is mutable, a small change centuries ago might grow into a temporal tsunami by the time it reached the present. Time travelers will need to be very careful not to cause any significant changes to the past."

After ordering everyone to clear the area near the platform, Warner activated the hyperdrive engine. He inputted the temporal-space coordinates for a time and place he had chosen weeks before. Warner summoned a tech who brought over the rolling cart Warner had ordered. He checked to see that everyone was at a safe distance from the door. Warner gradually brought the hyperdrive engine to full power. Waves of temporal energy swirled over the platform. They appeared blue and red to the human eye.

Slowly images formed in the door. It opened to a dark room illuminated by moonlight streaming through an open window. Gideon ordered Casey to aim an attractor beam at a huge book lying on a table. The beam slowly pulled the book through the Time Door.

Casey gently set it down on the cart. Warner, Casey, and the Speaker walked over to the cart.

"Check it out, Mr. Speaker," directed Warner.

The Speaker turned the cover and looked at the first pages. He stared at the book in wide eyed wonder and delight. "It's a Gutenberg Bible! It looks brand new."

Warner smiled. "That's because it is brand new. Bringing it through the Time Door spares the Bible the ravages of time. The Bible is yours. It's a small token of appreciation from all the people of Project Timestream."

For a moment, Marshall was too choked up to speak. "Gideon, how can I accept such a priceless gift?"

"With gratitude and humility would be appropriate," suggested Warner with a twinkle in his eye. "Take the Bible."

The Speaker tried to lift the book but found it much heavier than he imagined. "The Bible weighs seventy pounds," Warner informed him. "One of my people will deliver it to your house. I suggest that you put it somewhere no one will see it until the Time Door is unveiled."

"You can count on it!" promised Marshall. "Don't forget President Harrison. He deserves a special gift far more than me."

"We already obtained some Imperial Chinese artifacts for him," Warner informed the Speaker. "I'm confident that he and his wives will like them."

After completing the tour of the project, Warner escorted the Speaker to his private transporter pad. "You will be transported first to the Presidential Palace, then to your house. You and President Harrison are invited to witness the first human journey through time."

"Has the lucky man or woman been chosen yet, Gideon?"

"I have not yet decided who that will be," replied Warner. "I don't have to order anyone to make the first journey through time. Many of my people have already volunteered."

Marshall checked his watch. "I'm afraid I must go now. The Finance Committee is hammering out the final details of next year's budget. It's a lot harder when the Constitution requires the Solar Council to spend no more than it takes in except during wartime and clearly defined emergencies. At this point, negotiations become very testy. Thank you again for the Bible."

Amara joined Warner and the Speaker. "Our pleasure, Speaker Marshall," said Warner. "You are always welcome here." After the Speaker transported out Warner asked, "Are the temporal tracers ready for the next tests, Amara?"

"They are ready and waiting at the Time Door, boss," she informed him. "I checked them myself."

Warner noticed that she was looking at him curiously. He felt a bit annoyed but more curious. "Have I forgotten to trim my nasal hair or comb my hair?"

"Just curious," replied Amara innocently. "I was just wondering what the motivation was for your beard and long hair. Is it rebellion, affectation, indifference to your appearance or personal taste?"

The question both amused and intrigued Warner. "To be honest, I haven't really thought about it," he confessed. "I can't even remember what I look like clean shaven with a short haircut. I'm focused mostly on the what rather than the why of things. Affectation? God forbid! Laziness, most likely. That's enough philosophizing for today, Amara. Our work awaits us."

When Warner and Amara arrived at the Time Door, they found Gill and Casey waiting for them. The test objects lay on wheeled carts near the platform. "The engine is powered up and ready as ordered, Doc," reported Casey.

"The time-space coordinate software and controls are fully functional," confirmed Gill.

Amara attached the time tracers to the vase, metal bucket and plastic drum on the cart. Warner checked for the tracer signals. "All tracer signals are strong," noted Warner with satisfaction.

Casey wheeled the carts onto the platform just outside of the rift. He quickly retreated from the Time Door. Warner increased the power level of the hyperdrive engine to maximum. Seconds later swirling waves of temporal announced the opening of the Time Door. The objects on the carts vanished one by one into the timestream, each going to different times and places.

"All the objects have arrived at their destinations!" announced Warner triumphantly. He reversed the field and all the objects reappeared looking no different than when they began their journeys to the past. Casey scanned the objects and confirmed that they had not changed in any way.

Warner continually sent the objects further into the past at fifty-year intervals. The tracer signals stayed steady and strong. When Warner brought them back after each interval, scans revealed no change. Then he increased the intervals to one century. Each time the tracer signals remained strong. The objects suffered no ill effects from their time journeys. When the objects reached 1000 AD, Warner increased the intervals to five hundred years.

Even when the objects reached 5000 BC, the tracer signals remained strong. Scans of the objects after each journey indicated no change to them. It didn't surprise Warner or Amara. They couldn't imagine any possible bad effects to inanimate objects traveling through time. Living things were another story. Time travelers had to be monitored carefully. No one had any idea what effects time journeys might have on humans. Only time and experience would tell.

"The range of the tracers is better than I dared to hope for," noted Warner gleefully. "Thank you for the improvements you made to them, Chief."

"Any star cruiser Chief Engineer could have done it, Doc," replied Casey modestly.

"But you are the one who did," noted Amara. "Our doctors will have to monitor the effects of time travel on travelers very carefully. We are entering completely unknown territory with no knowledge or experience to guide us. Despite this, we will have no shortage of people who desire to go on missions to the past once our history gathering begins."

"We can bet our lives and my last credit on that," agreed Warner. "That's it for today. Tomorrow, we begin the tests on living subjects. The first ones will be plants. Amara let's think about which plants we will use. We will compare notes in the morning."

When Amara returned to Warner's office the next day, to her surprise and displeasure, she found a man wearing an expensive custom tailored cashmere suit studying a readout on Warner's computer screen.

"Sir, all visitors to Project Timestream must be accompanied by an escort at all times," Amara informed the man sharply. "Mr. Kern will get an earful the next time I see him."

The man turned around and smiled. "I'm sorry, Dr. Taft. It won't happen again."

"Gideon?" asked Amara hesitantly. "My God! You look so different without that long hair and beard." She laughed with delight. "Gideon Warner, you are the most unserious serious scientist I ever met, but I like it. That suit must have cost you a fortune."

"It did," acknowledged Warner ruefully. "I can't look like a bum when I accept the first Nobel Prize for Temporal Physics. Excuse me for a few minutes while I slip into something more comfortable." Ten minutes later, he returned in shorts and an Aloha shirt. "After our first successful human test, I plan to take a two-week vacation in Hawaii."

Amara sighed. "That sounds great, Gideon. We have a lot of work to do before we pack our bags for the Aloha state."

Was that a Freudian slip? wondered Warner.

Warner read with amusement Chief Casey's suggestion for an entertainment center. What would impractical scientists do without practical engineers? The bar, pool rooms and bowling alley proved to be an immediate hit. They boosted morale and greatly reduced tension and irritability. People didn't even mind the two-drink daily limit Warner imposed. The entertainment center turned out to be the cure for the project team's cabin fever.

People had begun to speculate about who would be chosen to make the first trip through the Time Door. Everyone who desired to make the trip communicated it to Warner. The people who had no desire to step through the Time Door wasted no time informing Warner about it. Amara gave Warner the list of twenty-five volunteers who had sufficient nerve and desire to pass through the Time Door.

Amara was no longer just a colleague to Warner. She had become someone he cared about. He had decided to be the first person to step through the Time Door as soon as Project Timestream began. Warner sensed that Amara suspected it. Subtly she let him know that she didn't like the idea of him serving as his own human guinea pig. The prospect of stepping through the Time Door to the past both exhilarated and frightened Warner. Nevertheless, he was determined to make the trip. Warner doubted that he would get another chance to pass through the Time Door.

Warner found it fascinating that while Amara loved animals, she sent them through the Time Door with no reluctance or regret. She never lost her scientific detachment, except in the case of the Director of Project Timestream. Warner thought Amara felt great relief every time the animals returned safe and unharmed by their journeys through the Time Door. Finally, Warner and Amara both agreed that the time for the simian test had come.

Warner, Amara, Casey, and Gill waited patiently for the simian 'volunteer,' Charlie the chimp, to arrive. Warner borrowed Charlie from the San Diego Zoo. The director of the zoo was reluctant to grant Warner's request when he couldn't satisfactorily explain what he wanted the chimp for. President Harrison intervened. He promised the director that not one hair on Charlie's head would be harmed. With that assurance, the director finally granted Warner's request.

"We stand on the threshold of a new age," reflected Gill soberly. "For centuries, mankind has dreamed of traveling through time. If the chimp passes the test, that dream will be just one step away from becoming reality."

"Truly, my friend," agreed Warner. "Ah, here comes our 'volunteer' at last."

A security shuttle drove up to the Time Door and stopped. Kern and Charlie disembarked. Kern looked annoyed and disgusted. "Dr. Warner, I never imagined that you and Dr. Taft would make a monkey out of me!" he complained.

Warner and Amara struggled not laugh. "You know the rules, Roy," Warner reminded Kern. "All visitors to Project Timestream must be escorted by the Chief of Security."

Kern reluctantly smiled. "I guess that I should be glad you didn't decide to use a gorilla."

Amara escorted Charlie to the Time Door. He seemed fascinated by the swirling colors. Amara placed a time tracer around Charlie's neck. Without any coaxing, he stepped through the door. Seconds later, Gill picked up Charlie's tracer signal. The chimp had arrived safely at his destination exactly one hundred years in the past.

"Life signs are normal," reported Amara.

She sent the chimp back five hundred years at a time until it reached 5000 BC. At each interval, he experienced no adverse effects from his travels. Warner let out a sigh of relief. Amara brought the chimp back slowly to the present. He waited by the Time

Door for Charlie. When he arrived, Warner escorted him over to Amara.

"Congratulations for being the first and only simian to step through the Time Door, Charlie," said Warner. "For your meritorious service to Project Timestream, I award you a year's supply of bananas. Expect the first shipment tomorrow."

Charlie seemed completely unimpressed.

Chief Casey completed the latest adjustments to the hyperdrive engine and sat down for a moment. Working on the Telmierian engine had been a real education. The more he worked with it, the more he appreciated the engineering that went into it. Captain Reynolds had recommended him for the engineer exchange program with the Imperial Navy. Hopefully, he would make the cut. Casey hoped to get well acquainted with a pleasant blue skinned Karani beauty.

The hyperdrive engine was Casey's main responsibility. In his all too abundant free time, he visited the different sections and closely studied what they were doing. Often he found opportunities to be useful. The engineers who worked with the fusion reactors appreciated both Casey's company and help. Just about everyone made him feel welcome and part of the Project Timestream family.

Casey became curious when he spotted an unusual connection between the main fusion reactor and the Time Door. Scrutiny revealed that it had a deadly purpose. Immediately he called Warner, Amara, and Kern. They arrived within a few minutes of Casey's call.

"What is the problem, Chief?" asked Warner anxiously.

"Doc, I help out the other engineers when I have spare time to make myself useful," began Casey. "I found something very disturbing." He showed it to Warner and Amara. "Someone rigged the main fusion reactor to become a fusion bomb. It can be detonated manually or by a timer."

"All of us are grateful for your diligence and conscientiousness, Chief," said Warner. "Had this sabotage not been detected, eventually everything and everyone in the cavern would have been vaporized."

"Dr. Warner, someone among us has both the desire and knowledge to destroy the entire complex," observed Kern grimly. "We better learn who he or she is and soon."

Amara shook her head. "I just can't imagine that any of our people could do this."

"I was going to test everyone with a truth detector, Dr. Warner," said Kern. "I changed my mind after Chief Casey showed me how the machine can be circumvented."

Warner and Kern studied the SBI and Earthfleet Intelligence background checks of every member of Project Timestream except themselves. Project Timestream was Warner's baby. Kern knew nothing about fusion reactors. None of the members of the project had a criminal background or any history of mental illness. Fifty people had the knowledge to rig a reactor to be a bomb. None had any apparent motivation.

"If being an arrogant, obnoxious jerk made a person a suspect, Brion Gill would be our prime suspect," said Casey.

Warner chuckled. "Brion will have more good job offers than he will know what to do with when the Time Door passes the human test. He will also get a flood of requests from the most prestigious scientific journals to write articles. Brion has hungered for recognition from his scientific peers as long as I've known him."

"My people found no fingerprints or traces of DNA on the reactor that didn't belong there," reported Kern. "I've ruled out Gill. Someone who is smart enough to blow us all to hell would be smart enough to keep as low a profile as possible. We could uncover the saboteur quickly if we had a Telmierian telepath."

Warner sighed. "That is unfortunately out of the question. Amara, Chief Casey, and I will keep a very close eye on the reactors and the Time Door. The human test for the Time Door will take place on schedule. I have complete confidence in you and your people to keep the saboteur from causing any more trouble."

At the end of his workday, Warner headed back to his quarters. He received a call from Amara on his com-link. "Please don't tell me you have another problem to report, Amara."

"No problems, boss," replied Amara. "Just an invitation to join me for a drink in my quarters. I'm sure you can use one."

"You got that right," muttered Warner under his breath. "I'll be there shortly."

"Your quarters are well ordered like your mind," declared Warner as Amara showed him around. "I like the Imperial Chinese decor. My quarters are spartan in comparison to yours. My only indulgence is my book collection. I love the feel and smell of old books." Warner thought he detected approval in Amara's eyes.

"I'd like to see your collection sometime, Gideon."

"Just choose the time."

Amara took a bottle of wine and poured a glass for herself and Warner. They sat down on her love seat. "An occasional bottle of expensive wine is my only indulgence."

Warner drank some wine and nodded approval. "Life is more than work and science," he reflected. "I seem to have forgotten that over the last five years."

Amara drank her wine savoring every drop. She finished her second glass of wine while Warner was still working on his first glass. "I've dated many men since I completed my doctorate, Gideon. None of them lasted for more than a few dates. They were either focused on my brain or my body. Apparently, they didn't understand that my body and brain are a package deal. The men who met my standards worked far away from me, so nothing ever worked out. Excuse me, Gideon. It doesn't take much wine to make me ramble."

This is a side of you I never suspected, Amara, thought Warner. She apparently wanted a serious relationship with a man. Did that also include marriage and children? "Amara, we must not get paranoid and let our imaginations run wild. Our efforts will be hindered by suspicion and distrust. Cooperation and trust have brought the project this far."

Amara sighed. "I hate having to be suspicious of almost everyone. We could be looking at the face of the saboteur and not even know it. I haven't heard anyone express any reservations about the Time Door. Have you?"

"Brion is concerned about the possibility of damaging the time continuum," recalled Warner. "So am I. Anyone who doesn't share that concern, concerns me. Let's just relax and forget about that for a moment."

"How about a little Mozart? asked Amara.

"Mozart and fine wine make a great combination," agreed Warner. "He's the Shakespeare of composers." A quiet pleasant evening with Amara was just what the doctor ordered for Warner.

Two weeks after the chimp test, Warner and Amara completed the final preparations for the human test. They checked, double checked and triple checked all the equipment. Gill did the same for the Time

Door software. Kern and his people guarded the reactors and the Time Door round the clock. Day by day, they struggled to keep paranoid suspicion from clouding their perception. Finally, the big day arrived. Warner went to meet the special guests.

Warner greeted and welcomed President Harrison and Speaker Marshall after they stepped off the transporter pads. He waited for the remaining VIP guests to appear. To his surprise, they hadn't arrived.

"Where are the Vice President, Majority Leader and the Chief Justice?" asked Warner. "Aren't they coming?"

"I'm afraid they couldn't make it," replied Harrison regretfully. "Vice President Grant had to attend a special meeting with the Telmierian ambassador in my place."

"The Majority Leader is in the middle of difficult budget negotiations with Democracy Party leaders," added Marshall. "The Supreme Court is hearing an emergency petition. The Chief Justice can't be spared."

Warner frowned. "I could have rescheduled the test until a time when all the special guests could attend." Warner regretted that Ellison couldn't be present. An emergency operation kept him from attending the grand opening of the Time Door.

Harrison shook his head. "A guest defers to the convenience of his host, not the host to the guest. The sooner we complete the human test, the sooner we can announce the Time Door to the galaxy."

Warner's shuttle quickly transported him and his guests to the Time Door. Harrison and the Speaker discovered to their surprise that none of Warner's people were present except Amara, Casey, and Gill. Warner chose Gill to be the Doorkeeper.

"Why are so few of your people here at this historic moment?" asked Marshall.

No one else is needed," explained Warner. What he didn't say was that he couldn't risk having anyone else present who might be the mystery saboteur. "It seems so strange to see you without any Secret Service agents hovering around you, Alexander."

"The agents were very unhappy about it," confessed Harrison. "If I had brought them with me, they would have had to stay here until the announcement of the Time Door. Until then, I want no one else outside of Project Timestream to know about it."

Harrison noted the smug look on Chief Casey's face. "You see the irony of a Chief Engineer knowing about Project Timestream while the Commanding Admiral doesn't."

Casey chuckled. "I do indeed, sir. Admiral Wallace will be mad enough to chew serenium when he finally learns about the Time Door. Earthfleet Command will hit the ceiling when it learns that it will have no control over it."

"All of us have been wondering for days who the first official time traveler will be, Gideon," said Harrison. "Who is the brave man or woman?"

"I am," announced Warner solemnly. Everyone but Amara seemed surprised by the announcement. Warner suspected that she had figured that out by herself.

"You are a brave man, Gideon," declared Marshall in awe and admiration.

Warner smiled and shook his head. "Be assured, jumping headlong into the great unknown of the timestream scares me more than anything I've ever done before. My curiosity and desire to visit the past exceed my fear. I am the one who began Project Timestream. It's only appropriate that I should be the one to finish it," said Warner with finality.

"Where will you go?" asked Harrison.

"To a significant day in the twentieth century. Brion, I've already inputted the time-space coordinates."

"I'm afraid that your journey to the past will be permanently postponed, Gideon," announced Gill unexpectedly. To everyone's surprise and dismay, Gill pulled out a strange-looking weapon. "Are you surprised, Gideon?"

Warner couldn't believe what was happening. "Frankly, yes, Brion."

"This is a 357 Magnum," Gill informed his captive audience. "It's a projectile weapon of the twentieth century. It causes a lot of damage to whatever it hits."

"I don't understand this at all, Brion," admitted Warner. "You have so much to gain from the success of Project Timestream. You could have written your own ticket. Why destroy the Time Door?"

Gill smiled grimly. "The time continuum has so much to lose, my friend. Can't you see the hubris of the Time Door, Gideon? We don't have the right or wisdom to tinker with the very foundation of reality.

It would be a disaster if the Time Door fell into the wrong hands. I'm not suicidal. Neither do I seek martyrdom. The galaxy must be protected from this Time Door folly. I'm the only one who can. I'm the only one who will."

Kern's eyes widened in understanding. "Your rudeness and obnoxiousness were just a pose! You deliberately fouled up procurement and the machinery to hinder the project. You rigged the main fusion reactor to become a bomb."

Gill laughed. "Your thinking is so two-dimensional, Kern. That's why you got blindsided. The bomb was just a red herring. I knew that Casey would discover the bomb even if no one else did. It kept everyone chasing their tails while I prepared my real plan."

"How can you destroy the Time Door without a bomb, Brion?" asked Amara.

Gill smiled triumphantly. "My calculations revealed that if the Time Door's polarity was reversed and someone entered the open door from our end, it would result in an explosion that would destroy everything in the cavern. I reversed the polarity during my final time-space coordinate software check."

He pulled out a remote device from his pocket. He pressed a button. All the generators powered up. The hyperdrive engine then powered up. Gill pressed a second button and the Time Door opened. He slowly backed toward the platform while aiming the gun at Harrison. Warner felt completely helpless and powerless. They had the choice of either being killed by a bullet or the explosion of the Time Door.

Gill stopped when he reached the door. "I'm sorry it had to be this way," he apologized.

Before Gill could step through the door, a man ran out the door and collided with him. The collision knocked Gil backward off the platform. He hit the floor with a thud and dropped the gun. Casey picked up the gun while Kern put binders on Gill.

Amara stared intently at the stranger. He looked very familiar. "You're the man who disappeared through the temporal rift a year ago!"

The man looked around the cavern in astonishment and confusion. "A year ago?!" he muttered. "It seemed just like minutes. What the hell happened to me?"

Warner chuckled. "Friend, you have had the honor of being the first unofficial time traveler. Dr. Taft and I will explain everything to you later. Amara, escort our guest to the infirmary so Dr. Sterling can check him out."

Warner looked sadly at Gill. "I don't know what to do with you, Brion. You aren't a criminal or a madman. Without the software you designed, we would have no Time Door. Your desire to protect the time continuum is commendable. Your willingness to kill over two thousand people to destroy the Time Door is not. I'd hate to see your talent wasted in prison."

Gill smiled wryly. "So would I."

"Confine Brion to his quarters, Mr. Kern," ordered Warner. "I'm leaving it up to President Harrison to decide what to do with him. I have a few suggestions for the President. Amara, change the polarity of the Time Door immediately!"

"I never expected to see that man again," commented Harrison. "How did he get back?"

Warner pondered a moment. "Either he was suspended in a temporal limbo, or he never left from the spot where he disappeared. He must have entered the door when it appeared on his side. The man must have been moving fast to knock Brion down the way he did. Amara and I will debrief him later. Meanwhile, I have a temporal journey to make."

Warner finished dressing and looked at himself in the mirror and shook his head. The drab looking gray suit and plain tie were appropriate for the time and would attract no attention.

Warner double checked his tie clip camera to be certain it was functioning. The video would be the first contribution to the Temporal History archives.

A soft knock on the door interrupted his train of thought. He opened the door. "Come in, Amara."

Amara sighed. "I had a feeling months ago that you would decide to be the project's human guinea pig. I know there is no reason to expect that anything will go wrong, but the possibility exists. You can still change your mind, Gideon."

Warner looked into Amara's eyes. "If you had been the project director, would you have chosen to take the first journey through time?"

"Yes," admitted Amara reluctantly. "But not for the glory. I would not want anyone else to take that risk."

"If by unhappy chance something goes wrong, the Time Door will continue through you. You would serve as well as me as guardian of time."

Amara gave him a lingering kiss. "For luck, Gideon."

Warner chuckled. "Do you think I need that much luck, Amara?"

Amara smiled. "You can never have too much luck."

Warner and Amara returned to the Time Door where their special guests waited. President Harrison and Speaker Marshall laughed when they saw Warner's clothes. "Did men ever really dress like that, Gideon?" asked Harrison.

Warner smiled. "Unfortunately."

The Time Door suddenly opened. Waves of temporal energy swirled over the platform. Warner walked slowly over to the door. He stopped for a moment, then stepped through it. An explosion of light and color burst upon Warner's senses. His entire being felt like it had been instantaneously turned inside out. Warner seemed to shoot forward at the speed of light. Warner soon became accustomed to it and he relaxed. Shapes and images slowly took form around him as he synchronized with the past.

Warner appeared on a side street near a newsstand. Neither the owner nor his customers noticed the arrival of Warner. After the customers bought their newspapers and moved on, Warner went over to the newsstand. He picked up a copy of the New York Times. It was dated December 5, 1933. Prohibition had officially ended.

"This isn't a library, pal," grumbled the owner. "You want to read the paper? That will cost you a nickel."

"Sorry, sir," apologized Warner. He paid the owner with a nickel from his own twentieth century coin collection.

The owner looked over the coin. "This nickel looks like it's a hundred years old. It's legit and that's all that counts."

More like two hundred years, thought Warner with amusement. "Politicians have come up with a lot of dumb ideas, but Prohibition takes the cake."

"You said it, pal! Those stupid politicians thought they could make people stop drinking, making, and buying booze. The government lost a lot of tax money on illegal booze. Al Capone and his pals made millions in tax-free money. It was nuts!"

"What dumb ideas will the politicians come up with next?" wondered Warner.

The owner shook his head. "I don't even want to think about it!" His mouth fell open as the temporal doorway appeared. He watched in amazement as Warner stepped through the door. He and the door disappeared. "I gotta stop drinking cheap booze."

Amara, Casey, Harrison, and Marshall cheered when Warner passed through the door. The men shook Warner's hand. Amara hugged him in relief.

"I see that you have a souvenir from your trip," observed Harrison. Warner handed the newspaper to him. Harrison took a quick look at it. "We haven't used newsprint for over a century and a half. This newspaper is brand new."

Warner sighed. "We still have a few things to do before we can announce the Time Door to the Alliance and the Telmierian Empire. We need to create a Time Council, an organization to regulate time travel and a Temporal Historian Academy. Before we do that, Amara and I are taking a break. We want to get reacquainted with the rest of the world."

Warner stopped by Casey's quarters to say goodbye. He wanted Casey to stay with the project, but he knew the chief engineer's heart lay elsewhere. Warner hadn't ever served in Earthfleet. He greatly respected the people who did. Casey had contributed much to the success of the Time Door. Hopefully, Casey would stop by from time to time.

"It's time for me to return to the Atlantis, Doc," said Casey regretfully. "I've missed my ship and shipmates a lot. At the same time, I wish I could stay a member of the Project Timestream team. I've made some good friends like you and Doc Amara."

"Amara and I will miss you too, but we know you want to return to your ship. The engineers you trained on the hyperspace engine can now take care of it properly. Thank you for your time and contribution."

Casey gave Warner a soldierly hug. "I was very upset when Captain Reynolds told me that I had been transferred to your mysterious project. I had been recommended for the Engineer Exchange Program with the Empire. It upset me because I thought that I would miss my chance if I was here when the next exchange was made. Thanks for passing on the message from Captain Reynolds informing me that I have been chosen for the next engineer exchange. Hopefully, I will get well acquainted with a blue-skinned Karani beauty. Thanks to you and Project Timestream, I will have plenty of money to wine and dine her. Things could not have worked out better for me. Visit me on the Atlantis sometime, Doc. Be sure to bring Doc Amara with you. I think you guys belong together."

Warner smiled. He hoped that Amara felt the same way. "So do I. I'll leave you to your packing, Chief."

Casey finished packing his uniforms and personal effects. His doorbell rang. When he opened the door, he was surprised to find Amara.

"I'm here to take you to the transporter, Chief." They reminisced about the experiences they shared during the project along the way to Warner's personal transporter. When they arrived, they walked slowly over to the transporter

Amara hugged Casey and kissed him on the cheek. "Please come back for a visit at least once, Bryan. You will always be a member of the Project Timestream family."

"I will," promised Casey. "You're a fool if you don't marry Doc Warner, Doc Amara. Never did two people belong together like you guys." A moment later the transporter beam whisked him away.

Amara smiled. "I'm no fool, Bryan."

After Casey returned to the Atlantis, Warner returned to the Time Door. He contemplated the journey he had just made. Warner wanted to make more journeys through the Time Door. He knew that it would never happen. That privilege would belong to the Temporal Historians. It was his job to serve as a guardian of the time continuum, not wander about the past. Warner hoped that Amara would join him as a fellow guardian.

Warner didn't hear Amara as she quietly walked up behind him. "It has been an eventful day, Gideon."

Warner turned around. The moment of truth had arrived. "Indeed, it has, Amara. I appreciate all that you have done to help make the dream of the Time Door come true."

"Where do we go now, Gideon?" asked Amara softly.

Warner looked deeply into her eyes and smiled. Where indeed, he mused. Warner understood that she spoke about their personal as well as their professional relationship. He wanted both to continue. It was clear to him that Amara did too. Warner took her hand. "I need someone to help me protect the Time Door and the time continuum, Amara. A permanent personal assistant. It's a lifetime commitment. If you think you can handle the work and me, you got the job."

Amara smiled. "Is this a marriage proposal, Gideon?"

Warner chuckled. "An offbeat one but yes."

"This isn't the first marriage proposal I ever received," Amara informed him. "It is the first one that I accepted. If you hadn't proposed, I would have. Do you think the project can get along without us while we take a couple of weeks off to get married?"

"I'm giving everyone a two-week break. They earned it, and they need it."

"So do we, Gideon," said Amara wearily. "I've been dying to go out for dinner since the project began. Steak and ribs would be wonderful."

Warner smiled. "You read my mind. Let's go!"

President Harrison gazed at the portrait of his grandfather David Harrison hanging on the wall of his office. His grandfather exhorted him and the Time Council to always be watchful and never allow the government or military any control over the Time Door. The President prayed that the enemies of the Alliance and the Telmierian Empire didn't declare war on the Alliance over it.

Harrison expected the Telmierians to take the news of the Time Door with their usual calm. While they publicly congratulated the Alliance for its great accomplishment, privately they would express their serious concerns about the Alliance's intentions for the Time Door. Not having any control over or even access to it would deeply trouble the Telmierians. In time, the Alliance had to give them access to it. Harrison and the Time Council decided to authorize Imperial Observers once Time Control was fully organized. Allowing Telmierians to travel through the Time Door would be the decision of a future President.

Throughout his political career, Harrison had always been honest with citizens, sometimes to the point of offense. He had worked very hard in words and deeds to earn their trust. Harrison needed to use all the political capital he had accumulated over fifteen years to allay citizens fears and concerns about the Time Door. At first, the news of the Time Door had shocked and dismayed the people of the Alliance.

Gradually, they got used to the idea of time travel. Shock and dismay had changed to curiosity and fascination. Most people grudgingly accepted that time tours were too dangerous to permit.

Harrison didn't look forward to informing the Solar Council and Earthfleet Command that Time Control and the Time Door would be completely independent of the government and the military. The Solar Council would have a measure of oversight as required by the Solar Constitution. Time Control would be a completely independent entity like Vatican City had been before the Solar Alliance. Never could government or the military be allowed to weaponize or politicize Time Control. Harrison smiled wryly when it occurred to him that the government prohibition also applied to him. He would see that Time Control remain independent of the government and Earthfleet for the rest of his Presidency. Vice President Grant would do the same after he succeeded Harrison.

Harrison felt very comfortable with Gideon and Amanda Warner as the heads of the Time Council they had organized. They had proven their character and probity. Unfortunately, they would not live forever. God willing, all their successors to the end of time would be equally trustworthy guardians of the time continuum. Harrison had no regrets about helping to turn the dream of time travel into reality.

President Harrison finished signing the last of the bills sitting on his desk into law. He leaned back in his chair. The day had been long, and the opposition leaders had been more tiresome than usual. He couldn't wait until he returned home to his wives and his newborn son. It had only been a year since he had returned from his involuntary sojourn on the Rigel Home World. A few months later, Gideon Warner came to him with his crazy time door proposal.

So far, none of the galactic powers had gone off the deep end after they heard about the Time Door. The Rigellians had been strangely and unexpectedly silent after hearing the news. Knowing his Rigellian counterpart, Harrison expected a Rigellian attempt to take out Time Control and the Time Door eventually. It would be a while before the Alliance felt comfortable enough to grant the Empire access to Project Timestream. Letting a Telmierian step through the Time Door. would take even longer. Harrison couldn't imagine a time when a Rigellian would be trusted to pass through the Time Door.

Just as he was about to leave his office, he got a call on a secure line. Harrison took the televiewer call. "It's always a pleasure to hear from you, Gideon. If you don't have serious trouble to report, the pleasure will be even greater."

Warner chuckled. "Everything is fine," he assured Harrison. "It's a great pleasure for me to get through to you directly rather than being screened by your secretary. Alexander, if you can spare the time, I have something I think you would be very interested to see."

"You've piqued my curiosity, Gideon. I'll be over in a few minutes."

Harrison summoned the operator of his personal transporter pad. By the time he arrived at the transporter, the operator was ready for him. "Where to, Mr. President?" asked the operator.

"Time Control," replied Harrison. "After you transport me, you can go home. I'll transport home from there."

Harrison materialized on Warner's personal transporter pad. Warner along with his shuttle and driver were waiting for him. Harrison shook Warner's hand.

"Welcome to Project Timestream, Alexander," greeted Warner. "Much has changed since your last visit. I'm happy to report that we can now determine the coordinates of any time and place we want to go. Presently, our biggest problem is deciding the priority of the historical missions."

"You could have informed me about that in your next report," noted Harrison.

"That isn't why I called you," said Warner. "There are some things a report just can't do justice to."

"Where is Amara, Gideon?" asked Harrison.

Warner smiled. "She is meeting with the Telmierian ambassador. "He is diplomatically being informed that for the foreseeable future, only Alliance citizens will work in Time Control, serve as Temporal Historians, or accompany historical teams on missions."

Harrison chuckled. "The Empire isn't going to like that. They will be patient. They know that in time they will get the access they desire. After all, we haven't known the Telmierians very long." Warner ordered the driver to take him and Harrison to Artifact Room One.

The shuttle arrived at its destination one minute later. Warner opened the door and Harrison followed him inside. Warner took

Harrison over to a large object covered with a tarp. "We brought back this artifact as a test," said Warner. He removed the tarp and revealed a statue. Harrison stared at it in astonishment and wonder.

"Venus De Milo," murmured Harrison. "So that is what she looks like with her arms. Wow!"

"We determined when the statue was damaged," explained Warner. "Then we took it before it got broken and replaced it with a copy of the statue without the arms. Now we can destroy the copy. Apparently, no one noticed the change. Will you promise me something, Alexander? Don't ever ask me to bring back the Colossus of Rhodes or a dinosaur."

Harrison laughed. "I promise."

Warner gazed earnestly at Harrison. "Alexander, I invited you here for another reason. The Time Council and I decided that we need a member who has a practical real-world perspective to counterbalance our academic perspective. Would you consider accepting a seat on the Time Council after you complete your second term?"

"A seat on the Time Council?" echoed Harrison in astonishment and disbelief. "That's a tremendous honor and responsibility. Being President of the Alliance pales in comparison with serving on the Time Council. Gideon, I'm just a politician. No politician deserves that honor."

Warner smiled. "My friend, you are a politician who governs like a statesman. I followed your career closely. Never once have you compromised your fundamental principles even when it cost you. We need your kind of person on the council."

"Perhaps my political perspective could be of value to the Time Council, Gideon," allowed Harrison. "There needs to be a balance of idealism and practicality. If my bosses agree, you have a deal."

Warner grinned. "I already discussed the proposition with your wives. They told me that you will gladly accept the nomination."

"How do the other members of the council feel about me joining it?" asked Harrison uncertainly.

Warner chuckled. "They told me to litcrally twist your arm if necessary."

Harrison smiled. "For the sake of my arm, I accept the nomination. Will I and my family have to live in Time Control?"

"All the other Time Council members do," Warner informed him. "We live here for security as well as convenience. Alexander, accepting a seat on the Time Council will require a great sacrifice of you. I know you wanted to return to Titan at the end of your second term. If you accept a seat on the Time Council, you must remain on Terra most of the time. Council members must be available at a moment's notice if an emergency arises. We have four alternate Council members who fill in so the permanent members can enjoy some rare vacation time."

Harrison sighed. "At least I can see my old home occasionally. Gideon, do you ever plan to send any Temporal Historians to the future?"

Warner shrugged. "I'm not even sure the future exists. If it does, I think we should leave it alone. Knowing the future would change it by changing the present. The temporal sword cuts both ways. You, Amara, and I will do all that we can to make sure the future we are helping to create is a good one."

About the Author

The author has earned a B.A. in English at Alvernia University. He also successfully completed Short Story Writing, Novel, and Advanced Novel courses of the Writer's Digest School. The author has lived in Hawaii, Taipei Taiwan and American Samoa. In 1985-86 he participated in a salvage operation. He has worked at a variety of jobs including taxi, driver, fundraiser, and English tutor.

You may contact the author at timedoor2023@yahoo.com